LADY IN WHITE

GOLD AND COURAGE SERIES
BOOK 7

KAREN S. GORDON

ISBN: 978-1-954296-10-7 (Ebook)

ISBN: 978-1-954296-09-1 (Print)

ISBN: 978-1-954296-11-4 (Audiobook)

"Such is the fate of all who are greedy for money;
it robs them of life."

Proverbs 1:19

1

MIAMI, FLORIDA
THURSDAY

Holidays in Miami sucked for the locals and this one was off to an especially bad start. The international airport was always a nightmare, and with this being the start of the long Memorial Day weekend, Vance Courage was glad he wasn't the one traveling. Taking a position behind a black Mercedes, he parked the Audi on an angle trying not to block lanes in the drop-off zone in front of Cayman Air. He checked the time. Just after 8 a.m.

An officer approached the Benz and spun his hand, motioning the driver in front of him to get moving. The cop's partner, a square-shouldered female with foot-long dreadlocks stepped off the curb. She opened her palm and gave the hood of the Mercedes a good smack.

Vance lowered the window to listen in as the driver got out to confront her. Lauren Gold glanced across at him from the passenger seat and shook her head.

"I said, move it!" the woman cop repeated.

"How am I supposed to drop my mother off? She's old," the driver said, taking a step toward her.

"Move back," she warned. "I'm gonna write you a ticket if you don't get back in that car." She blew her whistle hitting a note that tickled Vance's eardrums.

"You're getting pleasure from this," Lauren said, sticking her fingers in her ears and twisting them. "Roll your window up."

He didn't. He preferred to watch the man cower, plant a hand over each ear and slink from the female officer. But the crisp morning air was changing quickly and thickening like a sauna. A sweat broke under his shirt. He powered up the window and cranked the A/C to LO. Welcome to Miami where if you didn't like the weather, wait five minutes. If you didn't like the people, too bad.

Lauren's phone rang an odd tone. She held it so he could see the screen, then she yelled at it. "You have the wrong number." She stabbed the red dot with her fingertip ending the call. "Did you see that?"

He did. It was a video call with no one there. Just the empty background of a beach scene.

"Freaking spammers are hitting a new low," she said. "That's the second time in two days I got a call from the same number. Probably some timeshare scam hoping I'll hit redial. I hate video calls. If I wanted to be in front of the camera, I'd have done that years ago."

It was true. When he'd first met her, she produced videos for corporate clients working behind the camera.

"Can you block the number?" he asked.

"What do you think I'm doing?"

The Mercedes driver pulled forward slowly and stopped. An elderly lady got out and the driver who'd tangled with the cop popped the trunk and slung his elderly mother's bag onto the walkway, then drove off. Vance swooped in to take his spot. The female cop who'd rapped the hood of the Benz approached. He rolled down his window.

She was about to rip him a new one when she hesitated and flashed a grin. "I'll be damned," she said, "I ain't seen you in, hell, I don't know how long. Heard after you quit the force you went to law school or somethin'."

"Something like that," he said. The roots of her dreadlocks had turned salt and pepper since the last time he'd seen her. "I see you're still on the job."

"Not by choice," she said, leaning over and peering inside the vehicle. "You droppin' someone off?"

"I am."

"Looks like you're doin' okay these days," she said, shaking her head making a series of "mmm, mmm, mmm," sounds.

"Shouldn't you be retired by now?" he asked.

The driver behind him honked.

She sent a clenched fist that way. "Yeah, shoulda, but I got a daughter who's an addict and a sick grandkid to look after. Been moonlightin' as much as I can to stay ahead of it all."

"Sorry to hear."

"If you know of any side hustles, keep me in mind," she said, plucking a card from the shirt pocket of her brown uniform and handing it to him.

Back in the day, they dubbed her Zo. A derivative of

Haitian-Creole meaning '*hard to the bone.*' An apt description of Officer Jean Delgado.

She slapped the window frame. "Good to see you. I mean it. Keep me in mind."

"Will do," he said.

"Who was that?" Lauren asked.

"I used to work with her."

"I got that much," she said, before going back to checking the flight schedule on her phone.

He'd driven her Audi instead of his car at her request. What he'd learned later in life than most was the secret to a happy relationship was to figure out what she wanted, then insist on it. Besides, his Porsche 911 had almost no room for luggage.

It seemed like Miami was a lot angrier these days. It was a temperamental place before the transplants from New Jersey and New York invaded. With a little luck they'd tire of the hot summers and hurricanes. He smiled at the thought. Hurricane season was only a month away.

Back when he was a homicide detective, before he'd graduated law school, Miami International Airport was a safe zone in no need of off-duty cops. The police who moonlighted back then worked the doors at the discotheques and private clubs and were paid to look the other way when it came to illegal activity. When the drug cartels ran things, it was more lucrative to do business with them than with honest folks. Gunshot wounds were the leading cause of emergency room visits. Dirty cops ripped off drug dealers. Body bags were on back order. The city was so violent no one in their right mind wanted a job as a police officer. The department resorted to lowing hiring standards. Applicants with misdemeanors made the cut. Record keeping wasn't as good back then. Rumors swirled about felons graduating the academy.

But that was then, and this was now.

Lauren was flying to the Caribbean to visit her old friend, Davis Frost. He'd called several times over the last couple of months trying to sell them on a business venture to launder some of their dirty money through a scuba diving operation. The outfit, Sea Otters, was located on the small island of Little Cayman located some 133-kilometers east, southeast of Grand Cayman. According to Davis, the British couple who'd opened it thirty years ago were getting on in age and wanted to retire and return home to England to spend their golden years in the fog and rain.

It was probably a solid proposition, but when it came to business, he self-identified as a gifted chemist who could turn money into dust. Vance had given the prospect some thought. The business had potential. Little Cayman was remote. It had no military installations or international banks to attract outside attention.

Davis's proposal went something like this. Purchase a fleet of small dive boats, hire additional dive-masters, and cook the books by claiming tons of fake customers. Vance had been interested enough to google the business. The pictures on the website were tantalizing. The offer included a luxury villa, though the word *luxury* was up for debate. Visitors could snorkel and dive year-round. Tourists had contributed dozens of photos and videos of stingrays, sharks and reef fish. The monster grouper was his hands-down favorite.

But none of it hooked him. Scuba diving made him claustrophobic. During the ten minutes he'd spent thinking it over and looking at pictures he'd decided the greatest risk would come from the local population of a couple of hundred people who'd scrutinize them. Unlike the obese, hard-partying, flip-flop-wearing Davis Frost, newcomers like he and Lauren would attract attention. The other problem was it would probably work to launder a couple of hundred grand a year — not enough to make it worthwhile.

To entice Lauren, Davis promised to teach her how to scuba dive and, unlike him, she thought the business prospect had enough potential to check it out.

"Do you need any cash for the trip?" Vance asked.

"I'm good," Lauren said.

He inched closer to the drop-off lane. "You have your passport and ticket?"

"Of course."

"Do you plan to go to the bank and meet the eels that manage your moola?"

"They're not eels. They're bankers, and no I'm not going to meet them. Why risk it?"

"Agreed," he said, realizing he was going to miss her when she was gone. She was his first serious relationship, which was saying something for a guy pushing well into his forties.

"You know what my dad told me when I was eight?" she asked.

"I give up," he said.

"Never depend on a man."

It was probably good advice, but still, —it was harsh. "Text me your arrival information so I know when to pick you up."

The line of idling cars finally began to move, and he pulled forward to let her out.

"Stay out of trouble, Harry," she said, getting out.

He popped the trunk and hurried to help her with her bag. She hadn't called him that for a while, a pet name she'd chosen because she said he looked like the jazz singer, Harry Connick, Jr. "Don't do anything I wouldn't do," he said, uncertain about his resemblance to the singer, surer she could be mistaken for Gwyneth Paltrow.

"That gives me free rein," she said, kissing him on the mouth. "Don't forget to take care of Cash. I left a list of things to do. Walk him in the morning and evening, and give him a scoop of kibble —"

"I know what to do. Don't worry about us. Have a safe trip."

He got back in the car and watched a family with two children follow her into the airport terminal. His mind drifted to his childhood. By the time he was in fifth grade, being bullied on the playground was a daily occurrence. Kids called him half-breed though he'd never figured out how they knew he was half Cuban because he looked like his dad. Sometimes he'd lie to his mom. He'd tell her he had a stomachache, always making a remarkable recovery before his father-the-doctor got home from the hospital.

This morning he'd awaken with an actual pain in his gut. He'd promised to meet his old friend, retired Ft. Lauderdale PD Sergeant Daniel Ruiz for an early lunch. Sarge intended to ask for a personal favor, and the only clue he'd dropped was that it had something to do with his son-in-law being suspended by the Florida Bar. It was going to be hard to turn Sarge down; he'd accumulated a lot of debt service by way of asking and receiving a laundry list of personal favors.

The shrill of the off-duty whistle brought him back to the present. The male cop rapped his side window. He put the Audi in drive, looked over his shoulder and pulled slowly forward. He had time to kill before the meeting. He headed home to feed the dog and change into his bike shorts.

When he was five years old, he'd asked Santa for a crystal ball. Though his father scoffed at the idea, if he'd gotten what he'd wanted it would've saved him the boatload of trouble that was about to unfold.

After dropping Lauren off he had no clue it might be the last time he'd hear from her.

2

Thursday spin class at the indoor cycle studio started at 10 a.m. and barring some traffic disaster, Vance had enough time to make it. Dreading the meeting with Sarge and not having come up with a plausible reason to cancel — like death — he figured forty-five minutes of high intensity cardio might be a good way to blow off a little steam before the ambush at the Italian joint where Sarge had a frequent diner card.

He and Lauren had received a promotional offer in the mail for a free month of indoor cycling and Lauren had signed them both up. He checked his phone at the next red light, surprised he hadn't heard from her yet. The flight time from Miami to Cayman was approximately 90 minutes, but then again, the way the airline industry operated these days, her plane could still be on the tarmac at MIA.

Window-filling graphics of fit models in spandex made the cycle place easy to find. He entered through the front door, dropping his left shoulder to avoid bumping into a guy slurping green sludge through a fat straw. Following the sounds of the music, he entered the exercise room, more a bat cave, immediately recognizing the song playing on the surround sound system. The walls pounded as he looked for an available bike. Selecting one at the back, he set his bag down, tossed his towel across the handlebars and sat on the rubber mat to change into his new bike shoes.

The female instructor approached. "Do you need help setting up the bike?"

"I got it," he said, "but thanks."

She tipped at the waist to get closer. "I don't remember seeing you before."

He cupped his hands around his mouth. "I'm new. It's my girlfriend's idea."

"And she's not with you?"

His phone glowed inside his gym bag. Speaking of girlfriend, her name came up on CALLER ID. He held up the phone, pointed to the screen and mouthed over the music, "I have to take this."

He left his bag next to the bike and hurried out to the lobby where it was quieter. "Hey," he said, "how was your flight?"

"*Ju* need to listen up."

It was a man with a heavy accent. He must've dropped her call and answered one from a bot. He checked the screen. He was still connected to Lauren's phone number.

"I am going to send *ju* a text. Follow the directions," the man threatened, "or we will kill her."

"Kill who? Who is this?"

The caller was gone.

His phone pinged.

Meet at Vizcaya at 1 today. Do not be late.

He slapped the phone against his thigh, then jabbed the green redial dot on the screen. It went directly to voicemail: '*This is Lauren Gold. You know the drill.*'

Another text bubbled up.

Wait at the barge. Alone. Do not call the cops or we will kill her.

The barge? What was that?

Vizcaya Museum and Botanical Gardens was a popular tourist attraction located about ten minutes north of Lauren's condo in Coconut Grove. He replayed the events of the morning. When he'd dropped her at the airport, he'd seen her enter the terminal. Scenarios tore through his head, but none made sense. Unless she had been abducted in Cayman. If that was the case, the situation just got a lot more complicated.

He shoved the phone in his pocket, rushed to the cycle room, grabbed his gym bag and headed home. He played each sequence of this morning's events over. He and Lauren left their place a little after 7:15 a.m. and arrived at Miami International at approximately 8. He'd chatted with Zo for a half minute. He remembered seeing a family of four follow her into the airport terminal. Someone could've abducted her before she cleared security. Maybe they'd been followed. He hadn't been paying attention.

He remembered the meeting with Sarge. He dictated a messaged to his phone:

Need to reschedule

Two seconds later his phone rang.

"No way," Sarge said. "You can't do this."

"Something came up and I can't make it."

"No can do," Sarge said, "we're meeting in less than an hour. I can get there a few minutes early, but the place doesn't open until eleven."

He checked the time. If the lunch was short, he'd have enough cushion to make the meeting and get to Vizcaya on time. "Fine," he said, "I'll see you there, but I have to make it quick."

Vance arrived home and waited for the security gate to open, parked Lauren's car and rushed inside. Cashmere waited on the other side of the front door, cowering. He and Lauren had adopted the poodle-terrier rescue less than a month ago. He saw the yellow puddle and muddy footprints on the tile. Instead of walking him when he'd stopped to change for the gym, he'd left the courtyard door open just enough for the small dog to go in and out, but the poor little guy hadn't figured it out.

"Hey little buddy," he said scratching the pup's chin. "I know it was an accident."

Cash watched with droopy eyes as he wiped up the mess before stripping out of his bike shorts and changing into jeans and a short-sleeved shirt. He took his windbreaker from the coat closet and grabbed the key fob to his Porsche. Kneeling, he patted Cash on the head. "I'll be back."

He backed the Porsche out, wiping a droplet of sweat from his brow and drying his hand on his jeans. He checked his phone again. No new messages from Lauren's phone. He felt the 9-mil holstered under his left arm. Was *'the barge'* code for something? As he dropped the Porsche into reverse, his hands shook. His brain spun a wheel of thoughts. Nothing made sense. "Focus," he said aloud to himself, "you need to focus."

Halfway to the Italian restaurant, he checked his phone. Still nothing. Under normal circumstances, he would have shown the text messages to Sarge and asked him for help, but he couldn't. This was precisely how he'd become indebted to Sarge, and he couldn't dig a deeper personal-favor hole without first finding out what his friend wanted. Besides, the retired police sergeant would have company.

There had to be security and cameras all over the airport but getting access to the footage would take an act of God. Then he had an epiphany. At the next red light, he took the business card from his wallet and dialed the number.

"You find me a side hustle already?" Zo asked, letting out a hearty laugh.

"It's more of a personal favor," he said. "I want you to find out if my girlfriend got on that plane."

"What? It's been what, like two hours."

"Two hours and thirty-six minutes."

"If I go pokin' around, I might be riskin' a gig I *cannot* afford to lose," Zo said. "You understand what you're askin' me to do?"

"I do, and I pay better. Just do me a solid and find out if Lauren Gold got on the flight to Grand Cayman. Call in a favor. Say it's for a friend. Better yet, don't say anything. Miami PD has jurisdiction at Miami International. Get someone to check the passenger manifest or security footage. You must know someone."

"Been here way too long. I know everyone. If I was you, I'd wait twenty-four and report it. Do that and the first thing they'll do is check the footage."

"I can't do that, Zo."

"I ain't gonna ask why you can't wait 'cause I don't wanna know." She hesitated, then added. "Where you gonna be if we need to talk?"

"I'm having lunch with an old colleague of yours."

"That right?"

"Yeah. Sergeant Daniel Ruiz."

"You goin' to that endless-spaghetti joint?"

"How did you know?"

Zo let out a big laugh. "Oh honey, I told him he oughta buy stock in the place. How Sarge love that all-you-can-eat lunch special. Some habits never die. Where you livin' these days?"

"With my girlfriend in The Grove," he said, adding, "it's her place."

"Ah," Zo said. "So, Courage finally gone and got his self a girlfriend. Sarge always yakkin' that was never gonna happen. Well, I'll be," she said. "Wishin' I could join you and if I wasn't workin' and you was buyin' I'd fill up on endless shrimp scampi. Seein' as how you're shackin' up with this gal, I'll see what I can do. What's her name again?"

"Lauren Gold."

"We ain't never had this talk."

"What talk?" he said, hanging up.

3

When Vance arrived at the chain Italian restaurant on Coral Way, the parking lot was only a third full, the benefit of meeting early ahead of the lunch rush. He saw an open space next to a white Jeep Cherokee that looked a lot like Sarge's. Daniel was one of those guys who got the same new make and model every five years. He shook his head and chuckled at the bumper sticker.

WOMEN WANT ME, FISH FEAR ME

He entered the restaurant and while waiting for the hostess, spotted the sheen on the back of Sarge's brown bald head. He headed toward the booth in the back, near the restrooms, not recognizing the man sitting across from his old buddy. He assumed it was Sarge's son-in-law.

Sarge stood to greet him. The gray fringy hair circling the bottom half of his head needed a trim and his Mr. Potato Head glasses could've used a cleaning.

"You lose some weight?" he asked, messing with him.

Sarge patted his big belly and grinned. "My *madre* said if you're proud of something, build a porch over it."

He choked down the urge to laugh.

"Thanks for coming," Sarge said, giving him a two-armed bear hug, squeezing the air from his lungs.

"This is my son-in-law, Rafael Suarez," Sarge said, gesturing to the man sitting in the booth.

Suarez didn't stand. He was dressed in a pale blue polo shirt and wore a gold and stainless Rolex on his wrist. His black hair was short and spiked with gel and he wore cologne strong enough to overpower the scent of grease and garlic.

Sarge sat and scooted toward the smudged window to make room for him.

Keeping an eye on Suarez, he took the aisle seat next to his friend.

Sarge handed him the menu. "Get whatever you want. My treat."

Truth was, he wasn't hungry and even if he was, he didn't have time. "Vance Courage," he said, extending his hand across the greasy tabletop.

"I know who you are," Suarez said, reaching and grabbing his palm, squeezing it hard enough to show off the flexors on his right forearm. "My father-in-law says you had your own law practice."

"I did. Had a little place over on Bird Road."

"What made you give it up?" Suarez asked.

"More like it gave me up. I'm not cut out for the work."

"How so?"

"For one thing, I speak ten words in Spanish."

"I can see how that would be a problem," Suarez said. "Three-quarters of my clients don't speak English." Suarez eyed Sarge. "I don't understand. As I recall, my father-in-law said you're one of us."

He cocked his head. "Us as in lawyer?"

"No, us as in Cuban."

"On my mother's side."

"Well," Suarez said, nodding slowly, "you must favor your daddy's side of the family."

"Daniel said you have some sort of personal matter you want to discuss," he said, pushing the convo along.

"I do," Suarez said, eyes darting around the restaurant. "It's not exactly a personal matter, more a business problem. I've been suspended by the Florida Bar."

Sarge had already shared this with him. "Do you mind if I ask why?"

"I was stopped for speeding," Suarez said, "and I blew a blood alcohol level double the legal limit. Good thing they didn't search the vehicle."

"Why?"

"I had an ounce of weed in the glove box."

That was a strange detail to share. "You're a lawyer. You could've refused the breathalyzer."

Suarez shrugged. "There was no point. The cops had body cams and as much as I'd have liked to get out of it, the video would show me struggling to get out of the vehicle. I can barely remember the field test even though I didn't think I drank that much. If I refused, they'd have drawn blood at the jail, not to mention the possession charge."

He'd been around enough alcoholics to know most of them couldn't remember how much they drank. "You could've fought it by demanding a warrant. You would've sobered up by the time a judge signed it." It was lawyer 101. They could've suspended his driver's license temporarily, possibly up to a year, but it beat a DUI. Chances are it would've been dismissed.

"I've used my get out of jail free card already," Suarez said. "This is my second DUI. Last one was sixteen years ago. If it was less than five, I'd be facing mandatory jail time and a felony. Good thing the judge is a golfing buddy. I got a nudge from the judge."

"A nudge to do what?" he asked.

"Go to rehab, do community service, pay the fine. Do you have any idea how much a felony and a stint in prison would screw up my life?"

"I do," he said, checking the time.

"You need to be somewhere?" Suarez asked.

Sarge side-eyed him, acknowledging the talk they'd had earlier this morning.

"I'm listening," he said.

"I agreed to plead it down to a misdemeanor," Suarez said. "What's important now is to keep the matter private. The worst part is the Florida Bar suspended me for thirty days."

"What's any of this have to do with me?"

Sarge cut in. "It's sounds worse than it is. Ralph was just out having a little fun. It was Easter and who isn't out enjoying themselves, right? He was just driving in the wrong place at the wrong time."

Easter? What was he doing? Searching for eggs and found a bottle of scotch instead? For a retired cop, Sarge was like anyone. His judgment was impaired when it came to family matters.

"The Florida Bar is forcing me to do thirty days of inpatient rehab before they'll reinstate me," Suarez said. "After I graduate rehab, I'll be back to work like it never even happened."

"What do you get at graduation? An autographed bottle of Jack Daniels?"

Sarge took umbrage. "Is that supposed to be funny?"

It was supposed to be funny. He stared at the laminated

menu with splats of fossilized food. The purpose of the meeting was beginning to take shape.

Sarge laid his menu down and studied him, looking for a reaction to the news of his son-in-law's DUI and suspension.

He kept a poker face. It didn't take much of an effort because between being an ex-cop and a washed-up lawyer whose girlfriend had just been abducted, he was numb. "When I was in law school," he said, "I had a classmate who wanted to be a police officer."

"Is there a punch line?" Suarez asked.

"The academy rejected him because he had a felony conviction for heroin. His parents did everything they could to get the charges dropped but couldn't. He applied to law school instead. Today he's a judge. Imagine that, not qualified to make a traffic stop but approved to preside over peoples' lives. It's strange, don't you think?"

Suarez shrugged. "My father-in-law said you're the right man to cover for me while I'm gone. I need someone I can trust." The lawyer leaned in and spoke softly. "Someone with discretion. I heard you were a heck of a plaintiffs' lawyer."

"It doesn't matter if I'm F. Lee Bailey reincarnated, I'm not your guy," he said, fish-eyeing Sarge who twisted the fake diamond pierced into his right earlobe. "I told you. I don't speak the right language."

"I have people," Suarez said, "and the language won't be a problem."

"Look, I'd like to help you out, but I can't. I'm not sure my law license is active."

"I had my office check," Suarez said. "Your license is current and you're good to go. I plan to make it worth your while. It'll be low key. Keep my clients happy until I come back. It's a part-time gig. Just cover the basics. File motions for continuances and if you can't get delays, appear in front of the judge and find creative ways to buy more time. You know the drill. The courts are clogged. Dump documents, reschedule, do whatever you have to do to get continuances."

He looked at Sarge. He'd never seen him so stone-faced. If he agreed to do this, which was becoming increasingly impossible to avoid, any debt service to Sarge would be wiped out now and forever. "What did you tell your clients?"

A male server with turquoise hair appeared at the table, interrupting. "Are you gentlemen ready to order?"

"We're still looking at the menu," Suarez said, waiting until the waiter was out of earshot before continuing. "I'd rather not have to tell them anything. Most clients don't want a drunk for a lawyer."

"Is that what you are? A drunk?" he asked.

Sarge's brow folded into horizontal rolls of flesh. "No," he said in a tone bordering a growl. "Like I told you, Ralph was in the wrong place at the wrong time is all."

That's what the drunks usually said, not their retired-cop in-laws. His radar went higher, and he made a mental note. Maybe Sarge was embarrassed. Denial was a security blanket that kept people from the truth until they were ready to deal with it. On the other hand, he'd never known Sarge to be willfully blind. But he was human. The situation involved family. Suarez was the father of Sarge's two grand-daughters and Rafael was trusting his father-in-law with something highly confidential. And Sarge was trusting him. There was a saying about the direction sewage flows.

"It's okay," Ralph said to his father-in-law before addressing him, ignoring the 'are you a drunk question.' "You wanted to know what I told my clients. I haven't told them anything and when the time comes, they'll be told that

I took a leave of absence because my wife had a medical emergency."

On top of being a drunk, Suarez was a liar. On the other hand, that pair of character flaws often went together. "You said three-quarters of your clients speak Spanish."

"My crack paralegal Lola is fluent in English and Spanish and can brief you on everything. She knows every case file and client, and she's an ace at keeping things running. She can handle anything that doesn't require a lawyer. That's not true. She can handle anything a lawyer can, but she's not licensed and that's why I need you. I also have a part-time investigator, Franco, who can pitch in."

Sarge leaned sideways and spoke directly into his earhole. "You owe me, Courage."

It was true. He owed him big time. "Let me to think about it."

"What's to think about?" Sarge said. "Ralph doesn't have time for you to think about it. He has to leave for rehab at five o'clock tomorrow evening. How many times have you asked me for help and how many times have I asked you for anything in return?"

Ambushing him at the last minute was a strategy. Sarge knew if he gave him enough time to think about it, he'd have found a way out. *Time kills deals*. He'd rather drive a honey wagon on Spring Break, slurping sludge from port-a-potties with a fat hose—on an unseasonably hot day—than spend another minute in court.

But, but, BUT. Sarge was right. He owed him. "How many cases do you have and how many are set for trial over the next thirty days?" he asked Suarez.

"I have about fifty files in various states of litigation. I have a couple of probates. Three or four divorces. You know how the deep-pocket cases go. The insurance companies are always finding ways to delay."

Deep pocket was code for anyone worth suing regardless of how frivolous the case was. It was true, if they settled too quickly, it sent the wrong message. Plus, lawyers working for the insurance companies lived for billable hours.

"I have one case that will settle while I'm out," Suarez said. "I'll give you my contingency fee. Forty percent of two-hundred grand. That's a lot of clams for a month of part-time work."

It was good money, but he didn't need it. More importantly it meant Sarge hadn't shared his financial well-being with his son-in-law. Only a handful of people knew about his offshore bank account, and Sarge was one of them.

"What about your investigator? You said he works part time."

"That's right. Lola will handle him," Suarez said, plucking the corner of the plastic menu with his thumbnail.

"What's that supposed to mean?" he asked.

Suarez didn't answer.

Every muscle from the waist up felt like an overstretched rubber band. He placed his elbow on the table, cupped his chin in his palm and massaged his lower jaw with his fingers. "I guess I should look at the upshot," he said.

"Which is?" Suarez asked.

"You didn't ask me to hire a hit man to kill your wife."

Sarge's head snapped back, and his eyes narrowed.

"What?" Suarez asked, appearing royally pissed off.

"Haven't you noticed spouses looking for hit men always get caught meeting undercover cops in cheap Italian chain restaurants."

Suarez lightened up and laughed a little, but Sarge failed to see the humor.

"I'm taking that as a yes," Suarez said.

He let it hang in the air for a minute, buying a little time, cocking his head and grimacing, gazing out the window, tapping the tabletop, staring at the menu. It was all for show. They were not taking no for an answer. "Fine," he said, "but this isn't for you. It's for your father-in-law. As far as I'm concerned, you could lose your law license and train for the Mr. Universe competition at a Club Fed somewhere. Here are the ground rules. No nine-to-five. No going into the office unless I absolutely have to. Ditto for court appearances and no consultations with clients. No new clients. That's non-negotiable."

"Deal," Suarez said.

Sarge nodded slowly, as if digesting the answer. "I really appreciate this *gallego*."

"*Gallego*! Ha!" Suarez guffawed, "that's funny! That's *Cubano* slang for a guy who can't get laid. Good one."

It was also a very old inside joke.

"You still seeing that horsey chick?" Sarge asked, referring to Lauren.

He changed the subject. "I saw an old colleague of yours today."

"Is that right," Sarge said.

"You remember Zo?"

"Of course. She was my partner her rookie year up in Lauderdale before she transferred to vice. Busted the biggest child porn case in Florida history while staking out an illegal gambling operation. Broke the perp's jaw before cuffing him."

Zo's claim to fame went beyond the busted jaw when she rescued fifty immigrant kids being trafficked from a safe house.

"What's she doing these days?" Sarge asked.

"Still working."

"No shit." He wrinkled his brow. "She should've retired years ago."

"She's going through some hard times. Family stuff," he said, staring at Suarez.

The waiter returned. "Have you gentleman decided what you want?"

He felt his phone buzz in his pocket and discreetly checked CALLER ID. "Excuse me," he said, sliding out from the booth. "I have to take this." He stood, pulled a twenty from his wallet, changed his mind, exchanged it for a five and let it sail onto the table. "Enjoy your lunch," he said, hurrying toward the exit to take the call.

If she'd called thirty seconds earlier, he might've had a legit reason to turn Suarez down. Too late for that. His word was his word, and he could tell from the tone of his sister Kathy's voice something was wrong.

4

Shouldering past the swarm of hungry patrons hovering three deep around the hostess stand, Vance made his way out the front door. He stood on the sidewalk beneath an overhang in front of the Italian place looking at a wall of gray clouds gathering overhead. He held his phone close to his ear; Kathy's tone was stilted.

"Is everything alright?" he asked.

"Yeah, I'm just having a bad day," Kathy said.

"What's up?" he said, jogging, pushing the key fob and unlocking the Porsche.

"The roof is leaking."

"Where's Larry?"

Larry the husband that could never make ends meet. "He's at work."

"I can't come over now," he said as large raindrops splattered the windshield.

"That's not why I called. The boys are out of school tomorrow and Ethan will be home alone."

"Is something wrong?"

"No. Larry's taking the other three boys to a paintball

place and Ethan doesn't want to go. I just thought . . ." she trailed off.

"Let me check my schedule."

"You don't have a schedule." She lowered her voice. "I know what you're thinking. Larry's going to take care of the roof as soon as he gets his bonus."

The one he never seemed to get. "I told you I'd pay for it."

"I thought you might like to see Ethan. It might be nice for you to spend some time with him."

"Listen, Kat . . . I'm not sure it's such a good idea to keep pushing it."

"He asks about you all the time, but if you don't want to see him, I get it. If you say no, I'm sure he'll understand."

Jesus. He'd stopped by recently with Lauren and the Jones' household was practically a war zone. They'd dropped off presents for Kathy's birthday and didn't stay long. He should've given her a gift certificate for a roofing company, but he hadn't seen the ceiling damage and catch bucket filled with rainwater until they were on their way out. When he asked about it, Larry told him not to worry. Code for let Kathy worry about it. Larry wasn't a bad guy, but he wasn't a go-getter either.

"I know eight in the morning is probably too early for you," she said.

That wasn't it.

"Sorry I asked," Kathy said.

"No, no. I'll try to stop by. I'd like to see him," he said, as a hard rain pummeled the Porsche.

"He'll be happy when I tell him."

He spoke loudly over the noise. "Don't promise him, Kat, I'm not sure if I can make it or not."

"What's up with you?" she asked.

They were close like that; she sensed the anxiousness in his voice. "Everything's fine. I'll do my best to be there."

Ethan would turn eighteen in four years. That was the age Kathy and her husband Larry agreed to tell him he'd been adopted, and Kathy was trying to get ahead of it. Ethan didn't know Vance was his biological father, a fact that he himself didn't know until recently. The result of a fling he'd had with his married secretary who'd gone to Kathy in secret.

"I won't promise him," she said, "but it would be good for both of you to spend more time together."

He ended the call. The rain intensified and a powerful gust of wind snapped a GRAND OPENING sign tied to a post in the parking lot, the metal grommets barely missed the hood of his car. As the sign flapped, he fumbled for the windshield wipers and headlights. A loud thump on the driver's side window startled him. He automatically reached for the 9-millimeter Glock he'd stowed beneath the driver's seat.

A young man stood in the torrential rain, hunched over, stretching his jacket over his head like an awning. Vance cracked open the car window just enough to ask what he wanted.

"Your rear passenger tire is flat," the young man yelled, struggling to hold his coat steady over his head.

He got out and jogged around the back bumper getting drenched. The Porsche listed on an angle. "Freaking potholes," he said, heading back to the driver's side to take cover.

"I saw the guy who did it," the young man said. "I was sitting in my car checking my phone when I saw him crouching between the cars. It looked like he used a knife or something. I bet those tires cost you a bundle."

He rushed back to look again, squatting in the pouring rain next to the rear passenger side flat. Sure enough, the sidewall had a deep gash that matched the guy's story. The wind howled and he felt a chill.

"That's my car," the young man said, gesturing to the Tesla parked next to him on the side with the flat tire. "I can move so you'll have room to jack yours up to change the tire."

"I don't have a spare," he said. "It comes with a kit to inflate and seal the tire. It's supposed to be temporary, enough to drive somewhere to get a new tire. But there's no way I can seal a sidewall tear." It was obvious the gouge was a mortal blow. He needed roadside assistance, but he didn't have time to wait. He checked the time. Precious minutes slipped away. He couldn't be late to the barge.

Then he noticed the ride-share sticker on the windshield of the young man's car.

"Can you give me a lift to Vizcaya?"

"Um, sure," the stranger said standing in the rain. "Since you didn't use the app, this one is off the books. The company has cameras in our cars. To make it kosher, you'll need to sit up front with me and pay cash."

"No problem," he said climbing into the front passenger seat.

"Name's Logan," the driver said.

5

As Logan approached the pale-yellow wall surrounding Vizcaya, the sun winked through the gnarled tree branches forming a canopy across South Miami Avenue. Unlike the garish signage at most Florida tourist attractions, the entrance to the historic home and botanical gardens was understated.

Vance eyed the computer monitor attached to the dash of the Tesla. They were 100-feet from the entrance and as the traffic light turned amber, Logan rolled to a stop adjacent a decommissioned guardhouse with metal latticework around the windows. He craned his neck looking for the limestone pillars he'd seen a thousand times before.

"Did you get a look at the guy who cut my tire?" he asked.

Logan fish-eyed him. "It was raining pretty hard, and he was fast. Average height and build, I guess. I couldn't see his face because he was wearing a mask and a hoodie."

"You're sure you saw him do it?"

"I heard a pop and saw a guy run away."

When he'd talked to his sister during the storm, he could barely hear her over the pounding rain, but it was possible.

The light turned green, and Logan hung a right passing the tall posts flanking the entrance to Vizcaya. The winding road to the mansion was narrow and shaded with dense tropical foliage.

"How would you like to make some easy money?" he asked Logan.

"There's no such thing," Logan said.

"I'll pay you to go back to the restaurant and wait for a new tire." He flashed a wad of cash then placed it on the center console between the seats.

Logan eyed the money. "What's the catch?"

"There isn't one. I'll call the dealership," he said, getting out of the car, handing Logan the key fob to the Porsche. "Give me your number and when I'm done here, I'll call you so you can pick me up and take me back to my car."

"You got business here or something?" Logan asked.

"Something like that," he said rattling off his mobile number as Logan entered it into his phone. A few seconds later his phone rang with a call from the ride-share driver. "I bet the Porsche people will be there by the time you get back to the restaurant," he said, saving Logan's number in his contacts list.

As Logan turned the Tesla around, he trotted alongside the vehicle trying to get his attention. Logan powered down the window.

"Do me a favor," he said. "If anyone asks what happened, tell them you don't know. If they ask for ID, say you're my cousin or something. Call me only if you need to."

"No problem," Logan said, lifting his right hip to stuff his wallet in his pants pocket. The edge of a silver object stuck out from under his thigh.

"I'll call you when I'm ready," Vance said.

BEELINING past mazes of geometric hedges and life-sized nude stone statues covered with moss, he called the Porsche dealer and reported the flat. They promised to send someone right away to replace it.

The sun was out, and the walkway shimmered from the recent rain. He was barely aware of the electric colors of the orchids in bloom or the musky aroma of wet dirt from the thunderstorm. In the distance he zeroed in on a large group of people milling in the shade beneath a portico. He approached the mansion, a sprawling two- and three-story Baroque-style estate with a red clay roof. It was more impressive in person than in the photos he'd seen on the 'Net. He joined the line of tourists waiting to pay admission, inhaling the salty air wafting from the bay.

On high alert, he watched as throngs of visitors chatted and pointed, admiring the meticulously manicured gardens and endless architectural details. Weaseling his way to the front of the line, he ignored the dirty looks and searched for metal detectors. Not seeing any, he slinked to the end of the line pressing his left elbow against his ribcage, feeling the butt of the 9-millimeter Glock against his bones. He clenched his fists in his pockets and stretched his neck from side to side as the line inched forward, then checked the time. He had ten minutes to spare before the appointed hour of 1 o'clock.

When he reached the front of the line a middle-aged woman with raccoon eyes working admissions asked, "How many in your party?"

"Just one," he said, screwing his head left and right as he pulled his wallet from his pants pocket. "Can you tell me how to get to the barge?"

She grimaced as if he were an idiot, handed him the change and slapped a brochure on the counter. "You can find it on the map, or you can sign up for a guided tour." She tossed her head to one side, jutted her chin and glared over his shoulder at the folks behind him, signaling him to move it.

He entered the open-air walkway, merging to one side making way for the faster foot traffic. A row of tourists stood three deep behind a thick red velvet rope cordoning off a room. Tall enough to see over most of the tourists, he peered into the living area. People tilted their heads back at the fresco painted on the dome of the soaring cathedral ceiling; the Louis XIV furniture was topped with a dizzying array of valuable knickknacks and art pieces—all frozen in time.

He stepped to the side, inhaled deeply and leaned against the exterior wall. He pulled the brochure from his back pants pocket and unfolded the map to study it. A woman approached and sidled up next to him.

"*Ju* look lost. May I help *ju*?" she asked.

Her voice was husky, and her accent was heavy and familiar, like his mother's Cuban-Spanish dialect.

"Do you know how to get to the barge?" he asked, blotting his forehead with the sleeve of his windbreaker, suddenly conscious of the unpleasant aromas of the place, ones that reminded him of death and decay.

"I do. I'm going that way. I can show *ju*."

"You don't mind?"

"Not at all. Follow me," she said.

The rubber soles of her dirty white plimsolls squeaked on the marble floor.

"Have *ju* been to Vizcaya before?" she asked, the sounds of her sneakers mixing with the indistinct voices of tourists gathered in small groups.

"No," he said, noticing her purposeful walk. He followed her outside to the gardens, scanning the perimeter. "What is the barge?" he asked.

"*Ju'll* see," she said. "Did *ju* come with anyone?"

"No."

She led the way, stepping across large pavers lain in a checkerboard alternating with squares of green grass.

His mind turned quickly from the small talk to the strange phone call. How would he know the man he was to meet and how would he disengage from this woman to make contact? What if she hung around out of boredom, or curiosity, or whatever? They approached an old concrete balustrade built a level above the seawall holding back the waters of Biscayne Bay.

"There it is," she said, gesturing to a massive manmade structure the size and shape of a freighter rising from the water.

It was situated parallel to the bulkhead seventy-five, maybe a hundred feet from the water's edge. The middle section was in ruins. What remained was gaudy like every-thing else. Statues of bare-breasted mermaids sprouted at the bow. The middle of the fake ship was demolished almost to the waterline.

"What is it?" he asked.

"It's what's left of a stone barge."

"I can see that. But what's it doing there?" he asked, head rotating side to side, looking for the man, half listening to the woman.

"It was built as a breakwater."

"Ah," he said.

"They had a live camera on it during Hurricane Irma and *ju* should see the storm surge and waves breaking big chunks from the middle."

"It didn't work?"

"No, but nothing could've stopped the surge. It flooded parts of the house. *Ju* better turn around slowly," she said, looking past him.

He kept his eyes on her. "Why?"

"Just do it. Stay calm."

He lurched backward. "What the hell?"

"It's more scared of *ju* than *ju* are of it."

An iguana with horizontal green and black stripes hugged the top of the cement railing. It was over a foot long with small hands and long fingers that looked almost human. He took two steps away. "How long have you worked here?"

She narrowed her inky black eyes. "I don't work here."

"What?"

"*Ju* have a problem with people being friendly?"

Before he could answer, an elderly bespectacled gentleman donning a beret and plaid slacks approached. The man led two dozen or so tourists. The old man stopped a couple of feet from them, gripping a carved wooden walking stick with both hands. His followers surrounded him in a semi-circle. His voice was high-pitched and sharp like a cat in heat.

"*What you're looking at is what's left of the Vizcaya Barge. In its heyday James Deering hosted parties on it and—*"

He turned his back to the woman and the tour guide to survey the perimeter. He checked the time. His contact was now late. He shifted his attention to the twisted mangrove forests located along the north side of the property near the water's edge. He counted thirteen tourists standing on an arched wooden footbridge connecting the estate to the woodlands. He looked skyward. A blanket of white clouds gathered, blocking the sun.

He checked the time again. More than fifteen minutes had passed since he'd arrived. Did he misunderstand the directions for the meeting? Maybe the man saw that he was with someone. He'd been specific about him being alone.

"I appreciate your help," he said to the woman still shadowing him.

He took a few steps away from her, but she followed. For God's sake. Didn't she have something better to do? She'd been helpful so far but now she was in the way. He stopped and leaned against the railing, clenching his teeth, thinking of ways to get rid of her. The old guide chattered in the background. It was low tide and plastic bottles bobbed in the shallow water lapping against the seawall. For the first time he noticed the foul smell of the frothy bay water. Where was the man? A plane buzzed overhead and when it was out of earshot, his ears tuned back into the tour guide.

"Deering of the International Harvester fortune, built Villa Vizcaya as his winter home but he died in 1925 shortly after it was finished."

A ray of sun highlighted the front of the woman's loose-fitting white dress. He noticed a faint brown stain, from an old coffee spill he guessed. Wisps of threads sprouted from the shoulder straps. Why wasn't she picking up on his clues to leave? His phone pinged in his pocket. Using one hand to shade it, he read a text message from Lauren's phone number.

Look for the arch at 3 o'clock.

Using the hands of an imaginary clock for directions meant the stranger had eyes on his position.

He looked to his right and spotted a brick archway in the

distance, beyond the footbridge. A silhouette stepped out into a small clearing in the dense woodlands. The stranger's face was obscured by the forest shadows. He calculated the distance to be about a half a city block from where he stood. The man raised his hand in the air. He shaded his eyes and squinted to see better but in low light at five hundred feet, he couldn't make out any details. But the thing he held in his hand glowed in the dim forest.

"I hate to be rude," he said to the woman, "but I have to go." He spun and rocketed on foot toward the woods, shouldering people, apologizing as he skimmed the tour group. He bolted past pockets of distracted tourists, startling them.

He'd noticed the pop-up farmers market when he'd arrived and zigzagged on foot along the walkway between the portable tents with vendors and tourists milling around the folding tables. As he turned the corner toward the path leading to the forest, a young mother pushing a navy-blue baby stroller crossed in front of him. He cut hard left to avoid T-boning the infant, bumping into a wedding photographer hovering over the lens of a camera, almost knocking him over. The photog grunted.

"Asshole!" the groom yelled at him.

"Sorry," he shouted over his shoulder, spooking a flock of roosting seagulls that launched vertical and swooped horizontal over the bay water. He had eyes on the limestone archway in the distance where he'd spotted his contact and sprinted toward it. By the time he reached the opposite side of the footbridge, he'd lost sight of him. He felt his phone vibrate in his pocket. He read the message.

The lady in white is ur contact. Do what she says if u want to see ur girlfriend alive.

He stopped, out of breath, and held the wooden railing of the bridge for balance. The side he was on opened to a shaded tropical jungle and the man who'd taunted him was nowhere in sight. He sprinted into the forest, eyes darting, head twitching, before he stopped beneath the canopy of an old oak. He bent over, gripped his knees and panted. He looked at the text message again, then tapped the gray dot with Lauren's initials at the top of the screen, redialing the number. He heard a phone ringing.

He felt for the 9-mil, his shoulder muscles tightening as he drew it. Crouching, he followed the narrow sandy footpath, soggy leaves and palms squashing beneath his shoes. Heading toward the small clearing where he'd first spotted the man, he stopped to listen. On the sixth ring the mystery phone went to Lauren's voicemail. He redialed and cupped his right ear to tune into the sound. He saw something glowing in a pile of decaying palm fronds. He picked up the phone and tapped the red button to end the call. It was bare bones with a solid blue screen, no apps. A burner.

He dialed Lauren's number again from his phone. The one he'd just found rang in his hand. He stared at it.

How could this be?

He stuffed both phones in his pants pockets and jogged toward the bridge leading back to Vizcaya. People standing on both sides cleared a path and glared at him. Heading back to the barge to find the woman in white, he stopped near the base of the footbridge to regroup.

"Hey," the still photographer yelled, hands funneled over his mouth. "You're in my shot."

The groom turned and flipped the bird at him. His betrothed, a buxom woman wearing a low-cut satin bridal gown with breasts billowing like blooming dough rotated on her heels. She scowled, flailed her arms and bellowed, "Move it, you dick! You're in our pictures!"

He raised both hands with open palms in an apology

and headed back to look for the woman in white. When he arrived at the same spot, the old tour guide and his followers were gone but the lady was there, standing alone, gazing at the bay. As he approached her, a lone seagull dive-bombed a group of tourists forcing them to scatter and duck for cover.

"I am *jur* contact. Give me that phone." She held her hand out.

"Why didn't you tell me up front?"

"*Ju* need to know I don't work alone." Her tone hardened. "Give it over."

"I'll give it to you as soon as you tell me what you want."

"I speak for *Damas de Blanco.*"

"Who?" he asked, gritting his teeth, surveying the perimeter. He was exposed from every angle. A sitting duck. The stranger who'd dropped the burner could still be out there, somewhere. If something went down, there were dozens of tourists who'd be witnesses but that guaranteed nothing. They'd scatter at the first sign of trouble. He moved closer to the woman.

She backed away from him as she repeated herself. "*Damas de Blanco.*"

"I don't speak Spanish." He took another step toward her.

She stepped back. "*Jur* joking," she said, eyes narrowing.

"No."

"*Jur* name is Vance Courage. *Jur* mother was born in Cuba and left after the revolution. *Jur* aunt and *jur* uncle Tony fled the homeland with her. *Jur* uncle is an FBI fugitive. He's in Panama now. *Ju* used to be a cop before *ju* went to law school. Should I go on?" she asked, lifting a delicate silver crucifix hanging from a thin chain around her neck. She twirled it between two fingers before releasing it where it disappeared into the soft V between her breasts.

A tsunami of adrenaline flooded his system. "Who are you?" he said, fighting the impulse to grab her by the neck. He reached inside his jacket and walked his fingers up the inside of his windbreaker until he felt the hard polymer grip of the Glock holstered under his left arm.

"Don't be stupid," she said, folding her arms across her chest. "*Ju* don't know how many of us are here."

She was right. He didn't know. Relaxing his right hand, he slowly lowered his arm to his side where she could see it, then hooked both thumbs through the belt loops of his jeans. "If you hurt her, I'll kill you."

"Meet our demands and *ju* won't have to worry."

"What are your demands?" he asked, sucking saltwater air through his nose, inflating his lungs till they hurt. Her smile sent a chill down his spine.

"*Jur* fat American friend in Grand Cayman has a big bank account and a bigger mouth. *Ju* know the expression. Loose lips sink ships. For *ju*, loose lips bragging about rich friends will cost *ju* a fair share of your stolen *dinero*."

He stared at the waterline, at the ugly crumbling cement ship rising from the bay waters.

"Does the name Monkey Morales ring a bell?" she asked, cocking her head ever so slightly.

The hair bristled on the back of his neck. Morales had been dead for decades. Shot in a bar fight and died in a local hospital. It had been a big news story. When karma caught up with certain characters from Miami's sordid past, there had been a visceral euphoria that permeated the city. Like when terrorists and serial killers are caught. From suburban neighborhoods to newsrooms, the death of Monkey Morales evoked that sort of *cause célèbre*.

He stared at the wave of charcoal clouds erupting offshore, to the east. White caps churned along the tops of choppy waves, breaking against the fake barge before lapping at the seawall.

"What's Morales have to do with kidnapping my girlfriend?"

"He wants what *ju* stole from him."

6

S he had her facts wrong. He'd never stolen a red cent from Ricardo Morales.

"Maybe the *dinero ju* and *jur* friends took might help *ju* remember. *El Mono* wants it back."

That was one of the five words he knew in Spanish. *Dinero* = money. He hadn't stolen it. He and Lauren had been fairly compensated for helping salvage drug cash purported to be hidden in the hull of a powerboat sunk offshore in the 1980s. The loot was hidden inside the hull of a boat alright, but the rumor it was offshore in Key Biscayne wasn't accurate. It was true he and Lauren had been handsomely paid, but so had others. *El Mono*—The Monkey in Spanish— had nothing to do with it.

Not now.

Not then.

Damn Davis Frost and his fat mouth.

"If *ju* want to see *jur* girlfriend alive, give me that phone. Now."

He hesitated, then handed it over.

"The counterrevolution is coming, and *El Mono* needs his *dinero.*"

This was beyond nuts. "What counterrevolution?"

"Don't call me. I call *ju*," she warned. "Don't think about following me unless *ju* want to get *jurself* and *jur* girlfriend killed. *Ju* wait here for fifteen minutes before *ju* leave. *Ju* follow my directions and *jur* girlfriend will be okay. Understand?"

He could hear his heart beating. "When will you call?"

"By this time tomorrow. Wait fifteen minutes," she said, "*ju* try to follow me and we put a bullet in her *cabeza. Ju* understand me?"

"I do," he said, watching her disappear in the crowd. He couldn't think for a moment. The days of *El Mono* were a distant memory. He leaned against the cement balustrade recalling what he knew about Monkey Morales. There was his appearance, of course. Big ears. Even bigger teeth. If he were still alive, which he wasn't, he'd have to be in his late 70s, early 80s. Years ago in his prime, he was an enigma in the strictest sense of the word.

Cuban exile.

Intelligence agent.

FBI undercover.

CIA operative.

DEA informant.

Dope dealer.

Terrorist. Bomb maker. International assassin. A key architect of the failed Bay of Pigs invasion to topple Fidel Castro. Suspected enemy of Castro's Cuban government but no one really knew for sure what side he'd been on. If information on the internet was to be believed, Monkey was a master planner for Operation 40, a U.S. government-funded group of international assassins. The line between the intelligence agencies and the criminal syndicates was as thin as a human hair.

Monkey's son claimed his father knew Lee Harvey Oswald, recognizing him from a CIA training camp, and that Monkey was in Dallas days before JFK was killed. Rumor had it he told his son he had nothing to do with the assassination and that he'd been deployed by the CIA as part of a 'cleanup crew' in case something went wrong. Every Cuban counterrevolutionary with a checkered past claimed to be 6-degrees removed from the killing of the American president.

He'd seen *El Mono* for the first time at the Hotel Mutiny. There was a time when the Cuban and Colombian drug cartels ran the biggest drug trafficking operation in American history out of the swanky Upper Deck. More, recently, the era of the Cocaine Cowboys had experienced a renaissance by way of popular culture. A streaming channel had released a series based on Griselda Blanco depicting the narco-godmother as a Hotel Mutiny VIP, holding court behind velvet-roped stanchions.

What a load of crap. There was no reception line at the hotel, not even for the powerful *Dos Guapos* kingpins. Traffickers were discreet, placing a gold paper Burger King hat on the table to signal a big shipment of cocaine had arrived from Colombia.

In historical reality, the gatekeepers at the Mutiny denied Griselda access to the private club. They saw her as a low-class operative with a lust for violence. While it seemed nuts now, it didn't seem strange then to see drug traffickers and gunrunners rubbing shoulders with local law enforcement and U.S. intelligence operatives.

Monkey was a regular at the hotel. He spent late nights

hanging out at the Upper Deck, snorting blow, flashing wads of cash, orbiting *Dos Guapos*.

Miami's most powerful cartel, *Dos Guapos,* was run by a pair of Cuban-born high school dropouts, Chago Marino and his partner Tony Famosa. Tony also happened to be Vance's uncle. But like most things from that era, even that wasn't true. Tony was a blood relative, but he wasn't his uncle. There was a streaming series about them too, and it was well done.

The last Vance had heard about Morales was when news broke in 1983 that Monkey been shot during a bar fight at a Key Biscayne discotheque. He died days later in a Miami hospital. Described by his attorney as a "real world James Bond," given his reputation as an accomplished assassin and skilled bomb maker, he had more in common with Osama Bin Laden than 007.

The words echoed in his head. *'A counterrevolution is coming, and El Mono needs his money.'*

He checked the time. Fifteen minutes had passed. He jogged toward the open-air market to retrace his steps and work off the adrenaline wondering about the identity of the man who'd dropped the burner. He slowed as he approached the photographer whom he'd almost tackled earlier. The guy was packing up.

"Excuse me," he said.

The young man with a red beard turned around and cocked his head, not looking pleased. "Aren't you the dude who pissed off my wedding couple?"

"Sorry about that. I hope I didn't ruin their wedding memories."

"I wouldn't worry about it. Fifty percent of all marriages end in divorce, odds that help my business. It's me that hopes you're not in any of the shots. I'm already going to be stuck photoshopping every picture. She was sweating. Nothing worse than the rings of Saturn on the underarms of a bridal gown. If you're in any of the pictures, I'll voodoo curse you for every picture I have to digitally clean up."

"Can I get your card?"

"You need a wedding photographer?"

"Maybe, someday," he said. "I'd like to pay you a little something for your time, in case I wrecked any of your shots."

"Why would you do that?"

"I'm a nice guy."

"Right," the photog said, laughing, "my guess is this has something to do with whatever you're looking for."

"What?"

"You were chasing something," he said, reaching under a folding table and handing him a business card.

Kent Clark's name was printed on heavy white stock with a figure 8 embossed in gold. "I bet you get your share of wisecracks."

"A few," Kent said, "it's a bird, it's a plane, it's a wedding photographer. It gets old."

He turned away from Kent and studied the background where the bride and groom had stood. It had an unobstructed view to the coastal woodlands where he'd seen the man who'd dropped the burner phone. He pulled his wallet from his pants pocket, slipped the business card behind his driver's license and removed several one-hundred-dollar bills.

Kent saw what he was doing. "Seriously, dude, you don't have to pay me. It's part of the deal. I build it into the price. These days my clients choose the most touristy places and want me to work around it. You'd be surprised what I've seen in the background. Gophers, men mooning me, a guy taking a dump, drug paraphernalia, you name it. It's like those puzzles where you have to find the hidden objects. Not to mention the damn weather."

He spotted Kent's laptop on the tabletop. "I have something else in mind."

"What?" Kent asked, loosening the legs on his tripod.

"My girlfriend was kidnapped."

Kent stopped what he was doing. "No shit."

"That's why I ran through your shot. I was supposed to meet my contact, but he got spooked and disappeared in the jungle over there. How much to upload those wedding pictures to see if you might've gotten a shot of the guy?"

"I don't know about that," Kent said.

He glanced around, then dealt a one-hundred-dollar bill on the folding table. Kent continued to pack his camera gear while watching out of the corner of his eye. He set another hundred down. Kent stared at the money for a moment but didn't speak.

"Listen, I'll pay you five hundred bucks to help me out. Every minute that goes by, the chance of finding her goes down." He looked around for eyewitnesses and when he didn't see any, opened his windbreaker.

Kent's eyes widened when he saw the gun.

"If you got something that will help me, I'll need a high-resolution copy. That's all. Easiest money you ever made."

"Ah, yeah, okay," Kent stammered, grabbing the cash and stuffing it in his pants pocket.

Kent pulled a wooden barstool to the folding table. "You sit here," he said, "while I set things up."

A raindrop slapped the tabletop.

"Crap," Kent said, pushing a hard plastic shipping case under the table and snatching his laptop. "Come on, we can work out of my van. Kidnapped," he said, "that's some crazy shit."

"Yeah, crazy shit," he said, following him to a white Ford van in need of a wash.

Kent flung open the back doors and climbed in first. The sky opened and a lightning bolt struck. Dozens of tourists milling about the farmers market shouted as they took cover from the storm. Vendors scrambled packing their displays. Others carried what they could sprinting past the van heading toward the parking lot. As he stepped into the vehicle, he felt a clap of thunder rattle the roof. He squatted and leaned against one side of the interior of the truck while Kent clambered to the front and started the engine. Another lightning strike lit the windshield. He covered his eyes as the sky flashed bright green.

"Listen dude," Kent said. "I can't do this here. This storm's gonna get worse and I need to get out of here. I got a long drive home and my wife's expecting me. The kids are out of school for the holiday and she's gonna be pissed if I don't get on the road. I'll check the files as soon as I can, and I'll let you know. I promise."

"You better be good for your word," he said. "I used to be a cop and I'm also a lawyer." He pulled Kent's business card from his pocket. "And I know where you live. Unlock your phone and give it to me."

"What?"

"Just do it. Hurry up."

He entered his number into Kent's phone and texted a 'hello' message to himself to save the number. "I don't want my money back. I want those pictures. If you don't get back to me ASAP, I'll find you and I'll break more than your camera."

"No need to threaten me, dude. I have a wife and family.

I can't imagine how I'd feel if someone kidnapped one of them."

He returned the phone. The photographer's hands trembled as he looked at the screen. "Nice to meet you, Vance."

"I'll be expecting your call," he said, flashing the Glock one last time for good measure. Then he called Logan.

As VANCE CLIMBED in the Tesla, Logan tossed him a roll of paper towels and handed him the key fob to the Porsche.

"You were right, the roadside guys were already there waiting when I got back to the restaurant. They put a new tire on. This weather is nasty," Logan said turning toward the exit leading to South Miami Avenue.

Vance blotted his hair and clothes with paper towels while Logan clenched his hands on the steering wheel, driving slowly along the flooded street, craning his head over the dash, squinting through the windshield as sheets of rain covered the glass. A driver behind the wheel of a redneck truck with mud flaps passed them going over the speed limit, creating a tidal wave that splashed across Logan's windshield, dropping visibility to near zero.

As traffic snarled to a crawl, he had a weird thought. Monkey Morales died at Mercy Hospital. If the weather had been better, he'd have been able to see the hospital from where they were. When Vizcaya was donated to Miami-Dade County, a portion was annexed to a group of nuns who operated the only Catholic hospital in Miami. His own father had told him the story. His dad was a doctor on staff at Jackson Memorial, and for years he'd tinkered with the idea of moving his practice to Mercy because of its seaside location and charm.

Mercy was the first American hospital to allow exiled

Cuban doctors to practice medicine. It was the only one offering free medical care to veterans of the failed Bay of Pigs operation. That must have been why Monkey Morales was taken there after he took a bullet.

He and Lauren followed a podcast about true Miami crime and had caught an episode with Ricardo Morales' son. He told the hosts after his father was shot the hospital called to tell his mother that his father was on life support. They had to hurry because the hospital staff was keeping him alive long enough for the family to say goodbye.

The son told the story about the priest who waited bedside, and of the machine with big blue hoses attached to his father's face and the rhythmical sounds of forced air doing the work of his lungs. At the time, eyewitnesses claimed his mother had made a scene. The younger Morales confirmed that she had to be forcibly removed from the room after screaming that the man on the ventilator was not her husband.

Up till now, Vance thought it was a conspiracy theory.

7

L auren Gold's flight to Grand Cayman had been eventful. The commuter jet encountered turbulence and the fellow in the seat behind hers filled two barf bags which left her and other nearby passengers struggling to keep their pretzels down.

In the better news department, the flight had landed on time and the views of the ice blue water and pearly sand settled her stomach. It had been over a decade since she'd set foot on the island, and she'd forgotten how small it was and how claustrophobic she'd felt during her last visit. Located south of Cuba in the Greater Antilles—compared to Cuba—Grand Cayman was a microdot. Twenty-two miles long and four-miles-wide. Every time she'd seen a hurricane forecasted to hit the island, she'd thought about how there was nowhere to escape the winds and storm surge.

While she waited at the gate at Miami International, Davis Frost had texted to remind her that he didn't have a car and had asked her to catch a taxi. He'd sent her a link with directions to a popular local restaurant in George Town where they could have lunch together before boarding a charter flight to Little Cayman. She'd opened the link after boarding the plane and had decided on the jerk chicken.

"First time *'ere*?" the friendly taxi driver asked.

"I've been before," she said, "but it's been a long time."

"Welcome to *Caymankind* where everyone loves *de* Americans."

She smiled at him in the rearview. What they loved were American dollars. The open windows on the taxi invited the balmy weather inside. Being a month away from summer, the days were getting longer, and warmer. She stuck her head partway out and glanced up at the cotton balls of white clouds floating beneath a clear blue sky. She hadn't checked her phone since she'd landed, mindful of the nightmares about distracted travelers who'd lost luggage to scammer-jammers pretending to be skycaps, and even gotten in vehicles driven by shake down artists masquerading as cab drivers.

Fishing her phone from her purse, she expected to see a message from Vance. Instead, the screen was black. She tapped it and when it didn't light up, pressed the start button to bring it back to life. Nothing happened. That was weird. It'd worked when she'd left Miami. She was sure she'd charged it last night before leaving, but it had been a hectic morning. Then she remembered the bizarre video call she'd received just before Vance dropped her off at the airport.

She recalled the name of the restaurant and the driver knew his way around, expertly navigating a hilly driveway and letting her out at valet. The place was a converted pink colonial home built on a bluff overlooking the water.

She paid and tipped the driver cash for the fare posted on the vintage meter on the dash and entered the restaurant. Davis Frost saw her before she spotted him. He lumbered toward her, flip-flops slapping the white marble floor.

"How was your flight?" he asked, widening his arms, pulling her in and giving her a literal bear hug.

The wraparound sunglasses hanging from his neck dug into her chest. She gently pushed him away, eyeing him up and down. Though he was dressed casually in shorts and a parrot-print shirt, the expression on his face suggested something was wrong. For a grown man who towered over her, she'd always marveled at his facial expressions which did nothing to hide his feelings. Often, he wore a wide-eyed look of childish amazement; today his brow was furled, strands of wispy white hair hung over his ears and his pale blue eyes were dull and marred by dark circles.

"Are you okay?"

He nodded like a grizzly and adjusted the wire rim bifocals on his nose. "You hungry?" he asked.

"A little."

A waif of a hostess rushed over when she saw him.

"Hello, Mr. Frost," she said in a squeaky voice. "Would you like a table for two?"

The hostess studied Lauren with an ambiguous look on her face that might've been disapproval. Or simply curiosity.

"May I get my regular table," Davis said, reaching into his shorts and handing her a folded twenty.

"Look at you," Lauren whispered as they were led to a corner waterfront booth. "You're Mister VIP."

The waif gave her a dirty look as she set the menus down.

"What was that about?" she asked Davis.

"She knows my girlfriend."

"You have a girlfriend?"

"You look surprised."

She was surprised. Davis had discerning taste in women and as a morbidly obese, middle-aged guy with stringy hair, he'd never been interested in what she considered *realistic possibilities*. "No, I mean yes," she said. "But I'm happy for you. How long have you been seeing each other?"

"A few months."

"And?"

"And what?"

"Do you think you have a future together?"

Davis didn't answer. Rather he stared over her shoulder at something in the distance. She turned in her seat to see what but there was nothing other than a view of blue water and sky.

A waitress dressed in a yellow mini skirt approached.

After they ordered and the server was out of earshot, she asked, "What's wrong?"

"Who said anything's wrong?"

"You didn't have to say it for me to notice."

He ducked the question. "How was your flight?"

"It was on time."

"Best kind," Davis said.

"You still didn't answer my question."

"Nothing's wrong," he sniped.

She'd obviously hit a nerve and would come back to it later. "How do you like living on Little Cayman?"

He rolled his beefy shoulders in a display of indifference. "It's quiet."

His cavalier response wasn't what she'd expected. He'd gushed on the phone when he pitched the idea about investing in the Sea Otter dive outfit two weeks ago. Living on an island had always been his dream and he was living it.

She'd done some research before the trip. The only civilized way to get to Little Cayman was on a prop plane. To go by boat, one had to cross the Cayman Trench, an ominous deep-sea cave almost five miles deep. She'd bought her air ticket to the out-island online ten days ago and had sent him a copy of her itinerary. "I'm excited about scuba lessons," she said, "but I'm a little nervous."

"Don't be," he said, lifting one hip and pulling his cell phone from his shorts pocket. He tapped the screen and set it face down on the tabletop.

That reminded her. "Do you have a charger?"

"Not on me."

"My phone's not working and it's weird because I could swear, I charged it last night."

"Let me see it," he said. "Huh," he said, pushing buttons. "It looks like your battery might be dead."

"It was fine this morning."

"I mean *dead*-dead. There's a phone store a few blocks from the hotel."

"Little Cayman has a phone store?"

"We're not going to Little Cayman," he said, placing his elbows on the table.

"What?"

"Cancelled," he said in a monotone.

"Why?"

"I can't go back there."

"Why not?"

"I can't travel."

"What are you talking about?"

"They took my passport."

"Who took it?"

"The RCIPS."

"The *who*?"

"The Royal Cayman Islands Police Service."

"Why?" she said, pushing the menu off to the side.

"You remember the British couple I told you about, the ones who want to sell the dive shop?"

"Of course."

"They're missing."

"What do you mean, *missing*?"

"They disappeared."

"To where?"

"Now you sound like the cops. I spent two nights in a hell-hole jail cell where they interrogated me." He looked around, undid the top two buttons on his parrot-print shirt and pulled it one side revealing his right collarbone. The bruise was big and olive green.

"Oh my God. They roughed you up. Why?"

"The investigators somehow knew I was planning to buy the business. I only told a couple of people, and I hadn't made a formal offer. I've been wracking my brain trying to think of anyone who'd want to hurt the owners, and I can't come up with anything. Everyone on the island knows everything about everyone. I've been trying to figure out who would've tipped off the police. The cops think my interest in the dive shop was a possible motive to kill them."

"What? They were murdered?"

"I don't know for sure. Maybe the cops know something I don't."

"As in what?" she whispered.

He lowered his voice. "You know." He rubbed his fore-finger and thumb together. "When they interrogated me, they wanted to see proof I was in a financial position to buy the business. You know I couldn't do that," he whispered.

It was easy to see how Davis became a suspect. Plenty of rich people frequented the Caymans and he in no way looked wealthy. He'd lived modestly to provide cover for the large sum of money she and Vance had paid him to move their cash offshore and open their Cayman accounts. If the investigators did a background on him, they'd find no discernible way he could afford to buy the business. "Do you think someone killed them?"

"People don't disappear from Little Cayman. If they're leaving, they say goodbye. The whole thing stinks. The LeCroys were a fixture for decades and lots of people knew they wanted to sell their business. The year-round population is a hair over two hundred. You can't walk outside your house without someone noticing. It's fishy that they — poof, disappeared."

"Why didn't you tell me before I flew down?"

He cast his eyes on the table and stared at it for a long moment. "Because I knew if I told you, you wouldn't come."

Their server in the short skirt approached.

"Can we have a few minutes?" Davis asked, shooing her away.

"Is it possible they went offshore and got lost at sea?" Lauren asked.

"No." His tone turned irritated. "Like I told you, they were ready to retire. They hadn't been on the water for years and stayed back at the shop helping customers. They have dive masters, and all the boats were accounted for. I checked myself. I'm the one who reported them missing for Chrissake. You'd think the police would figure I wouldn't call it in if I was guilty of something."

"Unless they thought you were trying to misdirect them," she said, studying his face for a reaction.

"Come on, Lauren. You know I didn't have anything to do with it."

"What about the employees? Did the police question anyone else?"

"As far as I know, I'm the only one who was detained. A

constable came from the mainland to investigate the crime scene. The detective said the couple hadn't used their credit cards or phones since the day they disappeared. The business has been shuttered for almost two weeks. They never closed unless the weather was bad, and it's been good. I think whoever took them dumped their bodies offshore and they'll never be found. They're looking for someone to pin it on. Murders are bad for tourism and this one has been in the news."

It was a cynical outlook, but he was probably right.

"I didn't have anything to do with it." He placed his hands over his face for a moment. "I need your help, Lauren. I need a lawyer."

"You don't need me for that."

"I want you to talk to Vance. You need to convince him to come."

"He's retired. Even if he wasn't, he's not licensed to practice here."

"He could help me find someone. He'll know what to do. If they keep poking around, they're going to find out certain things." He lowered his voice. "This place is a tax haven. They have a whole unit dedicated to investigating financial crimes. That big cryptocurrency scam in The Bahamas was an embarrassment and there's a lot of pressure to make sure something like that doesn't happen here. I can't get on their radar screen."

He already was. Damn Davis and his big, fat mouth. He was right. If she'd known about any of this she wouldn't have come. She should've listened to Vance. He'd reminded her every time they got involved in a deal with Davis, it always went south. She'd defended him, reminding Vance that without him they wouldn't have been able to move tens of millions of dollars in cash to Cayman. If Davis had been honest with her, she might've been willing to help him while she was still in Miami.

Now she was mired in his mess. She shook her head slowly, thoughts spinning at the ramifications if he were arrested and charged. Local police would be surveilling him and by now they were watching her, too. She and Vance had interests to protect. Ones they'd worked very hard to keep secret. Ones if revealed, could be prosecuted as crimes.

"I hacked your phone," Davis said, looking sheepish.

"What? Why would you do that?"

"I'm sorry," he said. "I didn't know what else to do."

"How?" she asked, drumming her fingers on the tabletop.

"I sent you the link to the restaurant and when you opened it, I installed spyware."

She shook her head in disgust. "Then un-hack it."

"I can't. After I was sure you were coming, I tried to delete it, but I couldn't. Your phone already had another virus."

"I can't believe you. Maybe you do know something about the missing couple."

"Don't say that." His blue eyes turned glassy, and his voice cracked. "I had to make sure you were coming. Maybe should thank me," he said, sniffling.

"Thank you? Thank you for what?"

"Whatever's installed on your phone is something I've never seen before. It looks and acts like something that can turn your phone into a listening device. I saw a story about an Egyptian politician who found similar spyware on his phone before an election. When I saw it on your phone, I killed it and, in the process, killed your phone. And yeah," he said, nodding his fat, sad head, "you should thank me because who knows what the hell is up with that. Someone else is targeting you."

"I haven't opened any links other than the one you sent."

"The way the other one works is it redirects when you open a link and downloads malware, then sends you back to the trusted website. When you opened the link to this place, you wouldn't have noticed it installing malware."

"You mean I was hacked because you hacked me. Damn you, Davis. I can't believe this."

"I didn't mean for you to get mixed up in it, I swear. But I don't have anyone else I can turn to. There's this woman—"

"Your girlfriend?"

He nodded meekly.

"Does she know you have money?"

"Not at first."

"Oh, great."

"I lent her a hundred thousand dollars."

"For what?"

"She told me she needed the cash to get her daughter out of Havana —"

"— this woman is Cuban?"

"Yes."

"Why would you give her that much money? How well do you know her?"

"I married her."

"Jesus, Davis. How long have you known her?"

"A few months. My stepdaughter —"

She cut him off. "You're telling me it didn't occur to you she might be using you for your money?" The waitress appeared again. "We're not ready to order," she snapped, sending her away.

"I told you. I didn't tell her I had any and it's not like I flaunted it."

"Do you have a picture of her?"

He lit up like a neon sign and showed her a half dozen pictures on his phone.

The woman was a knockout. "So, you gave her a hundred thousand dollars. How was she going to use it to get her daughter out?"

"I don't know."

"You didn't think to ask?"

He shook his head.

"Did she know you were interested in buying the dive outfit?"

"Probably. But . . ."

Her brain switched off. His lips moved in slow-motion, but she wasn't processing the words. When it came to women, Davis was an idiot. The question running through her head now was whether he'd compromised her and Vance in the process. Davis likely told his wife that she'd be traveling from Miami to visit him, and the reason for the visit.

Davis was a notorious over-sharer and if he was high on lust, or testosterone, or whatever, there was no telling what he'd leaked in the way of confidential information. He'd disabled her phone leaving her with no way to contact Vance. Even if she wanted to help, which she'd already decided against, he'd made it next to impossible. Her blood began to boil.

"You're my best friend," he said, looking hangdog. "You have to help me."

"What about your wife? Why can't she help you?"

"Because she disappeared."

"Wonderful," she said, shaking her head.

8

FRIDAY MORNING

The morning drive in commuter traffic from the condo in Coconut Grove south to his sister's place in the burbs to visit Ethan bit the big one. As Vance glanced in the side mirror to merge onto US Highway 1 south toward Kendall, he felt a thud as the right front tire of his Porsche 911 dropped into a deep pothole jerking the steering wheel from his hands. That was going to cost a front alignment, and maybe another new tire. The idiot in a BMW next to him jumped lanes forcing him to jam the brakes. Keeping his hands off the horn he muttered "Asshole" to himself and pulled up an inch off the guy's bumper. It was becoming increasingly difficult to own nice things in the concrete jungle.

He took a shortcut west on Seventy Second Avenue passing a sign for Dadeland Mall, wondering how many who shopped there knew its history. In 1979 in broad daylight on a hot July afternoon, rival drug cartels opened fire gangland-style at a liquor store killing two and injuring two others. Some in the media blamed the Dadeland Massacre on the Cocaine Cowboys, but that wasn't true. *Dos Guapos* operated more like a corporate entity than a goon squad, careful not to bring unwanted attention. He believed it was the work of Griselda Blanco's thugs.

He entered the residential development where Kathy lived and parked the Honolulu Blue Porsche curbside in front of her house. He lowered his sunglasses, checking himself in the rearview mirror, gently touching the half-moons hanging beneath his eyes. He'd gotten one, maybe two hours of sleep, and to top it off, he'd done a couple of shots of whiskey and mixed it with Benadryl at about 3 a.m. in a last-ditch effort to put himself to sleep.

He rang the doorbell and waited. Normally mornings in her neighborhood were a beehive of activity with dog-walkers, yellow buses and parents hustling to work. But school was out Friday ahead of the Memorial weekend and other than a leaf blower humming in the distance, it was quiet.

Ethan appeared at the door in his plaid pajamas. He wriggled his nose to move his glasses higher on the bridge. "You smell like booze," he said, "and you look like crap."

"Good morning and right back at ya," he said, entering the house. "Got any coffee?"

Kathy emerged from the hallway with her purse slung over one shoulder. "He's right, you look like shit. There's a pot of coffee in the kitchen. Milk's in the fridge. I'll be back by ten. Thanks for doing this," she said, giving him a sisterly peck on the cheek.

Kathy leaned over and kissed Ethan on the top of his head, then tousled his hair.

"Mom!" Ethan ducked and backed away from her.

"You need a shower," she said to him. "Feel free to use mine and you two have fun."

He headed to the kitchen for coffee.

Ethan followed. "You didn't have to come, you know."

"I know. How are you doing, bud?"

"Better," he said, lifting his pajama top and showing him the 6-inch crescent shaped scar from the kidney transplant. It was still bright red.

"Impressive," he said.

It'd been stressful last year when Ethan was diagnosed with renal failure. Waiting for a kidney donor was hell. He'd tried to give Ethan one of his own and was a perfect match but was disqualified for an old health issue. That's how he found out he was Ethan's biological father when Kathy was forced to tell him.

"I'm going to get dressed," Ethan said. "Maybe you should put some cucumbers on your eyes. That's what Mom does."

"Who knew? Go on, go get ready."

Alone, he grabbed his coffee, opened the sliding glass door and sat on the wooden bench under the veranda in the backyard. The words the lady in white had spoken played like a broken record. '. . . *loose lips . . . will cost ju all your money . . . loose lips bragging about a sunken ship will cost ju all your money.*'

In the midst of his insomnia, he'd tried to call Davis at 2 a.m., but it went directly to voicemail to a woman speaking Spanish. Davis had been living in Cayman for almost two years and likely had a new number. He'd been around Davis Frost enough to know he was careless, and it was possible he'd shot his mouth off about the money.

'*Jur fat American friend in Grand Cayman has a big bank*

account and a bigger mouth. Ju know the expression. Loose lips sink ships.'

But it didn't explain how the lady in white knew so many personal details about him and his Cuban family. Davis didn't know any of that. His phone pinged. He fished it from his pocket and looked at the text on the screen.

You've been selected to win $100 by filling out this simple survey.

He stared at the link with the weird web address, then deleted it.

He'd tossed and turned most of the night getting out of bed once to check flights to Grand Cayman, but there weren't any available seats. He went back inside to pour more coffee. Ethan sat at the breakfast nook, dressed in shorts and a T-shirt, eating a bowl of rainbow-colored cereal.

"How come you didn't want to go to the karting track with your brothers?" he asked.

"You mean paintball," Ethan said. "I'm not inclined to partake in a game that causes bodily pain."

"Good point," he said. "Where's the sugar?"

"In the blue jar next to the coffee pot. You have to wear goggles and a jock strap to play. It's stupid."

"Ah," he said, grabbing a half dozen individual packets. Shaky from lack of sleep, he tore one open and spilled half.

"Do you want to play a game of chess?" Ethan asked.

That was the last thing he wanted to do. "No thanks. You'll kick my butt. I have a better idea."

"What?"

"Go get your laptop."

Ethan hurried down the hall and returned with it under his arm.

Vance chugged his sugar coffee trying to remember the name of the group. *Damas* something? *Damas de? De?*

Blanco.

Damas de Blanco.

"Fire it up," he said to Ethan, spanking the top of the breakfast nook with his palm.

The screen came to life.

"Now what?" Ethan asked.

"Search *Damas de Blanco*. It's spelled D-A-M—"

Ethan furrowed his brow. "I know how to spell it."

"How do you know that?" he asked, pulling his chair close enough to shoulder surf the boy's computer screen.

"That's easy," Ethan said, typing '*Damas de Blanco*' into his browser. "It means '*Ladies in White.*' He pressed the return key and the screen filled with results. Ethan clicked the top link and began to read, then shared aloud. "*Damas de Blanco* is a movement that began in Cuba about twenty years ago."

"What kind of a movement?"

"I'm still reading."

"I didn't know you could read Spanish?"

Ethan laughed. "Duh. Everyone does."

Everyone but him. He got up from the table and rinsed his cup in the sink.

"They're a group of Cuban women who dress in white and protest every Sunday in front of a Catholic Church in Havana."

"Protest what?"

"Something called the Group of Seventy Five."

"Seventy Five what?"

"Hang on," Ethan said.

A long moment later he said, "It stands for seventy-five missing dissidents rounded up by Fidel Castro. *Damas de*

Blanco was organized in Havana in 2003 to call attention to the disappeared. They got the idea to wear white from the *Madres de Plaza de Mayo* who demanded information from the Argentinean government after their children went missing."

He knew nothing about either group. He got up from the table and paced the small kitchen. "What kind of dissidents?"

The boy ran his finger beneath the text. "Mostly journalists, human rights activists . . . librarians, engineers, scientists, anyone who criticized the Cuban government. They were jailed and denounced as subversives and terrorists. The ladies wear buttons that have pictures of their loved ones with the number of years they've been missing or lengths of prison sentences."

"I've never heard of them," he said.

"That was by design," Ethan said. "According to this story Fidel Castro rounded them up on the same day George W. Bush invaded Iraq. Castro knew the international media wouldn't report it because they would be following the Iraq War news. It was called the Cuban Black Spring. It also says that hours before the American president visited Cuba in 2016, the women protesters were rounded up and detained so our president wouldn't see them. Look at this."

He sat next to the boy eyeing the bulleted list on the laptop screen. Dozens of men had been sentenced to long prison terms, many over twenty years.

Ethan closed out of the link and opened a Wikipedia page.

"It says here that some of the men were released and exiled to Spain. Their leader died in 2011. Her cause of death was reported by the Castro regime as dengue fever, but this story says some people think she was poisoned by the Cuban government while she was in a hospital."

"Is the group still active?"

"I don't know," Ethan said, scrolling farther down the page, studying the results. He opened a new link connected to an international human rights group. "Yeah. The women still protest every Sunday after Mass at Saint Rita de Casia Catholic Church in Havana."

"Are any of the men still in prison?"

Ethan turned the laptop on an angle so he could more easily share the screen with him.

He squatted next to the table to read the article written in English. He checked the date. It was less than a year old and someone had leaked information to at least one human rights organization listing dozens of detailed reports with names, times, dates and descriptions of the Cuban government's misdeeds. He read the fact-pattern detailing bogus arrests and detainments by the National Revolutionary Police. Unfair prison sentences, kangaroo courts, government surveillance, food rationing, fines, and cutting of Internet connections were examples of ongoing harassment. But the women were not deterred, even after the suspicious death of their leader.

Ethan looked at him. "Why do you want to know about this, Uncle Vance?"

His phone vibrated in his pocket. He took it from his pants pocket and leaped to his feet, nearly knocking the chair over. "Hey, bud, sorry but I have to get this."

"You're jumpy," Ethan said.

"Must be the coffee," he said, "I'll be right back."

9

Vance stood on the stoop at his sister's house looking at CALLER ID on his phone: *Maybe Suarez and Associates* showed on the screen. On the third ring he picked up.

"Mr. Courage?"

"Yes."

"Mr. Suarez said I should give you a call and touch base."

"Who is this?" he asked.

"I work for Rafael Suarez. My name is Lola. I'm his paralegal."

"Right, right," he said recalling Suarez mention his bilingual crack paralegal.

A dog barked in the distance while two women wearing pink visors pushed canopied baby strollers on the opposite side of the street.

"He wants to know if you can stop by today," she said.

"When?"

"Anytime."

"Is there a reason?"

"He'd like me to show you around."

"If you text the office address, I'll get back to you."

"Sure," Lola said.

He ended the call wondering how much she knew about her boss's upcoming sabbatical. His phone vibrated in his hand. Another call, this time from his sister Kathy.

"Hey," she said, "how's your visit with Ethan going?"

"Good."

"He told me you asked him to do some research about a group in Cuba," she said. "What's that all about?"

"Ethan wanted to play chess and I didn't."

"You're a lousy liar," she said. "Why don't you and Lauren come for dinner tonight. I'm making Mom's *ropa vieja*."

"That's tempting," he said, "but I have plans. How's your doctor appointment going?"

"The usual. I've been waiting for over an hour. The office was full when I got here and now it's standing room only."

"You'd tell me if something was wrong, right?"

"Of course," she said. "It's a routine screening. I'm glad you're spending some time with Ethan."

"He seems like he's doing great, but he's perceptive, Kat. I think you shouldn't try to push so hard to make things happen. He's going to know you're up to something."

"He gets that spidey sense from you. I don't expect you to wait for me. Ethan's fine on his own but you're going to miss a good dinner."

"Maybe next time," he said, "I'll talk to you later."

He heard a voice from behind.

"Who's perceptive?" Ethan asked.

"I don't know, but I know who's nosy," he said, grabbing Ethan's shoulders and mock wrestling with the boy.

"Push to make what things happen?" the boy asked.

"Ask me when you're twenty-five."

"Very funny."

"Your mom said it's cool for you to hang out on your own."

"Duh. I don't need a babysitter. I never get any time by myself, and I don't have anything in common with anyone living in this house. I swear I must be adopted," Ethan said, heading back inside.

His phone pinged. He looked at the screen and saw the link to the address at Rafael Suarez's Coconut Grove office.

"What am I not supposed to figure out?" Ethan asked.

"Nothing."

"Yeah, right, like anyone else under our leaking roof could be described as perceptive."

He messed the boy's hair.

"Don't do that. Next time you come over," Ethan said, "I want to drive your Porsche."

"Deal," he said, "soon as you get your license and that'll be in about two years."

VANCE LEFT his sister's place and took the shortest route back to The Grove, planning to stop at the house to check on Cashmere and swap vehicles. He parked the Porsche in the condo lot and hurried inside noticing dirty paw prints on the entryway tile. Cash cowered in the corner near what looked like the remains of one of Lauren's shoes.

He picked up a ball of mauled leather. "You're going to get me in trouble," he said, kneeling to scratch the dog's ears then sat on the bottom stair. "Come here," he said to Cash. The dog wagged his tail but didn't move. "I wish I knew where your mom was," he said. Cash got up, walked over and laid at his feet with his chin on his paws.

He'd overslept and hadn't walked him before he'd gone

to Kathy's to see Ethan. He'd been running late and left the sliding glass door to the walled courtyard open just enough for the dog to let himself out.

"How about a quick walk?"

When he lifted the leash from the hook next to the front door, the little dog sprang into action, twirling, chasing his tail. He'd restricted the walks to inside the gated area to avoid the mushrooming homeless encampment that had taken root at the public park across the street. Cash sniffed the hedges lining the private parking lot, balanced on one back leg, peed on the tires of the neighbor's parked car before spritzing the plants until his bladder was empty.

He grabbed the keys to Lauren's car, got behind the wheel and backed out. Waiting for the driveway gate to roll open, he tapped the link to the address Lola had shared. Suarez's office was just over three miles from the condo. He hung a right onto Shipping Avenue, headed east to Mary Street, then drove north on Bayshore Drive.

The morning rush hour traffic should have dissipated but the road was congested on both sides of the grassy median with cars traveling five miles an hour, tops. He'd have rolled his window down, but every time there was a small gap in traffic the guy in front of him driving a diesel pickup gunned the engine, spewing a cloud of black exhaust. As if that would do something to move things along.

The blue-black bay water was rough with white caps and sailboats in the bay thrashed in their moorings. As he approached the address Lola texted, he was surprised to see a ten-story modern waterfront high-rise overlooking Biscayne Bay.

When he'd practiced law, he'd worked out of a dump, a freestanding bungalow adjacent to a no-name strip mall near a Cuban cafeteria that did a brisk lunch business. The windows leaked. The traffic noise had given him temporary tinnitus. It never occurred to him during law school that he should have learned a second language, namely Spanish.

When he spoke to Lola she'd said any time worked and he intended this to be a reconnaissance run to get a lay of the land and size things up. He parked the Audi at the marina across the street from the high-rise office building to gather his thoughts.

God, he was tired. He tilted his head back and closed his eyes for a second. He must've dozed off and awoke in a panic, not sure where he was. He'd only been asleep for a few minutes, but he felt as refreshed as he might have been from a full night of sleep. He pulled his phone from his pants pocket and redialed the number he had for Davis Frost, giving it a second try. This time a woman answered.

"*Hola.*"

"May I speak to Davis Frost."

"*Ju* have wrong number. I dun know no Davis Rust."

Vance tossed the phone on the passenger seat and pressed the back of his neck against the headrest. Davis had a habit of not thinking before he spoke and had an alligator mouth to go with his elephant ass. If he'd shot his mouth off like the mystery woman claimed he did, he might've compromised his and Lauren's financial secret. He clenched his fists thinking about it.

'*Jur fat American friend in Grand Cayman has a fat wallet and an even bigger mouth.*'

A rich American expat living in Grand Cayman wouldn't be all that conspicuous, but Davis didn't look or dress the part. His weakness was he was reckless and gullible in a childlike way. A flock of seagulls mewled as they passed overhead. White droppings splashed the hood and wind-shield of the Audi.

The woman he'd met at Vizcaya promised to call in the next few hours. He checked the time on his phone. There was a missed call from Sarge. His phone hadn't rung and there was no text or voicemail. He redialed the number.

It rang once before a woman answered.

"I'm sorry," he said, "I must have the wrong number."

"You have the right number. It's Maria, Daniel's wife."

"Ah, hi," he stuttered, not expecting her. "How are you?"

She sighed into the phone. "I'm fine. I wish I could say the same about Danny."

"Why? What's going on?"

"I'm at the hospital."

"Why? What happened?"

"He was having chest pains, so I called nine-one-one. They admitted him to Jackson Memorial Hospital."

"When?"

"Early this morning."

"Did he have a heart attack?"

"I don't know yet," Maria said. "I'm waiting to talk to the doctor. Danny asked me to call you and let you know."

"He seemed fine when I saw him yesterday. Is there something I can do?"

"No. He just wanted me to let you know. Do you want me to give him a message?"

"No, no. That's not necessary."

"He'll want to know I talked to you, but if you don't want to leave a message, he'll understand," Maria said.

There was an awkward pause. "Maybe I'll come see him," he said.

"There's no need. You know how he is. A man of pride

who doesn't want anyone seeing him in a hospital gown eating pudding in bed."

"Will you call me as soon you get an update?"

"I will," she said, "and I'll let Danny know we talked."

"You take care of yourself."

He spotted a bench near the seawall where he'd parked across the street from Suarez's office. He got out and took a seat near the bulkhead watching a guy sailing a Hobie Cat, jumping the white caps. Poor Sarge. At least Maria had the good sense to get him to a hospital right away. He stared at his phone, then scrolled through recent text messages, rereading the ones from the kidnapper looking for clues he might have missed, but there was nothing.

He redialed Lola.

"I'm in the neighborhood. I could stop by now," he said.

"Like I told you earlier," she said, "anytime works."

HE WAITED for a break in traffic, crossed the grassy median, turned into the building's parking lot and drove around back. He saw an empty spot and as he prepared to park, saw a big man and a petite woman hurrying out of Suarez's office building. He backed the Audi into an available space and watched as the couple got into a Jeep.

There couldn't be very many white Jeep Cherokees in Miami with a *WOMEN WANT ME, FISH FEAR ME* sticker on the back bumper. He waited, then followed the vehicle onto the main road as it headed north toward Mercy Hospital. Staying two car lengths back, he gambled Sarge wouldn't recognize him in a black Audi sedan.

The Jeep stopped at the red light where Bayshore Drive turned into South Miami Avenue. He pulled up close enough on the rear quarter panel to see the back of the driver's head. He redialed Sarge's phone number. The passenger, a woman who fit Maria's description, showed the phone to the driver.

As the light turned green, a text pinged from Sarge's phone:

Still at the hospital. No news yet.

Unbelievable. Sarge wasn't in the hospital. He'd just left Suarez's office. At the next intersection he did a U-turn and headed back to meet Lola. He felt the sweat on his palms as the leather steering wheel slid through his hands. As far as he knew, Sarge had never lied to him, and this one was a whopper.

10

L auren awoke to the soft glow of an unfamiliar thermostat on the wall. She'd had difficulty sleeping at the hotel Davis insisted they stay at and hadn't been able to drift off until sometime after 5 a.m. She rolled onto her side and looked at the clock next to the bed. 9:32 a.m. She switched on the bedside lamp and massaged the joints of her jaw with her fingertips. A couple of weeks ago her mild case of TMJ — temporomandibular disorder of the jaw — had flared up and she'd followed her dentist's advice getting Botox injections. This morning the pain was back.

Davis wanted to stay in an American-owned hotel. She understood his reasoning though she doubted the hotel would provide any actual protection. He'd already been interrogated and roughed up by the police, and spent two nights in the local jail. Though he'd been living in Cayman for almost two years, he was still a U.S. citizen. The RCIPS must've thought the case against him was strong or they wouldn't have confiscated his passport. Randomly pulling travel documents from an American citizen risked a diplomatic nightmare not to mention what it could do to tourism.

She'd stayed awake most of the night doing mental gymnastics, running scenarios of what might have happened to the LeCroys but she had very few facts other than their disappearance. Davis stuck to the story that the couple planned sell the business and return to the U.K. There were only two plausible explanations. Either they fled the country for reasons only they knew, or something nefarious had happened. Hurting them wasn't in Davis's DNA. Maybe his cynical version of events was correct. Maybe the RCIPS didn't know who was responsible, figured they'd never solve the case and chose him as a scapegoat to make tourists feel safe. On the other hand, two people were missing, and without a body there was no proof of a crime.

Maybe there was a perfectly logical explanation for their disappearance. What if they had a family emergency back home and left without telling anyone? Then she remembered the LeCroys hadn't used their credit cards or phones since they went missing. If Davis had nothing to hide, he should have gone to the U.S. Embassy for help.

She called his room.

"Hey *dere*," he said with a hint of his old Minnesotan accent.

"I'm going to the phone store to see what they can do to fix my phone. Do you want to go?"

"No. I'm going to hunker down here until you figure out what we should do."

We. She held the hotel landline at arm's length and shook her head. There was a knock on the door. She'd left the room service door hanger on the knob last night. "I gotta go." She was about to end the call when she thought to ask, "Do you still have Vance's number in your phone?"

"I got rid of my SIM card last night. Flushed it down the toilet."

"Great," she said, hanging up and answering the door.

She tipped the bellman ten dollars for the $10 pot of coffee without letting him inside, set the tray on the table and opened the drapes. The hotel was in the middle of George Town and from the fourth floor she could see the western Caribbean Sea disappear into the horizon. She poured a coffee, took it into the bathroom and started the shower.

According to Frost, beyond confiscating his passport, his credit cards and bank accounts had been frozen. When she'd gone to his room last night to talk, she could see he was nervous. If the Cayman authorities seized his assets, interrogated him, pulled his passport and jailed him, there was a good chance they had him under surveillance. If that was the case, there was a good chance they had her on the same radar screen.

The mobile phone store opened at 10 a.m. and was within walking distance of the hotel. After Davis begged her to pay for his room, she'd put both on her credit card. Davis needed cash and she'd agreed to loan him some money. She'd withdrawn her daily limit at the hotel's ATM yesterday and planned to take out the max amount again today.

She should've listened to Vance who by now had to know something had gone wrong. He'd probably been trying to reach her. When he found out what had happened, he'd say 'I told you so' a thousand times and she had it coming.

She showered quickly, dressed and hurried to the elevator, riding it alone to the first floor. She spotted a young couple in the hotel lobby standing in front of the ATM. A pair of wrinkled, tanned senior citizens strolled past wearing hats and sunglasses, their noses painted white with SPF-a-million.

When she'd talked to Davis last night, she'd pressed him for more details on why he was a suspect in the case of the missing couple. He'd insisted he had no idea other than what he'd told her already. She'd known him a long time and one thing was certain, Davis was a lousy liar. When he was bullshitting her, his eyes widened, and he'd grin and blink. But the look on his face last night was different. He was jumpy. Twitchy. He seemed contemplative, which was out of character, and yet she suspected he wasn't telling the full truth.

"Sorry," the woman standing with a man at the machine said with a Southern drawl. "I swear this has-ta be the slowest ATM on the dang planet. I think it's running on solar or something."

"No worries," she said, scanning the lobby.

A minute later it was her turn. She inserted her debit card and waited. The machine buzzed. An ERROR message came up on the screen. INVALID ENTRY flashed in green letters. She tried again. Same result.

"Effing hell," she whispered, fishing inside her wallet for a different credit card. She tried a second, then a third. Each was declined by the cash machine. A young man in a maroon felt cap approached.

"May I help you?" the bellman asked.

"I think the ATM is out of order. Is there another one in the hotel?"

An older gentleman hunched over a walker shuffled his way toward the machine.

"Are you in line?" he asked in a gruff voice.

"No. But I think it's out of order."

"Let me give it a try," the old geezer said.

She stepped aside and watched him insert his card.

"It's the only one in the hotel," the bellman said, grimacing. "You might want to try the one at the liquor store down the street."

The old man balanced on the metal bars of his walker. "Christmas might come before this thing spits out my damn money," he barked.

The clack-clack-clack of an ATM spewing cash followed.

"Maybe you should try again," the old guy said. Gripping the walker with one shaky hand he used the other to stuff the money in the front pocket of his saggy shorts.

She headed for the revolving glass doors and once outside, took a deep breath. She looked over her shoulder aware the problem with her cards wasn't some random occurrence. Whoever was targeting Davis also had her in the crosshairs. She opened her wallet and counted the cash. It might be enough to get her phone up and running. As she walked toward the phone store, she passed three international banks located on a single city block.

A cool breeze blew wisps of hair in front of her eyes. She brushed the strands from her face and looked up at the pink neon sign she'd seen from her hotel room. The phone store display window was obscured by the long line of customers snaking around the corner. She took her place at the end of the line, her brain returning to the ATM. She took her dead phone from her purse, pressed the ON button and held it for a count of ten. Still, nothing.

Fifteen minutes later the line hadn't moved. There was an internet café across the street. She jaywalked to the place, paid cash, took a seat at a cubicle in front of a desktop computer and logged into her Gmail account. She pulled up

Vance's email from her contacts list and composed a message.

SUBJECT LINE: Greetings from Grand Cayman
    To: vancecourage@gmail.com
    From: themutinygirl@gmail.com
    10:29 AM

HI VANCE,

    I hope you haven't been too worried. There's something wrong with my phone and I haven't been able to check in. Send me a quick reply to let me know you got this email and I'll call or text when I figure something out.

    Love, Lauren

    P.S. I might have to buy a burner. Email your phone number. I don't know it. :-(

SHE WAS ABOUT to push the send key when she sensed a presence behind her. She turned in her seat and looked up to see Davis looming.

"Hey," he said, "I thought you were going to get your phone fixed?"

"The line was too long."

Davis spied her email. "I thought you were going to ask him to help me?"

"This is none of your business and, besides, I didn't say that." She turned back toward the screen, trying to block his view.

"Wait," he said, grabbing her arm.

She wrestled it away from him and pushed the SEND

key. "What is wrong with you?" she said. "Don't you ever put your hand on me like that again." It was out of character and she chalked it up to his desperation.

The shopkeeper who'd taken her cash and shown her how to log onto the computer hurried over.

"Is everything alright, Miss?" the man asked, glaring at Davis. "Do you want me to call the police?"

11

The visitor parking spaces at Suarez's office building were full and the car-sharks slowly circled waiting for vehicles to leave. Vance drove to the paid parking garage and found a spot on the fourth floor. Following the signs, he rode the rumbling garage elevator down to the first floor giving him a moment to process what he'd seen. It didn't make sense that Sarge had enlisted his wife Maria to lie for him.

The parking garage elevator opened to a gleaming lobby with white quartz walls and a second set of stainless-steel elevators that purred. He waited for the next car, pushed the button for the eighth floor and followed the directional placards to Suite 813. He turned the knob, but the front door to Suarez & Associates was locked. About to knock, he saw the buzzer on the wall and pushed it.

"Who's calling?" a female voice asked.

"Vance Courage to see Lola."

"Let yourself in," the voice said. The deadbolt clacked and he entered. The chair on the other side of the reception window was empty and there was no one to greet him in the waiting room. He strolled the faux wood floor gazing at the mass-produced modern art hung on the white walls. It looked more like a dental practice than a law office, smiling at the thought that attorneys were like dentists; they often dispensed more pain before relieving it.

His phone pinged.

Be out in a sec.

He glanced up and saw a camera attached to the wall above the door leading to the back offices. It wasn't unusual for lawyers to use security measures. If Suarez handled divorce cases, emotions often boiled over and disgruntled clients on both sides could be volatile. He'd had a college law school buddy who'd represented a father fighting his alcoholic ex-wife for custody. During a weekly visitation with her children, the mother showed up at her husband's lawyer's office drunk with her kids in tow, and a handgun. The woman fired two rounds before the gun jammed, but not before the attorney was fatally hit in the stomach.

He picked up a travel magazine and leafed through it. The frosted window slid open.

"You must be Mr. Courage," the woman said, eyeing him head to toe.

"That's right."

She had a black patch over her right eye and wavy brown hair loosely tied into a ponytail, held in place with a bright green scrunchie. He approached the window, then took a step back, away from the secondhand smoke wafting from her clothing.

"Come on back," she said, disappearing and reappearing as she opened the door leading from the lobby to the back offices.

"And you are?" he asked.

"Sorry," she said. "I'm Lola."

He tried not to stare at the eyepatch. "Where's Suarez?"

"He's not here. He had some last-minute business to attend. It's just me."

Suarez's rehab started at 5 p.m. and Vance thought Suarez might be at the office tying up loose ends.

He followed her to an office at the end of the hall. She walked like Frankenstein's sister with her granny skirt brushing the backs of her lace up combat boots.

She turned and pointed to the patch over her eye. "Don't worry. It's not contagious. Unless we share a pillow."

"Good to know," he said.

She stopped in the hallway and gestured to an open door. "This is the boss's office," she said. "You'll be working out of here."

As she waved him in, he noticed the Cuban flag tattooed on the inside of her right forearm. "How long have you worked for Mr. Suarez?"

"As long as he's been in practice."

"And how long is that?"

"Let's see," she said, narrowing her good eye. "Going on fifteen years."

Suarez's diplomas hung on the wall. He'd graduated from Florida Atlantic with a Doctor of Jurisprudence in 1984.

"He's not a drunk, you know," she said.

"I didn't say he was." But it was good to know she knew the score.

"If any of his clients ask, he's on vacation."

"Whatever you say. As long as you hold up your end of the deal."

"What deal?"

"I made it very clear to your boss that you handle everything that doesn't require a lawyer," he said, scanning the large office with the tasteful furnishings.

"Not a problem," she said, straightening the file folders on the desk.

"I only come into the office when I have to."

"Sure," she said, pulling the blinds. "Nice view, don't you think?"

It certainly was. The corner office had an unobstructed view of Biscayne Bay. There were no high-rises on the opposite side of the street. It wasn't because the city of Miami had building ordinances. It was because there was a seawall and no beach or land to build on. He looked to the left, north. He could make out the rooflines of Vizcaya and Mercy Hospital.

A fat high-powered telescope perched on a tripod faced east over the bay. She observed him eyeing it.

"You can see Stiltsville on a clear day," she said. "What's left of it, anyway."

Stiltsville had become popularized as a shooting location for the TV series Miami Vice. Located one-and-a-half miles offshore in Biscayne Bay, the houses built on stilts hovered above the water, but only a handful had survived the recent hurricanes.

"The other part of my deal is I'm only going to court when you can't get a delay and I expect you'll do everything in your power to get dates pushed."

"No problem," she said.

"And no consultations with new clients."

"Oh," Lola said, furrowing her brow. "Mr. Suarez didn't mention that."

"Now you know."

"You have a four o'clock consultation this afternoon," she said.

"Cancel it."

"I can't do that."

"Sure, you can."

"No, I can't."

"Get Suarez on the phone."

"I can't do that either."

He crossed his arms across his chest. "Suarez and I had a deal. No new clients."

"Technically she's not a new client," Lola said, sitting on the edge of the desk. "She's an existing client with a new problem."

"I'm sorry but it's non-negotiable. A deal is a deal."

"Just this once," Lola said, "and I'll make sure you don't have to talk to another client the entire time you're here."

"Under one condition," he said.

"Name it."

"You tell me what your boss's father-in-law was doing here."

"What are you talking about?"

"I saw Daniel Ruiz and his wife leaving the building when I arrived."

"I've never met them," she said. "We're not the only business in this building. Why don't you go home and come back for the meeting. You have time. I need to leave soon. I have an appointment with my doctor." She pointed at the patch over her eye.

"I might do that," he said, adding, "and I might not come back."

"You won't do that."

"Sit," he said, dropping into the ergonomic chair behind the desk, "and brief me on the meeting."

Lola took the client chair opposite him. He listened,

taking notes. "Wait a minute," he said. "I've never practiced immigration law."

"Mr. Suarez isn't an immigration attorney either, but sometimes he takes special cases for friends and family."

"This one will have to wait."

"It can't wait."

"Then refer it to another firm."

"I can't do that either," she said, fiddling with the green scrunchie holding her hair.

"Why not?"

"Because it's personal."

"If it's a personal immigration matter, you knew about it long before now and so did your boss. I told him I wasn't handling any consultations. No exceptions."

"I told you, she's not a new client. She's been out of the country and she's here now on a temporary travel visa that's going to expire in five days. I already confirmed the meeting."

"I don't know anything about visas."

"You don't have to know anything. I already filed the form I-907 for the revised H1-B. She paid for premium processing but there was a hiccup. You need to sign the G-28 form."

He vaguely knew what an H1-B visa was from news stories he'd read. It was the application corporations filed when they wanted to hire skilled workers from foreign countries. "What's premium processing?" he asked.

A man entered the room. "*Ju* can pay twenty-five hundred dollars extra to move the application to the front of the line. DHS USCIS processes the paperwork in fifteen days instead of six months, or longer. Years, sometimes."

"DHS . . . US-what?" he asked.

"Department of Homeland Security U.S. Citizenship

and Immigration Services," Lola said. "Franco, meet Vance Courage. Vance, meet Franco Frank, our PI."

The investigator was an unremarkable skinny guy with a nervous twitch.

"Good to meet *ju*." Franco set a business card down on the desk. "Call me anytime twenty-four-seven. I mean that," he said, before disappearing down the hall.

Lola pulled a file from the stack on the desk and pushed it toward him.

He opened it and scanned the USCIS Form I-907. "What's this for?"

"You need it for the meeting."

She pulled another file and set it down in front of him. He read the top line. '*U.S. Department of Justice, Notice of Appeal to the Board of Immigration Appeals . . .*'

Lola interrupted. "The short version of what happened is we filed the documents and paid the fees for fast tracking, but DHS denied the application."

"On what grounds?"

"It's all there. Like I said, she'll be here at four o'clock. You can go over it with her."

"This wasn't the arrangement."

"We're past that point," Lola said. "If you need anything, Franco and I are here to help."

His phone pinged. He pulled it from his pocket and looked at the screen.

"That's my cell number," she said.

He was rapidly recalling why he quit the profession. The paperwork and deadlines were a big part of it, not to mention that justice was for sale, even to speed up a visa application. He'd agreed to do this as a favor to Sarge, and in return his friend lied to him, and Sarge's son-in-law misled him. As a lawyer Suarez was trained to say whatever he needed to get what he wanted, but Sarge was a retired cop. A brother.

"Everything you need is in the file," Lola said, getting up to leave.

He looked at the label: *Natasha Popova-Morozova*. "A Russian?" he asked, scanning the first page.

"Only in name. I gotta get going to make my doctor appointment. I'll be back in time for the meeting."

"Hold up," he said. "When you said it's a personal matter, what did you mean?"

"It's all in the file."

"Sit back down." He gestured to the open chair on the other side of the desk.

Lola refused and stood with her arms clamped across her chest.

"I'm looking at this and it says here Natasha Popova-Morozova was born in Havana, Cuba in 1986 to Anastasia Popova. How is this a personal matter to Suarez?"

"Natasha is a doctor, a Cuban-born Russian-educated psychiatrist trying to emigrate to the United States. The Russian Ministry of Science and Higher Education selects a hundred Cuban nationals as students every year to attend the Russian university tuition-free. She's one of them."

"That doesn't explain what makes it personal."

"You're going to make me late."

"Why does she want to come here?"

"She's not the first Cuban to emigrate."

"The elites don't leave the country," he said. "If she's a Russian-trained Cuban doctor she has social and professional status."

"What difference does that make if you live in a third world country?"

"A lot, I would think."

"Right," she said, palming her forehead. "You can do wonders with mental health when there's no electricity or clean running water. Besides, the only good jobs are working for the government. Psychiatrists are often forced to ... —" she trailed off.

"Forced to what?"

"Just take the meeting and I promise you won't have any others."

He rubbed his brow. This didn't sit right. First *Damas de Blanco*, now some Cuban shrink trying to get a work visa. He posed the question again. "When you said her situation is personal, what did you mean?"

"There're hospitals here that can use someone with her background and training. Mr. Suarez told me what you did to save your sister's life. He said you sent her to Switzerland for cancer treatment. Oh no," she said, looking at her phone. "You're seriously going to make me late. Don't forget to sign the form G-28."

"The what?"

She handed him another file.

"The G-28 designates you as her new attorney. All you have to do is sign it. The meeting won't take long. Oh, I almost forgot. You'll need access to the building. Hold on."

Lola hurried down the hall and while she was gone, he thumbed through the file. It was true. Popova was Doctor of Psychiatry trained at the University of Moscow. Her H1-B application listed her future employer as a semi-conductor company based in Miami. That was weird. What did a place called Hialeah-Circuits need a shrink for? The job description listed a Director of Manufacturing Process Engineering with a starting salary of $215,000. The company was seeking an applicant fluent in English, Russian and Spanish. So much for the doctor story Lola told.

She reappeared. "You'll like her. She's smart, not to mention gorgeous. Here." She dangled the keycard over the desk. "To get in the office, hold it in front of the scanner and when you hear the pop, open the door. Remember to keep it with or you'll lock yourself out. If you need to use the computer, the login information is under the keyboard. Damn it. I'm going to be late," she said, scurrying out the door.

He hung the lanyard around his neck and stared at the files on Suarez's desk. When he was a plaintiff's attorney, the first assessment he'd make was determining whether the defendant had deep enough pockets to make the case worth his time. If so, he did things backwards. Most lawyers studied the merits of a case, then went to the law library searching for case law to support the theory. He often reverse-engineered lawsuits by first finding case law, then formulating the complaint to fit one already on the books. While it was creative, it was not what he'd been taught in law school.

He stared at the G-28 form. His Florida Bar license number had already been filled in. He had to hand it to Lola; she was thorough. *'Crack paralegal.'* Before he signed it, he read through the rejected application searching for the reason Natasha Popova's visa had been denied.

It didn't take long. DHS had rejected it because of a problem with her American husband, D. Morozov. In the comments section, the DHS officer who'd denied the application wrote: *'DHS is unable to confirm the identity of the applicant's husband. Further information is required.'*

The personal angle appeared on paper. It wasn't personal to Suarez; it was personal to Lola who was listed as Morozova's next-of-kin on the visa application. They were listed as half-sisters. Lola could have told him. If Natasha was married to an American, she could've applied for a spousal visa, and it should have been easy to verify his identity. Lola had a Hispanic last name while Natasha had a Russian one. Better question: why did her American husband have a Russian surname? He knew there were a few thousand Russian speakers living in Cuba dating back to the 1950s Cuban Missile Crisis. He checked the time. An uneasy feeling took hold. The 24-hour window had expired and the woman from Vizcaya still hadn't contacted him.

12

As Vance placed the visa documents back in the file folder, two passport-style photos of the applicant fell out and landed on the desk. Natasha Popova-Morozova looked nothing like Lola. The girl with the Russian last name had green eyes shaped like a cat. An idea of how they were related began to form inside his head. The logical explanation for the difference in surnames was that Natasha's mother or father may have been a Russian stationed in Cuba during the Cold War.

He drummed his fingers on the desk, then grabbed the Popova-Morozova file and headed toward the waiting room intending to leave, but when he got to the office lobby he backtracked and strolled the hallway reading the nameplates on each door. Franco's office was sparsely furnished with a metal desk and an empty bookshelf. He wandered around opening drawers and checking the trash. Other than a few office supplies, some yellow gum wrappers in the wastebasket and a stack of watercraft enthusiast magazines on the desk, there was nothing else in the investigator's workspace. He stepped into the hall and looked over his shoulder before slipping into Lola's office.

Her bookshelves were jam-packed with hardcover red law books perfectly arranged on a heavy-duty metal bookshelf. It was the full encyclopedic version of Florida Law—around 400 titles. He pulled a book from the shelf and checked the publication date. It was recent; the set must have cost close to fifty grand. He'd not been able to justify the expense when he was practicing, going instead to the law library to do legal research. He snapped the cover closed and returned the book to the empty slot on the shelf.

He picked up a framed 5-by-7 photo on the credenza behind Lola's desk. It was an old picture, with shades of black and white and sepia, and a spiderweb of cracks and scratches. The photograph showed three pencil-thin men wearing overalls over bare chests posing in front of a pair of oxen hitched to a primitive plow about the size of a push mower. All three wore straw hats with ratty fringed brims, their faces deeply wrinkled from the sun. He could see their ribs. They reminded him of scarecrows. The one with the widest grin was missing a front tooth. Another leaned on a pitchfork. The third one's hand rested on the oxen's neck. He wondered who they were, and how old the photo was. He turned it over and looked at the back but found no hints other than the tiny gold 'Made in China' sticker on the black cardboard backing.

He sat at Lola's desk and opened the drawers, starting on the left-hand side, skimming through her hanging folders arranged in alphabetical order. He checked the P's and M's but found nothing labeled Popova or Morozova. When he opened the bottom left drawer, he popped up like a gopher. The blast of secondhand smoke coming from an ashtray hidden in the desk drawer made his eyes water.

He turned his attention to the framed picture, picking it up again to examine it. The men were someone to her and it was the only hint of anything personal in Lola's office. They were too old to be her siblings. Uncles maybe. One of them could've been her father. He guessed Lola to be about forty and the men in the picture to be in their fifties at the time the photo was taken, but he couldn't gauge the age difference without knowing how old the image was. He set the picture back on the credenza and stared at it for a long moment.

Tucking the Popova immigration file under his arm he headed toward the exit. Then he had a thought; what if he *really* didn't come back to the office? What could they do about it? Fire him? Ha!

His phone pinged in his pants pocket with a text message. After more or less threatening the wedding photographer, he'd assumed the pictures were a dead end when Kent didn't call last night. He'd assumed wrong. He read the message from Kent Clark.

Got something. Call me. IMP.

13

"Never grab me again like that," Lauren warned Davis. "You realize that guy could've called the police." She got up from her chair and strode out of the internet café. The fellow who'd offered to call the cops watched her as she and Davis left the building together.

The line in front of the phone store seemed even longer now. Davis lumbered along next to her in silence.

"My credit cards aren't working," she said. "I might have enough cash to get a new SIM card."

Davis grimaced. "I don't think you can buy a SIM card if you have an American cell carrier. You could probably buy a burner. I could use one too."

She glared at him.

A bead of sweat was about to drip in his eye. He flicked it away. "I have an idea," he said.

"What, rob a bank?"

"Close. We could go to our bank and withdraw cash. It's walking distance from here."

She glanced around and lowered her voice. "I thought you said your accounts were frozen."

"My checking and debit accounts are but I don't know about my offshore account." He reached inside his pants pocket and removed something. He opened his palm and showed her a thumb drive.

"I didn't bring mine with me," she said.

"Come with me. I can withdraw cash and you can pay me back later."

"Do you think that's a good idea? Just because we don't have phones doesn't mean we're not being watched. Correction," she said, "doesn't mean you're not being watched. Go without me and I'll meet you back at the hotel."

"I could introduce you to our account manager," he said.

"I don't want to meet him."

"He's a good guy. They're very discreet and security minded."

"That's nice. It would be even nicer if I could get enough money to change my plane ticket and go home."

"You'd have to pay cash at the airport and that might raise red flags."

Red flags for whom? "How can you be so sure they haven't frozen that account too?"

"The privacy laws are tight for the offshore banks. I checked my bank balance online two days ago and it was all there. Come on," he said, "the bank is only a few blocks away."

She couldn't believe him. He knew he was being investigated for murder and he'd checked his secret bank balance online. He was paranoid enough to flush his SIM card down the toilet but willing to walk into the bank. She felt a raindrop smack her forearm.

"It's either that or we get soaked while you wait half the

day at the phone store for them to tell you they can't sell you a new SIM card for an American carrier. Besides that, if you buy a new phone, what good is it without your contacts list?"

She hated to admit it, but he was right. What she needed most was money. "Fine. I'll go with you, but I don't want to be introduced. If you can withdraw cash, you have to promise to give me enough to get home."

"Okay," he said, and then he perked up. "Last time I checked my balance, I was surprised. Did you know the dividends and interest we earn are tax free? It's enough for me to live comfortably without having to touch the principal."

The man walking in front of them turned his head. She smiled at the stranger, and when the man was done eavesdropping, she stood on tiptoes and spoke directly into Davis's ear. "Shut up," she said.

THE CAYMAN OFFSHORE BANK AND TRUST building looked more like a British colonial residence than a branch office . The lobby was airy with white tile floors and mint green paint. The only hint of security was the cameras housed in tinted domes in every corner of the building giving whoever monitored it a 360-degree view of the entrance and the lobby. There were three bank tellers standing behind shiny brass bars and a smattering of customers leisurely waiting in line.

"I'll wait here," she said, taking a seat near the window. Davis left to speak to a bank representative while she watched the rainstorm strengthen with brisk winds that bent the palm trees and cleared the sidewalk of pedestrians.

She turned her attention back to Davis who chatted with a petite, stern-looking woman seated behind a mahogany desk. While the woman made a call on the landline, Davis returned to talk to her.

"This is your chance to meet our banker," he said. "I told him you were coming for a visit."

"What? I specifically told you I didn't want to meet anyone."

"I already promised to introduce you when I was here last week." He leaned over and added, "before the problems began."

She gritted her teeth, fighting the urge to scream at him.

The small woman who'd made the phone call got up from her desk and approached. She was dressed in a gray power skirt and jacket.

"Mr. Green is ready to see you."

She looked at Davis and shook her head, then followed him as the woman showed them to a door leading past a large vault and offices.

An older man dressed in an Italian suit, mid-sixties she guessed, intercepted them and led the way to an office at the end of the hallway.

"I'm John Green," he said. "Very nice to meet you in person, Ms. Gold. Mr. Frost said you might be coming to visit. How long will you be staying?"

"I'm not sure," she said, forcing a half-assed smile.

"Have a seat," Green said.

When the banker's back was to them, she scowled at Davis who shrugged.

Green sat, then asked, "How can I help you?"

"I'd like to make a withdrawal," Davis said. "Can you issue a pre-paid debit card?"

"We can do that."

"Any chance I could get digital currency?" Davis asked.

"It can be arranged," Green said.

"Do a lot of places accept digital money?" she asked.

"Many do," the banker said. "The Cayman Islands Monetary Authority has granted custodial services to a lot more institutions."

Whatever that was.

Green continued. "There're ATMs all over the island that can exchange digital currency into cash if you need it. Most can convert into U.S. dollars if need be."

"I wonder . . ." Davis said, hesitating.

Oh no.

". . . does the local government have access to digital currency?"

"I'm not sure I understand your question," Green said.

Unbelievable.

"Could they cut off my debit card?"

She couldn't believe her ears.

"Theoretically, they could but our in-house legal team would require a court order before we would do that. Why do you ask?"

"Just curious," Davis said, looking over at her.

"Is that what you'd like to do?" Green asked. "Convert cash in your account into digital currency and have it credited to a pre-paid debit card?"

"Uh huh," Davis said, taking the thumb drive from his pocket and laying it on Green's desk.

"I don't need that when you're here in person," Green said referring to the thumb drive. "What about you, Miss Gold. Do you wish to make a withdrawal?"

"Sure. I'd like to do the same thing, if possible," she said.

"May I see your passports?"

She took hers from her purse and set it on the edge of the banker's desk.

Davis had a goofy look on his face. "I don't have mine on me."

"That's fine," Green said. "I know you and I believe we have a copy of yours on file."

He handed them each a document. "Fill this out," Green said, taking her passport. "I'll be right back."

She scanned the paperwork and when they were alone, glared at Davis. Part of her wanted to punch him. Instead, she said, "Maybe you should say a little less."

"About what?"

"About everything," she said, noticing the line on the paper where she was supposed to enter her account number. She didn't know it.

Green returned and set her passport down.

"I don't know my account number."

"Don't worry," Green said. "I need today's date, the amount, and your signature. We can fill out the rest. For digital currency we issue a Visa card. It looks like a normal credit card, but it's only accepted at approved ATMs and businesses. I recommend you ask the merchants first."

She filled out the form requesting $5,000 linked to the Visa card. That would be plenty to get her phone fixed, pay for a hotel for a night or two and go home. Her plane ticket was tied to the airline app on her dead phone. If she couldn't find the flight details for her return reservation some other way, she'd have enough to purchase a new one-way ticket back to Miami using a credit card.

The woman in the gray skirt returned and stood in the doorway. Green invited her in. She approached the banker's desk, leaned over, cupped her hand over her mouth and whispered into his ear. When she was done talking to Green, she said, "I have your card ready."

Davis reached for it, but the woman only had one and handed it to Lauren. It looked like a typical Visa debit card.

"You'll need to enter a six-digit pin number to activate it," the woman said. "When you're finished here, stop by one of the teller booths and we can set it up."

"What about mine?" Davis asked.

She left without answering his question.

When the woman was gone, Mr. Green asked Davis, "Did you get a new phone number?"

"No. Why?"

"Your wife was here trying to make a substantial withdrawal from your account."

"When?"

"The day before yesterday. We tried to contact you, but you didn't answer. Apparently, we sent several text messages, too. The bank also sent an email asking you to call us immediately."

"Did you, ah, . . . did you, . . . um, give her the money?" Davis stuttered.

"You added her to your account. As a joint account holder, she had access. So, yes, we authorized the withdrawal."

"How much did she take?" Davis asked.

"All of it," Green said.

14

Retired Fort Lauderdale police sergeant Daniel Ruiz stretched out on last year's Christmas present, the EZ chair his wife Maria generously charged on his credit card. It took up a big chunk of their small living room, but man-oh-man was it comfortable. Maria busied herself in the kitchen, drying dishes and tidying up. When the timer chimed, she opened the oven door; the aroma of cinnamon-chocolate chip cookies baking in the oven filled the room. His mouth watered.

"No, no, no!" he yelled at the television. "Damn it!"

The Miami Dolphins' quarterback fumbled the ball at the one-yard line. A Buffalo Bill player the size of a subzero freezer picked it up and lumbered down the field. Daniel straddled the wide chair with both feet planted on the floor staring in disbelief at the 70" screen that ate up one wall of the cracker-box house. The defensive tackle for the Bills made it to the Dolphins 20-yard line. Muting the TV, he grabbed his longneck beer from the chair's built-in cupholder and downed it in two swallows.

"Holy *madre* of God!" he hollered to his wife. "Close the damn window for crying out loud!

Maria hurried to the dining room and cranked the window shut. "What are you going to do about it?" she asked.

As far as he was concerned the smell of weed was worse than a dried fruit fart, not to mention possession was still illegal in Florida.

He leaned over, reached beneath the EZ chair and dragged out his old service revolver by the holster strap. He dismounted the chair, clamored to his feet, and pulled his shirt over his watermelon gut. Marching into the kitchen he searched the pantry. "Where'd you put that brownie mix?"

"Try the top shelf," Maria said.

"I'll be back," he said, slinging the holster over his left shoulder.

"*Ay yi yi*, do you think that's a good idea?" she asked, staring at the gun.

"Yeah, maybe they'll get the hint."

"What if they have one of those door cameras?"

"Who cares if they have one. It's not like I can be anonymous if I live next door."

"Why kick a hornets' nest, Danny? You've seen the kind of people coming and going from that place. They're probably cooking drugs or doing God knows what over there. What if they call the cops on you?"

"Pray Jesus they do. I'll be back." He walked twenty feet to the house next door and rang the bell. A minute later a skinny red-headed girl with bare feet and a halter top answered.

"What do you want?" she asked.

He held out the red box of brownie mix. "Ever heard of edibles?"

She stared at the gun holstered and hanging over his left shoulder.

He pushed the box at her. "Here. Take it. Tell your friends inside that stuff stinks and to either smoke inside or learn how to bake."

The scrawny girl grabbed the box and slammed the door in his face.

His phone vibrated in his pocket. He looked at the screen and sprinted home.

"What did they say?" Maria asked, as he rushed through the front door.

"Here," he said, ignoring the question, "answer it."

She glanced at the screen and held both hands up. "I'm not lying for you again. Let him leave a message."

She was right. It wasn't fair to put her in the middle between him and Courage. But that didn't stop him from pushing the phone at her a second time.

"Not unless you tell me why you've been lying to him," she said.

When he didn't offer an explanation, she said, "That's what I thought. You're up to something. You should really think about it. He's your only real friend."

A comment like that might've hurt, except it was true. He had contacts all over the city stemming from his long career as a Fort Lauderdale cop before retiring as sergeant. His sources ran the full gamut from the IT guys at the mayor's office, to the coroner, to entry level lawyers and senior administrative assistants working for the DA. But his relationship with Courage was different. They'd become friends after Sarge's only sister was murdered by a psycho Colombian drug dealer.

It was a long, long time ago, when both were still active

duty. Sarge had started hanging out at the Hotel Mutiny hoping to find her killer. Back then he and Courage were less than friends but more than acquaintances. More recently, they'd become buds.

The phone stopped ringing. He stared at the screen thinking Courage might leave a message, but he didn't.

He could've told Maria the truth about what was going on, but he wasn't in the mood for a month of I-told-you-so's. She didn't like Rafael Suarez from the moment their daughter Valeria brought him home to meet the family. Maria said he gave her the heebie-jeebies. He was certain if his wife had had the chance, she would've gelded Suarez. Too late for that. He was the father to their two beautiful granddaughters. Val had fallen for a lying, cheating SOB and was somehow blinded to what he and Maria saw.

"It's no big deal," he said. "Courage will never know."

"Seriously, Danny?" Maria clamped her hands on her wide hips. "You make me tell him you're in the hospital with chest pains? You call that no big deal? I call it a big fat lie. If you're not going to tell me what you're up to, keep me out of it."

He shrugged then reached around for a warm chocolate chip cookie.

She smacked his hand. "You can wait."

He glanced at the television. The Miami Dolphins were down another 7 points to the Buffalo Bills. It was hard to believe it was more than 50 years ago the team went 17-0, a perfect season ending with a Super Bowl championship. The only undefeated team in National Football League history. Like everyone else who could remember that glorious year, each season at the opening kickoff, he hoped it would happen again. He still had a stack of bumper stickers from their perfect 1972 season. He'd checked the price on eBay. They were only worth a few bucks, so he'd kept them.

"You should get ready," she said.

Good thing the game was a recording from last season, and he knew how it ended because his oldest granddaughters Leah's violin recital at the Catholic church started in one hour. The NFL season didn't begin for another four months, and there was no way he could wait that long to see the Dolphins play.

"Take a shower and put on a sport coat, Danny."

"Should I blow dry my hair?" He ran his hand over his slick dome.

"You could powder it."

Touché.

"Rafael will be there, and you know he always dresses like a peacock," she said. "You two can sit together. Better if he doesn't sit next to me."

Ralph drank too much. He worked too much. He was a womanizer, though Sarge had no actual proof of that. He was many things he didn't want in a son-in-law. On the other hand, he was a good provider, and Val and the girls lived the life he and Maria had never dreamt for themselves. As first-generation Cuban Americans who struggled to make ends meet and educate their two daughters, his and Maria's wish was always that their children and grandchildren would have a better life than they'd had. From a financial standpoint, Ralph measured up.

"If you text an update to Courage," he said, "I'll make sure you don't have to sit next to Ralph. Tell him I'm in the hospital and I'm going to live."

"You text him," she said, packing freshly baked cookies

in a small brown paper bag. "Hurry up and get ready. If you're a good boy, I'll give you a cookie on the way to church."

He smirked. "You know what I really want."

"When will you stop thinking about that all the time?"

He placed his hand over his heart and feigned a painful expression. "When I'm dead," he said, then sat on the edge of the EZ chair and typed a text to Courage:

He's still in the hospital. He's doing much better.

He pushed the send button and two seconds later his phone pinged. A thumbs-up icon from Courage appeared atop the blue text bubble. He felt bad for lying, but he sensed Courage was agitated when he'd left the restaurant, and he couldn't give him the chance to back out of the deal. He didn't care that Ralph was in a tight spot; he had his daughter and granddaughters to think about. If Ralph screwed up and didn't complete his rehab, he could be disbarred permanently. He and Maria were not in a financial position to support Val and the girls.

At Easter dinner, Ralph got so drunk he'd snapped at the kids for no reason. Val had left the table in tears while Maria comforted the children. His oldest daughter Gloria was there too, visiting from Santa Fe and had witnessed the event as it unfolded.

That night, Ralph was arrested for a DUI and had called Daniel from the jail. He and Maria had argued about it. She thought Ralph should spend the night and face the consequences, but Val came to the house and begged him to help. Against Maria's wishes, he went downtown and bonded him out. Ralph seemed distraught and confused. He claimed he didn't have that much to drink but that's what all the drunks he'd ever arrested had to say.

When the judge ordered Ralph to inpatient rehab, Val came to him again for help. It was Val's idea to ask Courage to cover for her husband. If he ran it by Courage privately and gave him time to think about it, he ran the risk he'd say no. That's why he decided to put him on the spot. It was also the reason he was ducking his calls and lying about being in the hospital.

On the days leading up to the lunch meeting at the Italian place, Ralph began to ask questions. How did an unemployed lawyer with no discernible income afford a Porsche? Daniel didn't have a good answer but thought it even weirder that Ralph knew Courage sent his sister to Switzerland for cancer treatment. Sarge suggested it might have been family money since it had been less than a month after Courage's father passed away. The answer about the pricey condo in Coconut Grove was easier. It belonged to Courage's girlfriend Lauren, who'd apparently inherited it from her uncle.

As Ralph pressed on with the questions, Val intervened, telling her husband to mind his own business. But he'd lain awake a whole night last week wondering how Ralph knew so much and why he asked so many questions.

Of course, he couldn't tell his son-in-law the truth. He'd never breathed a word about Courage's money to a living soul. He'd never told anyone he'd been offered a piece of the action, refusing a hefty chunk of the drug cash. Not because he was incorruptible and not because he didn't need the dough; rather if he got caught, he would lose his pension, and possibly even go to prison.

"Come on," Maria said. "You need to get going or we're going to be late."

He headed to the bathroom to freshen up and change clothes. He hadn't told Maria about Ralph's situation and was waiting for the right time. He'd told himself he'd kept the mandatory rehab from her because he didn't want her to worry but it wasn't that simple. Val was the one who made him promise not to tell.

DANIEL HURRIED out of the house ahead of Maria to open the car door for her.

"Good Lord," Maria said, bending over and picking up an empty box of brownie mix from the driveway. The mound of brown powder was piled on the hood of the white Jeep like an anthill.

"Gimme that," Daniel said, using the box to knock most of the cake mix off. It puffed into a chocolate cloud before dissipating. "Assholes," he said under his breath. He jogged to the garbage on the street and tossed the box in the can. On his way back to the vehicle he noticed the bumper sticker had been vandalized.

The '*Women Want Me*' part of the bumper sticker had been changed. The '*W*' and '*O*' of '*Women*' had been blacked out to read '*men*' and between the words '*Want*' and '*Me*', '*to blow*' had been added using a thick black marker. He squatted and picked at a corner of the sticker. A small piece tore from the edge leaving the vulgar part intact.

"What are you doing? We're going to be late," Maria said, walking his way to see what he was up to, rounding the corner where he squatted. "It's three-thirty and the traffic's going to get bad." She gasped as she peered over his shoulder. "I told you not to put that stupid bumper sticker on the car and I told you not to mess with those neighbors, Danny! See what they've done? *A veces pienso que estas loco.*"

Maybe she was right. Maybe he was crazy.

The skinny redheaded girl and her two emaciated male

friends sat on the stoop smoking a joint, whooping and cackling, as a stink as bad as skunk spray fouled the air.

"Get in the car and wait for me," he said, "and lock yourself in. I'll be right back." He slammed the driver's side door, swallowing the rage building inside.

15

The drive from Suarez's office back to the condo should have been a five-minute trip but at the rate traffic was moving, it might take a week. Vance watched the side mirrors waiting for the lane next to him to open so he could pass a slow-moving dump truck dropping dirt and gravel. He dialed Kent Clark from the Audi and listened as his phone connected to Bluetooth. A moment later Kent was on speaker.

"I looked through those files and I found some photos I think you'll want to see."

"Text them to me."

"They're too big. I already uploaded them to my server. Text me your email address and I'll send you a link. Open it and you'll see a bunch of thumbnails. You can zoom in and look at details."

"Any hints about what you found?"

"You'll have to see for yourself. Text or call if you have any trouble."

As he ended the call, the dump truck he was stuck behind hit a pothole spewing dirt, dusting the hood and windshield of the Audi. He activated the windshield washer; the wipers mixed a paste of fine dirt with seagull droppings. It took three more rounds of spritzing before he could see out the windshield.

At the red light he composed a text to Kent:

My email is vancecourage@gmail.com

A blue thumbs up appeared on the screen followed by a message:

Give me five minutes.

BACK AT THE CONDO, he hurried inside. Poor Cash waited at the front door, yelping softly. "Come on," he said, clipping the leash to his collar.

He walked Cash inside the gated area and as the dog squatted to do his major business, he turned to see where the loud rap music was coming from. Good grief. The electric foot scooters he'd seen buzzing around downtown had made their way to the residential streets. Three punk kids dressed in black wearing masks and wraparound sunglasses rode a lazy serpentine in front of the gate. The music came from small boomboxes hanging around their necks. They slowed in front of the condos and rode a tight circle in front of the gate. He ignored them.

There were more sets of dirty dog prints leading from the hallway to the sliding glass door. He stepped into the courtyard to inspect a shallow hole Cash had dug near a sprawling Pride of Barbados blooming dainty orange and yellow flowers. Using the sole of his shoe, he spread the dirt around the base of the plant making a mental note to water the plants in clay pots beneath the overhang. He pulled the sliding glass door shut, went to Lauren's home office and sat at her desk.

He jiggled the mouse to wake up the computer. A message appeared on screen requiring a login and password. He searched the top of the desk and drawers for the passcode. Cash sat next to him with his pink tongue hanging out and a throw-the-ball look on his face. "Where does your mom keep her password?" he said. The dog laid down on the tile. His eye caught a florescent pink sticky note affixed directly in front of him, stuck to the metal strip below the computer screen — so obvious he'd overlooked it.

He logged on, signed into his Gmail account and opened the message from Kent Clark Photography. Tapping the link, six thumbnail images from the bridal shoot appeared on the monitor. He moused over the first one and enlarged it to full screen. Ken had cropped out the groom and blurred the face of the bride-to-be but preserved the right side of the background. He selected the MAGNIFY tool, zoomed in and studied different areas of the backdrop, moving the mouse slowly until he came upon a fuzzy shot of what appeared to be a man wearing a ball cap holding something in the air. It was difficult to see details in the shady lowlight of the forest, but he was pretty sure it was the man he'd seen holding a phone over his head.

He tapped the next photo. It was another shot of the same guy, but in this scene, he looked down at something in his hand. He closed out of the second picture and opened the third. It was a stop-frame of the stranger turning to run. His heart pounded at the fourth and fifth pictures. He zeroed in on a bright green WaveRunner visible in the bay beyond the woodlands. He zoomed in 500-percent on the sixth and last picture in the file. A fuzzy image of a woman wearing white sat on the back of the watercraft, behind the man wearing the ball cap. That was how she'd made her escape.

He changed screens, pulled up Vizcaya on Google Earth and enlarged the aerial map. The concrete barge was clearly visible from the birds-eye view as were rooftops, buildings, gardens, entrance, parking lot, and woodlands abutting Biscayne Bay where he'd seen the man.

He zoomed in tighter. North of the barge was a narrow concrete walkway leading to a small over-water arched bridge attached to some kind of manmade structure. It was located about midpoint between the barge and where he'd found the burner in the forest. It might've been a small boathouse, but he couldn't be sure. Whatever it was, it had been reduced to large chunks of rubble.

Maybe it was damaged during the same hurricane that wrecked the barge. He dragged the mouse to the left and stopped over a marina that wasn't part of Vizcaya. It appeared to be abandoned. He moused past it pausing to study the residential mansions bordering Vizcaya to the north. Some had long wooden docks and luxury boats, tennis courts and Olympic-sized pools. He closed Google Earth and reopened the email from Clark, noticing another new message.

SUBJECT LINE: Greetings from Grand Cayman
    To: vancecourage@gmail.com
    From: themutinygirl@gmail.com
    10:29 AM
    Hi Vance,

I hope you haven't been too worried. There's something wrong with my phone and I haven't been able to check in. Send me a quick reply to let me know you got this email and I'll call or text when I figure something out.

    Love, Lauren

P.S. I might have to buy a burner. Email your phone number. I don't know it. :-(

He stared at the screen for a long moment. There was no way to know if it was legit. If the kidnappers hacked her phone, they might've been able to generate an email. He was about to delete it when he scrolled up the page to check the timestamp. He played the timetable from yesterday in his head. If his memory served him, the email had been sent around the time he got the kidnapper's call at the gym. It was possible she'd sent it. He composed a response.

Subject Line: Greetings from Miami
  To: themutinygirl@gmail.com
  From: vancecourage@gmail.com
  2:03 PM
Lauren, I've been trying to call you but there's something wrong with your phone. Where are you? Are you in trouble? I need to authenticate this is you. Please add the following information when you answer. What is the long and short name of the dog we recently adopted? What kind of car did I drive when we first met, and what was the nickname I gave it? If this is you, please add your new phone number and I'll call you.
  VC
  He stared at the screen for a second, then added:
  P.S. I miss you.

He pressed the send key, then checked the time. Just after 2 in the afternoon. He googled 'Jackson Memorial Hospital,' dialed the main number and asked to be connected to

Daniel Ruiz's room. On-hold music played before a woman got on the line.

"I'm sorry sir, but there's no one here by that name. Are you sure you have the right hospital?"

"Can you tell me if he checked out recently?"

"I'm sorry, but I don't have access to that information. Is there something else I can help you with today?"

"No," he said, ending the call and confirming his suspicion.

He opened the app to Lauren's online shopping account, searched *GPS tracking devices,* and selected a small magnetic one with free overnight shipping and no activation fees. When he pressed the BUY IT NOW button a message flashed on the screen. The online merchant declined her credit card on file. That was weird. He tried a second time. Same result. He pulled one of his from his wallet and charged it to his own card.

He grabbed a roll of paper towels and spray cleaner from under the kitchen sink and headed to the entryway to clean the muddy dog paw prints from the tile. While he wiped the floor he replayed the chain of events. He'd dropped Lauren off at Cayman Air, had gone to the gym, answered a call from her number that turned out to be from the kidnapper, met Sarge at the Italian place, and drove to Vizcaya to meet the woman at the barge.

He'd discovered the discarded phone in the woodlands, dialed Lauren's number from the contacts list on his phone and witnessed the burner ring. He wasn't tech savvy, but he knew hacking a smartphone wasn't easy. When the woman at the barge demanded that he return the disposable phone, he should have resisted. But she'd delivered a veiled threat reminding him he was a sitting duck. The new email changed things. He read it again. In the subject line it said,

'Greetings from Grand Cayman.' If true, it was a clue and meant Lauren had made the flight. It also meant she'd been abducted there.

He sat in front of the computer and scrolled through his email hoping to get a response from her, but it had been only a few minutes since he'd answered her email. He checked the time again; it had been more than twenty-four hours since the woman at the barge promised to contact him with the ransom demand. He tried Lauren's number again from his phone. A CALL FAILED message appeared on the screen. He googled '*Vizcaya hours of operation.*' It was still open.

He added kibble to Cash's dog bowl, refilled the water dish, stopped at the sliding glass door to the courtyard, hesitated, then left it open enough for the dog to go in and out. Hurrying to the Audi he opened the navigation app on his phone to check traffic. He had enough time to conduct a reconnaissance run at Vizcaya before meeting the Russian.

Passing Suarez's high-rise office building, he rolled down the car window and took in the saltwater air rehashing the recent barrage of strange, seemingly unrelated events. There were too many moving parts to make sense of anything. One detail did come to mind: If he'd remained at the seawall after the woman in white left, he might have seen her leave on the back of the WaveRunner.

The woman took a gamble that he'd assume she arrived by car and that he'd focus on the parking lot. She'd guessed correctly but she hadn't counted on his chance meeting with Kent Clark.

Or the wedding photos.

16

V ance parked and joined the line of tourists waiting to enter Vizcaya. The queue was shorter than before and within a few minutes he stood in front of the seawall surveying the perimeter using the concrete barge as his point of reference. To the north, his left, he spotted a short rainbow-shaped concrete footbridge that led to what appeared to be an old boathouse jutting out from the bay like a tiny island. He opened Google Earth on his phone and compared the aerial picture to the ground view where he stood. It was the same one he'd seen on the computer.

He walked toward the bridge hoping it might give him a vantage point to observe routes the pair may have used to escape by water, but it was cordoned off with yellow CAUTION tape.

Retracing his steps from when he'd sprinted from the barge to the woodlands, he headed to the spot where Kent had shot the pictures that captured the green WaveRunner in the background. Unlike the day he'd bumped into the photographer while running through the crowds, there was no farmers market and only a handful of people strolled along the walkway.

He stopped midway on the walkway to the footbridge leading to the woodlands and pulled up one of the wedding photos he'd downloaded to his phone. He compared the image on the screen to the view from the ground then jogged toward the wooden bridge leading to the forest to search for the abandoned marina he'd seen on Google Earth.

When he reached the other side, it was at least ten degrees cooler in the tropical shade and rotting vegetation mashed beneath his shoes, each step releasing a woody, musky smell. He swatted at a mosquito buzzing his ear, then used his hands to push away fronds and branches making a path through the foliage as he neared the shoreline. When he reached the water's edge, he squatted to examine the ground for shoe prints or other evidence. There were two sets of sneaker treads still visible after the rain, protected by the natural canopy; one set of tracks was bigger than the other. He touched the soft dirt and rubbed the sandy mud between his thumb and forefingers. A ray of sunlight glinted off a wadded foil gum wrapper. He pulled his phone from his pocket and snapped a photo.

A plastic soda bottle bobbed in the water near a small cove constructed from large boulders arranged as a barrier. He stood on the tallest rock, shaded his eyes and looked south, to his right, in the direction of the barge. He ruled it out as the path the pair used to land the Wave-Runner. The terrain along the shoreline in that direction was devoid of vegetation or buildings, making it too exposed to pull off a stealth water landing. The man who'd dropped the burner phone most likely came from somewhere to the north where the mangroves were dense, where the Vizcaya property line ended, and the residential mansions began.

Getting a visual on the abandoned marina, he stepped down from the rock and followed a path along the water's edge until he came to a clearing with a view to the dock. It was about 75-feet long, had no vehicle access and there were no boats. Water gently lapped at the trash bobbing along the pilings. He tested the footing. The dock swayed slightly, and he reached for the railing as he took a step onto it. The wooden plank beneath his left foot snapped and he lost his balance, his left leg plunging through the gap. He fell to one knee soaking one pant-leg and filling his shoe with seawater that smelled like rotten fish.

He crawled to the rail and palmed another plank, testing its strength before standing and grabbing a solid-looking piece of handrail. Small bait fish darted around the decaying pilings that resembled telephone poles, many reduced to nubs barely visible above the waterline. Squeezing water from his pant leg, he removed his shoe and sock listening to the mewling of passing seagulls overhead.

From this vantage point, in the distance he could see the Rickenbacker Causeway, the massive 6-lane overwater bridge more than a mile long connecting the mainland to the islands of Key Biscayne and Virginia Key. If he were trying to gain access to Vizcaya inconspicuously during daylight, he'd have launched a small watercraft from the island side of the causeway. He reopened the map on his phone and studied the surrounding topography.

The Rickenbacker bridge would've offered a point of reference and shelter during inclement weather. The map showed the causeway also linked to state parks on the islands, and he knew from experience that the one on Key Biscayne had a public boat ramp.

He considered the only other option. From this vantage point on the rickety dock he could clearly see what lay in the opposite direction. The southernmost side of the Vizcaya property line had an inaccessible beachhead too heavily forested with mangrove trees to land a watercraft. Farther in that direction the bulkhead and parking lots for Mercy Hospital and the adjacent Catholic school were developed up to the water's edge. If he were planning to enter Vizcaya surreptitiously by the bay, there was only one way; he'd have come from Key Biscayne and used the causeway for visual reference and shelter.

He'd have towed the WaveRunner across the bridge and launched it from the public boat ramp at Crandon Park. He remembered the storm the day he'd met the woman at the barge, and the white caps he'd seen topping the waves like whipped cream. If they'd come by water, it meant the man and woman were comfortable on rough seas. Recreational boaters wouldn't have been out at that time meaning they risked less chance of being seen from the water.

He checked the time. He had to get back to Suarez's office to meet with Natasha Popova-Morozova. He'd do a recon run to Crandon Park later, after his meeting with the Russian, before sundown. As he reached the apex of the footbridge, his phone dinged. A text from Lauren's phone number. He tapped the green bubble. A link appeared and a video played. Lauren's face popped up on the screen.

"Hey," she said. "I'm okay but you need to do what they say. I'll be fine as long as you follow directions."

"Where are you?"

The screen went black. He pressed redial attempting to reconnect, but the video call rang ten times before the call dropped. He searched his text messages but there was no record of the video.

His phone pinged with a new message from the same number.

You know what to do.

He held the screen in front of his face and yelled, "No, I don't!"

He stopped and leaned against the bridge railing, gazing over at the concrete barge. Closing his eyes, he played the video back in his head, again and again. It had been shot in front of a plain white wall. It could've been recorded anywhere; then it occurred to him that's why they chose it. There was no point of reference. He wanted to see it again, to study her facial expressions for hints about her emotional state, but it had disappeared from his phone.

He scrolled through recent texts and calls but there was no trace of the video. He had to find Davis Frost. He remembered the name of the place he'd pitched as an investment. Sea Otters. It would be easy to look it up on the 'Net.

But first, it was time to rattle Sarge's cage.

17

M aria hardly spoke to him on the drive to the church and when they arrived, the parking lot was mostly empty. Daniel Ruiz watched the onboard camera as he backed the Jeep into an available spot. If he'd had more time, he'd have used paint thinner and a putty knife to scrape the vandalized sticker from the rear bumper of the Cherokee. As a quick fix, he slapped on a *Miami Dolphins 1972 Undefeated Champions*' sticker to cover it.

"Hurry up. We're already late," Maria said.

When the back tires touched the curb, he put the Jeep in park and killed the engine. "It's not like there's a big crowd," he said. "I'm pretty sure there'll be plenty of seats left."

"I don't understand why you had to go and mess with those people," she said, letting herself out of the car.

Just as she had predicted.

INSIDE THE CATHOLIC SCHOOL AUDITORIUM, a dozen or so children with musical instruments sat on folding chairs on the stage beneath ancient lighting fixtures. Daniel spotted his daughter Val seated in the second row with their youngest granddaughter, six-year-old Ava. He felt for Maria's hand and led the way.

"Where's Rafael?" Maria whispered in his ear.

He shrugged and placed his hand across her lower back. "Excuse us," he said to the young parents sitting in the aisle seats, escorting Maria who sidestepped in front of them as the mom and dad craned their necks to see the stage. Maria crossed in front of Val and took the farthest seat next to Ava who spotted the top of the brown paper bag poking out of Maria's purse.

"How's my little angel?" Maria asked.

"I'm fine, Gamma."

Ava leaned forward in her seat and spoke past her mother, to him. "Guess what, Grandpa?"

"What?" he asked.

"I traded Sara five pennies for a quarter."

"Who's Sara?"

"My BFF," Ava chirped.

"Why did you do that?"

"To make twenty cents," Ava said, giggling. "Then I bet her two quarters it would rain today."

"It rains every day," he said.

"I know," Ava said, smiling at him.

"Ava," Val warned, "that wasn't nice a nice thing to do."

He fought the urge to laugh out loud. Ava looked like a little angel, reminding him of Val when she was that age; looks could be deceiving.

Sister Agnes dressed plainly in dark slacks with a navy-blue veil pinned atop her head doubled as the music conductor. Standing with her back to the audience and holding a wooden baton, she began to wave her hands gently, instructing the children. Ava reached into Maria's purse and stole a cookie. His wife pretended not to notice. Daniel leaned forward and peered past Val placing his hands over his eyes. Ava let out a naughty tee-hee as she bit a chunk of chocolate chip cookie.

"Where's your husband?" Maria asked Val loud enough for him to hear.

"Shhh," Ava warned, placing a tiny finger in front of her mouth. "We have to be quiet."

"Meet the Imperial Ava," Val said.

"Where's your husband?" Maria repeated.

The little boy and girl seated in the row in front of them watched a video on their phone and laughed aloud. Ava leaned forward and yanked the ponytail of the girl with such force she yelped. The little boy sitting next to her turned in his seat and flipped the bird. Ava laughed.

"Ava," Maria warned in a low voice. "That's not funny and you shouldn't do things like that."

Ava smirked. "Daddy's not coming."

Maria shot Val a look. "Is that true?"

"We can talk about it later, Mom."

A look of disgust formed on Maria's face as she pulled her shawl tighter around her shoulders and stared at the stage. He knew what his wife was thinking. She'd asked him to dress up because their son-in-law would be there. His phone buzzed in his pocket. He sneaked it from his pants pocket to see who was calling but even from a few seats away, Maria saw what he was doing. He stuffed it back in his pocket.

"Leah's solo's coming up," Val said in a loud whisper.

"She sucks," Ava announced. "She hates the violin."

"Ava," Val warned.

Leah the fledgling violinist sat in a chair near the middle

of the stage dressed in a white short-sleeve shirt and a plaid skirt covering her ankles. Leah picked up a bar of rosin and ran the pine tar over her violin bow, stood, bowed, and balanced the instrument on her left shoulder. The conductor—the nun—raised her arms. On cue, a young boy sitting behind the piano began to play *Over the Rainbow*.

Maria clasped her hands with a look of prideful joy. The woodwind section joined the piano and on cue, eight-year-old Leah, ran the bow across the strings of her violin making a noise he could only describe as a cat in heat. The audience groaned. Poor Leah. The only thing she liked about the violin was the horsehair strung taut to make the bow. She'd asked for a pony for her seventh birthday and her father gave her the violin instead.

The girl nearest Leah fell out of her chair, dropping her flute, and hit the stage floor with a thud. The small crowd gasped, and the music stopped as Sister Agnes rushed to help. Val jumped to her feet, grabbing the shoulders of strangers as she scrambled past, sprinting to the stage. Daniel scrabbled from his seat to follow her. The families rushed the stage and when he got close enough, he saw the child was face down on the stage floor, convulsing.

"She's having a seizure," Val yelled, dropping to her knees and rolling the girl onto her side, cupping her neck in the palm of her hand. "Give me that!" Val said to the teacher, waving her hand in the air.

"Give you what?" the nun asked with a look of terror.

"Your baton!"

Val inserted the wooden stick sideways inside the girl's mouth. Daniel knew what his daughter was doing. She was preventing the child from biting or swallowing her tongue.

The girl's parents pushed their way onto the stage. "She's epileptic!" the dad yelled.

Leah spotted her grandfather in the crowd and ran down from the stage. Her eyes were wild. He pushed his way toward her. "Hey," he said, kneeling to hug her.

"What's happening Grandpa?"

"Everything's going to be okay, sweetheart. Go get your violin."

Leah hurried back to the stage, hesitating for a moment as she passed her mother attending to her schoolmate.

"Go on," Sister Agnes said, waving Leah past.

He wanted to help but watched instead while Leah grabbed her violin, dropped it in the case and took a wide berth around the scene. She trotted down the stairs and handed him the violin. Daniel tucked it under his arm.

The seizure had passed and the poor child lay limp on the stage floor in the fetal position, whimpering. Her parents huddled around her trying to stop people from staring. A young boy held his cell phone over his head taking pictures.

Val clamored to her feet. "Give me that," she said, snatching the boy's phone.

The children who'd come to play had disbursed and huddled with their peers and families. A few of them— mostly adults—congregated near the stage trying to get a better look at the sick child. There were always a few that couldn't help themselves. He remembered them from his days as a cop. They jammed up traffic whenever there was an accident; the worse the wreck, the slower they drove. He'd taken his eyes off Leah for a moment and when he didn't see her, his heart raced as he scanned the room looking for her. He spotted her with a group of schoolmates. He approached the stage to check on Val.

"I don't know how we can thank you enough," the mother of the stricken girl said to Val.

Maria approached with Ava in tow. "Oh my gosh, that poor child," she said. "It's a good thing there was a doctor in the house."

"I know," Daniel said as two paramedics passed carrying an empty gurney toward the stage.

"I wish she never married that guy," Maria said. "Val's perfectly capable of managing her own life. She could do fine without him. This is a perfect example."

"Enough of that," Daniel said. "It's her life. You know how she is. She does what she wants."

"I'm telling Mommy you said she can manage her own life without Daddy," Ava said in a snotty tone.

"You should mind your own business young lady," Maria said.

It was true. Valeria was the daughter born with a mind of her own who could do just fine without Rafael.

"Mommy shops all the time and Daddy asks her not to, but she does it anyway," Ava said.

It was another truth: Rafael kept Val and the girls in style. New cars, clothes, vacations, a big house. All the things Daniel hadn't been able to give his own family.

"Children don't always understand what adults mean," Maria said to Ava trying to get ahead of the story.

"I understood it," the Imperial Ava said. "You think Mommy doesn't need Daddy."

Wow.

"If it wasn't for your father," Maria said, "I wouldn't have two beautiful grandbabies."

"We're not babies," Ava said.

Leah joined them. "Where's Mom?"

"She's talking to the parents," he said.

"I want to go home," Leah said.

"I know," Maria said hugging both children. "Which one of you wants one of Gamma's cookies?"

"I do, I do," Ava said.

She reached into her purse and gave Ava another. "What about you?" she asked Leah.

"Maybe later," Leah said, wandering off again.

He took one step to the side where he could keep an eye on his oldest granddaughter. He and Maria had scrimped and sacrificed to save up for their daughters' college educations. The oldest, Gloria, had graduated with a degree in theater and the arts and had moved to Santa Fe where she ran a struggling community theater. Val was the ambitious one, borrowing more money for medical school and graduating with honors. She was on a fast track employed as an ER doctor at one of the big hospital networks before she'd met Rafael Suarez.

"Those poor parents," Maria said, watching the mother and father follow the paramedics out the side door.

Maria eyed the violin case tucked under his arm. "Give me that," she said, holding Leah's violin bow. "It isn't right. She doesn't want to play the violin. It's what her dad wants, and he didn't even bother to show up today. What kind of *padre* does that?"

He left the comment about Ralph's absence unanswered. "We should stay out of it. Leah and Ava are too young to understand and if Ava tells Val what we said, it can only cause problems," he said.

His mind wandered to Easter dinner at the Suarez home. When he and Maria arrived, Ralph was already hammered on red wine. He didn't know what Val and Rafael had been fighting about that day, but it was serious enough that Val had left the table in the middle of the meal visibly upset. When he'd asked Gloria what happened, his oldest daughter reminded him it was none of his business. It was a valid point until it came time to bail Rafael out of jail.

It was the same evening he'd accepted Ralph's invitation to his man cave to imbibe in some Macallan 30-year-old scotch. He'd tried to beg off, but Rafael was wasted and wouldn't take no for an answer.

His phone buzzed in his pocket. He checked CALLER ID. It was Courage again. He'd ignored his last call thinking the recital was about to begin and he'd expected Courage to leave a message, but he hadn't. He let this call go, too. A text popped up on the screen. He took his readers from his pocket and looked at it.

Checking in to see how Sarge is doing.

Maria stood on tiptoes and spied the message.

He held his finger on the blue bubble and tapped the thumbs up icon.

She scowled at him. "Seriously?"

Another text from Courage followed.

Called the hospital. No patient with your name there.

He shoved the phone in his pocket. "I'll be right back," he said. "Stay with the kids while I use the little boys' room."

He passed the restrooms, slipped out the side door and redialed Courage. On the sixth ring, it went to voicemail. Without leaving a message, he returned to the auditorium to find his wife pacing.

"What's wrong?"

"I was packing Leah's bow in her violin case, and I found something," Maria said.

"What?"

She handed him a folded piece of paper. He read the typed note. The rush of adrenaline almost strangled him.

"Who did this?" he asked.

Maria raised her shoulders. "I have no idea."

"Does Val know?"

"I don't think so."

The girls were with Val and the threesome approached. He squatted and whispered to Leah. "Did you see a note in your violin case?"

"What note?" Leah asked with a puzzled look on her face.

"It's nothing, Sweetie," he said.

Val pulled him aside. "What did you ask her?"

He took the note from his pocket and showed it to her.

Keep your mouth shut or you'll be sorry.

"Where did you get that?" Val asked.

"It was in Leah's violin case," Maria said.

The music teacher interrupted, still frazzled. "I can't thank you enough," she said to Val. "I've been teaching that child all year and nothing like this has happened. Her parents said she hasn't had an episode in three years."

"Seizures can be spontaneous," Val said. "The good news is most kids grow out of them."

When the nun was out of earshot, he asked Val to step aside with him so they could chat privately. "Do you have any idea who would've left that note in Leah's violin case?"

"No. Maybe it's a joke. Probably one of the kids. You know how cruel they can be," Val said.

"Why would they do that?" he asked.

"Who knows? They're kids," Val said.

"You should report it to the school," he said.

"I don't see what good that would do. What could they do about it?"

Maria barged into the convo. "That's so cynical. If you don't report it to the school, I will."

"Mom, have you seen the stuff on social media? The kids get upwards of six hundred text messages a day on their phones. This is nothing by comparison."

"That's insane," Maria said. "And I politely disagree with you. It's a threat. I wish they didn't have phones. They're too young."

"I can't stop them, Mom. That's like you trying to stop dad from watching football. I need the app to pick the girls up from school."

It was true. He'd borrowed Val's phone once to get them after class the day Val had a medical procedure and couldn't drive.

"Kids these days need phones," Val said. "I have a tracking app on all our phones so I know where everyone one is all the time. No one has cyber-bullied either one of them. I'd know. If I don't let them have their phones, they'll find another way to get them."

His blood boiled. "Like asking their daddy," he said sarcastically.

"Exactly," Val said.

His own wife was familiar with social media. Two years ago, she'd reconnected with her high school sweetheart and had run off with him for almost a year before coming home. That was the worst year of his life. He'd moved into a shitty, cramped apartment and drank himself into a stupor most nights. His daughter Val was the only one who'd checked in on him regularly, bringing the girls on occasion, and delivering food. Val reassured him her mother would come to her senses eventually, and she was right. He changed the topic. "Good job up there, Val. I'm proud of you."

"Thanks."

"Come on Danny," Maria said. "Let's go home."

Keep your mouth shut or you'll be sorry.

Leah was in second grade. What second grader made a threat like that? Keep her mouth shut about what? He stuffed the note in his pocket and walked Val and the kids to her Range Rover. He surveyed the parking lot, watching over his shoulder. What did Val know about her husband's sabbatical? Rafael must have told her something, but she obviously hadn't shared it with her mother, and he had no intention of getting into the middle of that.

"What a day," Maria said when they were alone in the Jeep. "I wonder what excuse Ralph has for not being here. He's the one pushing that poor child to play an instrument she has no interest in."

He couldn't agree more with the first statement: it'd been a hell of a day. As for the second comment about Ralph's absence, he wasn't going there. On the third point, a medical emergency had spared the audience from suffering though Leah's violin solo.

An anonymous note that said *You suck at violin* was believable.

He wondered who had access to Leah's violin case, but he had no way of knowing. His son-in-law came to mind. He stopped himself. That was crazy thinking.

"When are you going to tell me what's going on between you and Courage?" Maria asked. "Why are you lying to him?"

18

Vance stepped out of the elevator onto the eighth floor of Suarez's office building. It was just after 3:30 in the afternoon leaving him a cushion time to review the client file again before the Russian was scheduled to arrive. He checked his phone for any updates. He'd missed a call from Sarge but his phone hadn't rung. The text he'd sent busting his chops for lying about being hospitalized with a heart problem must've gotten his attention. He'd deal with Sarge after the meeting.

Waving the keycard hanging around his neck, he listened for the door to unlock, then headed down the hall and entered Suarez's corner office. He stood in front of the window for a moment taking in the panoramic view overlooking Biscayne Bay. He could see the rooftop of the Hotel Mutiny where once upon a time in Miami, his blood relative Tony Famosa and his partner Chago Marino ran their drug empire. These days, Tony was a fugitive hiding in Panama while Chago was serving a 205-year sentence at the Supermax in Florence, Colorado. In a strange twist of fate—

decades later—their drug smuggling empire made Vance a rich man.

He hadn't thought about it in a long time, the day he'd accepted a fat envelope stuffed with cash. He, the once incorruptible detective who'd never taken an illicit dime nor snorted a line of cocaine, took the money without hesitation. He, the lawyer who stood on the highest moral summit, refusing a ridiculously generous offer right out of law school to join a 'white powder' firm specializing in defending drug dealers, had finally succumbed to temptation.

The moment he'd stuffed the first installment of dirty cash in his pocket, he'd waited for the heavens to open up and a lightning bolt to strike. But it didn't happen. No clap of thunder, not even a pang of guilt. Instead, he was glad he had the cash to replace Edgar, the hideous Nissan Cube with an amputated roach leg still bolted to the roof of the car he'd accepted in lieu of money from a client who couldn't pay.

Lately, he was beginning to see how it worked. The bad karma would come in dribs and drabs. Sometimes big, like million-dollar investments gone south; some small, like flattened tires. Others were huge. Ethan's nearly fatal kidney failure was an example. Lauren's abduction was another.

There was yet another inconvenient truth. He'd grown fond of the money, and he intended to keep it. Not to exert power nor be slave to magpie syndrome chasing shiny objects. Rather, he was married to the freedom and security it provided.

Financial air cover. FU money. Nice to have.

He turned away from the window and approached the desk, noticing something he hadn't seen before. A strip of gray metal was visible in the narrow vertical gap where two large barn doors hung behind Suarez's desk. He'd seen them when he'd met with Lola and assumed they were a façade. He rolled one side open, discovering a safe hidden in the wall. It was big, about five feet tall and four feet wide, reminding him of the gun safes at the old police precinct where they stored tactical weapons and contraband.

He opened the middle desk drawer and searched for a key or the combination to the safe but saw nothing but pens and paper clips. He inspected the decorative items atop the desk turning them upside down looking for clues finding the computer login and password information under the keyboard where Lola said it would be. He riffled through the rest of the drawers, searching every nook and cranny. He got on his knees and inspected the underside of the desk. Crawling out from under it, he stared at the safe for a moment, then jimmied the heavy handle.

It was unlocked. He pulled the door slowly open and looked inside. There were no weapons or ammo, no cash or jewelry, only a manila letter-sized envelope on the bottom shelf. He removed the document and scanned the cover page titled 'Manifiesto por la Contrarrevolución Cubana,' and beneath it on the same page, a subtitle, 'Bahía de Cochinos 2.0.' The first part of the translation was simple, even for him: 'Manifesto for the Cuban Counterrevolution.'

He flipped the pages.

All were written in Spanish.

He set the document down, sat and logged into the firm's computer system. Using an English-to-Spanish translation website, he entered 'Bahia de Cochinos 2.0' and waited for the result.

'Bay of Pigs 2.0.'

Wow.

Flipping the pages, he scanned for words and phrases he

might recognize but found nothing he could translate. He got up from the desk and paced, then walked to the window and peered through the lens of the high-powered telescope. It might have been possible to see Stiltsville, but not this afternoon, not through the smoky storm clouds brewing to the east.

Maybe this was the plan. Maybe Suarez banked on him finding it. On the other hand, maybe the lawyer had been in a hurry and simply forgotten to lock the safe. Either way, there had to be a reason he kept the document in a fireproof vault. He sat, placed the manifesto on the desk and signed into his Gmail account hoping to find a reply from Lauren. Still nothing.

He opened the browser, typed '*Damas de Blanco*' and waited. Dozens of hits filled the page, and all were in Spanish. He refined the keywords, adding '*English*' to the search terms.

He scrolled past the Wikipedia page and clicked on a story from the *New York Times*. It linked to a paid subscription. He backspaced and selected a free article published by a British online magazine dated 2011. It was an in-depth obituary for Laura Pollán, the deceased ringleader of *Damas de Blanco*.

He read on. Laura Pollán was born in a small village in Cuba in 1943, ten years before the Revolution. Like many young idealists of her generation, she was a strong supporter of the Castro regime. As a child she'd volunteered to participate in a government program enlisting a million young people willing to leave their homes to live with rural families, teaching them to read and write. The experience had led her to become a teacher.

But all of that changed during the '*Primavera Negra*,' the Black Spring of 2003 when her husband, a nuclear engineer and journalist, was arrested and jailed. The British article intimated that the Cuban government may have played a role in her death. He opened the Wikipedia page, the same one Ethan had shown him earlier, and noticed a recent update to her bio just hours old; her cause of death had been changed and was listed as cardiorespiratory arrest. There was no mention of dengue fever or the conspiracy theory that the Castro regime may have had her killed. It listed the date and time of the update but made no reference about who'd made the changes or what source material had been used.

He backspaced to the British story. Laura Pollán was survived by her jailed husband and a daughter from a previous marriage. He double checked Wikipedia. There was no mention of Laura having a daughter. He returned to the search page and clicked on a different link, loading a crudely translated blog written by a Cuban doctor claiming there was substantial medical evidence to prove that Laura Pollán had been poisoned by the Castro government. The blog had been updated with a footnote: the doctor had been stripped of his professional license and branded a dissident.

He logged out of the computer and opened the Popova-Morozova client file. Running his finger along each page of the work visa application, he located the line denoting next of kin residing in the U.S., then stared at the single entry: Lola Pollán. His heart ticked faster. It was possible Lola was Laura Pollán's daughter. He checked the time again on his phone. Exactly ten minutes before Natasha Popova-Morozova's scheduled arrival. He hurried to the copy room, powered up the machine and waited, but nothing happened. He held his finger on the power key for five seconds, then saw the electrical cord laying on the linoleum.

He plugged it in, powered it and fed the manifesto into

the tray. On the fifth page, the machine stopped, and a PAPER JAM message flashed. He opened the lid and pulled gently but the paper was stuck between the black rollers. He pulled harder tearing it, leaving half a sheet of the original document stuck in the copier.

He heard the buzzer.

The client had arrived.

He grabbed the original document and the copies, left the torn sheet in the machine and hurried to Suarez's office, placing the documents back inside the safe and closing the vault but not locking it.

The woman at Vizcaya had warned him. '*The counterrevolution is coming.*' Maybe the manifesto was the blueprint. Maybe Suarez left the document in the unlocked safe on purpose. Maybe he was supposed to find it. That was too easy. More likely it was a trap.

It was obvious what they wanted. The lady in white had told him.

Revolutions cost money.

Money that can't be traced.

Maybe Monkey Morales was alive, and this was *El Mono's* last chance to free Cuba.

L auren's mind drifted while Davis continued to question Mr. Green at the bank. When Davis raised his voice, she tuned back into the conversation.

"I want to see the withdrawal form," Davis demanded.

"If you'll take a seat, I'll have a copy of it printed." The elegant banker attired in the tailored Italian suit picked up the phone, turned his back to them and made a call.

A moment later two uniformed security guards arrived and stood on either side of the doorway to Green's office.

"Even if you have a document," Davis complained, "I didn't authorize you to deplete my funds. How could you possibly give her all of it?"

"When you were here with her in person," Green said, "you added her to your account giving her co-signing authority. I've already explained to you that we tried to contact you. We are not obligated to do so. We did so as a courtesy."

"This isn't happening," Davis said. "Tell me this didn't actually happen."

The guards took a step inside the office.

Lauren tried to lay a hand on his shoulder, but Davis brushed it away. "You need to calm down. Take a deep breath," she said.

"May I speak to you privately?" she asked Mr. Green.

"Of course."

"Wait out in the hallway," she said to Davis, "I need a minute."

"I'm not leaving," he said. "This is my money and my life you're talking about."

"You don't have any money," she said matter-of-factly. "Please, leave the room and let me have a moment with Mr. Green."

One of the armed guards approached. Davis glared at her, pushing his bifocals higher on his nose. He used the chair arms to raise his obese body and lumbered into the hallway. Green instructed security to close the door.

"I'm sorry," Green said to her when they were alone. "We followed all the protocols."

The banker had probably seen it all and Davis couldn't have been the first rich rube to get rolled by a hot woman. "I know," she said. "I want to talk to you about something else. This is embarrassing, but I dropped my phone in the tub this morning. Without it, I don't even know when my plane leaves for Miami."

Green nodded sympathetically. "I'd be lost without mine. How can I help?"

"You have Vance's cell number, and without my phone, I don't. Would you do me a favor and share it with me?"

Green hesitated. "I'm not authorized to do that."

"Why not? You know our situation. We opened our accounts at your bank at the same time."

"I'm very sorry, Miss Gold, but we have tight procedures

in place. Our clients value trust and discretion above everything."

"You know who I am. I'm sitting right in front of you. You saw my passport. What else do you need?"

"I can appreciate your situation, but I can't infringe on our customers' privacy."

"Then call him for me. Ask him if you can give me his number."

"Again," he said, "I can't do that. I am truly sorry for the situation you and Mr. Frost find yourselves in—"

"—I don't think you do."

"I can appreciate your frustration, but—"

"May I remind you," she said curtly, leaning closer to Green who sat behind his desk. "Mr. Courage and I have quite a bit of money in this bank. There are plenty of others I'm sure who would be more than happy to take our cash."

"You are more than welcome to move your account elsewhere but I'm not sure if you know what it entails."

She scoffed. "What? A phone call? An online application?"

"It's more than that. May I remind you that you deposited U.S. dollars delivered in duffle bags. It's unconventional, and it kept your account from certain outside scrutiny."

"What scrutiny?"

He hesitated, then said, "The money starts here, at this bank. A bit like the American expression of 'the buck stops here,' but in reverse. If you move the money, you'll generate an electronic trail."

"Are you threatening me?"

"Of course not. If that's what you'd like to do, I could get the process started right now. And please don't take this personally or the wrong way, but you're hardly our biggest customer. Back to what I was saying. It's much easier to deposit money than it is to transfer it to another bank and possibly catch the eye of regulators. Interbank transfers are conducted by SWIFT, and a multi-million-dollar transfer will create an electronic trail that might catch someone's eye. At the very least, there will be a digital footprint."

"SWIFT?"

"Society for Worldwide Interbank Financial Telecommunications, the agency that monitors all wire transfers. They are open to scrutiny by world governments that have anti-corruption units watching for terrorist organizations, sanctions and other suspicious activity."

"I see," she said, slipping the credit card pre-loaded with 5K of digital currency into her wallet.

"It's my job to advise you on how to best protect your assets."

"Like you did for Davis? I'm sure you know, he's not the first man to let a pretty woman cloud his judgment. Surely there was something you could've done to alert him."

Green leaned back in his chair and placed his hands on his desk. "I've been in your situation before."

"It's not my situation. It's Davis's."

"I was referring to your phone. It happens all the time here. People drop them in saltwater which is no friend to the electronic gadgets. Your SIM card is likely protected. If you get a new one, I'm sure your contact list will still be there."

"Right," she said, wishing it were true.

"Is that all I can do for you today?"

"Yes."

"We close at five o'clock and the private banking office is not open over the weekend so if you believe you'll need more money before Monday, I highly recommend doing it today."

"Good to know," she said, following Green's lead as he got up from behind his desk, signaling the meeting was over.

The banker opened the door for her. Davis leaned against the wall flanked by the beefed-up security guards stationed outside Green's office. Davis hung his head in a look of defeat.

"Come on," she said to him, "Let's get out of here."

THE STORM HAD PASSED, and the sidewalk glistened with fresh rainfall, bringing with it a wallop of humidity.

"We need phones," Lauren said.

"Did you fix it?" Davis asked.

"Fix what?"

"My bank account. I'm broke. I literally don't have a penny to my name. You always fix everything."

"I can't fix that, Davis. He wouldn't even give me Vance's phone number."

"What am I gonna do?"

"I don't know. You'll figure it out. In case you forgot, you'd still be living in some shitty rental in Key West if I hadn't brought you to the deal. I know, I know," she said, "you earned the money, but don't forget the day we met you didn't have two nickels to rub together. Don't get on the victim bus and act like someone stole the silver spoon from your mouth. You've spent most of your life barely getting by and you'll do it again. You know what?"

He stared at her with wide eyes. "What?"

"It was only a matter of time before some good-looking

woman was going to roll you for every penny. What's wrong with you Davis? Don't you have a mirror?"

"Ouch. That wasn't very nice."

"I know. I'm sorry," she said, meaning it, "but you've put me in a terrible spot."

"Only because I didn't have a choice," he said.

"Don't give me that crap. You had a choice. You could've kept your zipper up. If they arrest you, how are you going to pay for a lawyer? Did you think about that before you gave this woman you barely knew, access to your bank account?"

"You're right. It was stupid."

"How much was in the account?"

"A little over five million."

"Where's the rest of it?"

"I spent it."

"On what?"

"I dunno."

"You know what? I should find an ATM and get enough cash to catch the next flight out of here."

"You won't do that," Davis said.

She paced the sidewalk with her hands on her hips and punched the air. Two young men passing the opposite direction, saw her do it. They laughed, then mimicked her, giving the air a few comical upper cuts.

"Assholes," she said, under her breath.

"We need Vance's help," he said.

"Here," she said, opening her wallet and giving him all her cash. "Go buy a couple of burner phones."

"Where're you going?

"To have another talk with Mr. Green."

20

Vance hastily organized the immigration file on the desk wondering what the office was like when Suarez was there. He pegged him as a loudmouth who yapped on the phone all day, a show-boater who made Lola do all the grunt work. It certainly couldn't be as quiet as it was now. From what he'd seen, nothing about Suarez was understated. The office doorbell buzzed again.

As he headed down the hallway to answer it, he dialed Lola's number and let it ring six times. So much for the crack paralegal who was supposed to help him. The bell sounded again, this time in a continuous buzz that reminded him of a hornet's nest.

The woman at the door mostly matched the picture he'd seen on Natasha Popova-Morozova in the client file, but it was hard to say because she wore mirrored sunglasses and a hat. His eyes traveled down toward the sounds of heavy panting. Her left hand gripped the square handle of a leather harness attached to a guide dog. The black Labrador sat at attention, tongue hanging out, breathing loudly.

"You're early," he said, opening the door wide,

wondering why Lola didn't mention the client was blind. The dog stared straight ahead, not in a threatening way, rather as if waiting for the next command.

"I no recognize your voice. You my new lawyer?" the woman said.

"I am."

"I'm Natasha," she said, holding her hand out.

He grasped it, and having no experience with someone blind, wondered what he was supposed to do next. "I'm Vance Courage. Come in. You're a few minutes early."

"On-time late in my book," she said.

"Let's meet in Mr. Suarez's office," he said, confused about how this was going to work, starting with how to hold the door open while she passed through, wondering how he'd deal with making sure she knew what documents she was signing. From a legal perspective, he needed a witness and neither Lola nor Franco was there.

"If you lead way, Noir follow," she said, adding, "Noir is my dog."

He processed the insane situation. A blind woman wearing mirrored aviator glasses being led by a black dog named Noir. He waved the keycard opening the middle door leading to the back offices. At the sound of the clack, he shouldered it open, and as he sized up the doorway, wondering if the dog would lead or if he should—the front door flung open.

"Sorry, I'm late," Lola said, rushing ahead and holding the door open for the dog and the woman.

He hurried down the hall to Suarez's office to double-triple check he'd left no sign he'd been in the safe. As he sat at the desk and opened the Popova file, it triggered the things he hated about being an attorney. One big thing he didn't miss was the clients. Many needed a therapist more than they needed a lawyer. Grifters and crazies were the ones who often hit the jackpot. It wasn't random, or that the universe had it out for the good guys; rather most stable folks preferred to find a more amenable way to settle disputes. On the other hand, an immigration case was new territory and he sensed there was more to it than he knew.

Lola entered the office ahead of Natasha, pulled a chair for the blind woman, then turned to leave.

"I want you to stay," he said. "Miss Popova will need to review and sign documents and I need a witness. You'll have to read the documents out loud. You could record the audio to be safe."

"That won't be necessary," Lola said. "I'll be right back."

When Natasha released the handle to the harness, the animal laid down next to her chair. He watched as she felt for the chair arms, then sat, crossing her legs and smoothing her short skirt over her tan thighs.

"Did you look at file?" Natasha asked.

"I did. If you don't mind my asking, why didn't you apply for a spousal visa? It would have been simpler."

"My husband file for divorce. Mr. Suarez say that why they reject application. Mr. Suarez say my new lawyer fix it."

"I can't promise that."

"Lola say I need to sign paper to make you new lawyer. I sign it. No problem. I can pay."

Lola returned with an energy drink. At first, he hadn't noticed she wasn't wearing the eyepatch, and there was a lighter circle around her eye, like a farmer's tan. The white of her injured eye had a large red blotch around the iris, but other than that, looked normal.

He separated the papers that needed to be signed, and as he pushed them across the desk wondered how long they thought their little charade would last. Did they assume he wouldn't read the file? He might've been retired, rusty and beyond disinterested in filling in for Suarez, but he wasn't an idiot. While Lola arranged the pen in Natasha's fingers and guided her hand to the signature line, he watched himself become her new attorney. Lola signed as a witness.

"I'll show Miss Popova out," Lola said.

"No," he said. "May we have the room? I'd like to speak to Miss Popova privately."

Lola tilted her head as if confused. "Uh —"

"Please leave," Natasha interrupted, blindly staring straight ahead at the barn doors covering the safe.

The distorted reflection of himself in the lenses of her mirrored glasses was unnerving.

"Fine," Lola said, snatching her energy drink and shutting the door with a bang.

When they were alone, he said, "I read your file. You speak four languages."

"Yes."

"I only speak one, and not all that well. Let's see here," he said scanning her application. "It says you went to medical school in Russia."

"Yes."

"What is the nationality of your husband?"

"What of it?"

"I read your file, and it says your visa was denied because the U.S. government can't confirm your marriage."

"That's what Suarez tell me too."

"Do you know where your husband is?"

"No."

"Do you have a marriage certificate?"

"Husband have everything."

"Did you get married here, in the U.S.?"

"No."

"That complicates things," he said, tapping a pen on the desktop.

"Yes. I know. That why I'm here."

"I'm not an immigration lawyer, Miss Popova. I'm sure Mr. Suarez told you that. I'll have to do some homework."

"Home work?"

"Legal research."

"My visa good for four days. What do I do?"

"I don't know. But what I do know is that I don't think it's fair for immigration to hold up the process because they can't find your husband. It looks like the company that's sponsoring you wants to hire you, not your husband."

"I like your name. It mean brave, right?"

"Something like that," he said, getting up from behind the desk. He wanted to ask her why Hialeah-Circuits was hiring a blind person with a medical degree, but he couldn't think of a polite way to do it. He'd googled the company. They made RF and microwave components. "I'll let you know if I have any questions. Expect to hear something from me early next week."

As he stood and came out from behind the desk, the dog sat up, saliva drooling from both sides of its mouth. Natasha waved her hand feeling for the harness. He reached for it slowly, and when the animal didn't growl, placed the handle in Natasha's hand.

"I have four days. Not whole week."

"It's late on a Friday. Government offices are closed. The best I can do is make some calls first thing Monday morning."

"That mean you help me?"

"Yes," he said. "I'm going to help you. I promise. It was a pleasure meeting you, Miss Popova."

"Call me Natasha."

He reached for the doorknob and when he opened it, saw Lola standing just outside, eavesdropping.

"Would you please walk Miss Popova out," he said to Lola, following them to the bank of elevators. When the double doors whooshed open on the eighth floor, Franco Frank stepped out. As the two women and dog got on, the doors began to close before Noir was clear of the threshold. Franco offered no help; Vance lunged forward to stop the automatic doors from trapping the dog.

"It's after four on a Friday," he said to Franco. "Don't you have a cheating spouse to spy on?"

"What's it to you?" the investigator asked, chewing gum and smacking his lips.

He pressed the down button, waited for the next elevator and rode it to the second floor where he could observe the two women from the window overlooking the parking lot. A white Tesla was parked illegally in the fire lane. Natasha and Lola spoke for a minute, then hugged and kissed on both cheeks. The driver got out, opened the back passenger door and the dog jumped into the vehicle.

He bolted to the stairwell and raced down to the first floor. Shouldering the glass double doors open, he reached into his pants pocket and activated the phone on his camera. As the Tesla pulled away, he pointed the camera at the license plate but missed when he fumbled the phone. When it hit the pavement, the screen cracked.

"What are you doing?" Lola asked, as he knelt to pick it up.

He didn't have a good answer; paranoia was often a symptom of sleep deprivation.

21

L auren entered Cayman Offshore Bank and Trust alone. The Pretorian Guard-like security goons flanked the front doors, and she felt their eyes upon her as she beelined toward the woman in the power suit sitting behind the reception desk talking on the phone. When the woman saw Lauren, her hand sprung into the air instructing her to wait. When she finished the phone call, she motioned Lauren to approach.

"I'd like to speak to Mr. Green," she said trying to read the small name tag pinned to her jacket.

"Your name?" she asked, acting as if she didn't recognize her from a few minutes earlier.

"Lauren Gold."

"Just a minute," she said, picking up the landline. She turned away from Lauren and spoke softly into the phone making it impossible to eavesdrop on the convo. A moment later she swung her chair around and said, "Please take a seat Miss Gold and Mr. Green will be right with you."

Lauren didn't sit. She paced.

Ten long minutes passed before Green greeted her in the lobby.

"Hello Miss Gold. You're back," Green said. "If you need to make another withdrawal, you may speed up the process by presenting your Visa card and ID to one of our tellers. Fill out a withdrawal form and they can transfer the funds directly to your card."

"That's not why I'm here. I'd like to see my bank file."

"What file?" Green asked with a perplexed expression.

"I'd like to see a copy of the application I filled out online."

Green seemed annoyed at the question and rather than answering, approached the woman at the desk. "Sadie, would you please print out a copy of Miss Gold's application on file." He turned towards Lauren. "That should do it."

Sadie clacked away at the keys while she trotted behind him.

"Hold on," she said. "I'd like to speak to you. In private."

"Come along," Green said, as he marched to his office. "What is this about?" he asked as she followed him in.

Sadie hand-delivered a printed copy of the application she'd filled out on the bank's secure portal when she and Vance first opened their Cayman accounts.

"May I?" Lauren asked tilting her head in the direction of the document on his desk.

Sadie excused herself while Green pushed the application across the desktop. Lauren leafed through it, and without looking up asked, "May I use your pen?"

Green handed her a nice fat one with the bank logo on it. She stood, grabbed the notepad from his desk, copied Vance's phone number from the emergency contact line on her application, tore the paper from the pad and handed it to Green. "Would you please call him?"

"I'm sorry, Miss Gold, but I can't do that. I've already explained to you the bank has very strict privacy policies."

"He's a client and so am I. How is contacting him breaching bank policy? I don't have access to a phone, and I need to speak to him. Call him. Please."

Green shook his head no and pushed the note away.

"Listen, we're customers and I need to speak to him urgently.

"You are," Green said.

"I'm what?"

"A customer."

It took a moment to decipher what he'd just said. "What are you implying?"

"I've already gone out on a limb Miss Gold, and I can't say anything more about it."

"Vance isn't a customer?"

"I thought you knew when you came here but it has become obvious that you didn't. If you want more information, you'll have to ask him. You have his number. That's what you wanted."

"I see," she said, staring over his shoulder at a historic black and white photo of the bank hanging on the wall. "Did you warn him that it could expose him to . . . how did you put it . . . scrutiny?"

"We advise all of our clients about risk."

"I'd like to make another withdrawal," she said.

"Certainly."

"I'd like fifty thousand dollars U.S. in cash."

"I'll get that going."

"Is Davis Frost's account still open?"

"We keep zero balance accounts open for thirty days."

"Good. I'd like to transfer one hundred thousand dollars into his account."

"Anything else?"

"Yes. Can you refer me to an attorney?"

Green narrowed his eyes. "What sort of lawyer?"

"Criminal."

The banker didn't seem surprised. "I'll see what I can do. How would you like the cash?"

"Five twenties, ten-tens and the rest in hundreds."

GREEN RETURNED with a tan pouch with the bank's logo filled with cash and a receipt for the deposit into Davis's account.

"My brother is an attorney," Green said. "I put his card in with the money. He doesn't do criminal work, but he should be able to make a referral. But please," Green said, "I'd appreciate it if you didn't tell him who referred you."

"I understand," she said, taking the bag of cash.

"It's been a pleasure doing business with you, Miss Gold."

She passed Sadie's desk clutching her purse with fifty thousand U.S. dollars hidden inside.

"Have a nice weekend," Sadie said without looking up.

"You, too," she said, wadding the paper with Vance's phone number into a little ball and dropping it in the waste-basket on her way out.

22

V ance finished the bottle of water he'd taken from Suarez's office and tossed it into the back seat of the Audi. As usual, traffic heading north on I-95 to Broward County was crawling. He tuned into an AM radio station broadcasting regular traffic reports.

His phone rang interrupting the news program in progress. Bad Ass came up on caller ID.

"Hey, Zo. Any news?"

"Yeah. Called in a favor. Looks like your girlfriend got on the plane to Cayman. Watched the video myself."

"Can you meet me later so we can talk?" he asked.

"I'm workin' tonight. Barely gettin' enough free time to get six hours of shut-eye."

"Where're you working?"

"Nowhere you wanna to meet."

"Try me," he said, turning the A/C to LO.

"A concert. Shift starts at six at that casino where that old dog track used to be. Couldn't even tell you who's playin'. Some washed-up band from the eighties."

"I'll ping when I'm in the neighborhood."

"Pack your earplugs," Zo said.

He ended the call and dialed Sarge.

"Oye, *Gallego*."

"You're sounding pretty good for a guy who had a heart attack."

"It wasn't a heart attack. It was chest pains," Sarge said.

"I'm two minutes from your house."

"I'm not home."

"Too bad," he said, cruising slowly past Sarge's bungalow. "I was going to stop in for a visit."

"Try calling ahead next time," Sarge said, hanging up on him.

The white Jeep was in the driveway and a red Range Rover was parked curbside. Vance drove around the block and stopped at the end of the street where he could watch for a minute. A woman walked out of Sarge's house, got behind the wheel of the Range Rover and drove off. He pulled up and parked out front. He got out of the car, grabbing the weird document he'd found in the safe at Suarez's office and strolled past the back bumper of the Jeep.

It appeared that the 'THE FISH FEAR ME . . .' decal had been covered with a vintage Dolphins' Championship bumper sticker. He squatted and picked at the corner of the new one, pulling it back a couple of inches, far enough to confirm it had been slapped atop the distasteful one.

Turning on his heels, maroon dots glistened on the concrete. The spatter made a trail from the neighbor's place next door to Sarge's front door. He knelt, dabbed his fingertip in a droplet, rubbed his fingers together and sniffed. It was sticky with the metallic scent of fresh blood.

He unholstered the 9-mil from under his arm and tucked it in the waistband of his pants and covered it with his shirt. More drops led to the welcome mat on the stoop.

Careful not to step in the blood he rang the doorbell camera. No answer. He counted silently to five then called Sarge's phone. He was about to hang up when Maria answered the door.

"Oh my God! I'm glad you're here!" she said. "Danny's been shot!"

"What? By who?" he said, pushing his way into the house.

"I told him not to mess with the crazies next door, but he won't listen to me."

Sarge hobbled to the entryway with one pant leg rolled to the knee. His calf was dressed in blood-soaked gauze.

"He should go to the hospital," Maria said. "Maybe you can talk sense to him."

"It's nothing. Bullet grazed my leg. Got plenty of natural padding," he said, patting his belly.

"What happened?"

"It was nothing," Sarge said.

"It's not nothing," Maria said.

Sarge's shirt was ripped. He had a fat lip. His clothes were covered with dirt, and he had road rash on his left elbow.

"Who did this?" he asked.

"The drug addicts next door," Maria said. "He went over there again and this time they attacked him."

Again?

"They went for my gun," Sarge said. "And I got grazed is all."

"They jumped him," Maria said. "They could've killed him."

"Where's the gun?"

"They took it," Maria said. "They shot him with his own gun. I told him we have to call the police, but he won't do it."

"You need to get that leg checked out," he said.

"Already did. Val came over and looked at it. Said it's a flesh wound."

"Val?" he asked.

"Our daughter," Maria said, "she used to be an emergency room doctor. She just left."

The red Range Rover. "Is the gun registered to you?"

"What do you think, *Gallego*?"

Maria scowled at her husband. "Danny! Language!"

"What are you going to do?" he asked.

"I haven't figured that out yet," Sarge said. "What are you doing here?"

He handed him the document. "I want you to take a look at something for me."

Sarge downed a swig of booze from the bottle, then sat on the edge of the big recliner and began to read.

"What is that?" Maria asked.

Sarge held his finger up to silence her and turned the page.

Vance walked to the kitchen and looked out the window at the neighbor's house next door. Maria followed him.

"It's been a nightmare," she said. "The constant fights, the late-night parties blasting music, hooting and hollering and now this. I can't open the windows when the weather's nice because it smells like something died in the yard."

Sarge got up from the recliner and joined them. "What happened to the bottom half of page five?"

"Copy machine ate it. Can you tell what it is?"

"It looks like some kind of a battle plan," Sarge said.

"For what?"

He had a serious look on his face. "To invade Cuba. They're calling it Bay of Pigs 2.0. Whoever wrote it thinks it's a good time to try to topple the Cuban government before

China completes their military installations. Where did you get this?"

"I found it at your son-in-law's office."

"What were you doing there?" Maria asked.

Sarge made an ugly face, then said, "He's filling in for him."

"Doing what?" she asked.

"Lawyerly things," Sarge said.

"Why?" she demanded, untying her apron and tossing it on the kitchen counter.

"Ralph's gone to rehab," Sarge said.

"Is that why you've been lying to me, Danny?"

"I didn't want you to worry," Sarge said, twisting the fake diamond post in his earlobe.

"That's not why he's been lying to me," Vance said, "but now that you mention it, why did you lie about being in the hospital?"

"Because I knew you'd be pissed off I ambushed you and I didn't want to give you the chance to back out of the deal before he left for rehab."

"What ambush?" Maria asked.

"Val wanted me to ask Vance to cover for Ralph while he's out of the office. He's already left for treatment."

Maria planted her hands on her hips. "I knew this had something to do with him. I told Val she shouldn't marry that good for nothing *pedazo de mierda*. Who in this family ever listens to me?"

That was one of the few expressions he could translate. *Pedazo de mierda. Piece of shit.* "Do you think it's possible your son-in-law is involved in some kind of underground operation?"

"I don't know," Sarge said. "He's not much of a Cuban patriot, if that's what you mean."

Maria added her two cents. "He's never sent a dime to his poor relatives left behind in the old country. Not a red penny."

"Is this the whole document?" Sarge asked, holding it up.

"No. There's the half page that's stuck in the machine and a few others I wasn't able to copy before I left the office."

"There're no names, or dates or anything," Sarge said, "just numbers that might be code for people and places. The top of page five looks like the timeline. If you can get it out of the machine and bring it to me, I can translate it for you."

Maria interrupted them. "Val should've married a man like you, Vance." She turned to her husband. "You should check up on him, Danny. Find out if he really went to rehab. For all you know he's in Las Vegas gambling."

"Is he a gambler?" Vance asked.

"Who knows," Sarge said. "I'll try to check up on him but first I gotta get my gun back. Those people next door are nuts."

"My advice is to wait," Vance said. "Don't mess with them."

"Maybe they'll shoot each other," Maria said.

"No such luck," Sarge said.

"May I use your computer?" Vance asked Maria, pointing to a desktop computer on a postage stamp of a table pushed up against the wall in the tiny dining room.

"Sure," she said, then turned to Sarge. "May I speak to you in private?"

He watched out of the corner of his eye as Sarge downed another slug of whiskey before limping down the hall behind his wife.

He set his Glock on the edge of the table, opened the

browser, typed 'Sea Otter Little Cayman' and waited for the results to populate on the screen. Listening to the muffled sounds of Maria ripping her husband a new one in Spanish, he drummed his fingers on the table waiting for the search results to load. He opened the website for the dive operation and dialed the Cayman number from his cell. It went to voicemail.

"Hi, my name is Daniel Ruiz," Vance said. "I'm calling from Miami. I'm trying to reach Davis Frost. I talked to him the other day about an upcoming dive trip. Would you please make sure he gets this message and ask him to call me a soon as he can." He added his phone number to the message and hung up. The argument in the back bedroom continued, and while the words were indistinct, Maria's was the dominant voice.

A Ruiz family photo was perched on the windowsill. It had to have been taken around the time he'd first met Sarge. Daniel was shirtless on the beach dressed in shorts with a full head of black hair and six-pack abs. Maria wore a wide brimmed hat and sunglasses. Their two daughters—still little girls—sat on the sand with their buckets and shovels, the ocean in the background had faded to a pale blue.

Back in the early 1980s Miami was in chaos. He couldn't imagine what it'd been like working patrol while trying to support a family on a cop's salary. The streets of South Florida had become the most dangerous place in America.

A stack of yellowed newspaper clippings was partially hidden under an old *PC's FOR DUMMIES* book pushed next to the computer monitor. He looked over his shoulder, listening to Sarge and Maria still going at it. He lifted the book and carefully unfolded the top document, a crude black and white illustration of Monkey's face with an uncanny resemblance to a chimp with big teeth and wide lips. During the height of Ricardo Morales's infamy, a popular lifestyle magazine had put him on the cover. He set it down and sneaked a look at a more recent article, an interview with Morales's son published last year in the local newspaper.

Maria turned the corner, startling him.

"What are you doing?" she asked.

"Looking for pen and paper," he lied, slipping the recent article in between the pages of the manifesto.

She went to the kitchen, opened the junk drawer and returned with a pad and pen.

He copied the phone number for the dive shop onto the notepad.

"Who's Davis Frost?" Maria asked.

Vance hesitated. "He's a friend of my girlfriend."

Sarge stood behind his wife shooting him a look that could've burned a hole in his forehead.

"Why did you leave a message for him to call Danny?" she asked.

Sarge shook his head behind his wife's back, eyes big as silver dollars.

"Danny told me you were thinking about going on a vacation to Grand Cayman," Vance said.

Maria scoffed, turned and faced her husband. "What's up with all this lying."

"Baby monitor," Sarge said, pointing to a white cone on the kitchen countertop. "Maria babysits."

While Maria berated Sarge, he tucked his gun in the front of his pants, stuffed the phone number in his pocket, and grabbed the manifesto. His phone vibrated in his pocket. He checked it. NO CALLER ID came up on the screen. "May I use your restroom?" he asked.

"First door on the right," Maria said.

He hurried down the hall and once inside the bathroom, turned on the faucet and answered the call.

"I send *ju* a text," the woman said. "Download the link and wait for instructions."

It was the lady in white. "You're late. Where's Lauren? I want to talk to her."

There was no response.

"Where is she? I want to talk to her." He looked at the screen. The call had ended. A text popped up. It linked to a messaging app. He downloaded it and read the instructions.

Deposit $5 million crypto into this account and we let her go.

He redialed the number. The call rang once, then failed.

He composed a text:

Bank closed until Monday.

He didn't know jack-crap about crypto.

A new message followed:

You have 48 hours.

Monday was Memorial Day. The bank would be closed for the holiday.

23

L auren stood on the sidewalk outside the bank. As a cab pulled up to the light, she rushed to get the driver's attention, stepping into a puddle of rainwater. The cabbie spun his finger motioning her to hurry. Hugging her purse, she clambered into the back seat and before she had time to shut the door, the light turned green and the car behind them honked.

The cabbie stuck his arm out the window, made a fist, then asked, "Where to?"

"The Hilton."

"Dat is tree blocks from 'ere. You could walk it."

She unzipped her purse and took two twenties from the pouch and passed them to him in the front seat.

"Are you visiting?" he asked, snatching the money, keeping an eye on her from the rearview mirror.

"I am," she said politely, offering nothing more in the way of small talk.

A block and a half from the hotel traffic jammed up and as the cabbie got closer to the hotel, she saw a white RCIPS mobile communication van stopped in the middle of the road obstructing their view. She craned her head out the window. A half dozen police cars were parked every which way in front of the hotel blocking the entrance.

A cop on a motorcycle rode up to the taxi. "You'll have to turn around," he said to the driver.

"But I'm staying at the hotel," Lauren said.

"I'm sorry ma'am," the officer said.

"What's going on?" she asked.

"It's a police matter. The road's closed."

The cabbie turned around. "What do you want to do?"

"You can drop me here I guess." She opened the door and was about to step out when her heart stopped. Davis Frost lumbered onto the walkway in front of the main entrance to the hotel flanked by four uniformed police officers. His chin hung to his chest as gawkers gathered and took pictures with their phones. "I changed my mind," she said, closing the taxi door. "Do you mind waiting here until the road opens?"

"It tis by the minute," he said, pointing to the old meter on the dash.

"I know."

She watched quietly from the open car window feeling a sweat dampen the back of her blouse. Davis did nothing to resist as officers clumsily loaded him into the back of a marked Ford Interceptor.

"Is it possible to drive around to the back entrance?" she asked.

"I kin try," he said, putting the vehicle in reverse and backing up on a sharp angle to avoid the car behind them.

Pedestrians swarmed the streets trying to see what was going on at the hotel. The taxi driver expertly navigated around them tapping the horn gently to get their attention. He drove briefly on the wrong side of a one-way street before turning at the next corner to access the back entrance to the hotel. Two white RCIPS sedans were parked in a V-formation blocking the hotel parking garage.

She leaned forward between the seats. "I changed my mind," she said. "Keep going."

"Where do you want to go?"

"I don't know. I'm having a problem with my boyfriend, and I think I better find somewhere else to stay tonight."

"What kind of a problem?"

"He had too much to drink at the bar. I thought I had time to go to the hotel and get my stuff before he comes back."

"You're not safe?" he asked.

She shook her head.

"What 'bout your clothes?" he asked with genuine concern in his voice.

"I'll get my things later."

"I kin go back to de hotel and ask dem to bring your luggage down," he said, driving slowly past the back entrance and stopping curbside.

"No. Really, it's okay."

"Where should I take you?"

"I'm not sure," she said. "I'm having a bad day. I lost my phone this morning."

"I'm sorry," he said. "My cousin manages a rental place over on Seven Mile Beach."

"Do you think it's available?"

"I kin ask."

The cab driver made a call while one of the police cars that had been blocking the parking garage passed, followed by another.

. . .

THE RENTAL HOUSE was a two-story duplex built on stilts, a gem located along Seven Mile Beach north of George Town with an unlimited view of white sand and turquoise water. As the cab driver slowed to a stop, a blue Ford Taurus pulled up to the taxi and the two men spoke through open vehicle windows.

"Dis is my cousin Sven, de property manager," the cabbie said her. "I din't git your name."

"Lauren."

"How many nights will you be staying?" Sven asked through the car window.

"I'm not sure," she said. "At least one."

"Did my cousin tell you how much?" Sven asked.

"No," she said, peeling her sweaty blouse from her chest.

"Four-fifty a night."

Oof. "Four hundred and fifty U.S.?"

"That's right."

That was a lot more than she expected. "Do you accept digital currency?"

"We take it all," Sven said, tapping his thumb on the steering wheel.

"Do you mind if I go inside and check it out before I decide?"

"Sure," Sven said. "Let me park and I'll let you in."

She waited, then followed him up the stairs. The duplex was bigger than what she needed with a full kitchen and two bedrooms decorated with pastel fabrics and rattan furniture.

"There's a coffee maker, water in de fridge, clean towels, everything you need," he said.

She handed him the Visa card preloaded with $5,000. "Can you put one night on it and if I decide to stay longer, I'll let you know?"

"No problem. May I see your passport?"

She took it from the side pocket of her purse.

Sven opened it, eyes traveling from the picture on the document to her face. He took his phone from his pocket, inserted a portable credit card reader and swiped her Visa card. "I heard you lost your phone. That tis a bummer."

He showed her the screen. With taxes and fees, the total for one night was more than five hundred dollars. She signed for it. "What about internet?"

"The password and login are in de kitchen drawer. Do you need anytin' else?"

"Not right now."

"My cousin said you had a problem with your husband."

"Boyfriend. I'm sure he'll calm down when he sobers up."

Sven was about to return her credit card when he pulled it away. "Are you going to tell him where you're staying?"

"I hadn't planned on it."

"The owner lives right next door. If you need help, go to him."

"Okay."

"I'm serious," Sven said. "If that boyfriend bothers you at all, I want you to knock on Arthur's door."

"Alright."

"He's a nice guy." He handed her the Visa card. "You'll like him. He's a cop."

24

Another text chimed on Vance's phone; he flushed the toilet in Sarge's bathroom while he read the next set of instructions.

Open a digital wallet. Deposit 5 million cryptocurrency into this account.

He stared at the QR code on his cracked phone screen and composed a message.

I need proof she's alive.

A text bubbled up:

Sent a video.

He typed:

I need more than that.

Then he heard a knock on the bathroom door.

"You okay in there?" Sarge asked.

"Be right out," he said, running the water, washing his hands and buying time while he mentally processed the new instructions. When he opened the door, Sarge stood in the narrow hall leaning against the wall.

"Let's go for a beer," Sarge said.

"I wish I could, but I can't. Besides, you should stay off that leg."

Sarge lowered his voice. "Why did you use my name when you left a message for Davis Frost?"

Maria intercepted them. "Maybe you can talk him into filing a police report against those maniacs next door."

"I'm not doing that," Sarge said.

"I have to go," Vance said.

"I'll walk you out," Sarge said, hobbling toward the front door.

They stepped outside onto the stoop, into the baking afternoon sun. He gagged for a moment on the aroma of weed.

"I have to smell that shit twenty-four-seven," Sarge said.

"You and everyone else these days," he said. "One man's buzz is another man's buzz-killer. It's not worth getting shot over."

"I wanna know what's up with that call. Why'd you leave a message for Frost and drop my name?"

A single blast of gunfire erupted.

"Shit!" Sarge yelled, pogoing back inside the house.

Vance dove to the ground. The sound of metal-on-metal followed as the slug lodged into the passenger door of Lauren's car parked on the street.

The spent shell casing landed with a plink, then rolled along the driveway. Crouching, he used the Jeep for cover as he peered around the front bumper. He saw the nose of a pistol sticking out from an open window at the house next door. The occupants inside howled like hyenas. He drew his gun and staying low, zigzagged to Sarge's front door and turned the handle, but the door was locked. He rang the bell, then waited. Leaning with his back against the wall, he peered around at the neighbor's place then pushed Sarge's doorbell five times quickly. No one came to the door.

He squatted and duck-walked from the stoop to the hedges, sprinted to the opposite side of Sarge's house, away from the crazy neighbor's and pounded on the bedroom window.

A moment later Maria appeared, peeked through the curtains and pulled the window open. He punched out the screen, squatted and jumped, using his forearms to hoist himself up and in.

"I told him, Vance. I told him not to mess with them. What are we going to do?"

Sarge appeared in the doorway to the bedroom standing on one leg like a flamingo.

"What do you know about them?" Vance asked.

"They're punks," Sarge said. "Stoners and tweakers."

Tweaker was street talk for meth users. "How long have they lived there?"

"A month, maybe less," Maria said. "The man who owned the house passed away last year and his kids have been renting it out."

"Do you know how to contact the family?" he asked, walking away from the window into the hallway.

Sarge and his wife looked at each other, then at him and shrugged.

"Aren't you going to call the police?" Maria said. "You could've been killed."

"And tell them what? That the gun belongs to your husband?" he said. "I have go before one of your other neighbors calls the police."

"I wouldn't worry about that," Sarge said. "It sounds like the Fourth of July every weekend."

"He has called," Maria said. "Last time it took two days for an officer to respond."

"In that case, I really have to go," he said, adding "I wouldn't mess with them if I were you."

"That's what I've been saying," Maria said.

He used the back door, and as he made the turn toward the Audi, heard the three assholes sitting on the front porch howling and waving Sarge's gun in the air. He activated the laser on his Glock. As he jogged toward the car, he pointed his weapon and let the red dot dance all over them. They jumped to their feet and went nuts, skittering in place like insane marionettes, hands flailing — as if that would stop a bullet.

25

L auren removed the small bills and a few one-hundreds from the pouch, then stuffed the fifty thousand in cash under the mattress. She looked out the bedroom window at the rows of navy-blue umbrellas and lounge chairs evenly spaced on the pearly sand. The afternoon sun was beginning to drop and there were no signs of people on the beach.

The doorbell chimed. She hurried to see who it was, peering through the peephole. It was a man she didn't recognize. She waited quietly for a minute. The bell rang again. She cracked the door open enough to look out with one eye.

"Hi," he said. "I'm Arthur from next door. My property manager told me you lost your phone." He showed her his badge. "I'd be happy to help you out."

"How?"

"I can give you a lift to the phone store."

"Um . . . okay," she said. "You don't mind?"

"I couldn't function without mine," Arthur said. "I'd be happy to help."

"Will you give me a few minutes to get ready?"

"I'll bring the car around and wait out front. Take your time."

"You're sure you don't mind?"

"Not at all."

She washed her face, fluffed her blonde hair, applied lipstick then met Arthur who waited outside in an unmarked white Ford Crown Victoria.

"YOU'RE OFF TODAY?" she asked, getting into the passenger left hand side, on what would be the driver's side at home.

"I am," he said, pulling onto the road. "Have you thought about filing a report?"

"My phone wasn't stolen. I dropped it in the bathtub."

He looked over at her. "I was referring to the problem you're having with your boyfriend."

"Oh. I thought about it but if I report it, it'll just complicate things. I'm planning to go home as soon as possible," she said, noticing the blinking array of police electronics in the vehicle.

"When are you leaving?" he asked, keeping his eyes on the road as they passed two cyclists.

"I'm not sure. I haven't been able to check my airline reservation since my phone stopped working," she said, careful to keep the story simple.

"Does your boyfriend know where you're staying?"

"No."

"Sven said you left your bags at the hotel."

"I did. It's not worth going back for," she said, eyeing the peppering of gray hair at his temples and the bulging bicep as he turned the wheel. "I bet you have an interesting job with all the tourists."

"It can be," he said, offering nothing more.

"I dated an ex-detective for a while," she said, digging around her purse making sure she had her passport.

"Not the drunk boyfriend I hope," he said, stealing a sideways glance at her.

"No. Of course not."

"I'm Arthur McDonald," he said. "And you are?"

"Oh, pardon me," she said, chuckling at the oddity of getting in a vehicle with a strange man in a foreign country whose full name she didn't know. Not to mention poor manners on her part. "I'm Lauren Gold."

"Where're you from, Lauren?"

"Miami."

"Then you're probably not as impressed with this place as the folks from Ohio."

McDonald pulled into a strip mall and parked in front of a shabby electronics store, windows plastered with florescent pink and green posters hawking deals.

"These guys ought to be able to help you out," he said.

"I don't need anything fancy," she said, getting out of the car.

While she asked for help inside the store, she kept watch on McDonald parked out front. She paid cash for a burner and thirty days of unlimited international calls and texting then hurried back to the car. On the way back to the duplex, she opened the box and read the directions on how to set up the new phone.

"I don't want to be nosy," Arthur said, "but what are you going to do about food and clothes?"

"I don't know." Aside from having no clothing other than what she was wearing, leaving her things behind at the hotel would eventually arouse suspicion. The staff might be concerned something happened to her. On the other hand, her credit card was going to be declined and it might make sense she skipped out. It also might look like she disappeared because Davis had been arrested. Management or local police might review surveillance video and see her interacting with Davis. She'd gone to his room but couldn't remember if she'd been with him in the lobby or not. Arthur's voice brought her back to the present.

"The house isn't walking distance to anything. There might be a bike in the garage, but you have to be careful. Most of the tourists aren't used to driving on the left side and last week a local was killed when he was hit in the head with a side mirror."

"That's awful," she said. A bike ride sounded tantalizing. "What if I stayed off the highway?"

"I might join you," he said.

They rode in silence and when they arrived at the seaside duplex, McDonald offered to look for the bicycle. She followed him down to a small shed beneath the house. The bike had two flat tires.

"You're not going far on that," Arthur said. "I could go get a couple of inner tubes and fix it but I don't think you should ride it." Arthur hesitated. "On another note, I know you don't have a change of clothes and I know it's going to sound weird but I have an idea. I hope you'll hear me out."

26

It took thirty minutes to drive from Sarge's house to Officer Jean Delgado's off-duty gig in Little Havana. While he waited at a red light, Vance held his phone over the steering wheel and reread the ransom message:

5 mil US.

A souped-up Japanese import with tinted windows pulled up next to him idling loudly. He opened the digital voice assistant on his phone and dictated a question 'Siri, are banks in Bermuda open on Memorial Day?'

The automated female voice answered. *'Can you repeat the question.'*

He spoke louder. 'Siri, are banks in Bermuda open on Memorial Day!'

'I'm sorry, I don't understand the question.'

The driver next to him revved the engine; he despised the sound of street racers. Running out of patience, he yelled at Siri. "Does Bermuda recognize American holidays!"

'Bermuda is a British Island territory. It does not recognize American holidays.'

When the light turned green, the lowrider Japanese import drag raced ahead of him. He motored slowly searching for a quiet place to park on a side street near the casino.

Getting a lay of the land, he circled the block passing a shoe repair, beauty salon and three small used car lots where the prices were crudely spray-painted in white on the windshields. He passed the casino, a one-story affair that didn't hold a candle to anything in Vegas; maybe it looked better at night. He'd been to the dog track and had seen the welfare and Social Security recipients spending rent money hoping to hit a jackpot. He imagined this place drew the same clientele. He parked on a side street and texted Zo, then fished the newspaper clipping from inside the pages of the manifesto and began to read.

'MONKEY MORALES'S SON DROPS BOMB 60 YEARS AFTER JFK'S DEATH'

'DECADES after the failed Bay of Pigs operation, rumors about Cuban ex-patriots having been trained by the Central Intelligence Agency to topple the Fidel Castro Cuban government continue to circulate. Many Americans still have questions about the 888-page report known as the Warren Commission ordered by President Lyndon Johnson who succeeded President Kennedy after he was assassinated in Dallas, Texas on November 22, 1963.

One such individual is Ricardo Morales, Jr. who has criticized the last three presidents for failing to follow through on their promise to release classified documents relating to the 1963 assassination of President Kennedy. Ricardo Morales, Jr. is the son of the late Ricardo Morales, also known as Monkey Morales who was shot and killed in a bar fight in Miami in 1982.

"Every president for the last thirty years said they would but after they got into office, none of them ever did. You have to wonder why," Morales, Jr. said.

Morales went on to say the last time he saw his father was at the gun range when he was nine years old. "He told me it might be the last time he had a chance to spend time with me, that he'd spoken to a writer researching the JFK assassination and that he might have said too much about his work with the CIA in Venezuela."

Morales claims his father told him that he'd been sent to Dallas and was there the day Kennedy was shot and that the CIA organized it. "My father was a sniper with an assault team assigned to the Bay of Pigs operation. Later he went to work for the CIA training snipers. He said he recognized Lee Harvey Oswald from television news stories and that he'd trained Oswald as a sniper. My father said there was no way Oswald could have made the shot from the book depository. He was a terrible aim and couldn't hit the side of a barn. When the day comes and they finally release the report, I'm sure it will mention my father and other Cuban nationals. I just hope I'm still alive to read it."

His phone rang on Bluetooth.

"What up?" Zo asked.

"I'm here. Can you talk?" he asked.

"Where are you?"

"I'm parked across from a funeral home on Northwest Third."

"Gimme a minute and I'll meet you there. What're you drivin'?

"Same black Audi sedan."

While he waited for Zo, he scanned the rest of the newspaper article. He'd never realized the Warren Commission Report was 888-pages long. That seemed like overkill to make the case that Lee Harvey Oswald was a lone gunman.

It had been over sixty years since JFK was assassinated in Dallas and keeping CIA documents classified spawned conspiracy theories that wouldn't die. But his curiosity was more personal: What was Sarge doing with a trove of newspaper stories about Monkey Morales?

A white truck rolled up behind the Audi. He watched the rearview mirror as Zo dressed in uniform got out of the pickup and approached. He unlocked the passenger side door, and instead of getting in, she squatted on the passenger side of his vehicle.

"Mmm, mmm, mmm," Zo said opening the door and getting in. "Bullet hole looks and smells fresh, honey. This car sure got itself dirty since I seen you last. That bird shit on the windshield?"

"I see you're still doing good police work," he said.

"Mind tellin' me how that happened?"

"The bird shit or the bullet hole?"

"Don't fuck with me. I ain't got time."

"I was driving in Hallandale and caught a stray."

"You sayin' you got caught up in a drive-by? City's all invested in puttin' in new bike lanes while them drive-bys keep on keepin' on."

"Old problem, new mission" he said.

"Whaddya want from me?"

"My girlfriend's been kidnapped."

"How do ya know that?"

He pulled his phone from his pocket and showed her the ransom message.

Zo's eyes got big. "What the —? Five mil? You datin' a Walmart heiress, or what?"

"Something like that. They want to be paid in crypto."

"I kin see that, but I don't know nuthin' about it. Can you raise that kinda smack?"

"I have forty-eight hours."

"Report it, Courage. Miami's got a department that does nuthin' but cybercrime."

"What do you know about Monkey Morales?"

She looked at him like he was nuts. "What you askin' me for when you should be askin' your buddy, Daniel Ruiz."

"Why would I ask him?" he said, searching her face for visual cues.

Her chin snapped back, and she stared at him in disbelief. "Morales is related to Ruiz's wife."

"How do you know that?"

"Seriously? You gotta be the only one who doesn't and that's whack cause rumor has it you and Sarge is chummy. As I recall you got a shady relative of your own. You know what I say?" Zo asked.

"Don't leave me in suspense."

"I say you can pick flowers and you can pick lotto numbers, but you can't pick your damn relatives. Do me a solid. Run across the street to that gas station store over there and get me a Doctor Pepper. I need somethin' to perk me up and that clerk is always wastin' my damn time talkin' about how the po-lice ain't doin' nuthin' about crime. Nuthin' worse than being told you ain't doin' your job while you is on the job. You say no and we're done talkin'."

HE LEFT the convenience store with a 64-ounce plastic cup. Zo stood outside the Audi smoking.

"You didn't have to go all out," she said, snatching the monster drink as she got in the car, hammering the fat straw on her thigh, using one hand to break the paper cover.

"Do you think it's possible Morales is still alive?" he asked.

"You gotta stop smokin' whatever you been into lately and you need to report that kidnappin'. You playin' with her life."

"How much is left on your mortgage?"

"I dunno. A hundred-and-fifty Gs maybe," she said, sucking soda through the straw.

"How much do you need for childcare?"

"Where are you goin' with this?"

"You need money and I need someone with computer and banking skills."

"I don't know jack shit about either one of them things."

"Something tells me you know someone who does," he said, lowering the A/C.

"You for real?"

"Yep."

"You tryin' to bribe a cop," Zo said. "I could arrest your skinny pink ass right now." Then Zo let out a thunderous laugh and slapped the knee of her uniform. "Fuck yeah," she said, "I'm so tired of this shit, but if I get caught, I'm takin' you down with me."

"Seems fair," he said.

"How much smack we talkin' about?"

"Enough to take care of your mortgage, medical bills, day care and some to stash away for a rainy day. Maybe even a new F-150."

"It rain here almost every day and I sure could use a new set of wheels," Zo said. "You lay it out for me, honey and I'll figure out the rest. If you is bullshittin' me, you is goin' to regret it."

27

L auren waited for Arthur McDonald to finish pumping air in the bicycle tires. He knelt and held his ear close to the valve listening for air to escape. "That might do the trick," he said, leaning the bicycle against the shed beneath the beachfront duplex.

She'd been anticipating he'd share the weird idea he'd teased earlier, and he delivered.

"My wife passed away a couple of years ago," he said.

"I'm sorry," she said, wincing. It came as a surprise. She guessed McDonald to be in his late forties and wondered what had happened to his wife but didn't ask. She also understood loss. While her first divorce felt like a default, her last one felt like a death. She'd been in a dark place for months after it was finalized, never having dreamt she and Peter would break up. Though it was Peter's idea, she'd not been able to imagine herself with anyone else. But that was before Vance came along.

"What I was thinking," McDonald said, "is if you need a change of clothes, I have a whole closet full of hers. I haven't been able to give them away. You're about the same size."

Ugh. She hadn't seen that coming either. She folded her arms across her chest.

"I know," he said, "it's weird. Holding onto her belongings has given me comfort. Never mind," he said. "It's a bad idea."

"No, no, I get it," she said. "My uncle died, and I inherited his house. For the first year I didn't get rid of anything except the rotten food in the fridge."

McDonald laughed at that. "Speaking of food, are you hungry?"

"Starving."

"Why don't you let me take you out to dinner. I could find something for you to wear," he said.

She hesitated, thinking before she weighed in on the delicate subject. "Do you think it might be weird seeing her clothes on someone else?"

"I don't know. I've never tried. Like I said, I've had a hard time letting go. If you say yes, it might be good, you know, give me a little push to move on." He paused, then said, "It's up to you. Either way, I want to take you off the beaten path and buy you a proper Caymanian dinner."

"You don't have to do that."

"I insist. A lovely lady such as yourself deserves to be treated better."

She threw one leg over the bike, sat on the seat and tested the hand brakes, squeezing the levers. "I'll take you up on both offers," she said, "but only if you let me buy."

WHEN SHE WAS ALONE AGAIN in the duplex, she lifted the mattress and removed the pouch with the cash, took out the business card the banker had put in it, and placed a call to the law firm. A moment later the receptionist connected her to Sheldon Green.

"Who am I speaking with?" he asked.

"My name is Lauren Gold. I'm hoping you can help me."

"With what?"

"I need a referral for a criminal defense lawyer," she said, putting the burner on speaker.

"Are you acquainted with our firm?"

"Not directly. I got your number from a friend," she said, sitting on the bed.

"I see. We don't do criminal work, but I can certainly make a referral. There are only a handful of good criminal defense lawyers on the island. For full disclosure, I must tell you one of them is a relative. If you'll hold the line, I'll have my assistant help you."

A minute later she had three referrals. Two were men and one was a woman named Margaret Terry. She checked the time. 4:32 pm. Then she placed the first call.

"Terry and Sheffield. How may I help you?"

She introduced herself and the reason for the call.

"Please hold." A minute of mindless music later, the lawyer was on the line.

After she introduced herself, she said, "I'm trying to find a criminal attorney to help a friend charged with a crime. He's a U.S. citizen and so am I."

"Why isn't your friend calling me?"

"He's being held at the jail."

"What is he being charged with?" the woman asked.

"He was questioned about a couple who went missing on Little Cayman."

"Oh, I heard about that," the lawyer said in a velvety smooth voice.

"Is our conversation confidential?" Lauren asked.

"I can't guarantee it is unless I'm your attorney and from what I gather, I might become his. If that's the case and you're called as a witness, you'll need your own attorney."

"I promise you he didn't do it," she said. "How does this work? Do you need a retainer?"

"I would," Margaret said.

"How much?"

"In a case like this, twenty-five thousand U.S. and I'd need to be paid before I go to the jail and talk to him. It's Friday and it's almost five o'clock," Terry said. "You can stop by my office first thing Monday morning and arrange payment."

"What if I can get the money to you tonight? Can you see him sooner?"

"I can't promise, but I can certainly try," the lawyer said.

"I'm having dinner with a friend tonight. Can I text you and maybe you can stop by the restaurant to pick up the money?"

Margaret Terry paused. "Sure. Where are you having dinner?"

"I don't know yet."

"Is this your mobile number?"

"It is."

"I'll text you and you'll have mine. Give me a call with an update. Make sure you have your passport with you."

She ended the call and tossed the burner in the air. It landed on the bedspread and bounced before hitting the floor. She closed her eyes, laid back and placed the pillow over her face. Margaret Terry had asked to see her passport. She had no idea if that was standard operating procedure or if something else was going on. Paying Margaret Terry would connect her closer to the crime. It wasn't as if she had other options. She was mad at Davis, but she couldn't leave him in jail with no way to help himself.

She picked up the burner from the floor, searched the kitchen for an outlet, put it on charge, returned to the bedroom and took the pouch from under the mattress. Spreading the stacks of bundled hundred-dollar bills on the comforter, she counted out twenty-five thousand dollars, wrapped it in a washcloth and stuffed it in the bottom of her purse along with her passport.

The doorbell rang. She peered through the peephole. Arthur stood on the other side with women's clothing slung over his arm.

"I'm betting something fits," he said.

She took the pile of clothes from him, still on hangers. "Hang on a sec," she said, "let me give you my new cell number."

Arthur waited on the deck outside while she jotted it down. "Here," she said, handing him the note. "Call me so I have yours and I'll text you when I'm ready to go."

She heard the burner rattle on the tabletop, then hurried to the bathroom and showered. When she was done, she toweled off and tried on a couple of the late Mrs. McDonald's outfits. Everything fit to a T.

MARGARET TERRY PUSHED her rolling chair back from her desk and spread her lardy legs while bending over. She opened the bottom drawer, and using a gold letter opener, ripped the cellphone from a package of chocolate frosted cupcakes, stuffing half of one in her mouth. Turning her chair toward the window, she looked out over the center of George Town, and beyond. The endless ocean glittered beneath a setting sun, the wispy clouds casting a pattern of white lace with gold trim. Extraordinary natural beauty was one of the benefits of working out of the tallest office building on Grand Cayman. The other was being born into the bloodline that controlled half the island nation.

She took the second cupcake from the 2-pack and shoved it in her mouth. Struggling to her feet, she closed the door to her office then chased the creamy delight with a can of cola that had gone flat. She lifted the landline on her desktop phone and made a call. Sheldon Green answered on the first ring.

"Let me guess," he said. "She called you."

"She did."

"Did you ask for a retainer?"

"I did."

"How much?"

"Twenty-five thousand," Margaret said, trying to get one of her elephant legs up on the desk.

"She'll pay you in cash."

"How do you know that? Never mind," she said. "I don't need to know. She wants to meet tonight."

"Does that mean you're cancelling date night?"

She gave up putting her leg up and leaned back in her chair. "I certainly hope not."

"Did she tell you who referred you?" Sheldon asked.

"No."

"That's good."

Margaret smiled as she gazed out the window at the orange orb beginning to drop. "This is the kind of case that could launch my career into the stratosphere."

"Don't get ahead of yourself, Meg. You don't need the money," he warned. "Let me know about dinner. I have reservations at your favorite place, but if you can't make it, we'll go another time."

Margaret hung up the phone and twirled the curly black cord in her fingers. Sure, she didn't need the money but thinking about it tingled her spine. The referral had come through her husband Sheldon's brother who handled high net worth offshore accounts meaning there was money. More importantly, there hadn't been a case this big on the island, *maybe ever*. A U.S. citizen charged with murdering two British Nationals? It was a dream come true. She'd spent her entire life overshadowed by the Terry family dynasty.

Just because she was eighty pounds overweight didn't mean she wasn't a damn good criminal defense lawyer. There were only three good trial lawyers on the island, and she was one of them, and this was her big chance. She dug through the trash and hid the empty food wrapper under a recent edition of Conde Nast she'd tossed, then rubbed her palms together. She'd have taken the case for free, but getting the retainer was a guarantee she'd be the one representing a juicy double-murder.

28

On his way to Suarez's office after-hours to retrieve the missing pages and the half of one stuck in the copy machine, Vance ran into a jam of another kind. Headlights on the Audi reflected off florescent bands on orange traffic barrels funneling vehicles on North-west Twenty-Seventh Avenue down to a single lane. The trip from the casino where he'd met Zo on a side street to the high-rise building was only six miles, but a ten-minute drive had morphed into thirty. Traffic was déjà vu, all over again.

He cut east on Coral Way, south to Bayshore Boulevard, and parked the Audi in the nearly empty lot at Suarez's building. Waving the keycard to gain access to the high-rise, he rode the elevator to the eighth floor. Using the access card again, he entered the front door to Suarez's firm, then passed through the second door leading to the back offices. He stopped when he heard a noise like a radio playing, and it smelled like smoke. He drew his gun and crabbed the hallway with his back against the wall, clearing each office until he reached Lola's.

The door was ajar, and a light flickered. He approached

slowly and listened. The noise was coming from her office and so was the smoke. Standing with his shoulders pressed against the wall, he activated the red laser on the Glock, elbowed the door open, and pointed his 9-mil at the intruder.

"What the—" Lola hollered, scrambling to her feet and grabbing a blanket as she dove under her desk. Her tablet lay on the floor face up, flickering colorful light and emitting dialogue from a show she was streaming on her iPad.

"It's alright," he said lowering the gun and approaching the desk slowly.

Lola peeked her head out. "What the hell are you doing here?"

"I came to pick up Natasha's file. What are you doing here?" he asked, noticing a duffle bag next to her desk.

She crawled out dragging a sleeping bag, tapped the pause button on her tablet and said, "I was working late, and I got too tired to go home."

He flipped on the lights. She was barefoot, dressed in a tank-top and sweatpants. A pile of clothing was neatly folded on the floor next to her combat boots. A clear baggie with toiletries was on top of her desk, and she'd propped a pillow against the wall. "That's not what it looks like to me," he said. "How long have you been sleeping here?"

She grimaced and took a deep breath. "This is the first night," she said, wrapping the sleeping bag around her waist. Leaning against the wall, she slid to a sitting position and hugged her knees.

"Does Suarez know you're here?"

"No."

"Do you mind telling me what's going on?"

"My life is shit."

"Wait here," he said, recalling the bottle of good Scotch

he'd seen hidden in Suarez's desk drawer. "I'll be right back."

HE RETURNED, sat on cross-legged on the carpet opposite her and poured two shots of whiskey in paper cups he'd taken from the office water cooler.

"He'd kill us if he knew what we were doing right now," she said.

"Then we better drink up before he finds out."

They toasted with paper cones and downed the alcohol. The burn felt good on his throat.

"Ugh," Lola said. "This tastes like crap." She held out empty her cup. "Gimme another."

He poured and asked, "Why are you staying here?"

"It's just till I save up enough money for my own place."

"What's wrong with your place?"

"I let my ex-husband move in. Now he won't leave. I shouldn't have believed him when he said things would be different. They were, for about a week."

"Why did you let him move back in if you're divorced?"

"I have teenage son who's been running with the wrong crowd. He's involved in one of those smash and grab rings that moves stolen merch online. I thought having a man around the house might help. Instead, I got this." She pointed to her right eye, the injured one.

"What happened?"

"We were at a bar, and he got tanked and decided to try to put my eye out with a pool cue."

"Ouch," he said, wincing at the thought. He never understood why so many women went back to their abusers. That shit was sour milk. You couldn't put it back in the fridge and expect it to smell better a month later. "Listen," he said, "I can loan you money for a hotel if you need a place to stay."

She took umbrage, scrambling to her feet. "I'm not a charity case. I thought while Suarez was out for the month it would give me time to save up a little money. It didn't sound like you planned on spending much time at the office. And here you are after-hours, and you don't start till Monday."

"I'm an over-achiever."

"Is that supposed to be funny?"

"Where's your son now?"

"With my ex. Just until —"

"I get it." He stood, walked to the credenza behind her desk and picked up the framed photo of the three pencil thin men posing with the oxen and plow. "Who are they?"

"They're my uncles."

"When was this taken?"

"What business is it of yours?" she asked, standing and trying to take the picture from him while covering herself with the sleeping bag.

He set it down. "I'm curious why you have a picture of them and none of your kid."

"I can see my son every day. I haven't seen my uncles in twenty-five years."

That information gave him something to work with. "Where are they?"

"They live in a small town outside Havana."

He poured more whiskey for both. "Are they still alive?"

"As far as I know."

"Are they farmers?"

"They were until thieves came in the middle of the night and butchered their animals for food. They used to write me letters and I used to send them money but that stopped a few years ago. The last one I got they said they were eating grass and weeds. Can you imagine living like that?"

He couldn't. He also couldn't overlook the fact that her uncles, the woman in white, the manifesto, Lola, Natasha, Suarez, Monkey Morales and even Daniel Ruiz all had something in common: They were Cuban.

"I haven't heard from them in over three years."

"What about your dad?"

"I don't know. I never met him. I heard he died during the Cuban Revolution."

"And your mother?"

"What is this? An interrogation?"

"No. I thought maybe if you had family, you could —"

"Seriously? You think I wouldn't have thought about that before you did?"

"Right," he said. "Sorry." The in-depth obituary he'd seen, the one published by the British online magazine said Laura Pollán had a daughter from a previous marriage. If this was her, maybe she knew something about the manifesto. Or maybe he was barking up the wrong tree. Lola might've gotten her surname Pollán from the guy who tried to put her eye out with a pool cue.

"If you want to sleep here, I have no problem with it." He took a hundred-dollar bill from his wallet. "Treat yourself to something. Order some food and have it delivered. I'm going to get Natasha's file and I'll see you Monday."

"Why are you being so nice?" she asked, taking the money.

"I don't know if nice is the right word. I know Natasha is your half-sister because you're listed on the application as her next of kin. Why didn't you say so?"

"I figured you wouldn't read the file. Now I know better. I

didn't tell you because I was afraid if you found out, you'd blow off the meeting."

"You were wrong about that," he said, "I'll see you on Monday, and lay off the cigarettes." He stood outside her door for a moment, listening, thinking, taking in the new information.

He headed down the hall, entered Suarez's office, and closed and locked the door. Gently pulling back one of the barn doors, he opened the safe and removed the manila envelope with the original nine-and-a-half pages of the manifesto. He'd have to come back for the half-page still stuck in the copy machine. He stashed the document inside the folder with Natasha's immigration paperwork, stuffed the file under his shirt, closed the safe and spun the fat dial. He jimmied the handle, making sure it was locked, then headed to the elevator.

Riding it to the ground floor, he couldn't help but feel sorry for Lola. A single mother working her tail off, unable to get out from under an abusive relationship she'd gone back to in order to help her kid.

What if she was Laura Pollán's daughter? The age-math worked. Laura Pollán was 63 in 2011, the year she died. He guessed Lola to be in her late thirties, early forties. He wondered how she and Natasha Popova were related; it had to be on the paternal side. The more immediate question was whether Lola knew about the documents in the safe.

Maybe she didn't know about Bay of Pigs 2.0. Maybe it was Suarez's secret. If Suarez was so reckless he drove drunk as hell, maybe he was careless enough to leave the safe open. Anyone with half a brain knew the most important aspect of any battle plan was the element of surprise. Leaving the documents unsecured while he was away for a month was plain stupid.

His thoughts reverted to Lola. It was possible her ex might figure out where she was staying. He turned around and rode the elevator back up to the eighth floor, let himself into the office and knocked on her door. "It's me," he said, pushing it open a few inches. "Are you decent?"

"Yeah," she said, silencing her tablet.

She was sitting on the floor atop the sleeping bag leaning against the desk.

"Can you defend yourself if your ex-husband shows up?"

"He doesn't know I'm staying here," she said, lifting one leg and removing a small 38-caliber revolver. "But if he does, I'm ready."

29

The hop from Suarez's office to the condo was less than five minutes, enough time to call Ethan.

"Hey Uncle Vance."

"I need a favor, kiddo."

"That's the only time you call," Ethan said.

"That's not true," he said, feeling a pang, wondering if it seemed that way. "I want you to look up a last name for me and tell me how common it is."

"Why?"

"I'll tell you when you're twenty-five and meanwhile, don't tell your mom."

"I never tell her anything," Ethan said.

"The name is Pollán. It's spelled P-O-L-L-A-N. There's one of those slash marks over the 'a' that points—"

"It's called an acute accent," Ethan said, "in Spanish it always points to the right over an 'a'. Why do you want to know how common it is?"

"Just do it."

"Does this have something to do with the thing you wanted me to research earlier?"

"What makes you think that?"

"I'll do it if you let me drive your car."

"It's going to have to be at the Post Office, in the parking lot, at night. Two laps at ten miles an hour. And you can't tell your mother."

"Deal," Ethan said.

He waited on hold for a couple of minutes while the boy did his thing. Lola seemed close to her uncles yet didn't know much about her own father. Maybe it wasn't that strange. His own mother's family was torn apart when they emigrated from Cuba to the United States in the late 1950's after Fidel Castro came to power.

He pulled past the gate and parked the car at the condo waiting for Ethan to get back on the phone.

His own mother had told him that the Cuban people supported Castro because they believed he would improve their lives. Castro railed against capitalism and demonized the casino operators, tourism and the U.S. sugar companies that had gotten rich creating a vibrant economy. Castro made speeches claiming that Cuban citizens had been exploited, overrun by imperialists and he promised after the government was in charge, wealth would be divided and shared among the people. The government kicked out the American companies and seized their assets. A special police force was set up pressuring neighbors to watch each other and report unapproved activities to the authorities. Quality of life for citizens deteriorated and had never recovered.

"I got it," Ethan said, taking him out of the story in his head. "The name is very uncommon."

"What countries did you check?"

"I did a global search."

"Can you narrow it down by country?"

"Probably, but it will take me more time."

"Can you check Cuba and the U.S.?"

"I was right, wasn't I. This has something to do with *Damas de Blanco.*"

30

The restaurant Arthur chose was off the beaten path on a narrow, sandy road on a remote dead-end street where the endless blur of black ocean met a moonless sky.

"You picked one of Anne's favorite dresses," he said, opening the car door for her. "It looks nice on you."

The vibe inside the Liberty Inn was cozy with amber lighting and the flames of lit candles flickering against the windows. As the hostess in a red skirt led them to a small table for two near the kitchen, Lauren's mouth watered at the aroma of clove and garlic

"How long were you married?" she asked Arthur.

"Fourteen years."

"Any children?" she asked, laying the cloth napkin across her lap.

"No. How about you?"

"No," she said.

"Have you ever been married?"

"I'm divorced."

"I've heard people say it can feel like a death, except with a ghost," he said.

Their waiter arrived with a basket of crispy plantain strips and a pitcher of water. Arthur moved the candle to the middle of the table to make way for the menus.

"May I get you something to drink?" the male server asked.

"Would you like to share a bottle of wine?" Arthur asked. "There's an excellent merlot on the menu."

"No, thanks. Just club soda with lime for me," she said.

"I'll have a glass of the house red," McDonald said.

"The special tonight is the sautéed lionfish."

Gross. Lionfish were a popular aquarium fish before the idiots in South Florida began dumping them into canals where the population exploded and wreaked havoc on coral reefs as far away as Australia. "I didn't know people ate them," she said. The brown and white zebra stripe fish had a face like the cartoon phlegm character in the mucous relief ads, not to mention venomous spikes.

"It's part of a sustainable effort to stop them from damaging the reefs. They taste like grouper."

Poor grouper: it was to fish what chicken was to all weird foods.

After they ordered, she excused herself from the table. "I'd like to freshen up. I'll be right back."

As she left the table, she felt Arthur's eyes plastered on her. Weaving between diners she made her way to the ladies' room and texted Margaret Terry from a stall.

I'm at the Liberty Inn. If you can get here within the hour I can meet you. I'm with a friend and I'd like to be discreet.

Three gray dots danced on the screen showing Margaret had read the message, but she didn't answer immediately. A moment later, a message popped up.

I'll be there in 15 mins.

When she returned to the table, McDonald had already polished off his first glass of wine.

"Are you a Cayman native?" she asked.

"Fifth generation," he said. "The place you're staying has been in our family for over a hundred and fifty years. We've rebuilt it twice after storms. It used to my grandmother's house before we subdivided it as a rental."

As they exchanged more small talk, her mind fixated on Davis Frost. It wasn't like he was thirteen years old and had to crush on every pretty girl he met. It was hard to believe his judgment was so poor that he found himself destitute and accused of a crime he didn't commit.

She'd barely noticed that Arthur had downed the first two glasses of house wine by the time their main courses were served.

She used her fork and knife to cut the jumbo shrimp into smaller bites, and a fork and spoon to wind the ribbons of fresh fettuccine.

Arthur ate quickly and after he'd wolfed his food, he made small talk while she finished hers. He told stories about growing up on the island, and another about how he'd met his wife Anne while taking sailing lessons.

"Did you check your airline reservation yet?" Arthur asked.

"I didn't get a chance."

While Arthur motioned the waiter to the table to order another glass of vino, her phone chimed with a text. She sneaked a peak.

A message from Margaret:

I'm here.

She typed quickly under the table:

Meet me in the bathroom. I'm wearing a blue dress.

"Would you excuse me?" she said to McDonald.

"Is everything okay?" he asked, with a look of concern.

"Everything's fine. I'll be right back."

The restaurant was much busier than when they'd arrived, and a line had formed outside the bathroom door. Lauren joined the back of the queue with a view to the hostess stand. An obese woman dressed in a gray pantsuit entered alone, lumbered past reception and walked directly toward the restroom. She hadn't asked Margaret Terry what she looked like nor what she'd be wearing.

The woman took her place behind her and said, "You must be Lauren Gold. You're the only one in a blue dress."

"I am."

"Margaret Terry. It's nice to meet you. I hate to come across as rude, but may I see your passport?"

"Let's wait until we're inside," she said.

Margaret nodded and they didn't speak again until they were standing side by side in front a mirror and a row of sinks. "Do you have a business card?"

"I do," Margaret said.

Lauren eyed it, then slipped her passport to Margaret who looked at the photo page and returned it. She took a step sideways, closer to the lawyer and lowered her voice. "I brought cash. I'll pass it under the stall door."

"Is that necessary?" Margaret asked. "We could do it now."

In the mirror Lauren saw two women exit stalls next to each other, "Come on."

She entered an available stall, waited for Margaret to take the one next to her, and handed the twenty-five thousand wrapped in a washcloth to Margaret under the partition.

They met again in front of the sinks. "All good?" she asked the attorney, washing her hands.

"Assuming it's all there," Margaret said, patting her purse. "They're calling him the Sea Otter Killer."

"What? He didn't kill anybody."

"You know how the media is. Come by my office on Monday and I'll give you a receipt for my retainer."

"That won't be necessary. You can give it to Davis when you see him," she said, following Margaret out of the Ladies Room.

"As a lawyer," Margaret said, "I should advise you —"

Holy crap. McDonald stood outside the restroom leaning against the wall like some kind of creep.

"Hello Margaret," Arthur said. "Is Sheldon with you?"

They knew each other.

"No. I just finished dinner with a client," Margaret said. "What a nice surprise to see you out and about. How have you been?"

"Good," Arthur said. "There she is. You were gone from the table for so long I was beginning to worry."

A curious look crossed Margaret's face.

"Lauren, meet Margaret. Margaret, meet Lauren. Lauren is staying at my rental over on Seven Mile Beach."

"Is that right?" Margaret said. "I'm sorry, but you'll have to excuse me. I'm meeting my husband for cocktails and I'm running late."

When they returned to the table, the waiter set a fresh goblet of wine in front of Arthur.

"That was odd running into someone you know," she said.

"Not really," he said.

The waiter interrupted. "Have you decided on dessert?"

"I'm waiting for my date to decide," Arthur said.

Date? "Can you give us a minute," she said, pressing her credit card into the waiter's hand. The man nodded and left the table. If they didn't accept digital currency, at least Arthur would know she'd tried to keep her promise to pay.

"I highly recommend the chocolate eruption cake," Arthur said.

"That sounds good." She paused before broaching the subject a second time. "That was random running into someone you know."

"Not really," Arthur said. "The island is what the Americans call a small town. You can't go anywhere without seeing someone you know."

"How do you know her?"

"She's my second cousin twice removed. Her side of the family is a lot richer than mine. They own half of downtown. Meg's family opened the first bank on Cayman over a hundred years ago."

"Wow," she said.

"She's a lawyer," Arthur said.

"Is she a good one?"

"Rumor has it."

Lauren picked up the cloth napkin and placed it over her knees. "How long have you been a police officer?"

"I started as a constable twelve years ago," he said. "I made detective after four years, and five years ago I was promoted as a special agent in the CID."

"CID?"

"Criminal Investigations Division, in the FCIU."

"FCIU?"

"The Financial Crime Investigation Unit."

That tidbit released a rush of adrenaline. "I bet that's an interesting job," she said, trying to sound calm.

"Not really," McDonald said. "It's mostly boring, a lot of

small fry cases, like Internet fraud and stolen credit cards, but on occasion it gets interesting. Cayman is one of the biggest offshore banking and tax havens in the world. Now and then we're contacted by foreign intelligence agencies investigating international money laundering operations. Some people try to hide money here illegally and on occasion we get called in to help."

"Really?" she said, setting her hands on her lap where he couldn't see them shaking.

31

A rthur jogged to the Crown Vic. "Hurry up before the mosquitos have us for dessert."

Lauren felt the stinging sensation on her bare legs and high-stepped in place waiting for him to unlock the car door. Buckling into the front passenger seat she wondered if he was sober enough to drive. If he wasn't, there wasn't much she could do about it. Even if she bailed out and took a cab, she had no idea how to get back to the duplex. All she knew was the place was located somewhere along Seven Mile Beach.

The dirt road was rough, and McDonald drove slowly, cutting the wheel to avoid the deepest potholes. She powered her window halfway down letting fresh air in and the red wine on Arthur's breath out. She stuck her head out and gazed up at the starless sky, resisting the urge to scratch the fresh bumps swelling on her ankles.

Financial Crime Investigation Unit.

The restaurant accepted digital currency and she'd stupidly paid for their meal on her credit card leaving a paper trail to her Cayman bank account.

Arthur broke the silence. "Have you heard the weather report?"

She fish-eyed him. "No."

"There's a Category Three hurricane in the Atlantic."

"What?"

"It's forecast to strengthen overnight," McDonald said, keeping his eyes on the dark road ahead.

"How do you know?"

"I got a text alert on my phone while you were in the bathroom."

"It's not even June yet," she said, scratching her leg. "Where is it going to make landfall?"

"There's no way to know for sure but we're in the path. You're going to have a tough time finding a flight out. The government issued a travel advisory recommending tourists leave the island. A lot of them usually do and the airlines add flights. I might get called in to work tonight."

"Why?" she asked, still trying to digest the weather forecast.

"Police presence is increased at the airport during evacuations. They add more security as a precaution."

"I thought you were a special agent?"

"I am, but during emergencies, we all have to work."

She took the burner from her purse and opened the weather app. McDonald was telling the truth. The storm was south, southwest traveling on a north, northwest path toward Cuba, Haiti and The Dominican Republic. Grand Cayman was in the mix, but the tiny island was a speck on the computer models.

Hurricane season hadn't officially begun, and she was staying at an oceanfront duplex while a Cat Three churned offshore. Granted, the house was raised on twenty-foot stilts, but the storm surge could be higher, depending on wind speed and proximity to the eye wall.

"The chance of us taking a direct hit is remote," McDonald said. "My guess is it'll turn north and scrape Jamaica."

Chance and guess were the operative words.

The light ahead turned red. Arthur glanced across at her; the streetlights overhead cast a dark shadow on one side of his face giving him a resemblance to the joker from a deck of cards. "There's a hundred-percent chance you'll have trouble booking an earlier flight home."

That was the last thing he said before turning onto West Bay Road and following it past the brightly lit beachfront hotels. He slowed and turned into the driveway of the duplex, putting the Crown Vic in park. He left the engine running, hurried to the passenger side and opened her door. "Let me walk you up," he said.

"That's not necessary. I had a nice time this evening."

He grabbed her shoulders and reeling her in, planted a sloppy kiss on her mouth.

"Whoa!" she said, thumping him on the chest with the palm of her hand. She wiped the acidic stink of red wine from her lips.

McDonald backed away. "I'm sorry," he said. "I'm really, really, sorry. I just thought—"

"You thought wrong. What's the matter with you?" she said, fumbling for the house key. She turned away from him and climbed the stairs, shut the door and locked it.

Yuck.

She opened the fridge, grabbed a bottle of water, rinsed and spit in the sink then pressed the cold plastic on the bug bites dotting her legs. She peeked through the blinds.

McDonald stood leaning against the car gazing up at her place as if debating what to do next.

Dropping her purse on the sofa, she sat for a moment, then walked out onto the balcony to get some air. The ocean was an endless black void, and the wind breezy with a few light gusts helping to keep the mosquitos away. A high tide had rolled in, the foamy lip from the last wave dissipating under the house before the saltwater retracted into the sea.

Her burner rang. She went inside to answer. It was Margaret Terry, the lawyer.

"I wanted to give you an update," Margaret said. "I called the detention center and they're short-staffed because of the weather forecast. I'm sure you've heard by now we have our first hurricane. It's too early in the season if you ask me but Mother Nature never wants my opinion. We're not in the bullseye but that doesn't mean we won't get some rough weather. It's too late for me to visit your friend tonight. I hope to go first thing in the morning ahead of the storm. Do you want to go with me? I could arrange it."

"Is it necessary?" she said, standing in front of the window imagining what could happen if the storm intensified.

"No. I just thought I'd ask."

"I'm going to try to catch an earlier flight out."

There was an awkward pause before Margaret spoke. "I'd stay put if I were you. Trying to get out now will be next to impossible and you might get stuck at the airport. We'll know in the next forty-eight hours where Hurricane Anne is going make landfall."

Hurricane Anne.

"Will you give Davis a message when you see him?"

"Sure."

"Tell him I'm sorry I didn't come to visit and remind him he has enough money to get through this."

"Is he mentally challenged or something?"

"No."

"Wouldn't he know how much money he has?" she said, followed by, "It's probably a moot point because I have no idea how much bond will be, or if the judge will even grant it. It's a double-murder case."

It sounded as if Margaret had already convicted him. It wasn't a double-homicide case. It was a missing persons case, unless there was something she didn't know. "For what it's worth, I'll say it again. He didn't do it," she said, pulling the sliding glass door shut.

Margaret glossed over the comment. "I'm glad you found a safe place to stay. It's off the beaten path and having Arthur next door should give you a sense of relief. If things get ugly, you'll be in good hands. If you don't mind my asking, how did you find his place?"

Airbnb would've been the fib of choice, but Margaret and Arthur were related, and she couldn't afford to get caught in a lie, not even a small one. "Believe it or not, a cab driver suggested it."

"Imagine that," Margaret said, sounding surprised.

She peeked out the blinds again. Arthur walked a big dog on a leash along the grassy shoulder of the road on the other side the street.

"I shouldn't pry," Margaret said, "but I can't help myself. Were you on a date?"

McDonald scooped up the poop with a plastic bag and dropped it by the side of the house. Sheesh. What was it, twenty more steps to put it in the trash? "Heavens, no. He knew I lost my phone, and he offered to help me get a new one."

"And that led to dinner?" Margaret asked.

"Yes."

"I see," Margaret said. "I'll call you after I talk with your friend. I hope that's tomorrow but of course it will depend on the storm."

The chat with Margaret couldn't end soon enough. It wasn't Margaret's business who she went to dinner with. When the call was done, she set the phone down and squirmed out of the blue dress, letting it fall to the floor. Wrapping herself in a bath towel, she sat on the bed and downloaded the airline app. A banner appeared on the home page.

DUE TO THE HURRICANE ADVISORY, WE CANNOT CHANGE EXISTING RESERVATIONS OR BOOK NEW ONES. PLEASE CHECK FLIGHT SCHEDULES BEFORE TRAVELING TO THE AIRPORT.

A text alert popped on her phone.

Due to the hurricane warning, ORIA will close tomorrow at noon.

ORIA, Owen Roberts International Airport in Grand Cayman.

32

V ance parked the dirty Audi beneath a streetlamp on a quiet side street two blocks away from Tavern On The Grove. The dive bar was an old hangout of his located less than a mile from the condo. He grabbed the envelope with the manifesto and the GPS device that the delivery driver had tossed over the gate.

Sarge's Jeep with the crooked '74 Dolphins' decal slapped on the rear bumper was parked in on the street in front of the bar. He strolled past the vehicle, circled back, dropped his key fob, and used the back quarter of the Jeep for cover as he planted the magnetic tracking device beneath the rear fender.

After his chat with Ethan about Lola's last name, he'd called Sarge to see if he still wanted to meet up for that drink. Before he left the condo, he'd checked his email; still nothing from Lauren. Whoever was behind her disappearance knew a few key things about him — his identity, who his girlfriend was and that he had money. The list of people who knew all three was short.

He opened the door with the peeling red paint, his

throat tightening at the smell of sweat and mold inside the tavern. He spotted Sarge sitting alone in the corner near the pool table clutching a mug. It was a slow night with a smattering of patrons sitting at the bar. A guy two tables from Sarge sucked on an e-cigarette, exhaling a cumulous cloud of white vapor while staring at his phone,

"How's the leg?" he asked, taking a seat opposite his friend.

"Hurts. How's the car door?"

"Power window doesn't work."

"What did you tell the horsey chick?"

"Her name is Lauren, and I haven't told her anything yet," he said.

"You need to dig that slug out before she calls her insurance company. Some ambitious claims adjuster might turn it over to the police and I don't like the idea of what could happen."

"Either report it stolen and you won't have to worry about it or face the fact you're never getting it back."

The waitress stopped by the table. Vance ordered, then got down to the reason for the invite. "How come you never told me your wife is related to Monkey Morales?"

"You never asked."

"Give me a break."

"Who told you?"

"Doesn't matter," he said, drumming his thumbs on the tabletop.

"It matters to me and for the record, it's not me keeping a secret, it's my wife. He's family."

He felt a slow burn coming on.

"She'd rather not have people know. Monkey's not exactly *Santo Pedro* in the *Cubano* community. Besides, what would you know about keeping the wife happy?"

That was a well-earned barb. "How's she related?"

"Her sister was married to Monkey's half-brother."

"Was?" he asked, attempting to unravel the family tree in his head.

"She's divorced. They're twins."

"Maria has a twin? You never mentioned that."

"You know what they say. Double the—"

"Save it," he said. Sarge was the most unfiltered human he'd ever met. "Is it possible Morales is still alive?"

Sarge scoffed. "Right. The missus and I imagined we attended his funeral."

That was another secret Sarge had kept from him. "A funeral doesn't mean jack-all if he was CIA."

"You're like the rest of them. All the rumors about *El Mono*. He was a CIA spook. A gunrunner. International assassin. Can't think of anything he wasn't accused of other than being Jimmy Hoffa. I'm not defending him, just saying there's a conspiracy theory about everything. So how do you like playing lawyer again?"

Sarge was good at minimizing some things and deflecting others. He'd play along. "I don't start until Monday." He unzipped his windbreaker and set the envelope on the table. "Here's all nine and a half pages."

Sarge pushed it away like it was radioactive. "You went back to the office?"

"Just read it."

"Find someone else, *Gallego*."

"Lauren was kidnapped, and I think this has something to do with it."

"You're joking."

"She left for Cayman the morning before we met for lunch, and I haven't heard from her since."

"How do you know she's not ignoring you? Maybe she's having a good time. She might've figured out you're a diehard bachelor too afraid of forced refinement to make a commitment. Missing persons show up all the time and they always have a perfectly reasonable explanation. You know that."

"Not when there's a ransom demand."

Sarge was quiet for a moment. "You heard from them?"

"That's what I just said."

"When?"

"Right before lunch with your son-in-law."

A look of hurt came over Sarge. He tilted his head slightly to one side and was quiet for a moment. He gave him time to digest the new information.

Sarge pushed his mug of beer to the side. "Was she kidnapped in Cayman?"

"That's what it looks like."

"Jesus. What was she doing there?"

"She went to see Davis Frost," he said, taking a deep breath, forgetting about the foul smell in the bar.

Sarge knew the name. Frost was Lauren's friend who'd helped salvage the transport cases they believed were loaded with drug cash hidden in the hull of a powerboat sunk offshore in Biscayne Bay.

"Jesus," Sarge said. "You called him from my freaking house. You left a message using my name."

"I didn't call him. I called the dive shop where he hangs out and asked them to pass a message to him."

Sarge pounded the table with his fist. "If this thing blows up, there's geo tracking on your phone that'll put you at my house at the time of the call."

The bartender headed to the table. The guy was built like a WWF wrestler.

"No fighting," he said. "Pound the table like that again and you're outta here."

"Sorry," Sarge said.

When the gorilla was out of hearing range, Vance said, "Don't worry about the call. If this thing goes sideways, you won't be implicated."

"You don't know that," Sarge said, pausing for a two-count. "How much is the demand?"

"Five million."

"Five mil?" Sarge squeezed his eyes shut and pushed his fingers into his temples as if to pop what he'd just heard out of his head.

"I have forty-eight hours to deliver it."

"You have that kind of smack?" Sarge asked. "On second thought, I don't wanna know. Why'd you use my name when you left that message?"

"I couldn't use my own."

"Why not?"

"That should be obvious."

"It's not," Sarge said, reaching for his beer.

"I've done some banking in Cayman."

"Shit," Sarge said. "That's more than I need to know."

"I had a face-to-face with one of the kidnappers."

"When?"

"After our lunch meeting."

Sarge ran his hand over his slick head. "You talked to him?"

"Her."

"This is getting batshit-crazier by the minute. Who's *she*?"

"I didn't catch her name," he said.

"Where'd you meet?"

"Vizcaya."

Sarge rubbed his head briskly. "What did she say?"

"She said *El Mono* wants his money."

Sarge's hands began to shake. He set the mug down, the bottom of the glass rattling as it touched the tabletop.

"The woman claimed to know about a counterrevolution." Vance dangled the envelope in front of him. "That's why I need you to take another look at this."

"My daughter married the dumbest motherf—" Sarge caught himself mid-word and rephrased the next sentence. "You don't have the right to go through Ralph's stuff. Put that back in the safe and forget about it."

"What were you doing at Rafael's office yesterday?"

"Not that it's any of your business, I was getting my teeth cleaned. A dentist-buddy of Ralph's works out of the same building. He gives me a senior discount."

"I saw you leaving with Maria, and I followed you. I called your phone, and you didn't answer. You sent a text about how you probably weren't going to die of a heart attack. Correction. You had your wife send it because you were driving. I called the hospital. You were never there."

"Okay, so I lied. *Mea culpa.* I already told you why. I was worried you'd try to back out of the deal with Ralph."

The bartender remotely changed the channel to a soccer game. Vance could give a rat's ass about European football because he didn't understand the rules. "Have you ever heard of *Damas de Blanco*?"

Sarge didn't answer. He stared at the television. Vance waved his hand in front of Sarge's face.

"Ladies in White?" Sarge said absently. "No, why?"

"The kidnapper said she speaks for them."

"A minute ago, you said Ricardo Morales rose from the dead to start a revolution. Which is it?"

"I think it's all connected. The women are a group of

Cuban activists whose loved ones are missing. Their husbands, sons and brothers were jailed as dissidents for speaking out against the Castro regime. I think they're linked to the manifesto."

"That interesting," Sarge said. "Damn it!" he yelled at the TV.

Vance dragged the table to one side and placed his chair in front of Sarge blocking his view to the television. "It's more than interesting," he said. "What if the Bay of Pigs 2.0 is a plan for a coup? All revolutions need money and what if that's why Ralph kidnapped Lauren."

"That sounds *loco*," Sarge said. "Maria already told you Ralph doesn't have a patriotic Cuban bone in his body. Nor American for that matter."

He lowered his voice. "That might be, but you don't demand five million dollars ransom unless you know someone can pay it. The woman at Vizcaya knew details about me and my family. Someone leaked it to her."

Sarge leaned to the side to see the soccer game. "Crap! That's a bullshit call. They need to get rid of that ref."

Vance carried his chair beneath the wall-mounted television, stood on the seat and manually turned off the TV. The bartender noticed and glared at him but stayed behind the bar.

"You're worse than my wife," Sarge said.

"All I'm saying is only a handful of people know about the money and you're one of them."

"Hold up," Sarge said. "You're accusing me?"

"Simply pointing out a fact."

"I got some questions of my own," Sarge said. "Let's start with why you waited until now to tell me Lauren was kidnapped?"

"I couldn't say anything in front of your son-in-law.

When I tried to call you, Maria told me you were in the hospital with heart problems. When I figured out you were ducking my calls and lying, I wanted to confront you in person, look you in the eye so I could see your reaction. That's why I came to your house tonight. Then that other shit went down."

"You're implying I betrayed you?" Sarge said, looking genuinely hurt.

"Where's Rafael doing his rehab?"

"I don't know. Somewhere in Arizona or maybe New Mexico. My daughter Val knows. Listen," Sarge said, "you're implicating my family in something I can't get dragged into." He pushed his black-framed glasses higher on his nose. "I'm sorry about Lauren. I really am. But I don't see what I can do to help."

"You're already involved. I'm working for your son-in-law, and the woman at Vizcaya said your ex-half-brother-in-law is the one behind the ransom demand."

"That's on you. As far as I'm concerned, *El Mono* is dead. If you want to hallucinate without the benefit of smoking crack, be my guest."

This was how gaslighting worked, and he could sniff it a mile away. "Dead or alive, not a nickel of it was ever Monkey's money and you know it." He leaned into Sarge's personal space. "Who did you tell that I have money?"

Sarge raised his voice. "Fuck you," he said, struggling to his feet, pushing the chair over, hobbling on his good leg toward the exit.

The bodybuilder bartender raised the service bar hatch and beelined toward them. Vance threw three twenties on the table and followed Sarge outside.

33

Sarge staggered toward the Jeep parked beneath the streetlight. Vance jogged ahead and blocked him from getting in. "Who did you tell about the money?"

"Get out of my way," Sarge said.

"If you told Suarez, be honest," he said, refusing to move.

Sarge grabbed his forearm, but injured and overweight, he was no match for Vance. Sarge let go, then said, "Why would I do that?"

A blue BMW with blinding headlights stopped parallel to the Cherokee, blocking a lane of traffic.

"I'm not saying you did it on purpose. Maybe it was a slip."

The car stuck behind the BMW honked. "Find another spot!" Sarge yelled, then turned to him and said, "I haven't told a living soul. Val told him I recommended you as someone who could help while he was away. He asked me a few questions. I know, I know," he said, "maybe I should've given you a heads-up but if I thought if I did, you'd act like this."

It was reasonable for Suarez to quiz his father-in-law about the guy who'd be filling in for him for a month, but not about his finances.

The punk behind the wheel of the BMW rolled down the passenger window and hollered, "Are you leaving or what?"

"Fuck off," Sarge yelled back.

The BMW driver flipped the bird at them and laid down some rubber.

"What else did he want to know?" he asked, steering the convo back to the topic of Ralph.

"Like how you could afford your lifestyle even though you don't have a job."

Vance folded his hands across his chest feeling the 9-mil holstered beneath his windbreaker. "What did you tell him?"

"Nothing, really. I told him the condo belongs to your girlfriend. He wanted to know how you could afford to send your sister out of the country for cancer treatment. I told him I thought you inherited some money from your dad."

"How did he know my sister was sick?"

Sarge shrugged. "Not from me."

He couldn't think of anyone in Sarge's circle who would've known about Kathy's illness other than Sarge.

"If she was abducted in Cayman, it's FBI business," Sarge said.

"I told you. I'm not reporting it."

"You're a hypocrite. You tell me to report my gun stolen, in front of my wife, but you're going to try to drop a five-million-dollar ransom on your own. You should think that through."

"I already have."

Sarge stood on one leg like a fat flamingo and leaned

against the Jeep for balance. "My leg hurts and I'm tired. Get out of my way so I can go home."

"I have a plan. Hear me out."

"Make it fast," Sarge said.

When he finished presenting his idea, Sarge said, "Let me get this straight. You want me to use my wife to get my daughter and granddaughters out of their house so you can go in and search Ralph's home computer?"

"That's right."

"No," Sarge said, shaking his head. "I'm not doing that."

"If he's not involved, that'll be the end of it."

"What are you looking for?" Sarge asked, licking the wound on his lip.

"The demand is in cryptocurrency. The woman I met at Vizcaya sent a link to an account and I want to see if the information matches anything on Ralph's computer."

"You're making a big leap. Hypothetically speaking, what if my son-in-law has something to do with it? What's the end game?"

"To find Lauren and bring her home."

"If Ralph's involved, I'm not helping you prove it." Sarge pressed the key fob and unlocked the driver's side door. "What if you're wrong and you're barking up the wrong tree? Every minute you're chasing a dead-end, the less chance you have of finding her."

Vance clenched his fists and half his face twisted into an involuntary snarl. "What if it was Maria, or one of the girls?"

The red door to the bar opened. The extra-large bartender stood holding it open. "You two better get moving or I'll call the cops."

"We're not bothering anyone," Vance said, taking a step toward the beefcake, wondering what would happen if he accepted the dare.

"Finish your little soiree then hit the road," he said, disappearing inside.

Sarge grabbed the door handle to the Jeep. "You should've thought about this before you took a pile of drug money. You should've known there were people out there who'd never stop looking for ways to get their hands on it. There are guys still getting out of prison after serving twenty years. No one forgets about seventy-five million bucks, especially guys locked in a cage without much else to think about."

All valid points. He opened his arm in a gesture signaling Sarge was free to go.

Sarge yanked the car door open. "You had to know you'd be a target," he said. "I coulda done the same, you know. I coulda taken a couple of million as my cut. You know why I didn't? Because I have a family to look out for, and you don't."

"Someone in my inner circle told someone."

The BMW returned after making another lap around the block and honked.

"It sure the hell wasn't me. How do you know they haven't killed her already?"

He didn't, but he couldn't say it out loud. "I saw a video of her."

"Show me," Sarge said.

"I don't have it."

"You deleted it?"

The red door flung open again. "I warned you before. The two of you need to hit the road."

Vance approached keeping a safe distance under the streetlight. "This is a public sidewalk." He opened his windbreaker and flashed the Glock holstered under his left arm. "It's registered and I have a concealed carry license. Go ahead and call the cops. I'd love to see what happens. Response time is probably about two hours this time of night. Or maybe they'll get here in time to have a latte with you in the morning."

"Asshole," the bartender said loud enough for two girls with pink hair to hear as they approached. They made a wide berth around the goon.

"He's right," Sarge said. "You're an asshole, and for all you know Lurch's brother is a state senator. If Monkey's alive and he's got anything to do with this, you better watch your back."

"I thought you said he's dead."

"On the off chance he's not, he's CIA trained. If he's alive, he's an old man with one last chance to topple the Cuban Communists. You're on your own, *Gallego*."

"Fine." He stepped away from the Jeep. "I'll go see Val myself and show her this." He held the envelope in front of Sarge's face. "I'll tell her if she doesn't let me look at Ralph's computer, she can find someone else to cover for her drunk-ass husband for the next month."

Sarge used the back of his hand to wipe the sweat from his brow and dried it on his pants. "If I agree to help, then what? You're no computer expert."

"Zo's got someone."

"She's in on this?" Sarge said, shaking his head and making a fist. "Who else?"

"Just Zo and her guy."

"What guy?"

"He's one of her sources. He's got the skills."

"Why is Zo helping you?"

Before he could think of a way to deflect the question, Sarge reached into his pocket and looked at his phone. "I gotta get this," he said, limping to the front bumper of the Cherokee for privacy.

The call was brief.

"That was my other daughter, Gloria."

He'd forgotten Sarge had two.

"She operates a little community theater in Santa Fe that runs on hopes and dreams. She's staying with Val and that complicates getting in the house. She's in town meeting with someone who might throw a little money at her theater."

"Why would someone in Miami want to invest in a struggling theatre in New Mexico?"

"Hell, if I know," Sarge said. "What are you looking for on Ralph's computer?"

"I want to check his search history, get his IP address, see if he's set up a digital bank account."

"I hope you're disappointed," Sarge said. "Slime-ball, yes. Dumb enough to shake you down? I don't think so."

"Go back to thinking like a cop. You and I both have a good idea what a lot of people will do for a five-million-dollar payday."

"Most people would be tempted by a lot less," Sarge said.

He wanted to go through the list of arrows pointing at Ralph, starting with quizzing Sarge about where Vance had gotten his money, and the fact he'd found the document in Ralph's safe. He decided on a different course. "I get why your wife didn't want people to know her sister was married to Morales, but Zo said everyone knew but me. Why didn't you trust me? You and I were hanging out at the Hotel Mutiny when he was shot, and you failed to mention you spent Christmas with him."

"He was never at my house. Never. Not for Christmas, not for Thanksgiving. Not ever."

It was meant in jest, but man, Sarge got bent out of shape.

Suarez could've planned the whole thing. It would've been easy to set himself up to get stopped for a DUI. All he had to do was over imbibe and drive erratically. Sarge said Ralph and Val had a blow up at Easter dinner, but Sarge claimed he didn't know what it was over. He stepped into Ralph's head for a moment to see it from his perspective.

Ralph got drunk in front of his in-laws, had a fight with his wife in front of his kids then went out for a drive. He didn't resist the field sobriety test and allowed himself to be charged with a DUI. Suarez wasn't the type of guy to acquiesce to authority, especially drunk.

"Maybe your son-in-law went out and got himself stopped on purpose as part of a bigger plan to shake me down for money." He held the document up again.

"He's not that smart and you're insane," Sarge said. "I know you're worried about Lauren, but this thing is messing with your head. What about Lauren's friend, the fat guy with the boat who helped salvage the money? He lives in Cayman. Maybe he knows something. I'm assuming that's why you left a message for him when you called from my house. Lauren goes to visit him and disappears. Frost was part of the heist. He knows about your money."

It was a solid theory and one he'd been grinding on, but there were a couple of things wrong with it. First, he couldn't figure out how Suarez knew he'd sent his sister Kathy out of the country for cancer treatment. It was possible Lauren had mentioned it to Davis Frost, but Suarez and Frost didn't know each other. The more troubling aspect was the manifesto. Frost was from Minneapolis with no ties to the Cuban community, much less to a group of female freedom fighters he himself had never heard of until recently. Plus, Frost didn't speak a word of Spanish.

"My son-in-law's no angel," Sarge said, "but he's not a bad guy."

"Do you know if he has money problems?" he asked. "Gambling, extra marital stuff, anything that would make him financially vulnerable?"

"Nah, but it's not like Val would tell me. Look," Sarge said, "I know you're not going to take your foot off my neck until I agree to help you get inside the house. I'll do what I can but here's what you're going to do for me. One, you're gonna get my gun back from my asshole neighbors. Two, my wife and daughters are never going to know about this. And three," he said, taking a piece of paper from his wallet, "you're gonna find out who put this note in my granddaughter's violin case."

34

Lauren spied on Arthur in the dark through the blinds as he wrangled outdoor furniture from the beach to somewhere beneath his side of the duplex. Talk about awkward. She cringed at the thought of the unwanted kiss and the acidic taste of red wine on his mouth. She'd done nothing to lead him on and chalked it up to a mix of booze and loneliness. She observed him through the window a little longer as he dragged the blue beach umbrellas up the stairs and tied them to the balcony railing. After he was finished, she dressed into her own clothes and sneaked down the stairs for a walk on the beach.

A lot of what had happened up until now was her fault. She'd conjured the story about the abusive boyfriend to avoid going back to the hotel after Davis was arrested. That led to Arthur's generous offer to help her sort out her phone. She should've left it at that, but she'd accepted his dinner invite because she was famished. Margaret had seen them together and it was bound to raise questions.

What if Margaret called Arthur to quiz him? It wasn't a

paranoid delusion. Margaret and Arthur were related in what seemed to be a tight knit family and she appeared genuinely surprised to see him out on what looked to be a date. It would be natural for her to pry.

She rolled up her pants, left her shoes on the bottom rung of the stairs and stepped onto the wet sand feeling the sand squish between her toes. As the waves rolled in, seawater covered her feet up to her ankles. She'd been through enough hurricanes in Florida to recognize the calm before the storm. She jumped sideways as something brushed against her leg.

Ewww.

It was the bag of dog poop she'd seen Arthur drop near the house. It must have floated out with the step-up tide.

She had to prepare herself for a conversation with him. Margaret might tell him she'd hired her as the lawyer to represent Davis and it was a given Arthur knew about the missing couple on Little Cayman. Margaret might tell him she'd paid cash. Lauren was aware of attorney-client privilege but as the payee, Margaret had already advised her she didn't have the same right to confidentiality as a client. Worse, Margaret said if the case moved forward, she could be called as a witness by the prosecution.

According to what Davis had told her, the RCIPS investigators believed money was the motive for the crime, but it didn't make sense. It wasn't as though Davis was next of kin and would inherit the business in the event of the LeCroy deaths. It seemed more like Davis was the fall guy. An outsider unable to defend himself. At some point Margaret would wonder how she'd been able to access a large sum of cash on short notice. She took a deep breath and held it an extra moment as she walked along the shoreline feeling the cool water rushing over her feet.

This was a small town. Of course she and Arthur were going to talk. Everyone was going to talk. Margaret Terry was probably on the phone with Arthur right now. She clenched her hands and kicked at the saltwater, splashing her clothes.

She was concerned how Davis would behave when Margaret showed up at the detention center. He was needy on a good day, and behind bars he would be desperate. His default was diarrhea of the mouth and under duress, there was no telling what he would say. It was a little late to regret tossing Vance's phone number in the trash. He'd would've known what to do.

The temperature plummeted at least ten degrees and she lost her balance as a strong gust of wind erupted, buffeting the crowns of the palm trees. Shivering, she leaned into the headwind glancing back at Arthur's place. Thin ribbons of light emanated from the half-open blinds. He might be watching her. She shuddered at the thought, the uncomfortable feeling inside interrupted by a group of young people hooting and hollering from the balcony of a house a few doors down. The row of folded umbrellas staked into the sand behind their place had tipped over like dominoes and as another strong wave rolled in, three washed out to sea.

Another wave roared in the distance, the frothy crest fully formed before it broke and rushed to shore. She ran toward the wooden pilings near the neighboring house where the party was in full swing. A shirtless guy in swim shorts wobbled down the stairs, grabbed the railing and vomited before he made it all the way down. She couldn't outrun the wave. Calf-deep in the receding water, she held her arms out like the wings on an airplane trying to keep from losing her balance. When the water receded, she jogged back to the house, out of breath by the time she reached the stairs.

Grand Cayman might not take a direct hit, but the effects of the storm were already being felt. She opened the screen door, but the wind ripped it from her hands. It clattered and banged as more heavy wind gusts bent the trunks of the date palms, the fronds sweeping to one side like a balding man's comb-over. Waiting for a break in the wind, she held the aluminum screen door with both hands. A lightning bolt struck, blinding her for a moment followed by a boom of thunder that rocked the house. She wrestled the screen door and scrambled inside, pulling it shut. A series of lightning strikes turned the sky brilliant white followed by roaring thunder. The house lights flickered —

Then the house plunged into darkness.

Oh my God. She waved her hands in front of her navigating the unfamiliar floor plan.

The power could be out for hours.

No electricity meant no wireless internet, and possibly no cell service.

There was no food in the house.

Using her hands as a guide, she slowly padded her way to the kitchen and felt for her purse. She fished the burner out and checked the battery. It hadn't been on charge long enough and was already in the red with eighteen-percent power remaining. The only phone numbers stored on it were for Arthur McDonald and Margaret Terry. Her chest tightened and she could hardly breathe. The wind howled and the house on stilts shook. Lightheaded, she sat on the kitchen floor and ran scenarios in her head. Her only connection to the outside world was a pair of strangers.

Lights reflected off the windows. Lauren made her way across the living room to see who was arriving. No one was coming. Arthur was behind the wheel of the Crown Vic, and he was leaving. He backed out onto the dark road and the high beams on the sedan bounced as he looped around and headed toward town. She watched until the red taillights on his vehicle disappeared into the blackness of night.

Her phone pinged with a text:

I've been called into work and will be at the airport until it closes. Storm is strengthening and heading our way. Not sure how long cell service will work. Conserve battery. Power is out on most of the island. Stay inside. Should be back by daylight. I have enough supplies to get us through the storm. Arthur

Us?

Activating the flashlight on the burner, she headed to the bedroom and crawled under the covers. Her mind raced with a million thoughts all drawing the same terrifying conclusion. She was isolated on a small island in a foreign country with a hurricane in the forecast.

Unable to calm herself, she opened the weather app on her phone. The storm system was huge, a hundred miles in diameter, and Grand Cayman was now under a hurricane warning. She opened her email on the burner and saw a new message from Vance. Thank God.

SUBJECT LINE: Greetings from Miami

To: themutinygirl@gmail.com

From: vancecourage@gmail.com

2:03 GMT

Lauren, I've been trying to call you but there's something wrong with your phone. Where are you? Are you in trouble? I need to authenticate this is you. Please add the following information when you answer. What is the long and short name of the dog we recently adopted? What kind of car did I drive when we

first met, and what was the nickname I gave it? If this is you,
please add your new phone number and I'll call you.
VC
P.S. I miss you.

THAT WAS WEIRD. Why did he want to know the name and
nickname of the new dog? She didn't have enough battery to
worry about it.

She typed quickly.

*It looks like I'm stuck in Cayman because there's a hurricane
warning. Some other stuff is going on with Davis and I can
explain later. The dog's name is Cashmere. Cash for short. You
drove a weird car when we met. A Nissan Cube I think. It had a
cockroach leg on the roof. The name of the car was—*

She stared at the screen glowing in the darkness. The
vehicle had been part of an extermination fleet, and a
partial leg of a cockroach leg sprouted from the top of the
car where a giant bug had been bolted and sawn off at the
knee.

What was the nickname he'd given it? Come on brain,
kick on. It was from a movie. Will Smith was in it. So was
Tommy Lee Jones.

Gale force winds shrieked and rocked the house.

Men in Black! Vance had nicknamed the car Edgar! She
continued typing.

*—Edgar. I had to get a burner phone after mine died. Here's
the number—*

Opening the settings page on her phone, she copied the
new number and was about to add it to the email when a
bolt of lightning struck close to the house, followed by a
crack of thunder so ferocious it shook the bed. The phone
slipped from her hand and fell to the floor. She dropped to

her hands and knees and swept her palms across the tile, beneath the nightstand, and under bed. It couldn't have gone far but she couldn't find it it the darkness.

She scooted on the floor toward the bed, leaned against the mattress and closed her eyes. Another streak of lightning lit the room like a flashbulb revealing the outline of the phone that was within arm's reach. Grabbing the burner from the tile she gently tapped the screen with her fingertip to wake it up. But it didn't light. She thumbed the screen a few times, then stabbed it with her finger before smacking the phone with her open palm.

My God. The battery was dead.

She tossed the phone over her shoulder onto the comforter. There was no way to track the storm. No way to call for help. No way to monitor the airlines. She couldn't even get messages from Arthur.

The airport would probably shut down soon and there'd be no way off the island until the storm passed. If the airport suffered serious damage, then what? Margaret Terry was supposed to visit Davis tomorrow and give her an update. The latter was a moot point. With no power, the jail would be closed.

The surf pounded. She scrambled to her feet and used her hands to guide her toward the window, smashing her foot into the chair leg in the darkness.

Damn it!

She shoved it out of the way and looked out. The sea had morphed into snowcapped mountains of water with ten-foot waves roaring as they pounded the beach and crashed under the house. On the U.S. mainland, meteorologists could give people living near the coastlines ample warning. But storms formed quickly over open water leaving islanders more vulnerable with less time to prepare.

Her mind turned to Davis trapped inside a dark jail cell with no contact to the outside world. She'd seen a television series about Americans jailed abroad. The prisons were unimaginable, rampant with diseases, insects, rotten food, rats and human waste.

Her situation was scary, but Davis was entombed inside a living nightmare.

35

Vance leaned against the Jeep outside the tavern and read the note again.

Keep your mouth shut or you'll be sorry.

"Where did you get this?" he asked Sarge.

"It was in my granddaughter's violin case."

"Who put it there?"

"If I knew do you think I'd ask you to find out, numb nuts? She takes it to school with her. My wife thinks some kids might've done it but it's not the kind of thing kids Leah's age do."

"How old is she?" he asked, studying the rumpled piece of paper.

"Eight."

The note was old school, written in cursive. Hardly anyone under the age of fifteen could read or write script. Contemporary kids tortured their peers electronically. "The only promise I can make is that Val won't find out you helped us get in her house. I'll do my best to get your gun back. As for this," he said, referring to the note, "no promises."

"I know you'll do your best," Sarge said. "There's something else I need to come clean about." He tugged and twisted the cubic zirconia diamond in his earlobe. "I wasn't at the dentist when you saw me leaving Ralph's office."

"I know. I checked the directory and there's not a dentist in the building."

"I went there to introduce myself to Ralph's gal, but I got cold feet," Sarge said, slapping at a mosquito.

"Lola?"

"Son of a bitch," Sarge said, waving his hands in front of his face. "Hurry up and get in before these suckers eat us alive."

As Sarge unlocked the doors with the key fob, Vance felt a stinging sensation on his neck. He jogged to the passenger side and climbed into the Jeep while Sarge started the engine and lowered the A/C.

"I shoulda been honest with you," Sarge said turning the volume down on a Spanish-speaking station on the car's radio.

A shrill passed his ear and he felt a sting on his neck. "Son of a bitch," he said, spotting the mosquito as it landed. He swatted the dash but missed. "Why did want to talk to Lola?"

"I was gonna to tell her how important it was to treat you decent," Sarge said, reaching in the back seat for a roll of paper towels and mopping the sweat from his head and neck and throwing the used ones over his shoulder.

"What makes you think I can't handle my own business?" he said.

"Val told me Lola's a royal bitch and I knew you wouldn't put up with that crap for a month."

He was reminded of Lola's plight. "I don't know what Val's talking about. I met her and she's fine. Do you mind if I keep this?" he asked, referring to the note, thinking he could search Ralph's office for a writing sample and analyze it himself.

"Sure, keep it. I'd like to punch whoever did it in the face. My granddaughter is a little girl. Who does that?"

"I have no idea," he said. "Work on the plan to get inside Ralph's house."

"The girls have been bugging Maria to go see the new Disney movie. I'll drop a hint."

Vance reached for his wallet.

"You don't have to do that," Sarge said.

"Take it," he said handing him two folded hundred-dollar bills.

"Maria likes to go to the matinee," he said, taking the money, "but I gotta approach with caution. I swear my wife can read my mind. Val hates kids' movies, and my bet is she'll head to Bal Harbour to burn some of Ralph's dough on designer crap. Not sure why he puts up with her spending sprees, but he does."

"Here's an extra five hundred bucks. Tell Val to buy something nice for your wife."

Sarge hesitated, then snatched the money and stuffed it in his pocket. "My anniversary is coming up. I'll keep you posted."

"Figure out how to get me in the house ASAP."

"I'll do my best. Where'd you park?" Sarge asked.

"Around the corner."

"Let me give you a lift."

"No, thanks," he said getting out of the Jeep. "I'll walk." He set the envelope on the passenger seat. "Read the whole document and find out where Ralph's doing his rehab so I can verify his whereabouts."

"I'll try. If this thing goes south and you get caught inside his house, you're on your own," Sarge said.

"Deal."

"If my son-in-law is dirty, you have my permission to take him down."

"I don't need your approval," he said, shutting the car door.

As Sarge drove away, he was unable to shake an uncomfortable truth. He and Sarge had been friends for a long time but just because he'd known him a long time didn't mean he really knew him.

He checked his phone. No new messages. He wished he had a way to track down the woman in white, but he knew nothing about her. He had to figure out how to transfer the money from his bank account in Bermuda into cryptocurrency. He had a phone number for the bank and tried calling earlier but the automated recording said they were closed until Monday. The forty-eight-hour window to wire the ransom ended day after tomorrow, Sunday.

He read the threatening note again unable to come up with a rational reason why anyone would intimidate an eight-year-old child. He should've asked Sarge how he came to possess it. Sarge's recent behavior was out of character, and it was clear neither he nor Maria cared for their son-in-law. But, as with most situations, Vance didn't have all the facts. The note could've been planted for any number of reasons and although kids bullied each other electronically these days, it was possible a classmate did it.

As a former police officer, Sarge had had a front-row seat to the best con men working the streets. They'd been buddies for a long time, but their friendship leaned professional. Band of brothers' stuff from their days as cops. While Vance had never been married, Sarge had always been a family man. More than a family man; it was his main purpose in life. He'd seen it firsthand when Sarge went off the deep end after Maria ran off with an old high school flame she'd secretly reconnected with on social media.

It was the same year his own relative, deposed drug kingpin Tony Famosa, snuck into Miami from Cuba and roped Vance into helping him salvage seventy-five million dirty dollars the Dos Guapos cartel had stashed before Tony became a fugitive.

Sarge was a mess after Maria flew the coop. Vance recalled how he'd worried about him and how Sarge's daughter Val had checked in on her dad regularly before Maria finally came to her senses and returned home. He'd offered to cut Sarge in on the cash—a two-million-dollar bonus — mostly to keep quiet about Tony being back in Miami. But Sarge had turned it down.

He walked the side street to where he'd parked the Audi passing a guy on a bus bench in the fetal position clutching a black trash bag. The man's legs were exposed, oozing bloody sores that glistened under the streetlight. Vance reached into his pocket and took some cash from his wallet.

"Hey," he said, but the man didn't respond. He gently poked his shoulder, but the homeless guy didn't react. He tucked the cash in the pocket of the man's peacoat.

He jogged the rest of the way passing shops closed for the evening, stopping as he caught a faint reflection of himself in the window of a clothing store. He'd never been shy about making snap judgments about others. His sister should've married someone more responsible than her husband Larry. The guy on the bench should've had a job or gone to a homeless shelter. If it wasn't for Tony, he wouldn't be trying to figure out how to pay the ransom. It was Sarge's fault he was stuck covering for Rafael. As he stared at the ghostly reflection of himself on the glass it was as if looking at a stranger.

Sarge had needed money more than he did and had turned it down, worried how it would affect his family if he were caught. Sarge agreed he'd help search Rafael's home computer, but he was uncertain how far he would go to protect Val and the girls. Sarge said if Rafael was dirty, Vance should take him down. But when push came to shove, whose side would Sarge be on? He'd already gotten a sneak preview.

If Sarge had gone to Suarez's office for the reason he claimed—to grease the skids with Lola—why the sudden change of heart?

He unlocked the Audi, got behind the wheel and composed a text to Zo.

Getting it organized. Trying to get access to the house tomorrow. Firm it up with your guy. I'll call with details.

Next, he opened the app that came with the tracking device he'd ordered online and installed on Sarge's Jeep. The screen showed a yellow dot traveling north on Bayshore Drive heading toward Hallandale. Sarge was on his way home.

Zo texted back:

10-4

His phone rang.

Ethan came up on CALLER ID.

"I have the information you wanted," the boy said. "I searched a global database and Pollán is an uncommon name. It occurs most frequently in Cuba and Spain. In Spain, the ratio is one in 4.2 million and in Cuba it's one in

960,000. There's only one incidence in the United Kingdom and zero here."

"That narrows it down," he said. "Can you check another one for me?"

"Do I get to drive your car on the street?"

"Sure. After you get your learner's permit. Actually, two names. Check and see if the last names Popova and Morozova show up in Cuba."

"Only women?" Ethan asked.

"No, men and women," he said.

"Then that's four names. Russian women add an 'a' to their last names after they get married."

He'd never heard that.

"Why are you looking up Russian names?" Ethan asked.

"I'm looking for a bride," he said.

"Very funny. There's no one with those names living in Cuba."

"Is that a guess?"

"No. I'm looking at the database now. There're tons in Russia and Ukraine, and a lot here, some in Eastern Europe, Canada, and in the former Soviet bloc countries, but zero in Cuba."

He heard a voice in the background.

"Ethan, who are you talking to?"

He recognized his sister Kathy's voice.

"I gotta go," the boy said, ending the call.

VANCE DID THE MATH. The population of Cuba was around 11 million. One out of 900 thousand meant there were about 11 or 12 people with the name Pollán and zero named Morozov, Morozova, Popov or Popova.

36

D avis Frost lay on the bottom bunk atop a thin mattress, metal springs digging into his flesh. It was pitch dark and baking inside the cramped cell he shared with another inmate who'd introduced himself as Blackjack. When Davis had arrived handcuffed in the back of a police vehicle, the place didn't look like any jail he'd ever seen. But for the razor wire and chain link fence, the chalky blue one-story metal building looked more like a rundown storage facility.

The electricity had been out for over an hour and Davis flinched as something scurried against his thigh. He batted it with the back of his hand, then heard a squeak as the rat hit the floor and scampered for cover. Before the lights had gone out, he'd seen a ridge of dead cockroaches mixed with rodent hairs and droppings that had accumulated along the baseboards.

After he was booked, photographed, and fingerprinted he was given a prison uniform two sizes too small that wedged in the crack of his ass and itched his testicles. He unzipped the front and tied the sleeves beneath his belly giving his balls much needed relief.

He'd purchased two burner phones and had returned to the hotel to wait for Lauren and was about to step in the shower when he'd heard a knock on the hotel door. He looked out the peephole, and seeing the housekeeper's cart, had cracked open the door with the chain in place. Two Royal Cayman police officers stepped into view and pushed their way into his hotel room. While he dressed, they'd searched his belongings. Then they'd arrested him.

As he was escorted down the elevator and through the lobby by three uniformed RCIPS officers, the hotel staff and guests had gawked at him, some gasping. On the walk to the police vehicle outside, dozens of tourists and locals had lined the street trying to get a glimpse of him.

"That's the Sea Otter Killer!" a woman had yelled. The crowd chanted, "Killer, killer, killer!"

His throat had closed and as he gulped for air, he kept his head down, afraid to look up. He'd been loaded into the back of a police vehicle and told he'd be driven directly to the Fairbanks Detention Centre where he'd be held until Monday. That's all he could remember the arresting officer had said.

"Be grateful they didn't take you to Northwood," Black-jack said from the bunk above.

"What's that?"

"HMP Northwood. Her Majesty's Prison, or maybe it's His Majesty's now. Either way, trust me when I say the place is an overcrowded shit hole. I was transferred out ahead of the storm."

"What storm?"

"How do you not know we're under a hurricane watch? That's why the power's out. Rumor around her is the generator here has been out of service since Hurricane Grace," Blackjack said.

"How do you know?"

"We're in jail, you moron, not outer Mongolia."

"Great," Davis said rolling onto his side. "It's hot in here."

A red pin-light glowed from the ceiling illuminating the smoke detector.

Blackjack hung his head down from the upper bunk, the whites of his eyes glimmering pink. "Rumor has it you're being charged with murder."

"I didn't kill anyone."

Blackjack laughed. "That's what they all say. Where you from?" he asked, striking a match.

A flash of an orange glinted, and Davis smelled sulphur dioxide before the stench of ganja filled the cell.

"Here," Blackjack said, passing the lit joint down from the upper bunk.

"No thanks," Davis said, holding his breath. He'd been cautious about illegal drug use. Cayman's zero-tolerance policy was medieval with long prison sentences meted out for possessing even small amounts.

"My guess is you're an American," Blackjack said, before inhaling deeply. He held his breath, exhaled and said, "We don't have power or a backup generator. The surveillance cameras are down so we might as well go on a mental holiday."

"Aren't you afraid what'll happen if you get caught smoking weed in here?"

"Nah. How do you think I got this shit? Speaking of shit," Blackjack said hopping down from the bunk. "I gotta take one. Sorry."

Davis rolled onto his side and faced the wall. The toilet/sink was located a few feet from his bunk. Whatever

Blackjack had eaten gave him an audible case of diarrhea and noxious gas strong enough to overpower the smell of marijuana.

Davis waited for Blackjack to empty his bowels, then asked, "What are you in for?"

"Corruption. You got any toilet paper?"

Davis reached under his bed and felt for his roll praying not to touch anything alive and tossed it toward the toilet.

Blackjack lit a match and inhaled another hit of pot. "I was a politician. My opponent had me arrested for bribing a public official."

"Did you?" Davis asked.

"Of course not." Blackjack flushed the commode, stepped onto Davis's mattress and hoisted himself to the upper bunk.

"How long have you been in?" Davis asked, wishing there was a window he could open.

"It's my first day here but I spent more than a year at Northwood. This is a paradise by comparison. The prison at Bodden Town's been condemned by a dozen human rights organizations. I'm here because a couple of non-violent inmates had to be moved out of Northwood to make way for the Cuban immigrants."

Before the power had gone out, Davis had seen Blackjack. He had the appearance of a seasoned politician, tall and thin with a smattering of gray hair at the temples and somehow well-groomed despite the conditions.

"Your hope is your government will get you out of here," Blackjack said. "Otherwise, you might never leave this place. After pre-trial detention they'll transfer you to Northwood. There's only been one other murder case I know of."

"What happened to him?" Davis asked, listening to the sound of something rustling under his bunk.

"He was convicted and extradited to Great Britain."

"Why?" Davis asked. "Was he British?"

"No. He was a security risk," Blackjack said. "He was part of a gang in George Town that put out a hit on the mayor. He was caught smuggling contraband into the prison. If I were you, I'd try to contact the U.S. Embassy."

"I should've before they took my passport," he said, as a deeper sense of desperation took root.

"They had to have a good reason to pull it," Blackjack said.

"Like they had to have a good reason to charge you with corruption," he countered.

"Fair point," Blackjack said.

"They matched my DNA to samples found at the business," Davis said, "but I was working there."

"Working where?"

"I was living on Little Cayman helping an older couple who owned a dive operation. When they didn't show up for work two days in a row I reported it. Somehow, that made me the suspect."

"There has to be more to the story," Blackjack said. "How did they die?"

"How would I know? There's wasn't any evidence of a crime at their place of business. The police don't have anything to go on other than they're missing and haven't used their credit cards or phones for almost two weeks. They were trying to sell the shop so they could retire and go home to England. I was working for them so I could learn the ropes."

"Why?" Blackjack asked.

"I was thinking about buying it."

"If you had the money to buy the business, why haven't you hired a lawyer?"

That was a hard question to answer. "For one," Davis said, "I wasn't given the opportunity to make a phone call. I didn't do it, so I didn't see the need to go to the embassy. As for not hiring a lawyer, I screwed my chance to do that."

"How so?" Blackjack asked, cutting a loud fart. "Sorry," he said. "It's the food."

A new odor fouled the air. "I fell for a woman who cleaned me out."

Blackjack laughed so hard he rocked the upper bunk. "You're not the first fool to fall for that. Does anyone else know you're here? Friends or family?"

"No," he said as his eyes began to play tricks in the dark. He closed them trying to remember the last time he'd eaten. He had to take a piss, but he didn't want to step barefoot onto the concrete floor.

It was quiet for a moment before the bedsprings above Davis began to creak followed by muffled grunts. Blackjack was jerking off. Davis pressed his hands over his ears trying to shut out the sounds.

Beams of light pierced the prison hallway like search-lights. Davis laid motionless on the bottom bunk as footfalls drew closer. Two guards with flashlights stopped outside their cell. A set of keys jangled, the cell door opened, and one guard entered. Davis flinched as something dropped from the upper bunk and landed on his bare belly. He swatted the mystery object away. The guard who'd entered their cell rushed toward it, shining a flashlight on the bag of weed, then straight into Davis's eyes, blinding him.

"I saw you toss that," the guard said to Davis. "Hey!" he yelled to the second guard waiting in the hallway. "I found drugs."

His partner entered and shone his flashlight at the

baggie on the floor, then opened it and sniffed. "It's marijuana."

"You," the guard holding the weed said to Davis, "on your feet."

"It's not mine," he said. "Come on, tell them!" he yelled to the upper bunk.

Blackjack was silent.

The guard who'd entered the cell first pulled a nightstick from his belt and banged it on the concrete floor. "I said, on your feet! Now!"

Davis scrambled from the bottom bunk.

"We came to tell you your meeting with your lawyer is postponed until the weather clears and the power is restored. But this changes things," the guard with the baton said, holding up the bag of weed.

37

Late Friday night the heart of Coconut Grove beat with young people milling around the bay front bars and restaurants. Cashmere stuck close to Vance's heels as he threaded his way through the crowd stopping to look at a menu posted on a café window. Appetizers started at $18 for *pomme frites,* a florid name for thin cut French fries. In the distance, sailboats bobbed in their moorings, pin lights marking the tips of their halyard masts.

After meeting Sarge at the bar, Vance was too antsy to sit around the house. The last time he'd walked Cash in the neighborhood near the condo at night, they'd been accosted by a homeless man who'd set up house on a public bench in front of the park across the street. He'd decided to take Cash for a short ride in the car instead.

"Ahhhh," a young woman wearing a short leather skirt said. "Can I pet your dog?"

"Sure," he said, kneeling on the sidewalk, reassuring Cash who at first was timid and backed away.

"He's so cute," she said, stroking his back.

Cash dropped his head and licked her hand.

"What's his name?"

"Cashmere."

"He's so soft. What kind of dog is he?"

"I'm not sure but the rescue place said he's mostly poodle."

Cash wagged his tail. He felt his phone buzz in his pocket. Sarge's name came up on CALLER ID.

"Maria's taking the girls to the matinee at eleven in the morning. Val's not going with them. I asked her to come by my house and I'd give her the money to pick out something nice for Maria for our thirtieth anniversary. I told her she should go shopping while the girls are at the movies. You know how kids are. They can't keep a secret."

"Congratulations on thirty years," he said. "What's Val's address?"

"I'll text it," Sarge said. "I don't know where Rafael is doing his rehab because I didn't have the chance to ask Val."

"No worries. We'll know soon if it matters."

"They have one of those door locks with a passcode. I'll send the combination with the address. Don't get caught. Good luck," Sarge said.

A moment later his phone chimed with the address and combination to the door lock. He dropped his phone in his pants pocket and strolled with Cash to a casual joint at the end of the block taking a seat at a small metal table beneath a yellow umbrella. Cashmere lifted his leg and peed on the table leg, then laid down under his chair.

"May I help you?" the waitress with a gold nose ring asked.

"Give me whatever beer you have on tap."

After she left the table, he called Zo.

"Can't hear you!" Zo yelled into the phone. "It's a freakin' concert for deaf seniors in diapers!"

He cupped his hand around the speaker and spoke loudly, "I'll text you."

He hung up and composed a message.

Plan to meet me tomorrow morning at 10:30 with your guy. I'll text the address later.

Zo confirmed with a thumbs-up emoji. The waitress returned holding a molasses-colored beverage with a frothy white head. He sipped the bitter beer, grimaced, and looked at the menu unaware he'd chosen a British pub. He ordered the fish and chips to go with the Guinness stout and watched a parade of luxury imports cruising the boulevard looking for places to park.

His phone rang an odd tone. His sister Kathy's face appeared on screen. Ugh. A FaceTime call. He hated those but answered it anyway.

She said, "I have a bone to pick with you—"

"About what—"

She spoke over the top of him. "Are you an international spy or what?"

"What—"

"Ethan told me you asked him to look up Russian surnames and you said he could drive your Porsche. He's not old enough—"

"But—

"Don't make promises you can't keep."

Ethan appeared on screen laughing his head off. "You fell for it, Uncle Vance," he proclaimed with glee. "Nah, nah, nah, nah, nah."

"What are you up to?" He was pissed.

"That wasn't Mom. I made the video," he said, still amused. "You got suckered."

"Let me see it again."

He waited as Ethan cued up the video and played it.

When it ended, Vance said, "You better hope your mom doesn't find out or you'll be grounded until you graduate high school."

"You're not going to tell her, are you?"

"I won't if you keep it secret."

The waitress delivered a plastic basket lined red and white checkered paper loaded with golden fried fish that shimmered under the outdoor lights.

"Talk to you later, kid," he said.

He bit a chunk of crunchy fish remembering the weird video call Lauren received when he'd dropped her at the airport. She'd told him she'd gotten multiple calls from the same number and joked it might've been a timeshare salesman. It was possible the person on the other end of the call had recorded her face and voice. Maybe the kidnappers created a deep fake video of her. Something had seemed off about it, but he'd only been able to see it once. A shiver ran down his spine.

Something else didn't make sense. She'd emailed him to tell him she had a problem with her phone. But she still hadn't answered the email he'd sent with personal questions to prove it was her. Davis Frost hadn't returned the message he'd left at the dive shop using Sarge's name and his own actual number. He reached down and offered Cashmere a bite of fish. The dog sniffed, took a bite, spit it out and coughed.

His phone pinged again.

Have you seen the weather in Cayman?

It was from Sarge. He opened the app on his phone. He'd been so disconnected from the news he hadn't heard the island was under a hurricane watch. The airport was shut down and the power was out.

He pushed his basket of food to the side and gulped the

Guinness. An AI-generated video of Lauren was an effective way to keep him engaged long enough to get him to wire the money. He scrolled through recent calls and sent a blank text to the number with the link to the banking information the kidnappers had sent to test it. A red exclamation point appeared with a Not Delivered message. He smacked the screen that was already cracked on the tabletop then waved to the server to bring the check.

He paid using a credit card, and he and Cashmere were halfway to the car when he heard someone yelling.

"Mr. Courage!"

He turned around.

"You forgot your credit card."

Under normal circumstances he would've been annoyed with himself, but his mind was elsewhere. He had a hunch Rafael Suarez's computer would provide the clues he needed to find Lauren.

38

Zo backed her truck in front of HighJinks Ink tattoo parlor to wait for Jessy to show up, flattening an empty beer can in a brown paper bag in the parking lot. Half the stores in the strip mall had rusted bars on the windows, and most didn't open until 10 a.m. except the *supermercado*; it was open twenty-four-seven. She'd been on her feet until 2 a.m. working a side hustle for the geezer band playing at the casino where she'd taken an impromptu break to meet Courage around the corner last night. She reached into the glove box for Tylenol and swallowed two pills without water before heading to the supermarket bakery for a to-go cup of *café Cubano*. The place was nearly empty, and her stomach roiled as she passed the grocery meat department. There was something about the smell of blood.

Climbing back behind the wheel, she sipped the expresso, reached into the top pocket of her shirt and removed the 9-millimeter slug, rolling the metal between her thumb and forefinger. She'd taken the liberty of digging it out of Courage's car door last night without asking when he'd gone across the street to the convenience store to buy her a soft drink. She had a buddy at the Hallandale Beach Police Department and planned to give it to him. Bullets from drive-by shootings were often matched to stolen weapons and other crimes. It was next to impossible to collect latent fingerprints on strays, but lands and groove markings—the spiral indentations carved on the metal when a bullet is discharged from the barrel of a gun—could help identify a weapon.

She checked the time on the dashboard. It was seven minutes after 10 a.m. No sign of Jessy yet, but the dude would be late to doomsday. As Zo tossed the empty coffee cup in the back seat, the neon OPEN sign inside the tattoo parlor illuminated. She got out of the F-150 and entered Jessy's shop. The turquoise walls were filled with colorful framed drawings from snakes to Jesus and everything in between.

"Change your mind and decide to let me put that pretty butterfly on your thigh?" he asked, changing the trash bag at his workstation next to a black barber style chair. He was a tall, knock-kneed guy under forty with a resemblance to a scarecrow, or maybe an axe murderer.

"Nope. Visit is more official," she said, resting her hands on her hips.

"Oh?" he said, rolling a red metal mechanics' toolbox with skinny drawers.

Jessy had been working as a confidential informant for the last two years as part of an unusual plea deal he'd cut with the Florida Attorney General's Office. He was facing ten-to-fifteen for a cyber-attack that shut down a Tampa hospital group for more than 24 hours.

The first domino had fallen when Zo busted him for a DUI which led to his arrest. The thumb drive discovered in his possession when he was booked into the Broward County Jail was turned over to the Florida Cyber Fraud Enforcement Unit. It contained sensitive financial and medical information proving Jessy was involved in the hack on the hospital chain that had been bought out by a private equity group.

He'd sworn under oath he'd broken into the hospital's network for dragging their feet on the cancer treatment his mother needed, an expensive immunotherapy drug that could arrest her Stage IV melanoma. Instead, the hospital administrators kept putting her off. It was obviously more profitable if she died, which she did. Zo had a soft spot for him. If they'd done that to her mother, she probably would've killed them.

While it was a noble cause and probably played a role in the DA's sweetheart deal, Jessy also earned the dubious distinction of being the first cybercriminal busted for operating in the same jurisdiction where the crime had been committed. That allowed the State of Florida rather than the Feds to prosecute him. As part of a bargain to avoid prison time, he ratted out his cohorts. Since then, he'd been working as a full-time tattoo artist and part-time snitch.

"I need you to be ready to go on a job with me in thirty minutes," Zo said.

"I got a full day booked with clients," he said. "No can do. Tomorrow's better."

"Tomorrow's not an option," she said.

"I don't have time to cancel my clients," he said, pulling

on a set of blue disposable gloves. "My Saturdays are booked six months out." He rearranged needles and tubes as he wiped down his work area with rubbing alcohol.

"It might smell like it, but you ain't doin' brain surgery here," she said, resting her left wrist on the butt of her Glock. "They can wait, Picasso."

"What's the gig?" he asked, removing his gloves and dropping them in the trash.

"Need you to look at a home computer. Download search history, get me the IP address. Gig pays."

"It would help if you'd narrow down the search," he said, locking the cabinets at his workstation.

"Looking for banking info. Crypto, Bitcoin, whatever you call it."

"Who's it for?"

"That's not your concern," she said. "You open your mouth about this, and I'll tell the DA I caught you smokin' weed, and you know your skinny ass'll flunk a piss test. Place is over in The Gables. Cover up them tattoos and dress like one of them geeks from the computer stores 'cause I don't want you drawin' attention. You got time to go to the Walmart and get some low-key clothes. I'll text you the address. There's a public park 'round the block where we're supposed to meet. We're doin' a sneak and peek."

A sneak and peek was code for a secret law enforcement search warrant, but Zo left the part out about not having one.

"If we're breaking and entering who cares what I'm wearing?"

"I told you already. It's in a fancy 'hood. Grab what you need."

"All I need is my brain and my fingers. How long is this

going to take?" He reached under the reception desk and set a plastic WILL RETURN sign on the countertop.

"We gotta be out by 11:30."

"If you get me the IP address, I won't have to go in the house." He turned the red plastic hands on the flat clock sign to 12 noon.

"Make it one o'clock," Zo said.

"I hope this gig pays enough to cover lost business. Have you been to the grocery store lately?"

"Yeah, Edward Snowden, I got more mouths to feed than you do. You do me a solid on this and it'll be a nice payday for you, but I ain't givin' you a penny til it's done."

Zo left while Jessy hung the WILL RETURN sign in the window.

39

Vance took a left into a gas station and parked the Audi next to a drive-through car wash. He was ten minutes away from Val's place prepping to do a quick recon run when he decided to touch base with Zo.

"Where are you?"

"Me and my guy are on the way," she said.

After he hesitated, Zo said, "We still goin' in or are you pullin' the plug? You pull the ripcord, and you still payin' me you know."

He'd sent Zo the address for Majorca Park, not the Suarez residence, as the meet location. "What's your ETA?" he asked.

"We're stuck in some bullshit weekend construction traffic but we doin' good to get there on time."

"Park near the playground."

"You goin' in with us?"

"No," he said, as a wet VW exited the car wash tunnel. "I'll see you at the park."

"If this shit goes sideways, I'm takin' you down with me,"

Zo said. "You stiff me on my smack and I'm takin' you down another way."

"That's the deal." He put the Audi in drive and waited for a break in traffic on Coral Way. It was the second time this morning he'd agreed to go down with the ship.

He slowed at Alhambra Circle, double checked GPS, then took a right-hand turn, cruising past the Suarez residence. A red Range Rover like the one he'd seen leaving Sarge's place the night of the shooting was parked in the driveway. He drove around the block and stopped catty corner from the house where he could keep watch. He glanced at the rearview as a neighborhood patrol car slowed, then parked on his back bumper. The officer got out and approached.

He rolled down his window.

"How are you doing today?" the young officer in a well-fitting uniform asked.

He was a rent-a-cop working for the community, and he was observant. "Is something wrong?" he asked.

"No. Just patrolling the neighborhood and I didn't recognize your vehicle."

"I don't live around here," he said, reading D. Munoz's name tag on his uniform.

Munoz leaned over and surveyed the interior of the Audi. "Are you visiting someone?"

"I'm waiting for Mrs. Suarez to leave the house. She lives a few doors up the street and it's her birthday. Her sister's planning a surprise party. I'm meeting a couple of people who are helping to get things going."

"Well, then," Munoz said, "I'll keep an eye out for you. I wouldn't want to spoil a surprise."

He waited for Munoz to go, then searched *'party supplies'* on his phone.

. . .

THE DOLLAR STORE parking lot five minutes away was busy on Saturday morning and the line to the cash register was long. Vance grabbed a bouquet of inflated Happy Birthday balloons and waited in the checkout line, paying cash, then grappling with the shiny Mylars as he hurried to the Audi. He checked the time. Just after 11:00 a.m.

He texted Sarge:

Need an update.

His phone pinged:

Dropped them off myself. Val's going shopping. Picking wife and grandkids up from movies at 12:45. I read the document. Can't figure it out.

He dictated the next message into his phone. '*What do you mean*?' then he pressed the send key.

Sarge pinged back:

Didn't make sense. Don't know enough about Cuba to figure out the locations or targets. Names and places I never heard of.

He dictated another message. '*Did you see anything about Monkey Morales in the docs?*'

Ping:

Yeah. Let's save it for in-person. Btw. Val's dog should be friendly.

Dog? *Should be friendly*? He didn't remember anything about a dog. He ran back into the Dollar Store and bought a pack of bacon-flavored treats. Relying on the side mirrors and backup camera, he reactivated GPS on his phone and followed directions to Suarez's place. Val's red Range Rover was gone from the driveway and there was no sign of Munoz. He continued past the house looking like a clown with a car full of birthday balloons and headed to the public park to meet Zo.

40

The wind howled and the surf pounded, and what was paradise yesterday had turned mean and ugly. Lauren had barely slept, finally dozing off around daybreak when the black sky brightened to a medium gray. She had no idea what time it was. She looked out the window to see if Arthur had returned. His car was gone, and the step-up tide had risen to cover the road. She dressed, turned on the faucet in the bathroom and let the water run while she stared at herself in the mirror.

Good grief, she looked like hell with bags beneath both bloodshot eyes. She splashed cool water on her face and ran her fingers through her hair. A rattling started behind the wall and steadily got louder. The room vibrated to the banging of water pipes. Ugh. The tap ran dry. No water and no power. She shut off the faucet, plucked a tissue from the Kleenex box, and wiped her teeth.

A car horn blared from somewhere outside the duplex. She rushed to see who it was. A dark green Cadillac Escalade had stopped in the driveway in the half foot of salt-water covering the road. A woman holding an umbrella struggled to get out of the vehicle in the wind creating a Stephen King version of Mary Poppins. Margaret Terry fought to hold onto an umbrella as she waddled through the water wearing black rubber boots.

"I can't climb the stairs," Margaret hollered up to her, standing with legs splayed and her arms out to her sides like the Michelin Man —if he was a woman — being buffeted by 50-mile-an-hour gusts. "I've been trying to reach you by phone. I called Arthur and asked him to knock on your door. He's working at the airport and said you haven't been answering his messages. I came by to see if you're doing okay."

Lauren rolled up her pant legs and hurried down the stairs barefoot using one hand to hold the railing and the other to wipe her hair from her eyes. "Thank God you're here," she said. "There's no power and no running water."

"I know," Margaret said. "The entire island is impacted. I wanted to tell you the jail is closed. I can't get in to see Davis Frost and I don't know when I'll be able to." She duck-walked to the vehicle and opened the driver's side door. "Go on," she said, "get in."

Lauren climbed into the passenger side.

Margaret flicked on the windshield wipers. "The storm is stalled over open water about two hundred miles offshore and it's gaining strength. The rain is about to get worse." She glanced over at her. "Goodness. You're barefoot."

"I only have one pair of shoes," she said. "The battery on my phone died and I thought Arthur would be back by now."

"Arthur figured that's what happened. I can't in good conscience leave you here," Margaret said, as another rogue wave rolled in and swashed under the car. "The tide is rising fast. Hurry and go get your things."

"Where are we going?"

"Don't worry about that. Just go!"

Lauren sloshed through the water and raced up the stairs. She grabbed her purse, phone and shoes and sprinted back to the vehicle plowing through saltwater, almost losing her balance twice.

Margaret turned the Cadillac around and hovered over the dashboard, her large breasts pressing the steering wheel like deployed airbags as she squinted to see through the torrents of rain.

"This place is a ghost town," Margaret said, wet hair dripping.

"Can you drop me at a hotel?" Lauren asked.

"I doubt you'll be able to find a room," she said. "Arthur mentioned you left your suitcase at the hotel where you were staying. We should try and get it. Otherwise, you're going to have a hard time finding anything. The stores are sold out of most everything. We're running out of time and need to get to higher ground."

Shit. She'd forgotten to get the rest of the money she'd hidden under the mattress. "I forgot something. I need to go back."

"Is it life or death?" Margaret asked.

"Kind of."

"Good grief," she said. The back window of the car was fogged up. Margaret's eyes were glued to the car's side mirrors as she slowly backed the Caddy beneath the house. The water had risen to almost a foot above the base of the pilings holding the duplex. "Hurry up."

Lauren hopped out barefoot into ankle-high saltwater and headed to the house. Before she got to the stairs, she felt a terrible pain. "Awww! Awww! Awww!" She danced in place with her skin on fire as if she'd stepped onto a red anthill. She looked down but didn't see anything as the water from the last wave receded. Then she saw at least a dozen jellyfish.

Margaret slumped across the center console and pushed open the passenger door. "Get back in the car!"

Lauren climbed in and planted one ankle on the car seat, wincing.

Margaret said, "I'm afraid you've been stung by a jellyfish. If you touch it, you'll make it worse."

"Oh my God! What should I do?"

"Hold tight," Margaret said, as the sky opened, and ferocious winds growled, and gusts blew sheets of rain beneath the house in waves that splashed the windshield. Margaret reached over and opened the glove box, rifling inside and knocking half the contents out, before grabbing a small bottle of yellow liquid. "It's the best I can do. Splash this on your leg but don't scratch it or I promise you'll make it worse."

Lauren cracked open the bottle and doused her feet and ankles.

Margaret restarted the windshield wipers and put the Cadillac in drive. "It's going to hurt like hell before it hurts less."

"Oh my God! Awwwwww! What is this?"

"It's mouthwash," Margaret said, pulling onto the highway in near zero-visibility conditions. The Caddy rocked in the rain. "You're lucky you're on land. Lots of people who've gotten stung in the water go into shock and drown."

Death didn't sound that bad. The pain was excruciating, and the Listerine didn't do much to lessen it.

"Vinegar and heat are the best remedies, but I had to improvise."

Lauren wrapped both hands around her ankle and squeezed as hard as she could. It hurt like shit and her ankle had swollen where the tentacle had touched her skin. *Awww.*

"You can stay at our place," Margaret said. "We have plenty of room and a backup generator for the whole house."

"Are you sure?" she asked, gritting her teeth wondering how long the burning sensation would last.

"Of course," Margaret said creeping along the centerline of the road in blinding rain. "I'll tell my husband you're my client and you've been stranded. He'll understand."

"What time is it?"

"I can't look right now," Margaret said. "There's a clock on the dash."

Good, God. It was after 11 in the morning. She reopened the bottle of mouthwash and dabbed more on the wound. When she set it down, she saw a phone charger hanging between the seats on her side.

"Do you mind if I use your charger?" she asked loudly over the noise of the storm.

"Go for it!" Margaret said.

She plugged in the burner. Several text messages bubbled up and all were from Arthur, but they were old and there were zero bars on her phone. She'd been in hurricanes before, but she'd never attempted to drive this close to shoreline when storm conditions worsened. The car shook like a mechanical bull and blowing rain pounded the windows of the Caddy in waves. Somehow Margaret kept the car on the road.

A fallen tree appeared blocking the route. Margaret slammed the brake pedal, and the Caddie shimmied as the ABS brakes kicked in. Lauren white-knuckled the door handle barely aware of the pain from the burn from the jellyfish as the lawyer backed up and cut through a yard.

What she didn't know was Margaret Terry used her maiden name. Mr. Green at the bank had given her Sheldon Green's contact information to get a criminal defense lawyer for Davis. When she'd contacted Sheldon, he'd disclosed that he was related to one of the three defense attorneys he'd referred her to. Sheldon's last name was Green. It occurred to her there was a one in three chance it was Margaret, but it never crossed her mind that Sheldon Green was married to her.

She'd made her decision before discovering Margaret was second cousin to Arthur McDonald, a special investigator in the RCIPS Financial Crimes Unit in Grand Cayman. Lauren had thirty million dollars hidden in Margaret's brother-in-law's bank.

41

The recent rains had turned the manicured grass at Majorca Park almost chartreuse, and the lush tropical landscaping every other shade of green. Vance parked the filthy Audi near the giant cypress stump in front of the tiny playground. Designed equally for dogs and children, there were no pets, parents, nor kids today. He got out and strolled the sidewalk waiting for Zo.

"What-up with that?" Zo said, peering into the back window of the Audi filled with balloons.

"The community has a sharp neighborhood cop. I told him I'm organizing a surprise birthday party for the wife. Where's your guy?"

"He'll be here."

They heard Jessy before they saw him.

"What the hell?" Zo said, as a space-age three-wheel fireball-orange trike stopped behind her truck.

The rider removed his helmet. The smell of marijuana wafted from him.

"I told you to tone it down," Zo said, skipping the introductions. "You ain't ridin' that thing. You're goin' with me."

"I'll lead the way," Vance said. Zo pulled out behind him and followed a few car lengths back.

Five minutes later he turned onto Alhambra Circle, slowed, stopped and rolled down his passenger window. Zo pulled up alongside. "I'll park here," he said. "You go ahead. It's the big white house with the red clay roof on the right. Go to the end of the block and park on the side street."

As Zo continued driving past the Suarez residence, he planted a ball cap on his head and waited. When he saw Jessy and Zo turn the corner on foot heading toward the house, he grabbed the bouquet of Happy Birthday balloons.

His phone chimed with a text from Zo.

Doorbell camera.

He stepped back, unsure if he was in the line of sight. The camera was attached to the front door. He crossed the street with the balloons to meet up with Zo and Jessy.

"What's the plan?" Zo asked.

"The camera is on an unsecured wireless network," Jessy said, working the keys on his phone.

"Meaning what?" he asked.

"I might be able to bypass it. Give me a sec."

He studied the perimeter while Jessy typed on the keypad.

"Doorbell cameras come with factory settings," Jessy said. "I'm checking to see if they changed the login and password."

A car approached and a little girl hung her head out the car window. "Happy Birthday!" she yelled. He turned his back and waved to her over his shoulder.

"Good news," Jessy said. "The one on the wireless belongs to a different house. The doorbell camera at the target house is offline."

"You're sure?" he asked.

"I'm positive. It's a scarecrow," Jessy said.

He opened his phone to retrieve the message Sarge had sent with the combination to the door lock.

"Thought you weren't comin' with us," Zo said.

"I changed my mind." He headed up the walkway, looking over both shoulders as he approached the front door. He tapped the first number on the keypad. A dog barked on the other side of the door. "They have a dog," he said.

"I don't do dogs," Zo said.

"I got this," he said, while Jessy kept watch on the street.

Zo reached into her pocket and pulled a can of pepper spray.

"No," he said, shoving the balloons at her. "Take these."

The scent of Cashmere would calm Val's dog. He entered the full set of numbers into the pad and the pin light blinked green. As he cracked the door open, the dog growled. "Hey there," he said softly.

Zo pointed the can of pepper spray at the dog's snout.

"No," he said, taking it from her and reaching into his pocket for a treat. He held the door open a couple of inches, enough for the dog to smell and take the treat. He edged the door open another couple of inches and a long, black nose poked out.

"Nuh uh," Zo said.

"Animals can sense fear," he said to Zo, holding out another cookie; the dog took it. Offering his hand, the dog sniffed, then licked it. He opened the door wider, bracing it with his knee, reaching in and gently grabbing the animal's collar. The dog was excited but not aggressive. Jessy entered first and then disappeared down the hall. As Zo passed, the dog growled at her.

Jessy hurried back. "They have a home office." He held

up a blue thumb drive he'd brought with him. "Give me five minutes."

"Hurry," he said to Jessy, then turned to Zo who'd set the balloons on the hall table near the front door. She glared at the animal. "You keep an eye from inside the house while I take the dog out."

He grabbed the leash hanging next to the door, knelt and was about to clip it to the dog's collar when the animal broke away and bolted out the front door.

"Crap!"

He pushed Zo out of the way, sprinting out to catch the dog.

A car passed and the driver stared at him. He was almost to the end of the block when he saw a red Range Rover. His heart thumped under his shirt. The car didn't slow, rather it continued to the next block, rolled through the stop sign, and disappeared.

As he caught up to the dog, the black Lab lifted its leg and urinated on a trash can on the street. He approached slowly with another handful of bacon-flavored treats.

"Here boy," he said, taking one step, then another. The dog stopped running and he waited, offering more cookies, holding his hand out. As the dog took the bait, he snapped the leash to the leather collar. The green metal tag had the dog's name. "Good boy, Ebony," he said, scratching his ears. "What were you doing running out the door like that?"

A bombed-out economy car turned the corner. The driver stopped, got out and dropped a large box in front of a neighbor's front door, took a picture then hurried and drove off. As he passed the house across from Suarez, he saw a doorbell camera with a ring of blue light flashing.

A white SUV with Georgia plates approached from the opposite direction. It was too far away to see the person behind the wheel. The car slowed, activated the turn indicator, then turned into the driveway of the Suarez home. A woman got out carrying a bag of groceries. He pulled his phone from his pocket and called Zo.

No answer.

He texted quickly.

Get out now.

A DELIVERED message appeared below the message on the screen, but Zo didn't answer.

The woman in a sundress and heels stood on the stoop and peered into the open door, then pushed it all the way open.

42

"Are you sure your husband won't mind if I stay?" Lauren asked. "I feel like I'm intruding."

Margaret cut the wheel on the Escalade in a serpentine around storm debris scattered along the road. The driveway led to a sprawling colonial-style estate with white columns barely visible in the torrential rain. Margaret pressed the garage door opener revealing an exotic vehicle parked on the far side of the four-car garage. "Have you met my husband?" Margaret asked.

"No," she said, wondering how Margaret thought they would've met.

Rain poured from the rooftop of the garage like a waterfall, splashing the windshield as Margaret pulled inside and cut the ignition.

"If you'd met him, you'd know he wouldn't mind," the lawyer said.

"What do you mean?"

"Let me put it this way," Margaret said. "If my last name wasn't Terry he wouldn't have married me."

"I still don't understand," she said.

"Have you ever heard a man claim he married a woman because he liked her family?"

Lauren thought about it for a moment. "No."

"Honey, it's code for he likes her family's money or influence. Oh," Margaret said, "don't look at me that way. I knew what I was signing up for."

To Lauren, it was a form of settling. On the other hand, men did it all the time; it was reverse trophy-wife syndrome.

"Are you married?" Margaret asked, opening the car door and shaking the wet umbrella.

"No."

"Pretty gazelle like you should be. Have you ever been?"

Pretty gazelle? "A couple of times."

Margaret slapped the steering wheel. "Well good for you and I hope at least one of them had some money. My husband is a divorce lawyer and I put him through law school. I had to make a working man out of him, but I made him sign a prenup all the same. Let's go in and get you cleaned up. Do you like tea?"

"Sure," she said fighting the urge to dig her fingernails into the wound from the jellyfish.

"I've got something a little stronger if you want."

"No, tea is fine," she said, gathering her things from the vehicle. She followed Margaret into the house through the side door. It opened to a laundry room where Margaret leaned against the wall for balance as she kicked off her rain boots and slipped on a pair of clogs.

Lauren's heart thumped. The suitcase next to the cat dishes looked like hers.

"That's your bag," Margaret said, waddling toward the kitchen, her wide hips see-sawing. "Arthur told me where you left it and I had someone from the office go pick it up for you. Did you know you owed money for one night?"

"I did?"

Margaret filled an old-fashioned copper kettle with water from the refrigerator dispenser and turned on the gas stove. It was quiet inside the house, almost as if the storm had passed.

"I paid it for you. The receipt is over there." She pointed to a pie crust table, the type that folded in half, pushed up against a wall in the dining room. "You owed for two nights actually, which I find odd since you told Arthur you were escaping your abusive boyfriend." Margaret glanced over at her. "Unless, of course, Davis Frost is your boyfriend."

"No, no, he's not," she said, taking enough cash from her purse to reimburse Margaret for the hotel expenses and setting it atop the receipt.

"It's none of my business," Margaret said, "but while it's fresh in your mind, if there's anything you can tell me that might help exonerate your friend, I suggest you write it down while you're here. I have reason to believe Davis Frost occupied the other room you put on your credit card before it was declined," Margaret said.

Her attention turned toward the grand staircase right out of *Gone With the Wind*. A swashbuckler with a pencil thin mustache and slick dark hair descended and entered the kitchen. He kissed Margaret on the cheek, while eying Lauren from head to toe.

"Lauren, I'd like you to meet my husband, Sheldon. Lauren is the one who called you for a referral about the double-murder over on Little Cayman."

"Right," Sheldon said. "Hi."

Lauren opened her mouth to speak, but no words would form in her brain.

"Lauren was staying at Arthur's rental over on Seven Mile Beach," Margaret said. "The power is out and there's no running water so I told her she can stay with us until she can make other arrangements."

A low hum buzzed in her brain, like static.

"You're lucky you chose Meg," Sheldon said. "I don't think any of the other referrals I gave you would have rescued you from the storm."

"That's not the reason she picked me," Margaret said, hitting back at him.

"Of course not," he said, giving his wife an atta-girl side hug across the shoulder. "Meg's one of the top defense attorneys in the country."

"I appreciate the hospitality," she said, finally able to complete a short sentence. "You're Sheldon Green?"

"Indeed. My brother referred you."

Margaret took her phone from her purse and typed while she spoke. "I just messaged Arthur to let him know you left something at the duplex."

The words faded into background noise and another wave of adrenaline raced through her body.

When her attention returned, she saw Margaret standing on tiptoes trying to open a cabinet above the sink. She reached for something but couldn't.

"Let me get that," Sheldon said. "What are you looking for?"

"A dishtowel."

Margaret poured hot water from the teapot onto the towel. "Put this on the wound," she said, then turned to her husband. "The jellyfish that stung her was right in the middle of the road."

"Ouch," Sheldon said. He took the linen towel from his wife, pulled a wooden barstool from the kitchen island and gestured. "Sit."

Lauren sat, crossing her injured foot on the opposite

knee. Sheldon laid the hot towel across the wound, reacti-
vating the pain.

Awwww.

"Would you like cream or sugar?" Margaret asked her,
holding a floral teacup with a thin gold handle.

She gritted her teeth from the pain.

Margaret asked again. "Your tea. Would you like sugar?
We have milk and cream."

"No, black is fine," she said, taking the cup from
Margaret as she set the matching tea set on the island
countertop.

Sheldon left the room for a moment and returned with a
crystal decanter and pulled the glass stopper. "How about a
splash of brandy?"

"No, but thanks," she said, sipping the hot tea.

"I could use a shot," he said, pouring one for himself and
throwing it down his throat.

"Hand me that towel," Margaret said to her.

She gently removed it from her ankle. Margaret
squeezed it over the sink and freshened it with more hot
water. Arthur took it from his wife.

"I'll take that," Lauren said, preempting him, draping the
hot compress over the red welts resembling a lightning bolt.

"Those lines are where the tentacles touched your skin,"
he said, inching closer to her.

"Do you have cell service or internet?" she asked,
changing the subject.

"We have a dedicated satellite connection that should be
up and running in the storm. At least that's what they told
us when they installed it." Sheldon took his phone from his
pocket and checked.

An uncomfortable feeling began to eclipse the pain and
fatigue. It was Sheldon. He gave her the creeps. "It's so quiet

in here," she said, sipping her tea. "I can barely hear the wind or rain."

"The hurricane shutters are closed, and the windows are bulletproof glass designed to take a direct hit from anything a Category Five storm can throw at us." He paused, then added. "The house is one of the first ever build on the island and it's on the highest ground."

"This home has been in my family for over a hundred and fifty years," Margaret said. "How's the ankle?"

"Better. Thanks."

"I'll be right back," Margaret said.

MARGARET RETURNED with what she thought was an expensive bottle of liqueur. "Here," Margaret said, handing her a cotton ball with the dark liquid on it. "Put this on the bite."

"What is it?"

"Fourteen-year-old vinegar from Modena. White vinegar works but it's all we have."

She swabbed the bite. It burned at first, then the stinging subsided.

"Good news," Sheldon said. "The satellite is connected." He opened a kitchen drawer and removed a pen and paper. "Here's the guest password."

It meant she could finish the email to Vance. "Do you mind if I charge my phone?" She'd connected it to Margaret's car charger, but it had barely any power now.

"Not at all," Sheldon said, grabbing her purse without asking. He set it on the counter near where she sat. "My brother said you're a client at his bank. Did you know Margaret's family owns it?"

She wondered what else Mr. Green the banker had

mentioned to his brother. Her fingers trembled on the teacup.

"Sheldon," Margaret scolded, "don't discuss money." She turned to Lauren. "You must forgive his manners."

Oh no! The teacup slipped from her fingers and hot tea splashed her clothes as the delicate china shattered on the marble floor. "I'm so sorry," she said.

Shelden leaned toward her. "Let me help you," he said.

Wow. Margaret's family owned the bank and her brother-in-law works there.

43

"Where're we going?" Davis asked, handcuffed, sitting cross-legged on the floor of the panel van, the tight jumpsuit wedging farther up the crack in his ass over every bump in the road.

The redheaded driver dressed in a guard uniform didn't answer. His partner, another corrections officer Davis had never seen before either, sat quietly in the passenger seat. The sky was dark gray, and rain pummeled the windshield as the one driving sawed the wheel avoiding tree branches in the road. A bolt of lightning lit the clouds followed by the rumble of thunder.

This was the first time Davis had been able to see outside four walls since he'd been arrested at the hotel yesterday.

Yesterday.

It seemed like weeks had passed.

"The marijuana wasn't mine."

"Yeah, right," the guard in the passenger seat said.

These were two different guys than the ones who'd discovered the bag of weed Blackjack had tossed.

"You can give me a drug test and I can prove it wasn't mine."

"It might prove you didn't smoke it, but it won't prove it wasn't yours," the driver said. "You should shut up."

"I will if you tell me where you're taking me."

"You don't get a say in this," the redhead driving said.

The shocks on the van groaned every time they hit a pothole.

"Are you taking me to Bodden Town?"

There was no response. Fear struck like a knife. Blackjack had told him about the prison at Northwood. *That fucker*. It was his weed and he let him take the fall for it. The wind whipped the sides of the van and rain pounded the roof. Wipers slapped the windshield, unable to keep up with the rain. The inside of the van felt like a greenhouse in summer and the guard riding shotgun wiped the fog from the glass with his sleeve. In the distance, red and blue lights flickered against the blurry windshield. The driver pulled up to the scene and stopped. Emergency vehicles blocked the road going both directions. A cop in yellow rain gear approached. The driver rolled the window down a few inches and Davis struggled to listen in.

"The power lines are down."

"We're transporting a prisoner from HMP Fairbanks to Northwood," the guard said.

"Sorry, but the road is closed," the cop said. "It's impassable from here. High water."

The driver rolled up his window and turned around in his seat. His eyes were slits, like a snake. "It's your lucky day," he said to Davis.

A radio crackled up front, but Davis couldn't make out the words. The guard riding shotgun held the radio to his ear, then answered the call. "10-4. We have the prisoner." He leaned across the center console and whispered to the driver, so Davis couldn't hear. The guard behind the wheel made eye contact with him in the rearview mirror.

"What's going on?" Davis asked, streams of sweat dripping down his face.

"Shut up back there," the driver said.

"That wasn't my weed. I know the laws here, and I know what happens. I'm not stupid. If I had a lawyer, he'd demand you give me a drug test."

The snake behind the wheel did a tight three-point turn in torrential rain, avoiding tree limbs in the road. He pointed the van in the direction they'd come and stomped the gas. Davis fell backward in a half-somersault, handcuffs digging into his tailbone before hitting his head on the metal flooring—

He blacked out.

"You got a lawyer, fatso," the driver with lizard eyes said, "and I hope you got a good one because they found the bodies."

But Davis didn't hear him because he was unconscious.

44

V ance looked both ways and when the street was clear of traffic, he released the dog. "Go, go, go," he said, as Ebony galloped home, startling the woman standing on the porch in front of the Suarez residence.

He tossed the leash over the fence into a neighbor's yard and checked his phone. No response from Zo. He texted her again.

Get out now.

Ebony ran circles on the walkway in front of Val's house before darting from the woman, and back toward him. He pulled the brim of the ball cap down as the woman chased the dog in high heels. "Ebony! Come back here!"

He walked toward the side street with his phone in his hand hoping not to be seen but it was too late. The dog arrived first, then the woman. Ebony sniffed the treats in his pocket.

"Dumb dog seems to like you," she said, holding her shoes. The stem of one heel was broken off.

"Babies and dogs always know," he said.

"Know what?" she asked, looking at him strangely. She grabbed the dog by the collar and began to pull. Ebony squatted and growled at her.

"Let me help," he said, gently taking ahold of the collar, and taking a sly picture of the woman's face. He released his grip on the collar and took a step forward testing the animal. Ebony followed him. "Is he your dog?"

"No, I mean yes. He's my sister's dog. I can't imagine how he got out."

"He's probably scared is all. I'll walk you home if you like."

She debated the offer silently, then shrugged. "Why not."

She led the way walking on the balls of her feet, carrying her broken shoes.

When they reached the driveway, he turned to leave but the dog followed him. He walked halfway to the stoop. The front door was ajar; the bouquet of balloons flew above the credenza.

He tilted his chin toward the house. The woman looked inside the entryway, then back at him with a puzzled look on her face. Ebony panted with his long pink tongue dangling from one side of his mouth before trotting into the air conditioning.

"Thank you," she said, turning her back to him, grabbing the bag of groceries before disappearing inside the house.

"You're welcome," he said under his breath, noticing Georgia license plates on the white SUV.

He checked his phone. No response from Zo. He walked slowly toward the sidewalk, listening. Nothing —

Zo and Jessy turned the corner on foot. Fighting the urge to run, he strolled to meet them.

"Jesus, that was a close call," Zo said.

"I thought you said we had a half hour?" Jessy wiped his forehead with the back of his sleeve.

"Did you get what we need?" he asked.

"I'm not sure," Jessy said. "I was in the middle of cloning the hard drive when we had to abort."

"Who the hell was that?" Zo asked.

"Sarge's daughter."

"I thought you said she'd be gone," Zo said, pissed off.

"He's got two," he said. "Do you know if she saw you in the house?"

"Don't know but you payin' me either way."

45

Jets of hot water shot from the spigots on the shower walls pummeling relief into Lauren's back and shoulders. She squatted, stretching her legs, then stood and tilted her head beneath the water rinsing the shampoo from her hair. It was weird that Margaret's husband hadn't accompanied her to the duplex, letting his wife brave the storm conditions alone. But intimate relationships were like black boxes and wormholes. Most were mysteries, and once inside it was hard to get out.

She stepped out of the shower and wrapped herself in a plush bath towel, pulled another from the rack and blotted the water from her hair. She opened the Ziplock bag with the travel items she'd brought on the trip, squeezed a dollop of moisturizer on her hands and massaged her face. She turned on the overhead fan to dry the mist from the mirrors.

Everything was surreal. The imprint of the jellyfish tentacles on her ankle had turned magenta, and the burning sensation returned. Running hot water in the sink, she made a compress out of a washcloth. Lowering the toilet seat, she laid the cloth over her ankle, reached across the vanity, took her phone off charge then opened her email and checked the draft folder. A copy of the message she'd written to Vance during the power outage at the duplex wasn't there. Ugh. She reopened the one she'd received from him two days ago and composed a new response with answers to his questions. Mindful her email might not be private on the Green-Terry satellite network, she crafted a concise missive revealing minimal information.

Hi, Sorry for the delay. I'm sure you've heard about the storm in Cayman. The island is out of power and I finally was able to charge my new phone. I remember when we met you had a Nissan Cube you dubbed Edgar from Men in Black. How's Cashmere? I miss you both. Give Cash a kiss from me. Here's my new number. Please call ASAP. I can explain more on the phone. It's a long story but I've met a very nice couple who are allowing me to stay in their home. Miss you, XO, LG

She copied and pasted the burner phone number into the email, then pushed the send button.

Placing the phone back on charge, she opened the cabinets looking for a hair dryer. Plugging it in, she turned her head upside down and ran her fingers through her hair, fluffing it with hot air while her mind drifted to Davis stuck in a jail cell. Maybe Margaret could make a call and get word to him that he had a lawyer and to sit tight until the storm passed. She hung the towels on the hook and opened the door leading to the guest bedroom where she'd left her suitcase. A spike of bad chemistry coursed her veins and her face burned red. She froze, unable to speak —

Sheldon sat on the edge of the bed gazing at her nude body.

"What are you doing in here?" she gasped, covering herself with her hands and rushing back into the bathroom. She slammed the door, grabbed a bath towel and stood in front of the mirror, heart pounding. What the hell was wrong with him? He'd sat there as if nothing had happened. She put her ear against the door, listening, thinking he would leave. But all she heard was the ambient hum of the air conditioning and the whir of the bathroom fan.

She opened the bedroom door an inch and peeked out. Sheldon was still sitting there staring at his phone. She tightened the bath towel around her chest and stuck her head out.

"Excuse me. What are you doing in here?"

"I wanted to talk to you," he said.

"About what?"

His legs were crossed, and he placed his hands behind his back, palms planted on the comforter as if he were hanging out with an old friend.

"Don't make such a big deal about it. I saw you nude. So what?"

"So what. So what!"

"What are you going to do? Tell my wife?"

If she could've gouged his eyes out, she would've. "What do you want to talk about?"

"Who are you?" he asked, narrowing his eyes.

What kind of question was that? "Will you please leave so I can get dressed. I'd be happy to answer any questions you have with Margaret present," she said, faking civility.

He shifted position, covering his groin with one hand. "My brother only handles high net worth clients. I googled you and there's nothing other than an address for an older condo in Miami and a video production website with your picture. You're not wearing a wedding ring and you paid quite a bit of cash to my wife to represent your friend."

"I'm not having this conversation," she said from the

small gap in the doorway to the bathroom. *Geez, what a two-timing gold digger*.

"My wife and I have an open relationship," Sheldon said. "She must've told you. I assumed that was the reason she brought you here." He placed both hands over his crotch.

"Knock, knock."

Sheldon leaped to his feet.

Margaret let herself in. "What on earth are you doing in here?" she said to him, then turned toward Lauren.

She braced herself for what would come next.

"Sheldon, you leave this room now," Margaret said. "I'm so sorry," Margaret said to her.

When they were alone, Lauren spoke first. "Is it true?"

"Is what true?"

"Your husband says you have an open relationship and that's why you—"

"In his dreams," Margaret said matter-of-factly. "I came to talk to you about your friend. I called the jail at Fairbanks where Davis is being held for pretrial detention and he isn't there. I asked why and found out he was caught in possession of illegal drugs. They were transporting him to North-wood HMP on the other side of the island—"

"Northwood?"

"It's a more secure facility."

"In this storm?" she asked, still wrapped in a towel.

"Yes. The road was closed, and they had to return to Fairbanks when he had some kind of accident and hit his head."

"Oh my God. Is he alright?"

"He's fine. It's a bump is all. They treated him at the infirmary. He's adamant the drugs aren't his and belonged to his bunkie. I've ordered a drug test."

Davis wasn't that reckless. If he'd had illegal drugs on

him when he was arrested, they would have discovered them when he was searched before being locked up.

"I've requested both he and his cellmate be tested for marijuana."

"How long will that take?"

"There are test kits at the jail, but the power is out, and the backup generator is out of commission so I'm not sure." Margaret walked closer to the bed and pressed her hand on the comforter, straightening the dip where her husband had been sitting. "Anyway, get dressed. You must be hungry."

Margaret turned to leave, then paused. "I almost forgot. The internet is down. Apparently, the satellite we paid a bundle for couldn't handle the wind and rain after all. We're going to have to sit tight and wait to see what happens."

When Lauren was alone, she checked her email. The new one she'd sent to Vance was unsent.

fter the close call at the Suarez residence, they'd agreed to split up and meet back at the public park to regroup. Vance was first to arrive, passing Jessy's orange trike where he'd left it and stopping the Audi in front of the yellow slide near the playground. Waiting for Zo and Jessy to catch up, he selected the blurry photo he'd secretly taken of the woman with the broken high heel and texted it to Sarge.

Sarge pinged instantly:

Where did u get that?

He skipped the where-question and went to who:

Do you know her?

It's my daughter Gloria.

His phone rang.

"How did you get that?" Sarge asked, on edge.

"She came back to the house while we were there." He shared what had happened with the dog. "Don't worry. She didn't see me take the picture and she doesn't know who I am. She thinks I'm some guy her dog likes more than her."

"Her sister Val's dog," Sarge corrected. "You're positive she doesn't know anyone was in the house?"

"I don't think so," he said, leaving out the part about the birthday balloons Zo had left behind.

"She's not an idiot," Sarge said.

He gave him a moment to cool off, then waited, letting Sarge control the convo.

"I guess if she thought someone was in the house, she would've called me by now." Sarge took a two-beat. "While I was alone, I read through the document again. It sounds nuts but I think it's a coordinated plan to destabilize the Cuban government."

"How?" he asked.

"Using tactics for a color revolution."

A color revolution was a term for regime change designed to topple an existing government using propaganda, rigged elections, youth protests and other covert means to spread chaos, and ultimately a coup. The CIA had been doing it for decades all around the world. "Any idea why it was in your son-in-law's safe?"

"No clue, and I don't want anything to do with it. People who get involved in this kind of shit wake up dead one day," Sarge said.

"Is there any mention of Monkey Morales?"

"Not by name, but no one is. There are code words and I think they're cover for people and locations."

He saw Zo in his side mirror as she rolled up behind him and parked.

"I've held up my end of the bargain helping you get in the house. I'm done now," Sarge said.

"I don't know what they found on his computer yet. I'll keep you posted," he said, killing the call and getting out of the Audi.

Jessy hopped out of the truck and held up the blue flash drive. "I'm going to my shop to look at the files,"

"Shop?" he asked.

"He's a tattoo artist," Zo said, looking over her shoulder. "I'm goin'. Join us if you want."

"What's the name of it?" he asked.

"HighJinks Ink. High is spelled with a G-H," Jessy said.

"We need to leave at different times and use different routes to make sure we're not being followed," he said.

"You're gettin' paranoid in your old age," Zo said.

"I'll meet you both there," he said.

Jessy left first on his rumbling three-wheeler. To kill some time, he walked around the block, working up a sweat in the sweltering midday heat. About seven minutes later he got behind the wheel of the Audi, entered the location into GPS on his phone and took an indirect route, passing the condo, making certain he wasn't being followed.

VANCE DROVE past the tattoo parlor located in a downscale shopping center; the parking lot was full and there was no sign of Zo's truck or Jessy's three-wheeler. He cruised around the block hitting two big potholes before spotting Jessy's weird bat mobile parked next to a dumpster in the alley behind the building. A white truck like Zo's older F-150 was parked in the public lot across the street. He circled the block again then backed into a spot in front of the Cuban supermarket at the other end of the strip mall. He reached under the seat and tucked the Glock in the waistband of his jeans and pulled down his shirt to cover it.

The front door to Jessy's shop was locked and the lights were out. A WILL RETURN at 1:00 p.m. sign hung in the window. He checked the time. Half past noon. He called Zo.

"Go 'round to the alley," she said. "I'll let you in the back way."

He rested his hand over the Glock hidden under his shirttail and strolled toward the alley, head on a swivel. He knocked on the back door. Zo let him in.

Using a wooden utility spool for a chair, Jessy sat behind a makeshift desk with a plywood top. He approached and looked over Jessy's shoulder. A thin line with a progress bar inched across the screen of his laptop.

"Did you get what I need?" he asked Jessy.

"Don't know yet. Still transferring the files."

He looked around. The back storeroom could've been a curio shop from the 1800s, dimly lit with dusty glass bottles on shelves and antique furniture stacked on wooden slatted boxes. His eyes returned to the glowing computer screen, transporting him back to the current century.

"Do me a favor," Jessy said to him. "Go change the WILL RETURN sign in the window to two o'clock."

He walked the dingy corridor toward the lobby, peering into a side room with a narrow, padded bed reminding him of the chiropractor's office. Another had a barber style chair with a red metal rolling cart and a steel tray with tools laid out atop a white towel.

He removed the WILL RETURN sign from the window, set the hands to 2 p.m. and was about to rehang it when a woman showed up at the door. She pulled the handle then shaded her eyes placing her face an inch from the glass. He ducked behind the reception counter. She knocked on the door and jiggled the handle again, then stepped to the side and looked in through the picture window. A moment later she turned and walked away. He jogged from the hallway to the storeroom and closed the door.

"Are you sure no one followed you?" he asked Zo.

Zo hovered over Jessy's shoulders. "Don't think so," Zo said. "Why?"

"The lady who showed up at the residence is here knocking on the front door."

"You sure 'bout that?" Zo asked.

"Ninety percent," he said.

"Lemme handle this," Zo said.

Zo SLIPPED out the back door and hustled down the alleyway, stopping at the corner where she had a view to the front of the building. The woman paced the walkway talking on her phone. When she saw Zo, she ended the call.

"Is everythin' alright?" Zo asked, flashing her badge long enough for the woman to see it. "I saw you knockin' on the door. Just makin' sure everythin' is okay."

"Yes," the woman said, "I had an appointment, but it looks like the place is closed."

"What time was your appointment?" Zo asked.

The woman hesitated, looked at her phone and said, "Um, twelve-thirty."

"Accordin' to my watch you're late. I'd call and reschedule if I was you. This ain't the best neighborhood to be loiterin' in."

She took offense. "I'm not loitering. I told you, I have an appointment."

Zo folded her arms across her chest. The odds this woman was getting a tattoo was about the same as Zo scheduling a boob job. "What kinda tattoo you gettin'?"

"You're right," the woman said. "I'll call and reschedule."

That's what Zo thought. She watched her hurry across the street and get into an SUV with Georgia plates.

47

"It looks like I got most of the files," Jessy said after Zo had left to deal with the woman at the door. "Pull up a chair."

Vance unfolded a gray metal chair and sat. "Can you search for banking information, or bitcoin or cryptocurrency?"

"Let me think," Jessy said, pulling a half-smoked joint from a hiding spot under the plywood desk. "Do you mind?"

He did mind.

"It helps me focus," Jessy said.

"Then go ahead."

Jessy flicked a pink disposable lighter, took one long hit on the fat doobie, then knocked the orange head off using the edge of an empty Coke can. He held the smoke in his lungs and closed his eyes. "I need to narrow the search using keywords. I'll start with banks."

He typed 'bank' into the search bar and pressed the return key. Hundreds of hits filled the screen. He typed 'digital bank,' and nothing came up. On the third try, he entered 'smart wallet' into the search browser. A moment later a tiny blue envelope appeared on screen — a file.

"Open it," he said to Jessy.

Jessy clicked the folder. "This isn't going to help," Jessy said. "It's encrypted and password protected."

It did help. It proved Rafael Suarez had opened a digital bank account. "Can you tell when the file was created?"

Jessy selected the information tab on the browser and checked the date. "It was created two weeks ago."

"Did you get his internet search history?" he asked.

"I did. It's stored in a separate file. I have an app that locates search history. It's the first thing I downloaded off the computer."

"And?" he asked.

"I haven't looked yet. Do you mind?" He held up the joint and lighter. "Just one more hit?"

"Sure," he said.

Jessy took one another drag of weed, coughed and opened the folder with the browser history, then scrolled down a dozen or so pages with single line entries before pausing. "I don't think they've cleaned up their search history for a long time. Maybe never," he said, continuing to page down the results.

The files began to look never-ending. "Check the last two weeks," he said.

Jessy relit the weed and sucked in the smoke, holding it in his lungs while he knocked the lit head off the head of the joint. As it sizzled in the aluminum drink can, he leaned over and stashed the roach in his secret spot somewhere under the desk.

There was a knock on the back door. Vance got up and let Zo in.

"Did you find out what she was doing here?" he asked her.

"Said she had a twelve-thirty appointment. Jesus, what's that smell? You gotta be kiddin' me," Zo said. "You smokin' dope in here?"

Jessy changed screens on his computer and opened a digital calendar. "Are you sure she said twelve-thirty?"

"Mmm hmm," Zo said, contorting her face at the odor.

"I didn't have anyone scheduled for that time." He reached under the desk, placed an incense cone on top of the Coke can and lit it with the disposable lighter.

"That shit smell even worse," Zo said. "Gonna give me a migraine."

"What did she look like?" Vance asked, watching Jessy tap the backspace arrow and return to Suarez's search history.

"Hispanic, thirty-five to forty, longish hair," Zo said. "Tall, nice legs, fake tits."

Those were strange comments. On the other hand, it was Zo talking.

"Had Georgia plates on her car. Toyota RAV4," Zo said.

His heart skipped. "What color?"

"White. Why?" Zo asked.

"You sure no one followed you?" he asked.

"This ain't my first day on the job," Zo said.

The description of the woman and the vehicle fit Gloria.

"Maybe someone followed your skinny ass here," Zo said. "Have you thought 'bout what your gonna do if the clock runs out?" Zo asked.

"Meaning?" he said.

"Zo says the ransom is five million. Is that true?" Jessy asked.

He didn't answer.

"You should have a contingency plan," Jessy said.

"Enlarge the font," he said, "and go to the most recent searches."

"Let's assume you have the money," Jessy said. "You can't just transfer cash from a bank to a crypto wallet. First you have to buy cryptocurrency from an exchange—"

"How long does it take?" he interrupted.

"I'm not sure," Jessy said.

"Can you print out his search history?" he asked, now pacing.

"I can do you one better," Jessy said. "I copied a backup to my hard drive. Here," he said, ejecting the flash drive from the computer. "You can keep this."

"Show me recent search history," he said, tucking the thumb drive in his pants pocket.

He stood over Jessy's monitor, watching. The newest search was for movie theaters and matinee showtimes.

After that the browser history began to paint a much different picture.

48

D avis came to in the darkness; his body crumpled on the metal floor. His head pounded, and he was motion sick. Sheets of rain slapped the windshield and water drummed the roof of the van. The last thing he remembered they'd been forced to turn back to Fairbanks because of a road closure. It hurt to move his neck and his left arm was hung high above his head as if he'd been partially crucified, his wrist cuffed to a metal handle near the top of the cargo van.

He scooted sideways to relieve the pressure and leaned his back against one wall of the van. Running his free hand on the back of his head, his fingers felt damp and gooey. He looked closely to see what it was, but there wasn't enough light inside the van. He rubbed his fingers together and sniffed. A bolt of lightning pierced the blanket of storm clouds on the horizon like a flashbulb. He saw blood from where he'd hit his head before a boom of thunder rumbled.

The driver cut the wheel hard right and Davis lost his balance, toppling to one side, torquing his shoulder. "Awwww!"

The guards ignored his howl; he righted himself wondering if he'd dislocated the bone from the shoulder socket. As the van slowed, he massaged the joint with his good hand and squinted at the windshield straining to see through the foggy glass. A palm tree lay across the road. He clenched his teeth as the van bounced, front wheels first, and again as the rear tires rolled over the trunk. The guard behind the wheel made a slow right-hand turn and stopped. He recognized the blue metal building barely visible in the blinding rain. They were back at Fairbanks.

The guard on the passenger side climbed between the seats and unlocked the metal cuff holding Davis's sore arm to the handlebar. He cupped his left elbow with his right palm, moving it an inch, testing it. He winced, then held the injured arm steady.

The guard released the metal cuff holding Davis's left arm to the handle and snapped it to his own wrist.

"Awwwww!" Davis said. "Aw, aw, aw, aw," he panted.

"Get up," he barked. "Let's go."

"I can't. My shoulder might be dislocated," Davis cried, sitting on the floor of the van, bringing his knees to his chest, bending forward and rocking, clamping his good hand on his bad shoulder.

"I don't give two shits. Move it," the driver with slits for eyes said.

The guard cuffed to him grabbed Davis's good arm and tried to pull his ass up from floorboard.

"Take it easy and cuff my good arm," Davis pleaded.

While the one guarding him obliged, the reptile released the back door of the cargo van from the inside, forcing it open against the wind, and jumped out. A gust ripped the ball cap from the lizard's head, and it disappeared into the wind. While the driver struggled to hold the door open

Davis duck-walked like a Sumo wrestler to the opening at the back of the van. He stopped near the edge and sat where he could lower himself to the ground. The wind howled and a white flash of lightning struck, followed by thunder that shook the ground like an earthquake.

"Get moving!" the driver ordered, water dripping from his red hair into his eyes, uniform soaked. "There's no one here to look at your shoulder," he yelled over the roaring wind. "We're gonna have to wait for the storm to pass and we can't get you to a hospital now."

A frond tore from a nearby palm tree and whirred past the guard struggling to hold the cargo door open. "Come on already!" the snake on the ground shouted as hurricane force winds howled.

Davis gritted his teeth and scooted on his tailbone, placing one foot on the back bumper. Bracing his injured arm against his chest he stepped down, rain pelting his face. The guard cuffed to Davis hopped down, leaned into the wind, and lead him toward the building. His partner unlocked the front door to the jail, and they lead Davis by flashlight to a cramped cell with a dirty, deflated blue mattress next to a toilet.

The reptile pushed the cell door wide open. "Here," he said, holding a small wax cup with a paper lid.

"What do you want me to do?" Davis asked, grimacing, trying to steady his injured shoulder.

"Piss in the cup," the snake said. "You're getting the drug test you wanted."

Davis braced his left shoulder steady as he fumbled to unzip his pants. Some piss went in the cup while the rest dribbled down his prison jumpsuit and trickled onto the concrete floor.

"You got a lawyer," the redhead said, snapping a glove on

his hand and placing the lid on the urine sample. "She got you the test."

"A lawyer?" Davis said. "When can I see her?"

"Not up to us," the snake said.

"How long does it take to get the results?" Davis asked.

"Five minutes," the ginger-head said. "We'll know if you smoked weed today, yesterday or if you're a daily user."

"Then you'll know I'm telling the truth."

"Don't be so sure," the lizard said. "Your lawyer asked for two tests. We're getting a sample from your old cellmate to find out which one of you pieces of shit is lying."

"How could I smuggle anything in when I was searched and booked just hours before you found his dope?"

"I don't know," snake eyes said, holding up the dixie cup. "It's awfully dark in here. I hope we don't mix up the results."

49

Vance blocked the Jeep with the crooked Dolphins bumper sticker in the driveway in front of Sarge's house, got out of the Audi and rang the bell. Sarge answered the door wearing baggy shorts exposing his left calf wrapped in an ace bandage. His lip had swelled and the road rash on his elbow had crusted with a fresh scab.

"You coulda called," Sarge said.

Sure, he could've, but he wanted to see his reaction. "I have proof Rafael is up to something."

"What are you talking about?" Sarge said, ushering him inside.

"I have the search history from his home computer."

"And?" Sarge asked, sitting on the edge of his recliner and muting the audio on a replay of a Dolphins game on his DVR.

"He opened a Smart Wallet."

"What's that? A wallet with an IQ over a hundred?"

"No," he said, in no mood for wisecracks. "It's a bank account set up to deposit cryptocurrency."

Sarge scoffed and side-eyed the game on the flat screen

TV. "That doesn't prove anything. The mayor of Miami was trying to get the city to go crypto. He might've opened an account for a client at his law practice. There could be a lot of reasons."

"The mayor was pushing crypto two years ago. Your son-in-law opened his account two weeks ago."

"Still doesn't prove anything," Sarge said.

"He searched travel to Cuba."

"Yes!" Sarge yelled, holding both arms over his head.

The Dolphins had kicked a field goal. The score was three-zip, Dolphins over North Carolina.

"So, he was thinking about going to Cuba on a family holiday, so what?" Sarge said.

That was bullshit. "He also searched Sea Otter Grand Cayman."

That got his attention.

"When?"

"The searches all occurred over the last couple of weeks. Any idea why he'd look for information about seeing eye dogs?"

"No," Sarge said. "No clue."

"I had a consultation with one of Rafael's clients. She's blind."

"I thought you weren't doing that?"

"I wasn't," he said, walking to the tiny kitchen. He opened Sarge's fridge and helped himself to a beer.

"Gimme one of those," Sarge said.

He twisted the tops from both and passed one to Sarge who sat sideways on the recliner with his back to the television.

"I did have a deal with your son-in-law. No consultations with new clients. When I stopped by the office on Friday to meet Lola, she roped me into meeting the blind client. Lola said the meeting was already confirmed. The client is a Russian-trained Cuban doctor with an immigration problem."

"What kind of a problem?" Sarge asked.

"Ralph's been handling her work visa and Homeland Security hasn't been able to locate her husband to verify her marriage. Thing is, she showed up with a seeing eye dog."

The look on Sarge's face changed to one of concern, as if denial was vacating his brain and reality was setting in.

Sarge swigged the cold beer. "That's three too many coincidences. I asked Val where he's doing his rehab and she said she didn't remember."

That seemed strange, but on the other hand, she was probably pissed at her husband.

"I'll press her, and I'll find out." Sarge looked at the digital clock on the stove. "I gotta go," he said. "I promised to pick Maria and the girls up from the theater. I'm going to the house to drop my granddaughters off. I'll corner Val and find out where her husband is now."

"Soon as you know, call me," he said.

"Hang on," Sarge said.

Sarge left the room and returned with the manila envelope he'd given him outside the bar.

"Take this with you," he said. "You might need it."

SUAREZ'S OFFICE was on the way home. The pharmacy on the lobby level was open but most of the businesses located in the high-rise office building were closed for the weekend. He took the elevator to the eighth floor and rang the buzzer. Lola came to the door wearing sweats, hair piled atop her head and held in place with a neon green scrunchie.

"Guess you can't stay away," she said.

"Do you know anything about this?" he asked, handing her the envelope with the manifesto.

She took a seat in one of the armchairs in the lobby and removed the document. She read the first page then looked up. "Where did you get this?"

"I asked you first."

"I've never seen it before," she said, thumbing through the pages. "It's a plan to invade Cuba but that's nuts."

"Is it?" he asked. "I imagine you would support it."

"What's that supposed to mean?"

"You have family in the old country."

"You still haven't answered my question. Where did you get this and why are you showing it to me?" she asked.

"It was in the safe in your boss's office."

"How did you get in it?"

"It was unlocked."

"He never leaves it unlocked. Maybe that's why she was here," Lola said, standing and pacing.

"Who-she?"

"His wife. She let herself in this morning."

"Did she see you?"

"No," Lola said, wringing her hands.

"Was she alone?"

"Yes."

"What did she do?"

"She went into his office and closed the door. I don't know what she did. They've had their problems," Lola admitted, flopping into the chair.

"What kind of problems?"

Lola pulled the tie from her hair and let her hair fall to her shoulders. "The usual. Money, extramarital stuff."

Wow. Those were big ones.

"It's weird he got that DUI," Lola said. "I've been

working for him for a long time, and I never saw him drunk."

"Did you socialize with him?"

"What do you think?"

"Then you really don't know him, do you?"

"You sound like a lawyer," she said, running her fingers through her hair.

"Keep the document and read it with a fine-tooth comb. I'd like your opinion."

"How so?"

"I want you to tell me if you think it's possible your boss wrote it." He stood to leave. "One more thing. Do you have a sample of his handwriting?"

"Probably somewhere in my office."

"I'll wait while you look."

50

GEORGE TOWN, GRAND CAYMAN, CAYMAN
ISLANDS
SUNDAY MORNING

Lauren awoke to the droning of a small gasoline-powered engine humming outside the window. She got out of bed and looked out the curtains. The storm shutters had been removed and workers wearing oranges vests and thick gloves cleared the garden of storm debris while another crew with chain saws cut fallen tree limbs into stacks of firewood. Spears of sunshine pierced the wall of tired storm clouds on the horizon. The weather had finally taken a break.

She'd spent the night bunkered inside the guest bedroom at the private residence with both doors locked to keep Margaret's creepy husband at bay. She went into the bathroom to check her phone for battery, cell service and a weather update. Seventy-two percent juice with four bars. The hurricane advisory had been lifted and the storm had moved northeast, toward Jamaica. She set her foot on the toilet seat; the swelling from the jellyfish sting had gone down, and with it, the pain.

She opened Arthur's barrage of texts and sent him a question:

Is the airport opening soon?

He called immediately.

"I was worried about you. I phoned Meg and asked her to go to the duplex," Arthur said.

"I'm at her place now."

"I know," Arthur said. "Sheldon called and told me. Over dinner you didn't mention anything about your friend being arrested. Why not?"

"I guess I was trying to protect him."

"Is that why you lied about the reason for leaving the hotel?"

She sat in the red velvet chair in front of the dresser. "I didn't know he was in trouble until I landed in Grand Cayman."

There was a knock at the bedroom door.

"Hold on a sec," she said to Arthur.

It was Margaret.

"Can I call you back?"

"Sure," Arthur said.

"I got through to the supervisor at Fairbanks where Davis is being held," Margaret said, "and found out more about what happened. When an inmate is caught with illegal drugs, they automatically move them from pretrial detention to a more secure facility. The good news is the road to Northwood was impassable, and they had to turn back so he's at Fairbanks."

"Something doesn't add up," Lauren said, walking to the window and looking out with her back to the lawyer. She turned and faced Margaret. "Davis knows the drug laws here are zero tolerance. They must've searched him before they locked him up."

"I tend to agree with you," Margaret said. "His cellmate blamed it on him, and he accused his cellmate. I've asked for another drug test. I'm headed to the jail to see him and wondered if you'd like to go with me."

"Let me get my things," Lauren said.

THE STREETS WERE war-ravaged from the storm. Margaret sawed the wheel of the Escalade making last minute maneuvers around road debris and high water. She hit the brakes when a stray dog darted across the street. Plastic bottles and other garbage floated in the culverts. Lauren powered down the passenger side window and looked up. The sky was white with mottled patches of baby blue and the air was as crisp as an apple.

"Keep your window up," Margaret said. "The mosquitos are out in force."

They rode in silence for a long moment, the hum of the Cadillac almost a lullaby after 24-hours of hell. One car passed going the opposite way. A woman swept water from the open door to her ramshackle house while her children tossed a ball in the yard.

"Do you have kids?" Lauren asked.

"I couldn't," Margaret said.

"I'm sorry."

"I had an IUD injury and had a hysterectomy the year before we married. Sheldon knew."

IUD. Intrauterine Device.

"What about you?" Margaret asked.

She shook her head. "No. No children."

"Why not? Don't you want them?"

"It's complicated. Right now, all I want is to go home."

"I bet you can get out tomorrow," Margaret said. "On another note, I'm sorry about Sheldon's behavior yesterday."

That was the pink elephant riding in the car with them. "Has that happened before?" she asked.

"I'm sure it has but that's the first time I've seen it with my own eyes."

She glanced over at Margaret looking for a reaction, but the lawyer was stone-faced behind the wheel. "You seem okay with it," Lauren said.

Margaret slowed the Cadillac and crossed to the wrong side of the road to avoid a large pothole filled with rainwater. "That's been there for months," Margaret said. "I feel for the people who have to avoid it every day and sorrier for the ones who don't see it first."

The conversation stalled. Lauren gazed at the rows of shotgun houses on cinderblock foundations jamming both sides of the street. Up ahead an elderly man stood barefoot in the dirt, hunched over, clearing branches with green leaves off an old car.

Margaret broke the silence. "I've looked like this since fourth grade. Sheldon was one of the most eligible bachelors on the island. He married me for my family money. Have you ever had sex with a drunk?" Margaret asked, side-eyeing her. The lawyer waited for an answer and when none came, she said, "I'll take that as a no. I'm married to a man who has to get hammered to touch my naked body."

"You're okay with that?" she asked.

"I knew what I was getting into."

"You don't mind what he did yesterday? Coming on to me?"

"Only if you do," Margaret said, slowing to let an emergency vehicle pass.

"I never had the options like you," Margaret said. "When you get to be my age, those things don't matter so much. Would you believe Sheldon tried to convince me you have more money than I do?"

Her heart raced and her stomach roiled.

"Of all the mind games he's played, and all the passive-aggressive moves he's made about my social standing, comparing us financially is a new low—even for him. If you had that kind of money, you'd have found a way off the island and you sure wouldn't be staying at that duplex Arthur owns." Margaret looked over and smiled like a Cheshire Cat. "I did a background check on you. You're a pretty girl who makes videos for a living. More money than me. Ha! Imagine him saying that."

Margaret slowed, turned onto a gravel driveway and parked in front of a blue metal building.

"Here we are."

THE AIR inside the jail was muggy and stank of ripe socks. Lauren waited in the lobby behind a security door with a small window leading to the bowels of the jail. She took shallow breaths trying to acclimate to the smell, watching through the glass as Margaret spoke to a man in uniform. The door opened.

"This is my associate," Margaret lied. "She'll sit in on the interview."

She followed Margaret into a small windowless room where Davis waited dressed in an orange jumpsuit. Margaret pulled the door shut.

"What are you doing here?" Davis asked Lauren. "How did you find me?"

Margaret interrupted him. "I'm your lawyer. My name is

Margaret Terry. I got the results of the drug test. You tested positive for THC."

"That's impossible," Davis said, eyes welling, hands trembling, handcuffs jangling.

"I'm ordering another drug test," Margaret said, planting her palms on the rickety metal table and pushing herself to her feet. Rings of sweat had formed under the arms of her dress. She opened the door and stuck her head around the corner. "Guard!"

One appeared in the corridor.

"I want another drug test," Margaret said.

"That's not possible," he said.

"Why not?"

"We're out of them," he said, with a smirk on his face.

"Lauren," Margaret said, "bring me my bag."

She brought it and Margaret reached inside, producing two unopened test kits. "Here," she said, handing them to the guard. "Come on Davis, and let's try this again."

Alone in the cramped room Lauren took her phone from her purse and opened her email again. Rumor had it three times was a charm. She began to write an email to Vance, then changed her mind and deleted it.

Her phone chimed with a message from Arthur.

Margaret said you left something at the duplex. I'll look for it.

51

MIAMI, FLORIDA
SUNDAY MORNING, 9:57 A.M.
14 HOURS AND 3 MINUTES BEFORE THE DEADLINE

"Come here, Cash," Vance said, sitting on the bottom stair at the condo as he set his empty coffee mug on the tile. Exhausted and barely aware of the day or time, he clipped the leash to Cashmere's collar and followed the dog outside where the animal sniffed the hedges of the enclosed driveway. A squirrel leaped from the telephone wire to a tree, exciting the dog who yanked on the leash, almost knocking the phone from his hand. He recovered from the near miss and opened the GPS app on his phone.

The Jeep appeared as a yellow dot one block from the condo. When the Cherokee appeared at the gate, Vance punched the code on the keypad and the wrought iron fence wobbled open.

Sarge's wife Maria stepped out of the vehicle. "I'm sorry to bother you on a Sunday morning but Danny told me you were inside Val's house. He told me why and I have some information that might help you."

"Does he know you're here?"

"No," she said.

"Let's go inside and talk," he said, as Cashmere tugged on the leash and led the way.

"What's his name?" Maria asked.

"Cash. Short for Cashmere," he explained.

"Is this your place?" she asked, following him through the narrow, covered courtyard to the front door.

"It's my girlfriend's place but I live here."

"Danny told me she's been missing for three days, and you think Rafael knows where she is," she said, taking a seat at the dining room table.

He moved a stack of papers from the glass tabletop and set it on the kitchen counter. "What do you know?" he said, uncertain how much Sarge had shared with his wife.

"Danny said she's been kidnapped. I didn't know until last night when he told me what you found on Ralph's computer. I think this could be my fault."

"I doubt it," he said.

"I showed Danny a note I found in our granddaughter Leah's violin case, but I lied."

"What? Why?"

"It was never inside the violin case. I thought maybe Danny would blame Ralph and I hoped he'd tell Val. I thought it might push her to leave him. I've never liked him, and God knows, Danny and I have tried to get her to see him for who he is, but she loves him." Maria picked up a ball-point pen and began to tap the glass tabletop. "She's been upset about Ralph going away for a month. He could lose his law license."

"I know. Who wrote the note?"

"I did," she said, casting her eyes down. "I hid it in my purse and took it to the church. I had no idea Danny would give it to you. I never intended to get you involved."

"Does Sarge know?"

"No, and you can't tell him. I'll tell you what I know if you promise never to tell him."

This from the wife who'd run off with an old high school sweetheart and left Sarge devastated. He'd never tell him, but not because of his promise to her, but because it would rock Sarge's world. "You have my word."

"Danny said you're trying to find Ralph to talk to him."

"That's right," he said, leaning against the kitchen counter. "Do you know where he is?"

"I do."

"I need the name and address of the place."

"Danny said the ransom demand is five million dollars. Are you going to pay it?"

"I might not have a choice."

"I think Ralph has something to do with that document you found in the safe at his office. Val told me he's been converting his money into digital currency. She told me he opened an account about two weeks ago and has been taking an online course about investing. I think he's hiding money from her."

"Do you have any evidence?" he asked, wishing she'd stop tapping the damn pen on the glass.

"I think you're the one with the proof. Danny told me what you found on his computer. He said the ransom demand is for cryptocurrency."

"Do your daughters know about any of this?"

"Val doesn't know I planted the note, and they don't know Danny helped get you into the house."

"Does Val know someone was inside?"

"Gloria told her the front door was open, and someone left birthday balloons inside. The neighborhood security company is going through surveillance video and one of the patrolmen said he saw a man in a black sedan who said he was a friend of Val's. Something about a surprise birthday party."

Wow. Maria knew a lot.

"Why don't you just pay the money?"

"It's not about the money," he said. "I need to know she's alive."

"I don't think she's dead," Maria said, in an unwanted attempt to make him feel better. "But if you don't pay it . . ." she trailed off. A moment later she said, "He's at a detox center up in Boca."

"What's the name of it?" He took the pen from her.

"I can't remember," she said, taking her phone from her purse, using her fingertips to search for it. "It's called Gateway to Life. I don't know what good it will do because they don't allow visitors."

He jotted down the name of the place. "Let me walk you out."

As he opened the Jeep door, Maria made her final pitch. "You'll be wasting your time if you try to see him. Danny told me you refused to get the police involved. I think you should pay the money while you still have time."

"Point taken," he said to Maria, dialing Zo on his way back inside the house.

She picked up on the first ring. "I need you to meet me in Boca. Suarez is at a rehab place up there."

"Sweeten my deal," Zo said.

"You'll be able to retire."

"Text me the address," she said.

"I'm also sending a screen shot with the banking information from the kidnappers. Tell Jessy to go ahead and set up the accounts in case I run out of time and have to pay the money."

"You takin' a big risk doin' it this way," Zo said. "They might just keep the dough and kill her anyhow."

"You got a better idea?"

"Don't go gettin' all crossways with me, Courage. I done already told you what I woulda done. I woulda reported it. I'll tell Jessy to set it up but you gonna have to do better by him too, meanin' you gonna have to put some more cookies in his jar."

His phone chimed. He read the message. "I gotta go."

Damn.

It was as if the lady in white had ESP.

You have till midnight to transfer the money or you'll never see her again.

Then, the message vanished from the screen.

52

"That's what I figured," Margaret said, looking at the test results.

Lauren could no longer ignore the rancid smell inside the jail nor tolerate the stifling heat and humidity in the cramped interview room. Margaret showed her and Davis the second round of results proving Davis was negative for THC, but his bunkmate tested positive for heavy use.

"Did you call him yet?" Davis asked Lauren.

Her mind was on Arthur, wondering what the chances were of him looking under the mattress and finding the twenty-five grand she'd left behind.

Davis asked again and spoke louder. "Lauren, did you call Vance?"

"No. Why would I when I hired Miss Terry to represent you?"

Margaret struggled up from her seat and closed the door to the interview room. "Does the name Daniel Ruiz ring a bell?"

The question was for Davis, but her skin prickled from the rush of adrenaline.

"Vaguely," Davis said.

"Any idea why he might've called the Sea Otter dive shop and left a message for you?" Margaret asked, shifting her eyes between them.

Davis shook his head.

"He left a call back number," Margaret said.

"How do you know?" Lauren asked, hands trembling.

"From the investigators who are monitoring the missing couple's business phones."

"What did else did he say?" Lauren asked.

"He said he wanted to talk to Davis Frost and inquired about taking scuba lessons. You see, the thing is," Margaret said, "he was calling from Miami." She turned her attention to Davis. "Why would someone you claim you don't know call and ask for you by name?"

"How should I know?" Davis said.

"Let me remind you, you're a suspect in a double-homicide case," Margaret said.

Lauren interrupted. "He didn't kill anyone. I don't know the laws here, but how can you accuse him of a murder when there're no bodies."

Margaret ignored the comment. "Here's the other problem," Margaret said. "The cell number doesn't belong to a Daniel Ruiz. It belongs to someone named Vance Courage. Since Davis asked you if you called *Vance*, I assume you're both familiar with the caller."

Davis attempted to sneak eye contact with Lauren, but Margaret caught him.

"You know him," Margaret said to her in an accusing tone.

"Excuse me," Lauren said, getting up from the interview

table and pushing the chair back; it screeched on the concrete floor. She tried the doorknob, but they were locked in from the outside.

"Where do you think you're going?" Margaret asked.

"Out for air."

"I suggest you stay here. Cool your jets. I'm Davis's lawyer and I'm on his side which means I'm on your side. At least I hope the two of you are on the same team."

The problem was, she wasn't so sure about Davis. She doubted he killed anyone, but he'd married a woman who'd cleaned out his bank account and disappeared. The owners of the dive shop he was interested in buying vanished shortly before he lost his money. His hands couldn't be spotless.

"I can explain," Lauren said, standing in the room and pacing. "Vance is my boyfriend and he's probably worried about me. I lost my phone the day I arrived. I don't know his number from memory and haven't called him since I left Miami three days ago."

"Does he know about Davis's situation here?" the lawyer asked.

"I told you, I haven't spoken to him," Lauren said.

Davis interrupted, "I asked Lauren to —"

Margaret held her chubby hand in the air to shut Davis up. "Why would he call the dive shop and use a fake name?" Margaret asked. "Why not use his real name if he was trying to find you?"

"I don't know," she said.

"Who's paying you?" Davis asked Margaret.

"I am," Lauren said, then turned to the lawyer. "Davis was arrested at the hotel where we were staying, and then the storm—"

"I know," Margaret said. "That story about the abusive

boyfriend was a lie. We can't afford to waste valuable time revisiting all that. I have a copy of the charges against you," she said to Davis. "Are you aware they've found the bodies?"

"No," Davis said, sitting up in the metal chair, shifting his weight from one buttock to the other and tugging at the fabric around his crotch. "Where? What happened to them?"

53

BOCA RATON, FLORIDA
APPROXIMATELY 45-MILES NORTH OF MIAMI
11:52 A.M.

I t took about an hour to get to Gateway to Life Recovery located inside a two-story Addison Mizner building reminiscent of a Spanish fortress with arched windows and an orange tile roof. From the outside it appeared Rafael Suarez wasn't exactly roughing it. He was about to ping Zo to check her ETA when he saw her strolling along the sidewalk in front of Gateway scoping out the perimeter. He composed a text:

Look for me on the west side of the street.

Zo climbed in the passenger side. "What are we doin' here?"

"This is where Suarez is doing his rehab," he said, scanning the building, noticing the blinds were pulled on all the windows.

"Could figure that," Zo said.

"I might need your help getting in to see him."

"Mmm, mmm, mmm," Zo said. "I doubt havin' visitors is part of his treatment plan. I had to leave a side hustle I can't afford to lose for this shit. My grandkid is sick again. My daughter is in some dark alley rentin' God knows what body part to get high. I'm goin' in," she said, getting out of the Audi. "No matter how fancy these places are, they is used to seein' the cops."

He watched her strut to the front door and disappear inside. A moment later she headed back to the car.

"They sayin' there's no one here by that name."

"Do they know you're a cop?"

"You deaf? They sayin' he ain't here," Zo said. "Even if he here, you can't do nothin' if they're protectin' the identity of a patient. You need a warrant and you ain't got cause or time. I already goin' out on a limb for you. This ain't my jurisdiction. This place don't want trouble and neither do I. What makes you so sure he's here?"

While he contemplated the question, Zo's phone rang.

"For you," she said, handing him her phone.

He hesitated.

"It's Jessy, take the damn call," she said.

"Hey," Jessy said, "I got a wallet set up and it's ready whenever you are. I dug a little deeper into Suarez's hard drive and I found some interesting stuff. It looks like he's in debt."

"How deep?"

"Credits cards are maxed out. AmEx is suing him for over a hundred-grand past due. He crashed his 401K last month. They haven't made a mortgage payment in almost a year. His Bentley was repoed a week ago. Kids' tuition is past due —"

"Anything else?"

"Yeah. He took out a life insurance policy on himself three months ago."

"Who's the beneficiary?"

"His daughters."

"What about the spouse?"

"Nope," Jessy said.

That put a new spin on things. Suarez was broke. More than broke. He was drowning in debt — but he had enough to take out a life insurance policy.

"Can you search any cash apps?" he asked.

"Sure. I already saw a Venmo account."

"Go to last Thursday and look for any payments."

"Can I get a hint?" Jessy asked.

"Look for the name Logan."

"Not sure if you know, but the login and passwords for crypto wallets are a mile long. I copied them to a flash drive. I'll give it to you in person."

He waited a moment.

"Nope, I don't see a payment to anyone named Logan, but I see a payment with a note for a tire repair."

"Can you text me the phone number the payment went to?"

"Sure," Jessy said. "Let me know if you need anything else."

He dropped the phone in his pants pocket.

"I'm outta here, Sherlock," Zo said.

When she was gone, he called Sarge. He had another card to play.

54

T he muscled guard standing outside the interview room at Fairbanks unlocked the door and stuck his head inside. "Time's up," he said.

"May I have another minute with my client?" Margaret Terry asked.

"Five minutes. That's it," the guard said.

Now that the missing couple had been found, Lauren figured it might be good news for Davis. Or bad, depending upon the evidence. "How did they die?" she asked Margaret.

"The deceased have identities," Margaret said. "Martin and Betsy LeCroy. If you knew them," she said to Davis, "I find it odd you haven't referred to them by their names. Why not?"

"No reason," Davis said. "What happened?"

"The bodies were discovered in the mangroves at the Booby Pond Nature Preserve over on Little Cayman. A group of Chinese tourists spotted their remains from the observation deck at the park," the lawyer said. "Bones and clothing mostly. They were positively identified using dental records and DNA."

"How long have you known this?" Lauren asked.

"I requested the report from the coroner's inquest late Friday afternoon after we spoke. It was delivered to my office email but the building lost power during the storm and I didn't see it until this morning."

"You had power at your house," Lauren said.

"The office has its own server. When it's down, it doesn't forward my email," Margaret explained.

Davis turned the convo back to the LeCroys. "The preserve is off-limits to boats and people," he said. "How did they die and how did the bodies get there?"

"Unknown," Margaret said. "Like I said, the remains were spotted from the observation deck. As for cause of death, the medical examiner is listing it as undetermined. The preserve is one of the largest habitats for the red-footed booby, and the land is protected in perpetuity. It's a delicate situation."

"How so?" Lauren asked.

"It's a national treasure and finding murder victims there is unthinkable."

"Have you been?" Davis asked the lawyer.

Margaret shook her head.

"It's a mosquito infested swamp, and it stinks," Davis said, which was saying something coming from him. "It's good if you're a bird watcher, I guess, and not so much if it's a dry hole the day you go."

"My niece works for the Cayman Daily Press," Margaret said. "The inside information is the chief biologist suggested the birds may have pecked the flesh from the bones. The Cayman Islands National Trust would rather not have the story in the news."

Gross.

"What happens next?" Davis asked. "Will I be released?"

The beefy guard stuck his head in. "Time's up."

"You're not getting out today," Margaret said. "We have a hearing in front of the High Court in the morning."

TWENTY MINUTES after leaving Davis at Fairbanks HMP, Margaret followed the signs for valet at an elegant Victorian hotel in downtown. Like magic, the lux resort was abuzz as if the storm had never happened. Margaret parked beneath the porte cochere flanked by ribbed white columns in perfect harmony with the hotel architecture.

"Are you hungry?" Margaret asked, "because I'm starved."

"I could eat," Lauren said.

"Cool wheels," the young man parking cars said. "I like the dark green color."

The valet helped Margaret out of the Escalade and once inside the restaurant, the hostess recognized the lawyer, and they were seated straightaway.

"Getting back to your friend's situation, there are very influential people who fund the preserve," Margaret said, sipping sweetened tea. "The powers that be don't want a story coming out about our prized colony of red-footed boobies eating human flesh. We take our news ledes from the British press and '*Boobies Feasting on Rotting Human Corpses*' would make for a sensational headline."

"I'm sorry," Lauren said. "But I'm not following you."

Margaret lowered her voice. "The good news is you hired me and I'm one of those influential people. We have high net worth individuals from every walk of life trusting us to shelter and safeguard billions of dollars in Grand Cayman. It's our lifeblood. We can't have scandals."

She was uncertain where Margaret was going with this.

"The plan to charge your friend with possession of a controlled substance would have put him away for long time. Long enough for the news to die down and for people to assume the killer had been caught."

"You think he was framed for the drug test?"

Margaret shook her head as if frustrated by the question. "Never mind, it didn't work. I can make the drug charges go away, and that gives me a leg to stand on in court."

"What are his chances?"

"Decent, I'd say. The storm was a distraction, and the news cycle has moved on. I'll contact the U.S. Embassy first thing in the morning. Detaining Americans isn't good for business either."

The food arrived. Margaret dove into her meal while Lauren picked at hers.

"Have you booked your flight back to Miami?" Margaret asked, sawing a lobster tail into quarters and dunking it in a ramekin filled with liquid butter.

"I haven't. I might as well stay another day to see what happens with Davis."

"He's lucky to have a friend like you," the attorney said. "I perish the thought of what would've happened if you'd hadn't intervened, though to be honest, I wanted very much to represent him in criminal court." The lawyer stabbed a hunk of African lobster with her fork. "It's not often there's a double-murder in the Cayman Islands. Who's to say I won't still get the chance?"

The chance to do what?

"The LeCroy deaths could've been an accident," Lauren said.

"Exactly," Margaret said, speaking with a mouthful of tail meat, "though I'm having trouble figuring out how." She chewed, swallowed and said, "but that's precisely what I'm going to argue in front of the judge."

She'd stay another night. She probably couldn't catch a flight out anyway. Maybe it was wrong, but she didn't care if Vance was worried. He lied about his identity when he left the message at the dive shop. He moved his money behind her back. She could've asked Margaret for the phone number he'd left at the dive shop, but why take the chance? It seemed like all he cared about was himself. She'd let him sweat a little longer.

55

MIAMI, FLORIDA
3:15 P.M.
8 HOURS AND 45 MINUTES LEFT

The interior of the Suarez residence offered no hint of imminent bankruptcy. An original Mark Rothko painting with wide lines of primary colors and sharp edges hung on the entryway wall, and below it, the wilting birthday balloons draped from the credenza like dying tulips. Vance carried a box of fresh meals that had been left on the doorstep by one of those online delivery services.

"Where's Val?" Sarge asked.

Gloria ignored the question. "I'll take that," she said to Vance, grabbing the package. "Girls, go to your rooms."

Ava spouted back at her. "But —"

"But nothing. You heard me. Both of you. In your rooms. Now."

"But I want to see Grandpa," Ava argued.

"Listen to Aunt Gloria," Sarge said.

Vance watched the girls climb the winding staircase and disappear.

"What are you doing here?" Gloria asked him.

"I talked to Val," Sarge said, "and she knew we were stopping by. Where is she?"

"She had car trouble," Gloria said.

"What kind of trouble?" Sarge asked, following Gloria to the kitchen.

Vance had called Sarge on the way back from Boca and had asked him to set up a meeting to confront Val to confirm Suarez's whereabouts. He'd kept Maria's promise and mentioned nothing to Sarge about his wife's visit to the condo. He also left the part out about the run he'd made with Zo to Gateway to Life.

"I'm not sure what happened to her car," Gloria said. "Help yourself to something to drink," she said, carrying the box of meals to the garage.

"You want anything?" he asked Sarge, who declined. He opened the fridge. Inside it looked like a bag of neon Post-Its had exploded. Dozens of sticky notes were affixed to stacks of plastic containers with directions how to reheat. He looked over his shoulder, took a couple of the notes, stuffed them in his pocket and grabbed a bottle of water.

He peeked around the corner to see where Gloria had gone. Backpacks, a violin case and several pairs of shoes were piled haphazardly along the baseboard in the mudroom. The door to the garage was ajar. He took four steps in that direction before Gloria slid past him and pulled the door shut, but not before he saw the hood of Val's red Range Rover parked in the garage.

"It's such a mess with all this stuff all over the place.

Kids," Gloria said, kneeling to straighten a pair of small sneakers in the middle of the hallway. "I don't know how my sister does it."

Sarge stood in the entryway to the mudroom. Gloria looked up at her dad, then glared at him. "Val's upset you let people in the house without her permission."

"I don't blame her," Sarge said. "But —

He interrupted. "Just tell me where he's doing his rehab and I promise to leave you and your sister alone."

"It's none of your business where he is," Gloria said. "If Ralph wanted you to know, he would've told you. You're supposed to cover his law practice, not snoop around in his private life. Val's worried you're going to screw up his recovery. I don't know what you know about in-patient treatment, but Ralph couldn't even take his phone with him. He's allowed one supervised phone call per day. How could he possibly orchestrate a kidnapping from rehab?"

There were, of course, a lot of arrows pointing in that direction, not the least of which was motive. He'd played his cards closely on the ride over to Val's, keeping the Suarez financial situation secret from Sarge. He assumed Gloria would tell Val she'd seen him in the neighborhood. His thoughts were interrupted by a strange noise.

"That damn dog," Gloria said. "He paws the glass when he wants to come in."

She walked to the sliding glass door and yanked it open. Ebony bounded in, lapped at the bowl of water, then jumped up on him, slobbering on his pants.

"Get down!" Gloria swatted the black Lab on the haunches.

The animal cowered and retreated from the room.

"That dog likes you," Gloria said.

"Dogs and babies," he said. "Any idea who'd leave a threatening note in Leah's violin case?"

"Jesus, Dad. You told him that?" Then she turned to him. "That's personal family business and something else that's none of your concern."

Sarge fumed. "That's enough," he said. "I didn't come here to argue with you, I came to talk to your sister. Let's go."

"Take your birthday balloons with you," she said.

As Sarge headed to the door, Vance stopped to collect the wilted bouquet of balloons. He spotted a phone in the candy dish. He glanced over his shoulder, and on a hunch, took it, hiding it in his hand amid the balloon strings.

"WHAT WAS THAT ABOUT?" Sarge asked him on the ride back to his place in The Grove. "Why did you shoot your mouth off about the note?"

There wasn't much use in pointing out the obvious which was Gloria was covering for Val who was protecting her husband. Still, something seemed off. He wasn't sure Maria was telling the truth about forging the note found in the violin case either. He used his thumbnail to mute the audio button on the phone he'd taken from Suarez's house.

"Gloria's right. You're sticking your nose a bunch of places it doesn't belong. I know you're trying to find Lauren, but you need to stop dragging my family into it. You have no proof Ralph had anything to do with it."

Technically, Sarge was right. He had no hard evidence, but his gut said otherwise. He debated in his mind whether to tell Sarge he'd seen Val's red Range Rover parked in the garage but decided not to. Instead, he asked, "Do you have Ralph's number?"

"What do you think, numb nuts? He's my son-in-law," he

said, twisting and pulling the fake diamond post in his right earlobe. The driver in front of him hesitated when the light turned green, and Sarge laid on the horn.

"Jesus, Sarge, take it easy."

Sarge gunned the engine.

"Call Ralph's phone."

"You're losing your shit, Courage. You heard Gloria. He doesn't have it on him," he said, tapping the brakes, slowing the Jeep for a construction delay.

"Humor me," he said.

"I'll do you one better. I'll call him and I'll put it on speaker."

While they both listened to it ringing on Bluetooth, Vance felt the phone he'd taken from Val's vibrating in the pocket of his windbreaker.

It went to voicemail. "No answer," Sarge said. "What a shocker."

56

Lauren stood next to Margaret waiting for valet to bring the Escalade around. A bellman in a gray uniform pushed a garment cart loaded with leather luggage to a hotel shuttle idling under the portico. Two gardeners in crisp overalls carried a large ceramic container filled with blooming flowers, carefully aligning it atop a round stain on the walkway.

"Have you decided if you're staying another night?" Margaret asked.

"I think I should. I'd like to see what happens with Davis in court."

"Do you want to stay with us tonight?"

Us, meaning her and that dog-husband Sheldon. "Thanks for the offer, but I think I'd like to go back to the duplex."

"I'd probably make the same decision," Margaret said, pressing cash into the palm of the young man who'd parked the Caddie at valet. "I'll take you to the house to get your things," she said, "and I'll give you a lift to the duplex."

On the way home, Margaret took three detours where the roads were closed from storm damage and debris. They didn't speak much on the short trip back, mostly because in Lauren's mind, there wasn't much to say. As Margaret pulled into the winding driveway leading to her estate, she pressed the remote on the visor opening the garage door. Sheldon's swoopy red Corvette was gone.

Lauren hurried down the hall to the guest bedroom and quickly gathered her belongings. When she was finished, she found Margaret standing in the kitchen talking on the phone.

"That was Arthur," Margaret said. "I thought I'd call ahead and let him know you'd be staying with him another night."

"What did he say?"

"He said he's getting the place ready."

A LAYER of sand covered the road leading to Seven Mile Beach obscuring the painted center line. Margaret slowed as she approached the duplex, then turned into the driveway, cutting the wheel to avoid a screen door that had washed up with the storm surge.

"What a mess," Margaret said, putting the Caddie in park and popping the hatchback.

The high tide had receded, and the ground was littered with an array of weird junk: a wooden pallet, a white sneaker, an orange life preserver. Lauren stepped out of the vehicle and slung her roller bag out of the back of Margaret's SUV. She closed the hatch eyeing Arthur's unmarked RCIPS sedan parked under the adjoining house.

Margaret powered down her window. "If you need a ride to court tomorrow, let me know and I can swing by and pick you up. I should advise you if we're seen together, people may talk. I expect the media might turn out."

. . .

SHE CARRIED her suitcase up the exterior stairs. The A/C had been set to low and there was a note on the kitchen countertop.

I'm off work today. I searched the house and think I found what you were looking for. If you need anything, let me know. Arthur

Heart pounding, she dragged her bag to the bedroom. The linens had been stripped from the bed and the clothes Arthur had lent her hung neatly in the closet. Peering around the window frame, she looked but didn't see any sign of him. She pulled the blinds and lifted the mattress to look for the money.

57

Cashmere stood near the front door of the condo wagging his tail with so much vigor he might've won a doggy Hula-Hoop contest. Vance grabbed both phones, tucked the Glock in the waistband of his jeans then headed out the door. He hesitated. "Alright," he said. "Come on."

He snapped the leash on Cash's collar. "I wish I knew where your mom was." The dog whimpered as if he understood.

He set the pup on the front passenger seat of the Audi. Activating the flashlight on his phone, he shone it where the bullet from Sarge's gun had entered the side door of Lauren's car; tiny specks of rust had formed but the slug wasn't visible where he'd seen it lodged. It'd probably vibrated loose.

"Let's go see Jessy," he said, reaching over and scratching Cash's chin. "Your dog-dad is running out of ideas, and time."

He rolled the passenger window down a few inches and Cash stood on his hind legs with his nose poking out into the warm night air.

Fifteen minutes later he knocked on the back door of HighJinks Ink.

"Cute dog," Jessy said, as Cash hid behind his left leg.

"He's a little shy when he meets new people." The smell of freshly burnt incense couldn't mask the smell of dope, an odor he'd decided was essential to solving this strange mystery with too many moving parts. "Did you get my last message?" he asked Jessy, coaxing Cash into the back room of the tattoo parlor.

"I did. Did you bring the stuff?" Jessy asked, sitting on the wooden spool behind the plywood desk.

Vance reached under his shirt and set the Glock on the tabletop.

"Whoa," Jessy said, leaning back.

"It's legal." He removed a folded sheet of 8-by-10-inch paper from his pants pocket.

Jessy laid it flat next to his computer and typed the information from the document onto his laptop. "I need your password."

Jessy stood and stepped aside while he typed in the login information, opening his Bermuda bank account.

Damn," Jessy said, taking a seat and eyeing his $37,854,813.04 bank balance. "What did you do, rob the Vatican?"

"Something like that. You breathe a word about this, and you and Zo are going down with me."

"No worries, bro. How much crypto do you want to buy?"

"Five hundred thousand."

"I don't want to throw shade on your plan but how do you know she's still alive?"

It would be nice if Jessy would spare the commentary. "I want my ducks in a row to pull the trigger on the money if I need to. Transfer the cash." He watched the progress bar on Jessy's computer. The money moved seamlessly into the new account.

"That's not enough to pay the full amount."

He ignored the remark.

"You really think Suarez is the kidnapper?" Jessy said.

"Might be."

"Zo says you and his father-in-law go way back."

Meaning Sarge. "The three of us do." Cash came out from under his chair and sat. Vance reached down and lifted the little dog, placing him on his lap. "I have some words of wisdom," he said, gently petting Cashmere on the head. "Money isn't all it's cracked up to be."

"Dude, I know," Jessy said. "I'm not sure if you heard my story but I got busted for hacking a hospital group. I wasn't shaking them down for money. I was squeezing them to stop dragging their feet on my mom's cancer treatment. It's a moot point now but if I'd had the smack, she'd still be alive."

"I didn't know," he said, reminded he'd had the money to pay for his sister Kathy's experimental cancer drugs, saving her life.

"What's the plan?" Jessy asked.

He didn't have one. At least not a solid one. His gut told him to sit tight, and his stomach was always smarter than his brain. "I'm going to wait and see if I hear from them. Do you mind if I hang out here awhile?"

"I have nowhere I need to be," Jessy said, "do you mind?" he asked, reaching under the plywood desktop for his dope.

"Knock yourself out," he said, moving to an old plaid sofa pushed against the wall. Cash jumped up and curled next to him. He couldn't remember the last time he'd slept.

Jessy lit a fresh joint and sucked it, held his breath and closed his eyes. Exhaling the smoke, he offered it to him

"I'm good," he said, watching as the computer screen with the banking information timed out and a picture of a beautiful snowcapped mountain took its place. "Did you set up the other accounts?"

"Yep. One for Zo, and one for me. How much are you paying me anyway?"

"I haven't decided." He'd thought about it some and it depended on what happened next.

VANCE AWOKE to the sound of his phone ringing. Sarge came up on CALLER ID. He let it go. "Jesus. How long was I out?" he asked Jessy, rubbing his eyes and scrambling to his feet.

"A half hour. The supermarket next door is open. Do you want me to go get you a coffee?"

"Did you convert the cash to crypto?"

"Yep," Jessy said.

"I'll go. Keep an eye on my dog." He needed some fresh air.

He checked his phone for a voicemail; Sarge hadn't left one and still nothing new from the lady in white or Lauren. Or anyone. As he entered the store, the woman passing him grimaced and shook her head. The stink of secondhand marijuana smoke, he figured. He ordered two Cuban coffees, downed one in two gulps then headed back to the shop.

He placed the other cup of joe next to Jessy's computer and sat. "Transfer fifty grand to the kidnappers. Add a note that it's a test deposit."

Jessy cued up the smart wallet, typed in the amount and had him verify the information was correct. "Once I hit send, the money is gone. There's no way to dispute it."

"I know."

Jessy let it rip.

Ten minutes passed and nothing happened.

The phone he'd stolen from Val's candy dish pinged. He didn't need a password to see the incoming text and showed the message to Jessy before the screen timed out.

Courage deposited $50K into the account.

He couldn't tell who'd sent it. A moment later his own phone chimed with a text from an UNKNOWN sender:

Partial payment received. Send the rest by midnight or she's dead.

"Dude, that's freaking weird," Jessy said. "What do you want me to do?"

"Nothing." He tapped the screen on his own phone to look at the message again. A picture of Lauren holding Cashmere appeared on the display.

Jessy stared at it for a long moment. "Is that your girlfriend?"

"Yeah."

"I might be able to help you," Jessy said. "While you nodded off, I found something you need to see."

58

L auren awoke disoriented to a loud knocking on the door at the duplex and it took a moment to gather her bearings. After Margaret had given her a lift back to the rental, she'd checked for the money under the mattress surprised to see the bed stripped of linens and relieved to find the cash still there. She'd searched the closets for clean sheets and after not finding any, was so wiped out she'd laid down on the couch for a moment and must've fallen asleep. Half awake, she clambered to her feet and looked through the peephole. Arthur stood outside with an armful of bedding.

"Thank you," she said, reaching for the blue and white striped sheets.

"I'm sorry," he said, letting himself in. "I meant to take care of it earlier, but I got carried away cleaning up the mess outside."

He headed to the bedroom where he set the stack on a chair, took the bottom fitted sheet and placed it near the middle of the mattress.

She hurried to the foot of the bed near where the cash

was stashed and pulled her corner taut, then stretched the sheet toward the headboard. Arthur was quicker than her, finishing his side then grabbing the top sheet from the stack. He snapped his end where it billowed over the top of the mattress like a sail.

He moved to her side of the bed, leaned over and was about to lift the corner.

"I appreciate the help," she said, grabbing the edge of the top sheet and trying to take over. "I can take it from here."

"It's no trouble at all," Arthur said.

A rush of adrenaline passed through her body as he raised the mattress high enough to tuck the corner near where the money was still hidden. He folded a neat hospital corner, paused then said, "I think I know what you were looking for."

Her mind raced, thinking of a way to explain the cash.

He reached into the back pocket of his pants. "You wouldn't have gotten too far without this," he said, placing her passport on the nightstand.

Oh my God. She must've dropped it in her hurry to get out of the duplex during the storm.

"Margaret said you might go to the hearing tomorrow to support your friend," he said, slinging the comforter on top of the bed and smoothing it with his hands. "I'm still a little surprised you didn't mention anything about him, but either way, the case is going to be heard before the Grand Court and the setting is formal. The dress code is strict. I see you found your luggage," he said, side-eyeing her roller bag. "Do you have something suitable to wear?"

"How strict?" she asked, averting eye contact.

"Dresses for the ladies. Sport coats and ties for the men.

After I spoke to Margaret, I took the liberty of putting a few more of Anne's things in the closet for you."

Taking liberties seemed to be Arthur's specialty. She fluffed a pillow on her side and propped it against the headboard.

"No pressure," he said. "I'm sorry about the other night. I don't know what I was thinking."

Cringing at the thought, she had a pretty good idea what was on his mind when he'd planted an unwanted kiss on her mouth. Reminded of the taste and smell of fermenting wine on his breath, she turned away to hide her gag reflex.

"I work out of the same building and would be happy to give you a ride to the courthouse." He paused, then said, "Unless you have other plans."

"I don't want to inconvenience you any more than I have already."

"You wouldn't be. I'd be happy to help."

"Let me think about it."

After Arthur let himself out, she lifted the mattress and pushed the bag of cash deeper beneath it and stepped out onto the balcony into the misty air listening to waves crashing under a clear night sky.

There were no ride-share services in Cayman, and she could probably call a taxi service to get to the courthouse in the morning. Weighing her options whether to accept Arthur's offer or ask Margaret for a lift, her thought process was interrupted when headlights beamed next door.

Squatting in the shadows, she held onto the balcony railing and craned her neck. A red Corvette pulled in and parked behind Arthur's Crown Vic.

Sheldon Green was paying Arthur a visit.

59

MIAMI, FLORIDA
7:47 P.M.
4 HOURS AND 13 MINUTES ON THE CLOCK

Jessy inserted the flash drive with Suarez's files into a slot on his laptop giving Vance a quick lesson on how text messages between smartphones and desktops could be linked.

"Either Suarez didn't know SMS messages were being simultaneously saved as texts on his home computer, or he never thought they'd be discovered." Jessy pulled up a video and pressed the play button. "Is that her?"

Holy shit. It was the proof-of-life video of Lauren the kidnappers sent, the one that had played a single time before disappearing.

"Play it again," he said, massaging his temples with his fingertips. Seeing it a second time, it was obvious now. Her voice lacked inflection, and her face showed no signs of emotion. "I'm going to kill Suarez."

"Before you do that, try answering the text he just sent confirming the first payment. See if you get a response."

He was pretty sure what was going to happen but answered it anyway:

The 50K is a deposit to make sure the account is clear for a bigger transfer.

He hit send and a red UNDELIVERABLE message appeared on screen.

"That's fucked up," Jessy said. "How did you get Suarez's phone?"

"From his house."

"Jesus, you went back? Who knows you have it?"

"You do." Cash came out from under his chair and whimpered. "I'm taking him out for a walk," he said, tucking the Glock in the waistband of his jeans. He went out the back door to regroup.

THE NIGHT AIR was steamy and misty halos glowed from the tops of the shopping center lampposts like giant white lollipops.

Maybe rehab was a cover story. Maybe Suarez planned to take the money and run. He hadn't known until a few hours ago that Suarez was deeply in debt. He replayed the meeting with the lady in white in his head. It seemed like ancient history, but it had been only three days since he'd met her at Vizcaya. If Suarez was extorting him, how did *Damas de Blanco* and Monkey Morales fit in? Cash lifted his leg and peed on the dumpster while an army of kamikaze insects buzzed the streetlights.

Seeing the synchronized text messages between his

and Suarez's phone, it was obvious Suarez wasn't working alone. He rubbed the back of his neck. If Lauren was dead, the gig was up. If she was still alive, the first fifty-grand would be enough to string Suarez along a little longer. Insurance. The back door opened, startling him.

Jessy stuck his head out. "You okay out here?"

"Yeah."

"I can't unlock Suarez's phone, but I found a couple of emails," Jessy said. "There's correspondence from a rehab place called Last Chance Mental Health and Recovery up in Delray. Suarez filled out an application and was accepted." Jessy looked both directions in the dark alley. "Why don't you come inside."

If Suarez was there and didn't have his phone, that threw a wrench in the new theory. Suarez probably wasn't there, and it was likely another rabbit hole, but he had to explore it. He checked the time. Almost 8:30 p.m. "Text the address to my phone."

"Why?"

"I'm going up there to hunt down Rafael Suarez."

"I'm going with you," Jessy said, grabbing his laptop.

VANCE STOPPED at the condo to drop Cashmere off, then he and Jessy headed north to Delray Beach. He checked the navigation map on his phone. 52.3 miles. Drive-time 55 minutes. ETA 9:54 p.m., if he drove the speed limit.

"What's your game plan when we get there?" Jessy asked.

"Depends on whether or not he's there."

Jessy took a rolled joint from his sock and was about to light it.

"No smoking in the vehicle." His phone rang on the car's speaker; Lola came up on CALLER ID.

"I'm at the office," Lola said, "and I had an unexpected visitor."

"Hold on," he said, taking the phone off Bluetooth and putting it to his ear. "Your ex?" he asked.

"No. Mrs. Suarez came back again."

"What was she doing there?"

"I don't know. She went into Ralph's office and closed the door."

"Did she see you?"

"No, but she scared the shit out of me," Lola said.

"Text me Suarez's cell number."

There was a long pause. "Lola?"

"I can't do that. He has a strict policy of me not giving it out."

"Okay. Thanks for the update." He killed the call.

There could only be one reason Val went to the office twice. She was covering her husband's tracks.

"What was that about?" Jessy asked.

Flashing blue and red lights appeared in his rearview mirror. He activated the turn signal and changed lanes to let the trooper pass, but he got on his ass and whooped the siren. Vance slowed, pulled onto the shoulder and watched from the side mirror as the officer got out and approached the Audi. "Don't say a word," he warned Jessy.

The cop shone a flashlight in the car and swept the interior.

Vance powered down his window.

The trooper leaned away from the doorframe. "Step out of the car, sir, and away from the vehicle."

"Is something wrong?" he asked, obeying the command.

"Driver's License please," the cop said.

He moved slowly, removing the billfold from his back pocket and handing his ID to the officer.

The trooper looked at it, then walked around the sedan, pausing on the passenger side before aiming his flashlight at Jessy and continuing around the front bumper.

"Wait here," the officer said to him.

The dome light flicked on in the patrol vehicle. Experience told him the trooper was running a check on the plates. The patrolman stepped out of vehicle with the flashlight tucked under his arm and approached.

"Are you aware you were doing eighty in a sixty-five?"

"I could've been."

"Are you aware there is what appears to be a bullet hole in your passenger side door?"

"Yes."

"Did you report it?"

"No."

"How did it happen?" he asked, as a tractor trailer rumbled past.

"My neighbor shot at a home invader and missed."

"Are you aware there's a strong smell of cannabis coming from your vehicle?"

"It's possible."

"Are you aware it's illegal to drive under the influence of a controlled substance?"

"Yes, but —"

Another patrol unit appeared, slowing as the second Crown Vic activated the strobing blue light bar and parked in front of the Audi, pinning him in. Two more cops got out and pointed flashlights at his vehicle. They approached the passenger door and ordered Jessy out of the car.

"You need probable cause to search my vehicle," Vance warned.

The cop who stopped him said, "The vehicle smells like marijuana and a firearm is visible on the floor mat beneath the driver's seat."

Legally speaking, both were probable cause. He watched from the corner of his eye while the other two troopers tossed the Audi.

"Where are you going this time of night?" the one who'd pulled him over asked.

"To see a friend."

The patrolman pointed the light in his face, then at the ground, and again directly at him. Vance was familiar with the field sobriety test for weed — the officer was checking his pupils for dilation.

"Cross your eyes," the cop said.

It was another test, and he passed.

The two officers who'd searched his car approached and the three cops huddled. The pair who'd arrived last got into their unit and waited.

"It's your lucky day. I'm going to write you a ticket for speeding."

The cop knew the gun was legal when he'd run his license, and he wasn't high on drugs. It wasn't exactly his *lucky day*. But it might've been Jessy's. He leaned against the driver's side door gazing at the passing headlights, wishing the trooper would hurry and write the ticket when a white SUV changed lanes and slowed as it passed. It looked like the same vehicle he'd seen Gloria driving, and it had Georgia plates.

60

DELRAY BEACH, 52 MILES NORTH OF MIAMI
10:12 P.M.
ONE HOUR AND 48 MINUTES REMAINING

Vance cut the headlamps on the Audi and motored past Last Chance Mental Health and Recovery located in an elongated, one-story bungalow. Surrounded by unkempt hedges and tall weeds, the rickety wooden fence was lit by crooked solar lights planted in the dirt. A pair of rocking chairs on the porch moved gently in the steady breeze. A naked yellow lightbulb burned above the front door. All told, the place appeared to be living up to its name.

He circled the block and parked several houses down the street. "Wait here," he said to Jessy, tucking the Glock under his shirt and stuffing the two phones in the pockets of his pants.

Prowling the sidewalk and using the bushes for cover, he

scoured the perimeter searching for eyewitnesses. Sensing no one, he turned up the walkway leading to the front door. A blue light glowed on the doorbell camera. He pressed the button, then waited, looking over his shoulder. He rang the buzzer a second time. Then a third.

A moment later a man's voice came from the speaker box. "Can I help you?"

"I'm looking for a patient named Rafael Suarez."

"We're closed."

"It's an emergency," he said, glancing around.

"What kind of emergency?"

"A family emergency," he lied.

"Wait there."

A FEW MINUTES later Suarez appeared at the door dressed in sweats accompanied by another man.

"What's wrong?" Suarez asked, fear in his eyes.

"I need to speak to you privately," he said.

Suarez turned to the other man. "Harold, may I have minute?"

"Do you know him?"

"He's my lawyer," Suarez said.

Which was a variation of the truth.

"Make it quick," Harold said, leaving the door ajar, taking a few steps back, keeping watch.

"Are my girls okay?" Suarez asked, lines forming on his brow.

"They're fine."

"Is it Val?"

"She's fine. Where's your phone?"

"At home."

Vance pulled the one he'd taken from the house from his pocket and showed it to Suarez. "Who's been using yours?"

Suarez took it from him. "I have no clue what you're talking about. This isn't my phone. It's my daughter's. What are you doing with it?"

Between his years as a cop and a lawyer, he'd seen world-class grifters and con men. Rafael Suarez was good. He had to give him that. "I know it's yours. I had your father-in-law call your number and this one rang. I'm going to you five seconds to tell me where she is."

"Who-she?"

"Three days ago, my girlfriend was abducted."

"I swear to God I don't know what you're talking about."

"You asked your father-in-law about my financial situation. Why?"

"I was curious. Daniel was the one who brought your name up. He said you'd be the perfect guy to take care of my affairs while I was away. Why *wouldn't* I ask questions?"

Valid point. "What about the document you left in your safe at the office?"

"The safe was empty. I left it unlocked."

"I transferred fifty thousand dollars into an account set up by the kidnappers. Confirmation of payment was texted to this phone. How do you explain that?"

Suarez's eyes bugged out. "I don't know, but that's crazy. If I kidnapped her, do you think I would put my child in harm's way?"

"Who has access to the login information on this phone?"

"Me. My wife does. My kids, anyone with the password," Suarez said, unlocking the phone with a code. "We all share the same one. It was my wife's idea. Val worries about the girls. She has ways to keep tabs on them."

Apparently on her husband, too. What a lying piece of shit, trying to pin it on his wife. "I know you're broke," he said, poking the bear to see what happened.

"You don't think I know that? If I had money, do you think I'd be here rehabbing on a twin bed with rubber sheets if I could be at Canyon Ranch? Look," he said, returning the phone to him. "Read them."

Suarez had searched messages time-stamped from four days ago, and they were his daughter Leah's. "Give me the password."

"I can't do that."

"Your family is in danger."

Suarez hesitated. "It's the month and date of my wedding anniversary. January ninth, nineteen ninety-nine. On my mother's grave I have no idea what's going on."

"Give me your cell number."

Suarez opened the contacts list on Leah's phone and handed it to him. "I'm DAD."

Vance copied the number and dialed it from his phone. Leah's rang. "How do you explain that?"

Suarez appeared confused, shaking his head slowly.

Harold the house manager appeared. "Time's up."

"I swear to you I don't know where she is," Suarez said, as Harold pulled the door shut.

The night air was thick as Vance jogged to the Audi where Jessy waited for him. He had a weird thought. More of an epiphany. What if Suarez was telling the truth?

61

"Did you see him?" Jessy asked as Vance got behind the wheel of the Audi, the stink of dope fouling the cockpit. He couldn't believe he had the balls to smoke weed in his car.

"Yeah, he's here," he said, handing Jessy the phone. "He says this is his kid's phone. The passcode is one-nine-one-nine-nine-nine. Unlock it, go to the contacts list, pull up DAD and call the number from your phone."

While Jessy did that, he motored past the rehab place with the headlights off, slowing at the stop sign at the end of the street. A moment later, Leah's phone rang.

"That's fucking weird," Jessy said. "The only explanation I can think of is someone forwarded Suarez's phone to this one, but there's no way to know for sure without checking Suarez's."

Vance flipped on the headlights and hung a right, toward the interstate. A white SUV appeared in his rearview mirror.

"What are you going to do now?" Jessy asked.

Leah's phone chimed with a text.

Jessy held up the screen for him to see.

Time is running out.

"Transfer a hundred grand."

Jessy turned on the dome light, set his laptop on his knees and logged into the account.

Vance held his phone over the steering wheel and checked the tracking app to see where Sarge was. Expecting him to be home this time of night, his heart skipped when he saw the yellow dot in the vicinity of the Suarez residence.

"Done," Jessy said.

Then it dawned on him—

He gritted his teeth until his jaw might crack and pounded the dash with his fist.

My God, it was so obvious.

Sarge knew about his money.

He was the one who'd introduced him to Suarez.

He'd convinced him to cover his son-in-law's practice.

Sarge lied about being in the hospital.

He'd seen him leaving Suarez's office building, and he'd lied about that too, claiming he was there to grease the skids, accusing Lola of being a bitch.

None of it was true. He'd played right into his hand. The note in the violin case. He'd put Maria up to it, then sent her to the condo to muddy his tracks.

The *Damas de Blanco* bullshit. Monkey Morales. The manifesto. Sarge knew Lauren had gone to Grand Cayman.

Davis Frost. The cash. The phones. The trip to Val's house. Sarge had to know she was home, and her Range Rover was in the garage. Sending Maria with a bullshit story that Ralph was at a rehab place up in Boca. A web of lies that could only have been fabricated by his old friend. A strategy meant to run out the clock, forcing him to pay.

Shock morphed into despair then ignited into rage.

If Sarge needed the fucking money, all he had to do was ask.

"Check that phone for a tracking app."

While he waited, he opened RECENTS on his phone and scrolled through the list until he got to Thursday. He paused the screen with the call from Kathy in the parking lot of the Italian restaurant where he'd first met Suarez.

"There's one of those parental monitoring apps on the phone," Jessy said.

"Does it track locations?" He asked, switching screens and comparing Logan's phone number to the Venmo account. The ride-share driver who'd been conveniently parked next to the Porsche when his tire was slashed was a match. Two thousand dollars had been transferred into his account.

"It tracks everything," Jessy said. "Locations, text messages, social media accounts."

"Give it to me."

Jessy handed it over and he tossed Leah's phone out the car window.

"What the fuck, man?" Jessy said.

62

SUAREZ RESIDENCE 11:53 P.M.
SEVEN MINUTES LEFT ON THE RANSOM CLOCK

Vance killed the headlights on the Audi as he turned onto Alhambra Circle. Sarge's white Jeep was parked in the driveway in front of Suarez's house; there was no sign of the SUV with the Georgia plates. The blinds were pulled, and threads of light leaked from the windows. He completed a lap around the block and parked five doors down.

"Wait here," he said to Jessy. He reached under the driver's seat for the 9-mil and the loaded clip, and prowled toward the house, squatting behind the bushes. He ducked, remaining motionless as a car traveled slowly past. Taking a position directly below the picture window with a view to the kitchen and living room, he peered in through a gap in the blinds. Sarge stood next to the refrigerator talking to a woman whose back faced the window; he guessed she was Val.

He cupped the screen on his phone to shade the light and typed a text to Sarge.

Let Lauren go and I'll wire the money no questions asked.

He watched as Sarge took the phone from his pocket, read it, then showed it to the woman. They appeared to argue, and she stormed out of the kitchen, and out of view. Sarge dictated a message on his phone.

A moment later, his phone lit with a response:

Don't know what you're talking about.

The front door opened, and the woman stepped onto the porch and lit a cigarette. He held his position, heart beating, listening, calculating the distance before making his approach, taking one small step. Then a another. A branch crackled beneath his shoe. He froze as Val turned and looked in the direction of the noise, then away.

Prey and predator.

She dragged on the cigarette, the tip glowing orange in the darkness.

A dog barked in the distance. She tapped the ashes in the hedges and sat on the stoop, the outline of her profile visible in the shadows as she exhaled a plume of smoke. He took another small step toward her. He was fifteen, maybe twenty feet from the porch.

He ran his hand gently along the ground, feeling leaves and dirt, careful not to make a sound. He touched a small rock and picked it up. Aiming for the walkway, he tossed it; the stone bounced on the concrete, distracting her. She scrambled to her feet, dropped the cigarette and stomped it with her shoe as she reached for the door.

He pounced, grabbing her from behind, locking her

neck in the crook of his elbow, covering her mouth with his hand.

"You scream and I'll kill you," he said, pressing the gun against her cheek. "I'm going to take my hand away," he said, releasing the chokehold and moving the barrel into her periphery, testing her. He put his lips close to her ear and spoke softly. "We're going inside to talk to your father. I'm going to walk behind you and you're going act as if nothing is wrong. Do you understand me?"

She nodded but didn't speak.

"Open the door."

She obeyed, turning the handle and pushing it open slowly.

He lowered the gun, pressed the tip behind her ear and followed her in.

He heard Sarge's voice. "Val?"

She didn't answer.

Sarge turned the corner and saw them.

"What are you doing here?" Sarge eyed the gun. "What the hell? Let her go, you asshole!"

Sarge rushed him but stopped a few feet away.

"I don't want to hurt her," he said. "Tell me where Lauren is, and I'll let her go."

"I don't know what the fuck you're talking about!"

"If you needed the money, all you had to do was ask," he said to Sarge, nudging Val forward. "Tell me where Lauren is, and I'll walk out of here. Keep what I've already sent. No questions."

"I swear to God," Sarge said. "I don't know what the hell you're talking about!"

Val let out a blood curdling scream and spun, kneeing him in the groin. He went down on all fours and looked up.

He knew her, he'd seen her before. His thoughts

whirled. He was sure she was the lady in white. Rage erupted. He sprang to his feet, and he tackled her to the ground then —.

The pain!

"Get your fucking shoe off my wrist!" he screamed, rolling onto his side.

Sarge kicked the Glock away.

It slid on the tile.

Sarge picked it up and pointed it at him. "Get the fuck up and get out of here! Now!"

Val scrambled to her feet and rushed her dad, clasping her hands like a hammer and pummeling him beneath the chin. His jaw crunched and his head snapped back. Sarge lunged, grabbing her shoulders with his hands, restraining her. Val kicked his injured leg, directly in the wound.

"Ahhhhhhh!" Sarge howled, dropping on the tile, using his hands to break the fall.

He dove for his gun but she belly-flopped atop it, getting control.

Sarge hopped on one foot, doubled over, panting. "Put it down, Val! It's over. Give me the gun!"

Vance scrambled on the floor, clamped a hand on her ankle and yanked. She fell; the gun clattered. They grappled, but the gun was out of reach.

Val got it and clambered to her feet. She pointed it at him.

He stood. "Go ahead," he said calmly, taking a step toward her.

Maria entered the room. "Oh my God, Val! What are you doing!"

Val gripped the gun with two hands and kept her eyes on him.

"Go on," he taunted.

"Where's the rest of the money?" she demanded. "I told you five million and you sent fifty-grand."

"A hundred and fifty," he corrected.

"What are you talking about, Val?" Sarge demanded. "Are you nuts?"

"Shut up, Dad! I want the rest of it. Now!" she said, placing her finger on the trigger.

"Not happening until you tell me where Lauren is," he said.

"Val!" Sarge shouted, trying to get her attention.

She kept her eyes on him, head cocked, looking down the sight of his gun as she spoke to her father, her voice rumbling with anger. "Who looked after you after Mom ran off, Dad? Night after night after night you drank yourself into a stupor. I brought you food. I brought the girls to see you, and did you ever thank me?"

"Put it down, Val," Sarge said, taking a step toward her.

"And you," she growled at him, "You used my dad to make yourself rich. He helped you get that money. He covered for you. I overheard you talking to him, and my dad was too drunk to even realize I was at his shitty little filthy apartment listening to him play the boy scout, turning down the money to protect his family." She raised the gun an inch and activated the laser.

A red dot danced between his eyes.

Maria shouted, "Val! You need to stop!"

"He offered you five million dollars, Dad, and you said no. It was your share. You earned it. It was money Mom needed. Money our family needed."

"We didn't need the money," Sarge said.

"Is this true, Danny?" Maria asked.

He ignored his wife. "You might have your mother fooled," Sarge said. "But not me. You're the one who spent your family into bankruptcy, not your husband. That's what you were arguing about that night at the table before your husband got arrested. You're over a million dollars in debt. Your house is in foreclosure. You keep your car in the garage to keep the repo man at bay. The credit card companies are suing you. You think I don't know? That's why Ralph got drunk and took the car that night. You drove him over the edge. It was you!"

Vance heard a new voice in the room, a small one. "Don't hurt my mom," the little girl said, cowering in the corner in the entryway to the living room.

"Get back to bed, Ava!" Val ordered.

Ava was defiant. "No."

Another girl entered the room, an older one. She sobbed uncontrollably.

"Come here, Leah," Maria said, opening her arms, coaxing the older child.

"This is your life," he warned Val, eyes glued to his weapon. "I'd be very careful what you do next."

"What are you doing, Mommy?" Ava asked, with a bewildered look on her face, walking toward them, breaking her mother's focus for a moment —

He pounced, knocking the gun from Val's hand.

It landed at Ava's feet and the child picked it up with two hands.

"Put . . . it . . . down," Maria said, slowly approaching the girl.

"Where is Lauren?" he asked Val, cooly.

"What is wrong with you!" Sarge shouted. "Ava has a gun!"

"Where is she?" he repeated as Ava clutched his weapon with two small hands. Val held her hand out to take it, but Ava turned away, waving it clumsily.

"Tell me where Lauren is," he repeated.

"Give it to Mommy," Val said, reaching for the gun.

Ava paused, then obeyed, and Val trained the Glock on him.

He looked down at the red laser dot on the left pocket of his shirt. "Think about this," he said to Val. "*Ju* don't want to do this in front of *jur* family," he taunted.

"You missed the deadline," Val said. "Whatever happens now is on you!"

"Val!" Sarge yelled, "Stop! Think about the girls!"

"That's exactly what I'm doing. Thinking about my family. It's so easy," she said to him, jabbing the air with his Glock, then aiming it at him again, the red dot bouncing off his chest. "Wire the money and everything goes back to the way it was."

"That's not going to happen," he said, testing her, pushing the issue. "That little charade was good. That shit about Monkey Morales. *Damas de Blanco*. The counterrevolution. All of it."

"Shut up!" she warned.

"I'm just warming up," he said. "Did *ju* write the manifesto *jurself*, or did *ju* hire a someone to help *ju*?"

"Don't do it, Val!" Sarge said, pulling Ava away —

The front door blasted open. "What the —?" Zo morphed into a bull and charged Val, ramming her in the shoulder, spinning and knocking her to the ground. Zo kicked his weapon across the tile and stood with her boot on Val's back.

"What do you wanna do here?" Zo asked him, eyes on Sarge, her expression getting meaner as she saw the children in the room.

"I want her to tell me where Lauren is. After that, I could give a rat's ass," he said, releasing the magazine plate and holding the empty pistol grip so Sarge could see the gun was never loaded. "Did you really think I'd endanger your family?" he said to Sarge, reaching in his pocket, taking the full magazine and palming up and in.

Ebony bounded into the room and growled at Zo. "Nu uh," she said, drawing her can of pepper spray.

Leah beelined for the dog, tears streaming down her face and hugged Ebony's neck.

Sarge took a deep breath puffing up his chest. When he exhaled, he looked like he might cry.

"This could go a whole lotta different ways," Zo said. "And it ain't up to you, Sarge. I'd tell the man what he wants to know," she warned Val.

"She's in Grand Cayman," Val said. "Dad, get my phone from the kitchen."

Sarge hurried.

Val made a call and handed Vance the phone.

"I've been trying to call you," the woman on the other end of the call said. "I lost him. He must've ditched the phone."

Vance looked at the name on the screen. *Gloria.* "That's right," he said. "I tossed it. Where's Lauren?"

"Who is this?"

"You know who this is. I'm at your sister's house. I need proof Lauren is alive or you're both going down."

"I'm five minutes away," Gloria said.

63

Vance ducked outside to get some air and check on Jessy while Zo held the fort down, but Jessy was nowhere to be found. The Audi was idling curbside beneath a streetlight. He got in, took a breath and powered down the windows. A cell phone, a set of keys and a folded note were left in a pile on the passenger seat. He lit the flashlight on his phone to read.

Zo will be there by the time you find this. I transferred the balance of the $500K into my account. Taking it as payment for my services seemed fair. Closed your offshore account and exchanged all of it for crypto bc the first transfer could be traced to whoever got the $150k. When I was done, I wiped my computer clean. Don't bother looking for me or the $350K because you'll never find *us*. I *set up a hot wallet for Zo with instructions to move payment into her account. There's a flash drive in the ashtray of the car with all the information you need. I would appreciate it if you'd get rid of my phone so that I can get a head start. Hope you find Lauren and she's safe. Tell Zo to take care, and good luck.*

Jessy

Three hundred and fifty grand seemed like fair compensation for his work. It was enough money for Jessy disappear from the grid and exit a lifetime of servitude to the state for trying to save his mother's life. In his mind, intent counted for something.

A white Toyota RAV-4 passed and parked on the street, blocking Sarge's Jeep. Gloria jumped out and ran to the residence. He waited, then headed for the house, stopping to look in the vehicle window. It had a rental car decal in the windshield. He tried the passenger side door. The car was unlocked. He unzipped the duffle bag on the back seat and riffled through the contents, turning it upside down. He grabbed a square leather handle and two more items, then stormed into the house.

Gloria stood in the entryway, beneath the Rothko painting. There was no sign of Maria or the children. "We're sorry," Gloria said to him. "We're really, really, sorry. We needed the money."

"You're not sorry. You got caught," he said.

"We'll give you your money back." Gloria said. "If you turn us in, we could go to prison."

Val said, "We could cut a deal. We could tell them where

your money is and how you got it."

"Go ahead," he said, holding up the props — a dog harness, mirrored aviator glasses and a wig. "That was you impersonating the Russian," he said to Gloria. He should've put the acting job together sooner. Gloria, the theater major, in town to meet with a donor. What a load of crap.

Zo loomed large with her arms across her chest, observing.

"What about our dad?" Val asked, playing the family card.

Zo's face contorted as if she'd smelled something foul.

Sarge was silent, hangdog. Any mercy spared now would be for his friend.

"Tell me where she is. Until then, there's nothing to negotiate."

"She's in Grand Cayman," Val said.

"I need proof," he said.

"I don't know how we can prove it," Val said. "Franco installed malware on her phone. He made the video of her."

Franco Frank, Suarez's P.I. He'd met him briefly at the office.

"We were supposed to have the money by now. The storm wasn't supposed to happen," Val said. "We never abducted her. It was just supposed to look like we did."

"I need proof," he repeated.

"She's trying to help Davis Frost," Gloria said.

With what, he wondered? "How do you know Davis?"

'Loose lips sink ships. Jur fat American friend.'

"What does it matter how I know him," she said, shrugging.

It mattered because it's how the story hung together.

"I have a friend keeping an eye on him," Gloria said. "Davis is in jail in George Town. His hearing is in the morning."

"You should shut up," Val said to her sister.

"Why is he in jail?" He trained the loaded gun at Gloria.

"Whoa," Gloria said, cowering. "Don't point that at me. The owners of a business he was looking to buy disappeared. Rumor has it he's a murder suspect. Look it up on the internet if you don't believe me. They're calling him the Sea Otter Killer."

"I gotta go," he said.

"Whaddya want me to do?" Zo asked, blocking the doorway.

"Hold them until I confirm she's alive." He turned to leave, then hesitated. "I got a question," he said to Val. "Who was the man in the woods at Vizcaya?"

"Franco."

Another piece fell into place. The only stuff in Franco's office were gum wrappers in the trash and a stack of watercraft enthusiast magazines on his desk. He'd arrived at Vizcaya on a WaveRunner. The high-powered telescope in Suarez's office would've given anyone, including Franco, a bird's eye view of Vizcaya. "Was Lola in on it?"

Val nodded. "She's desperate. She has a kid to think about. It's easy for you. You have millions and no one to worry about but yourself."

"What about her uncles in Cuba?"

"Cover story," Val said.

"Her eye injury?"

"That was real," Val said. "Her ex did it."

"The immigration documents?"

"Lola doctored them. The manifesto was her idea —"

Gloria interrupted with a weird smile on her face. "Do you know what Morozova means in Russian?"

"No," he said, wishing Zo would get out of his way.

"It means *frost*."

Ah. *Davis Frost. Ebony. Noir.* His blood simmered.

"Where you goin'?" Zo asked, moving out of the way.

"To find Lauren."

WALKING TO THE CAR, he searched contacts in his phone and placed a call.

"I never expected to hear from you again," Blade said.

"I need you to fly me to Grand Cayman in the morning."

"You couldn't pay me enough," Blade said.

"You might be wrong about that," he said, making an exorbitant offer.

"Meet me at the Homestead FBO at sunrise," the pilot said. "They've had bad weather and I gotta find a place I can land."

64

MIAMI-HOMESTEAD FLIGHT BASE OPERATIONS
MONDAY MORNING, MEMORIAL DAY

A glow of light in the east was on the cusp of breaking night into day. Blade licked his teeth and scratched his gray beard as he stepped up onto the wing of the six-seater Cessna and raised the door.

"No talking," Blade said, grabbing the dull green headset from the pilot's seat.

"Good idea," Vance said. He'd helped put Blade's kid behind bars on a murder-for-hire charge. There was a saying. Money talks. Everyone knew how the rest went.

THE WEATHER WAS CLEAR, and Blade touched down at the small private airport adjacent the international airport in George Town. A sedan waited for him on the tarmac.

"I'm gonna fuel up. Gonna cost you a lot more for the return trip home," Blade said.

"Deal."

In minutes he was on route to the Criminal Records Office in downtown. If what Val and Gloria had said was true and Davis was being held at the jail, he'd start there. The driver dropped him at 80 Shedden Road. The CRO was located in the same building as the Royal Cayman Islands Police Service headquarters, a bland four-story reminiscent of a Holiday Inn Express.

The line was long and slow. He google-searched while waiting, discovering a link to the Coroners Court on the Cayman Islands government website. The two most recent inquests showed autopsies had been performed on Elizabeth LeCroy and Martin LeCroy. Cause of death was listed as Undetermined. If Davis was a suspect, the conclusion would be in his favor. A follow-up search on his phone confirmed they were the couple who owned Sea Otters, the dive operation Davis Frost had pitched to him and Lauren.

Twenty minutes later, the line hadn't moved and at this rate, he'd be there for hours. He bailed, and on the way out, glanced at the building directory. It housed the FCIU, the Financial Crime Investigation Unit. He hurried, heart ticking faster as he caught a cab heading to the Grand Court located at 61 Edward Street.

On route, he searched the Court website for criminal cases. He knew almost nothing about the structure of the Cayman Islands justice system nor the complexities arising from Davis Frost's U.S. citizenship, but he did figure out Davis was on the docket for 10 a.m. He checked the time. It was 10:21 a.m.

As the cabbie pulled up to a featureless concrete

building reminiscent of a U.S. embassy in a more dangerous place, a satellite truck had already taken a position. Smaller news media vehicles and RCIPS marked sedans occupied every available inch of street parking. He paid the driver and hurried toward the building but was blocked by the scrum of newshounds packing the entryway.

He was tall enough to see over the mob. A whale of a woman wearing a gown and a British style white wig stepped out from the courthouse, swarmed by reporters pushing and shoving and yelling questions.

"Where is the Sea Otter Killer!"

"When will he be tried!"

"What do you have to say about —"

"The charges against Mr. Frost have been dismissed!" she announced, elbowing her way through.

He pressed his way toward her and yelled, "I'm looking for Lauren Gold."

She stopped. "Who might you be?"

"My name is Vance Courage."

"She's inside the courthouse," the woman said. "She's leaving for Miami. You'd best hurry."

As he pushed his way through foot traffic, a guard at the door stopped him. "I'm sorry sir, but you are not permitted to enter."

"I'm meeting someone."

"You're not dressed properly. Gentlemen must wear jackets and ties," he said, with a whiff of arrogance.

He saw her heading toward the front door. "Lauren!" He held his hand over his head and waved. "Lauren!"

She spotted him and hesitated, then strode toward him pulling her carry-on bag. "What are you doing here?"

He grabbed her and tried to hug her, but she rebuffed

him, and twisted away. "I've been looking for you," he said. "Are you okay?"

She smoothed the black skirt and tugged the sleeve of the matching jacket. "How did you know where to find me?"

"I'll tell you later. Let's go," he said, grabbing her roller bag.

"I need to get to the airport," she said, blowing him off.

"Forget about it," he said, walking in front of a cab, forcing the driver to stop. He took hold of her hand, opened the cab door, tossed her bag on the back seat and climbed in.

"Where are we going?" she asked, confused.

"Home."

She was pissed at him, that much was clear, giving him the cold shoulder and staring out the side window. He wasn't sure why but gave her some time.

"You didn't tell me you changed banks," she finally said.

"I was trying to protect you."

"From what?" she snapped, as the taxi driver jammed the brakes and cussed at a jay walker from the open window.

Now was not the time to explain. "I'm sorry," he said.

"I have twenty-five thousand dollars on me," she whispered.

That was a problem. She couldn't fly commercially with that amount of cash. Her burner phone buzzed. He leaned across and looked. The name Arthur M. came up. "Who's he?"

"It's complicated," she said, explaining she'd rented a room from him before she knew he worked in the Financial Crime Unit.

"Don't answer it," he said. "We're not going to the

international airport. Give me the money and the phone. I'll take care of it."

He'd ditch the burner at the FBO in George Town, and the cash would be the most generous tip Blade ever received.

EPILOGUE

"**W**hat is this place?" Lauren asked as he parked the 911 out front. "Are you going to tattoo my name on your bicep?"

"I was thinking of a more private place only you and my doctor would see," he said.

He'd explained what had happened while she was away — the kidnapping hoax — and apologized for not telling her he'd moved his money from Cayman to Bermuda. He also shared that he'd converted his cash into cryptocurrency and advised her to do the same.

When Jessy disappeared, he'd ditched his keys in the Audi along with his phone and the note. "It's a business prospect," he said, taking a set of keys from his pocket. "All we need to do is find an artist and pay the bills to keep it going."

He'd found the lease in Jessy's desk. It was good for the next ten years.

"Great," she said, rolling her eyes. "With our track record for business, I'm sure we'll be selling franchises by this time next year."

"Come on," he said. "Be positive. The place already has clientele. Let me give you the tour."

"Who's going to manage it?"

He looked out the front window, through the burglar bars. An F-140 pickup backed into an available parking spot next to the Porsche.

Zo came through the front door. "You must be the squeeze," she said to Lauren.

Lauren hesitated and narrowed her eyes. "I remember you, from the airport."

It seemed like a long time ago he'd dropped her off at Cayman Air.

Zo handed him a 9-millimeter Glock, like his. "Belongs to Sarge," she said. "Dropped in the 'hood and paid the neighbors an unofficial visit."

He didn't want to know more than that.

She reached into her pocket and handed him the slug. "Was gonna surprise the boys in Hallandale with some evidence but this ain't gonna tie to a bad guy."

He traded the bullet for a piece of paper with numbers on it. One set had a dollar sign in front of it.

"You still funny." Zo let out an earthshaking laugh. "Don't mess with me Courage. Can't count that high."

He handed her an orange flash drive. "Don't lose this or the money will disappear."

"Yo," Zo said. "You tryin' to bribe a cop?"

Lauren gasped.

"I'm jus' fuckin' with him sweetie," she said, letting out

another massive chortle, lifting one knee and punching the air.

"I'm serious," he said. "If you lose the codes, you'll never recover them."

Zo sobered up. "You for real on that amount?" she said, looking at the note again.

"For real."

"What about Jessy?" Zo asked.

"He's good," he said, leaving out the self-dealing.

"Where is he?" Zo said. "I ain't seen or heard from him in days. He here now?"

A young man entered through the front door with an intricate Elizabethan collar tattooed around his neck. "Hi," he said with a soft voice that belied the ink on his body. "I'm looking for Jean Delgado."

Zo side-eyed him, looking for an explanation. "That's me," she said.

"I'm here about the job."

Vance stepped in. "Did you bring a resume?"

The artist took a binder from his backpack. "It's all here."

"Have a seat," Vance said. "We'll be right back." He pulled Zo aside and they stopped in the hallway where they had privacy. "Quit your job. Your retirement is vested. Work here until things settle down."

Zo leaned against the wall, thinking. "Could send my daughter to rehab I guess," she said. "Ain't sayin' it's gonna help but you never know. Did I tell you about my grandson?"

"No, just that he's sick."

"Got cystic fibrosis. Don't know who the daddy is 'cause ah my daughter's addiction. My wife gotta clear his lungs four times a day and it's been hell on her. What you done is gonna change all that." Zo shook her head, as if trying to process the thought. "Used to be most folks that got the disease don't see thirty, but these days, he might make fifty. The extra stuff, you know, like eatin' the right way, drugs. I ain't been able to swing it on a cop salary. Now I could."

A tear welled in Zo's eye, and she sniffed.

"Thank you," she said, wiping her eyes with the back of her hand. "That's love, brother."

"Am I interrupting?" Lauren asked.

"Nah," Zo said. "Gimme that." She took the binder from him. "Gonna go meet with that kid who's waiting."

When he and Lauren were alone, she seemed rattled.

"I just got a call from Davis," she said.

"And?"

"He's being investigated for money laundering."

"How did that come about?" He'd kept Val and Gloria's threats a secret.

"His wife surfaced and is cooperating with RCIPS investigators."

"Wife? You didn't tell me Davis was married."

He followed her into a side room. Lauren perched on the edge of the barber chair and held her head in her hands. "You know Davis. He made another bad decision."

"Who did he marry?"

"I don't know. All he said is she emptied his bank account and disappeared. He showed me a picture. She's not in his league, if you know what I mean," Lauren said. "When I put my car in the shop this morning, I found this when I cleaned out the center console."

She showed him a passport photo of Natasha Popova-Morozova. It must've slipped out of her file when he'd taken the file home to study it before the meeting.

"Who is she?" Lauren asked.

"Why?"

"I think I've seen her before."

He took his phone from his pocket and showed her the picture he'd secretly taken of Gloria when the dog escaped the house.

"That's her," Lauren said. "That's the woman Davis married. He showed me photos. He told me they met in Cayman. They had a whirlwind romance, and he loaned her a hundred thousand dollars before she emptied his bank account. Where did you get the pictures?"

Wow. Jessy had found 'traveling to Cayman' in the search files for Suarez. He'd briefed Lauren on the immigration ruse. "She's Sarge other daughter, the one who played the part of the Russian."

"Oh my God! She's going to turn Davis in." She laid prone on the barber chair and covered her face. "You need to back out of the deal with Suarez. You can't keep covering for him."

The plot to rip him off ran deeper than he'd thought. On the other hand, five million dollars was a big incentive. Sarge's daughters must've used Davis's money to put the plan into action. A guy like Franco Frank wasn't working for free.

"You can't help Davis. Neither of us can," he said, "and I can't back out of the deal." If he did, he risked turning Sarge and Rafael from allies into enemies. Plus, he hadn't told Lauren every detail. It was a matter of time before Suarez figured out Lola and Franco had stabbed him in the back, and he'd leave it to the troubled attorney to sort his business out after he completed rehab.

Sarge had gone to see Rafael at the treatment center and told him what had occurred. Rafael decided to file for divorce from Val. The settlement was straightforward: there were no assets left to split, just debt. He'd filed the papers for Ralph, and Val had already hired a big-time lawyer to wage a battle for custody and alimony. He'd wondered where she'd gotten the money to pay her lawyer. Now he had an idea.

He'd left it up to retired police sergeant Daniel Ruiz how to handle Val and Gloria. Not due to his benevolence, or even loyalty to his friend though there was a tad of the latter; rather because if the sisters retaliated, he and Lauren might be compromised.

He'd let the snakes eat their tails. Meanwhile, he'd followed Jessy's instructions, and with her consent, closed Lauren's account in Grand Cayman and converted her fortune into digital currency. He'd bought a subscription to a VPN app — virtual private network — that encrypted all incoming and outgoing communications on both his and Lauren's devices. It was easy.

His phone rang. Ethan came up on CALLER ID.

"How long until you get here?" the boy asked.

He'd promised to give him a driving lesson today. He checked the time. "I'll be there in one hour."

"That means two," Ethan said.

"I'll keep my promise if you keep yours. Not a word to your mother."

"Deal," Ethan said, "Mom will be happy we're spending time together. She's so weird about it."

That reminded him of one piece of the puzzle he hadn't solved. Was Lola the daughter of Laura Pollán? He and Ethan could work on figuring it out together.

"Your mother's not weird," he said, "she's just being your mom."

One day soon Ethan Jones would learn why, but for now a driving lesson would do.

ABOUT THE AUTHOR

Reviews are very much appreciated.

Karen S. Gordon has written several award-winning thrillers starting with *The Mutiny Girl*. If you enjoyed *Lady In White*, she would appreciate it you left a review. *Lady In White* is the sixth installment of the Gold and Courage Series.

Go to the series link here: https://amzn.to/3qci2k7

The adventures of Vance Courage and Lauren Gold continue with another installment in 2024. Title and publication date to be announced.

Please sign up for the newsletter at <u>karensgordon.com</u>

ALSO BY KAREN S. GORDON

The Mutiny Girl

"An outstanding debut thriller that has it all: misdirection, intrigue, murder, and family. Captivating and engrossing." — *The BookLife Prize*

"A taut, thrilling drama told exceptionally well." — *Steve Berry, NYT Bestselling Author*

"An engagingly written series starter with a bounty of plot twists and Miami vices." — *Kirkus Reviews*

Killer Deal

"A ripped-from-the-headlines legal thriller that John Grisham fans will love. Highly recommended." — *BestThrillers*

" . . . a fast-paced thriller . . . an intriguing look at the hunger for power, the ego of control, the persistence of greed, and two unlikely heroes whom we can cheer for . . ." — *BookTrib*

Express Intent

"Fast-paced, evocative and urgent from the get-go, Express Intent is the best Gold and Courage series book yet." — *Bestthrillers*

Sick Money

"The Bottom Line: A heart-pounding, adrenaline-spiking medical thriller that takes the series into new territory. Highly recommended." — *Bestthrillers*

Money For Nothing

THE BOTTOM LINE: " . . . a provocative, tightly-wound crime thriller that seems destined for its own streaming series. A must-

read for both fans of the series and the series' growing fan base."
— *BestThrillers.com*

"A brilliantly woven plot mixed with a rich cast of memorable characters make Karen S. Gordon's MONEY FOR NOTHING a must-read for anyone in search of an unputdownable reading experience." — *Ryan Steck, The Real Book Spy*

Liable

THE BOTTOM LINE: A captivating destination thriller with all the ingredients for a perfect beach read: betrayal, sex and deadly games on an exotic island. — *BestThrillers.com*

"Smart, quick, and wildly entertaining, LIABLE is Gordon at her very best." — *Ryan Steck, The Real Book Spy*